PALOMINO

Tank Gunner

Tank Gunner is the pen name of a retired combat cavalry trooper, awarded a Combat Infantry Badge and decorated with a Silver Star, three Bronze Stars, one for Valor, and a Purple Heart. He served his nation with pride and honor for more than a quarter century as an enlisted soldier and officer. An award-winning author, Tank wrote and published *Prompts a collection of stories* at age 76, *Prompts Too another collection of stories* at 77, and *Cookie Johnson*, his Vietnam historical fiction novel, at 78. At age 79, *Palomino* is his Second World War historical fiction novel and fourth book. He and his wife live with Toby, 100 miles southwest of Palomino.

OTHER WORKS

PROMPTS
a collection of stories
(fiction)

PROMPTS TOO
another collection of stories
(fiction)

COOKIE JOHNSON
(fiction)

WAR STORIES of an ARMED SAVAGE
(nonfiction)

ANY NAME BUT SMITH!
(play)

DIRECT HIT
(newspaper column)

For Sylviane, Rich, Rob,

and

for Terry, Chloe, Zak, and Toby

ACKNOWLEDGMENT

This is my special salute to Capn Lee Sneath, a former newspaper editor, corporate communications executive, public affairs spokesperson, and a college instructor, word coach, editor, and patient friend.

and

A grateful nod to Wayne Peterson – author of his hard science fiction trilogy *Canopy of Hope, Canopy of Mystery*, and *Canopy of Destiny* – a talented storyteller, colleague, and friend who shared his passion of the craft and provided ears, eyes, and reactions during the development of *Palomino*.

Palomino Cover
by
Lynsey Dreis

PLAYERS

Sergeant Willow "Twig" Chestnutt
Military Policeman

Teresa Chestnutt
Wife & Cafe Waitress

Tina Chestnutt
Daughter & Grade School Student

Ruby Bostick
Owner, Palomino Palace & the Porter House

Major Clay Monroe
WWI Hero & Cotton Farmer

Casey Shipp
Palomino Mayor

Estelle Kerns
Boarding House Madame

Eliot Thurgood
Palomino Tormenter

Milton Douglas "M D" Draggert
Petty Criminal

Artemis "Arty" Canton
Car Thief & Petty Criminal

Franklein Rosser
President, Red River County State Bank

Judy Jones
Vice President, Red River County State Bank

i

PLAYERS

Myrtle Sherman
Vice President, Red River County State Bank

Maybelle Winters
Owner, Editor, Publisher of the *Palomino Press*

Henrietta Draggert
Milton Draggert's Mother

Martin Church
Cotton Field Hand

Odessa Church
Daughter, Former Paris Jr. College Rangerette

Dallas Church
Daughter, Senior Palomino High School

Preacher Adams
Cotton Field Hand, Minister

Waldo Sutherland
Paperboy

Wolf Hunter
Gas Station Owner

Pearson Keenan
City Meter Reader

Caleb Joiner
Gas Station Helper

Carsey Belew
Palomino Switchboard Operator

PLAYERS

Betty Crane
Bogata Switchboard Operator

Delilah Wheeler
Entertainer

Ginnie Tyler
Entertainer

Billy Don Owens
Gas Station Owner

Aubrey Roach
Ranch Owner and Hunter

Julius Watson
Chauffer

Ethel Watson
Housekeeper

Kraus "Duke" Hopplendagger
Wehrmacht Sergeant, POW

Edwin "Eddy" Becker
Wehrmacht Corporal, POW

Wilhelm "Will" Weiss
Wehrmacht Private, POW

Deputy Logan Amesa
Red River County Sheriff

Deputy Walter "Pop" Crawley
Red River County Sheriff

PLAYERS

Deputy Stephan Stanton
Red River County Sheriff

Deputy David Sunday
Red River County Sheriff

Deputy Mavis Raymond
Red River County Sheriff

Sheriff Billy Blake
Red River County Sheriff

Sheriff Jim Dudley
Lamar County Sheriff

Brainard D. Baldwin
Attorney at Law

Tonya "Tiny" Talbot
Owner, Tiny's Cafe

Bobbie Jo Evans
Manager, Jeeps Cafe

Dora Kline
Co-Owner, Kline's Drugs

Kingston Kline
Co-Owner, Kline's Drugs

Nate Dulfeine
Co-Owner, Dulfeine's Grocery

Margie Dulfeine
Co-Owner, Dulfeine's Grocery

PLAYERS

Martha Parker
Council Representative

Patricia Ann "Patsy" Parker
Daughter

Paula Pinkston
Rayfield's Mother

Rayfield Paramore "Pinky" Pinkston, Jr.
Son and Paperboy

Jeannie Rider
Nurse, Bogata Hospital

Kitty Pratt
Nurse, Bogata Hospital

Doc Anson Bledsoe
Doctor, Bogata Hospital

Doc Garland Burns
Doctor, Palomino Hospital

Linda Thomas
Nurse, Palomino Hospital

Brigadier General Charles Pace, Jr.
Deputy Commanding General, Camp Maxey

Colonel Benicio Sardanna-Sanchez
Provost Marshal, Camp Maxey

Colonel R. J. Jones
Administrator, Camp Maxey

PLAYERS

Captain Fred Morris
Military Police Company Commander

First Sergeant Kenneth Kinnison
Military Police Company First Sergeant

Henry Wilson
Pie Shop and Domino Hall Owner

Corporal Oliver "Ollie" Schultz
Military Police Guard

THE ARRANGEMENT
July 1943
Largest tank battle in history in Kursk
B-24 Liberators bomb Japanese again

"German soldiers? Here? In Palomino?"

"Yes, I'm afraid so."

"Are you sure, Maybelle? The enemy is going to live here?"

"Yes, Henrietta. That's what the special meeting is all about tonight at the schoolhouse."

"I had no idea, Maybelle. When Rayfield brought the flyer by, I thought the meeting was going to be about rationing. Goodness sakes. I had no idea. German soldiers, in Palomino."

"Mayor Shipp is going to make the announcement. Then Casey and the council members are going to Camp Maxey to meet with the Army. Casey and the council are going to represent the town, and Casey asked me to come along to represent Palomino as a member of the press. We're going to talk about the arrangement for the Germans."

"Here? In Palomino? The enemy is going to live

here — in Palomino."

"Henrietta, you do know there's a war going on."

"Goodness sakes, Maybelle. You don't have to be so mean. Of course, I know that. Rayfield delivers your paper every week, I listen to Edward R. Murrow over there, and I see the newsreels and *Movietone News* with Lowell Thomas at the *pitchursho*. My nephew, Oscar Fant, you know, Marline's oldest boy, is flying bombers over there *someplace*. God knows where."

"These German soldiers are part of a new government program. You remember when those Liberty ships brought over five-thousand prisoners of war from North Africa to Boston? Well, about a month ago they were divided up and put on trains going to camps from Massachusetts to California."

"And there are some at Camp Maxey?"

"Yes, more than a thousand, maybe two thousand. And a lot are going into another two dozen camps in Texas towns, too."

"Goodness sakes. What are they going to do here?"

"Some are gonna work. They'll do some of the jobs left open when our boys go into service. The war effort needs cotton and people need food. They'll work on Bastion Albert's farm picking sweet corn, watermelons, and beets, and for Major Monroe, picking cotton. And when all the picking is done, they'll work with Bastion hauling vegetables to Paris. Or in Major Monroe's gin to process and bale the cotton."

"They might kidnap and kill somebody."

"Who?"

"The Germans. I've seen the newsreels at the

pitchursho. I saw how mean they acted with Humphrey Bogart and Ingrid Bergman. She looked so gorgeous, poor thing. I know she loved him and wanted . . ."

"They might do, Henrietta. But they sure as hell ain't going to escape. There's no place to hide. They know that. All we got around here is fields and wide open country. They'd be hunted down, slaughtered, and hung up on a bob-wire fence if they hurt anybody."

"Well, I guess you're right. I reckon one man wouldn't have a chance even if he looked cross-eyed at a woman here."

"Well, it'll be more than one, Henrietta. Casey said the figure was three available to come here. Maybe more, if we wanted them. Casey said the ones selected for local communities have gone through tough government screening. It's called a residency program where prisoners are released to live and work in Palomino."

"My, my. Goodness sakes, Maybelle. Of all things. The enemy is going to live among us. Where in the world are they gonna stay? We don't have a hotel."

"Well, that's gonna be told about tonight. It depends on the agreement with the Army at Camp Maxey. If you ask me, I'd say they gotta stay at Ruby's place. Either in her barn or the Porter House."

"Well, the Porter House is big. All them bedrooms. Her mansion is the biggest there is in two counties, as big as some I seen in Dallas."

"All the bedrooms are taken right now, but Edgar and Vincent got their draft notices so they're moving out next week. Major Monroe wanted them to claim an exemption to pick and bale his cotton, but they said

3

no."

"Instead of going into the Army, they told me they're going to join the Navy, Maybelle. Vincent's daddy was a soldier in the first war."

"When they leave, that'll free two of the eight tenant bedrooms. Henrietta, you've been all through her house, you know how spacious those bedrooms are."

"They are nice. Ethel takes good care of Miss Ruby's house. She's a good cook and housekeeper."

"Teresa and Tina are there, they rent a room."

"And the two boys who work out at the Talco oil rig, Otis Bassett and Ernest Blackmon. Of course, they've been talking about moving out, to be closer to their work."

"Right, Henrietta. So, that leaves Caleb, Jake Little, and Pearson Keenan."

"Jimmy Madison left."

"Yes, that's right. Teresa and Tina took that bedroom."

"Poor Pearson, working out there in all kinds of weather and all the while his wife is . . . Since Madison run off with Pearson's young wife we don't have a constable no more, neither. The Germans will have a free hand. They'll be ravaging and raping all the women here before we know it."

"I promise you, Henrietta, you and I won't let that happen. We still have *The Calaboose* if we need it. Anyway, we still have able men here. And everybody in town has pistols, rifles, and shotguns. The enemy don't have any."

"Why didn't Casey call the meeting for the

pitchursho instead of the school gym?"

"Gym seats more and the stage is bigger. We expect a lot of people to come since we didn't say in the flyer why we're gonna have a special meeting."

"Well, you better make sure Leon attends the meeting so he can write the story for your . . ."

"He is, and I told Stan to bring his camera to the meeting to get Casey's picture. It's going to be a late night for us here at the paper. I haven't published a special edition this important since December Eight, Forty-One. Tomorrow the *Palomino Press* will run front page, headline news."

"Everybody is going to be in for a big surprise."

"I think they'll be more shocked than surprised, Henrietta. I'm going to print a special bulletin for the two counties. I'll even send some copies over to Paris and Mount Pleasant and down to Fort Worth and Dallas. My headline will be a one-inch bold font above the fold, and shout — *ENEMY COMING TO PALOMINO* — or something like that."

"Goodness sakes, Maybelle."

At the front end of the school's gym was a thirty-six-foot wide theater stage. Heavy maroon curtains hung stage left and stage right. Gray drapes formed the backdrop. A prairie dog, Palomino sports teams' mascot, adorned the center of the white masking curtain above the opening. Plays, recitals, band performances, and community auctioneers used the stage. So an audience could see when those and other occurrences took place, the basketball backboard was

5

raised.   Out on the floor, Halloween booths and Christmas cakewalks were the town's favorites.

Casey Shipp stood behind the town council table. From the school gym stage, he looked down at his flock. He held the gavel in his left hand, chest high, casually lifting it and letting the head drop into his right palm with the consistency of an oilfield pumper. Never once did he tap the small block of wood with the gavel.

The packed space settled down, became hushed.

In less than 12 seconds, calm rustling eased as the men ambling about found vacant folding chairs among the rows set up on the gym floor — in spite of basketball coach Floyd Byrd's chagrin and fussing, and complaint that "you'll scratch my damn floor". Men paused and looked, searching for openings in the right or left side bleachers.

Kids stood near the right and left double doors, six Boy Scouts acted as door handlers. To earn merit badges, four Cub Scouts volunteered as ushers for seating, and six Eagle Scouts offered arms as escorts for anyone, young or old, who acquiesced. The greater majority of girls and women sat in the more comfortable chairs while the boys and men high-stepped to mount the hardwood bleachers when a spot appeared. While there was talk and how-dos, everyone was respectful of the meeting and their elected council perched on the stage.

Several waved church fans under chins, their own and flanking neighbors. Various fans oscillated in a slow, pendulum rhythm while others swung with the rapidity of wings of a hummingbird. Baptist fans had an artist's interpretation of God's human face, His

6

graceful, clean hands with trimmed nails formed in prayer. Presbyterian fans had colorful images of what heaven and angels might look like. Church of Christ fans had short verses printed on thin cardboard. The Methodist fan was white silk with a short string attached to its handle. The Pentecostal fan was round with strands of yellow straw. The eight Catholics in attendance held no fans; they dabbed at moisture above the top lip and swiped beads of sweat from their brows.

Some Baptist and Church of Christ fans pelted rambunctious toddler's heads to encourage compliance of the command to quit squirming and sit still.

Four Mexican men and four black men, all heads of households, stood shoulder to shoulder next to the rear wall flanked by the double doors. Their backs did not touch the paneling. As if instructed to pose, they stood solemnly, feet spread apart for balance. In rough hands with broken or cracked nails, the black men clasped the front brim of their sweat-stained, gray fedoras and the Mexican men clasped the brim of their ragged, sweat-stained, split-straw Panama hats. None were dressed in trousers or jeans; all eight wore worn, but Sunday clean, faded blue overalls. They did not attempt to look for a place to sit.

The 371 people sitting and standing surrendered the moment to the town's leadership. On Mayor Shipp's near right, sat Section 1 Representative Clay Monroe, decorated, disabled World War One hero, and retired Major, United States Army Reserve. On the Mayor's near left sat Section 2 Representative Ruby Bostick, owner of the Palomino Palace, otherwise known as the *pitchursho*, in addition to the Porter House. The Major and Miss Ruby were the two senior members of the council.   On the Mayor's far right sat Section 3 Representative Wolf Hunter, owner of the Gulf gas station, the only gas station in town. On Mayor Shipp's far left sat Martha Parker, Section 4 Acting Representative and housewife, who lived with daughter Patsy, formally known as Patricia Ann. She occupied her husband's council seat by default while Mr. Parker was an infantry rifleman with the 1st Marine Regiment presently camped on the Melbourne, Australia Cricket Ground after Guadalcanal. Wolf and Martha were the two junior members of the Palomino council.   The school's mascot-emblazoned banner covered the long table.

"Thank you for coming to this special meeting, my fellow Palominoans. Tonight, my duty is to make an extraordinary announcement that will have a significant impact on our community. What I want to tell you was decided by your elected representatives, on your behalf, in a closed, executive session."

Mayor Shipp paused and silently counted to five before continuing.   "But we are ready to hear your concerns. I, along with your council, will meet with the Camp Maxey Commanding General's representative, Colonel Sardanna-Sanchez, to complete arrangements to accept three German prisoners of war to live and work in Palomino."

He heard deep gasps and nodded at the whispered exclamations, but did not pause.

"In preliminary discussions ten days ago, we received assurances these three German POWs went through a thorough screening and approval process to live and work in our community. You and I well know we need the money and labor. The Army charges a dollar-fifty per day for each prisoner, for his labor. The Army pays the prisoner eighty cents and keeps seventy to pay for this new program. The Army will buy groceries from Dulfeine's to feed them, work clothes and boots from Wilburt's clothing store, toiletries and sundries from Kline's drugstore, and pay room and board to house them."

The gym erupted in an uproarious jumble of indistinguishable words uttered by male and female voices. Mayor Shipp permitted cussing, hollering, and angry yelling for 122 seconds before he slammed his ceremonial gavel down with great force six times on the small block of wood.

He held a hand up, palm out, and waited.

The cacophony of calamitous composure calmed.

He spoke quietly. "Now, that's good. Thank you for calming down, I know this is a shock for some. We've looked at this carefully and decided this is a situation our town can benefit from. In good order, I'll recognize a raised hand, listen to a concern, and respond the best I can. I won't have all the answers to your questions until after our meeting with Colonel Sanchez. Now, everybody please be patient. Let's start."

Mayor Shipp scanned the attendees but saw no raised hand immediately.

"That's great. No one has a question or concern so I guess we can close this special meeting of the council."

"Over here, Casey, on the right. A hand is up,"

Major Monroe said.

"Yessir, what is your concern?"

The man stood in the bleachers on the right side, near the entrance. He spoke quietly and politely. "Martin Church. I stay over on 4th Street. My concern is how come we got no say, no vote, on this matter. Ain't this a democracy, Mr. Mayor?"

"Thank you, Martin. We had no time to present this for public hearing, discussion, or vote. Our government and our Army have their hands full. They don't know where to put all these prisoners coming in every week from Africa, Germans *and* Italians. Most of the places are crammed full. They're living in temporary tents while building their own living quarters in the camps. Called up to go fight, our boys, able men, are sailing to England and Hawaii. Our workforce is diminished and harvest time is just around the corner. Quick decisions had to be made on the Army's offer, and we made them."

A female voice rose from among the chairs on the gym floor. "When are we going to be invaded by the enemy?"

"I would think in a week or ten days. The agreement will be finalized in our meeting at Camp Maxey."

The voices, polite and quiet, came from the women. No hands raised and Mayor Shipp did not admonish for that oversight.

"Are they Nazis?"

"We are told these three prisoners are not Nazis. They come from North Africa, Rommel's Afrika Korps. But it is hard to know what is in a man's heart. We

10

have to trust the vetting process conducted by those who are trained to do the interviewing and interrogating."

"Where are these boys gonna work?"

"In the beginning, in my fields picking cotton, and at the gin," Major Monroe said, "sorting seeds and baling cotton. There may be other needs that we'll consider when the time comes, like drainage ditches and such."

"Whose gonna keep watch on these Germans?"

"That has not been decided, but . . ."

"Since Jimmy Madison run off we don't have no law in town," another voice spoke. "We need a lawman, Mayor."

The vision of masculine Jimmy Madison with flirtatious Mary Lou Keenan, along with sympathetic feelings for cuckolded Pearson Keenan, probably flashed through many minds. They were a wild couple envied.   Foremost though, women formed their perfectly potent portrait of Jimmy, while the men visualized, fanaticized the tantalizing Mary Lou.

"As I was going to say, that has not been decided, but I have a solution that I'll present at our meeting. I think my idea will be welcomed and approved by Colonel Sanchez," the Mayor said.

The gymnasium grew silent. Mayor Shipp and the council — and the men, women, and children — knew there were dozens of questions, hundreds maybe, but no one voiced them or spoke their minds.

"Let me say how proud I am at the way everyone here has conducted themselves. We know there are concerns not yet voiced, but we could not reject this opportunity to bring men in to work here and receive the government money coming into our businesses to buy things. If there is nothing else, I'll close this meeting."

"Where're these Hitler-lovin, goose-steppin Krauts gonna stay?" The threatening tone of the male voice, from the left side bleachers, was easily recognizable. Men, women, and children turned to look warily at the questioner.   He stood, menacingly poised, fists clenched, chin jutting. All reached the conclusion Eliot Thurgood appeared ready for a fight. They knew he was a bully, maybe even a killer, and avoided him as best they could. Women in Palomino referred to Eliot as crazy, men said he was a mean son-of-a-bitch.

"At the meeting we might be able to come to an agreement with the Army for them to stay at my place, Eliot," Miss Ruby said. "Really, there is no other place with enough room for three men except the Porter House or in my old barn."

"I think we ought to just line em up, shoot em, and feed em to the hogs," Eliot said to the uneasy silence.

THE TENANTS
April 1942
Heavy bombing by RAF of Hamburg
Japanese attack Bataan

On December 8, 1941, regardless of status, the way of life in America no longer remained routine. The Japanese air attack on the island of O'ahu gave folks in Palomino pause. Not fear, per se, but people no longer felt safe and secure. Worry gained a resurgence many thought well behind them. Anxiety plagued cities, towns, and farms, unease became a daily companion.

President Roosevelt requested, and Congress declared, that a state of war existed between the United States and the Japanese Empire.

In the German Reichstag on December 11, with his declaration of war with the United States, Adolf Hitler dropped the other shoe.

"The First World War, the crippling Depression, the choking Dustbowl, and now this, the killing of sailors, airmen, marines, and soldiers on a little island way over there in the Pacific Ocean," the Palomino grocer said. Nate Dulfeine shook his head and looked up and down

Main Street, his white shirtsleeves neatly folded up to his biceps, in spite of a chill in the morning air. He stood on the sidewalk in front of his grocery store. "A lot of our boys are going to Mount Pleasant and Paris and signing up. David, Earl and Nancy's boy, left this morning. He just finished high school last May."

Kingston Kline nodded. "My oldest boy joined the Navy yesterday, Nate," the Palomino druggist said. "He said he wanted to fly airplanes off aircraft carriers."

"How old is Curtis, Kingston?"

"Eighteen. He and David were classmates. I tried to stop him, told him I needed him to help run the store. I wanted him to be a pharmacist, take over the store in a few years. He was seventeen when Hitler declared war. Birthday was two weeks ago. He was old enough for the Navy, didn't need my signature."

"Maybe if he joined the Army he could've stayed at Camp Maxey."

"I told him that. But his mind was made up. In a way I'm kinda proud he was headstrong about it. Gave him character, I thought. Dora gave me a fit about it, about not stopping our boy from volunteering."

"I know how that went, Dora is headstrong herself."

Kingston nodded and grinned. "Yeah, I know. But I told her that Curtis was growed up now and she needed to let him be a man."

"Well, I hope Curtis gets his wish to fly for the Navy. He's a smart young fellow. He'll be safe, Kingston. Don't you worry none."

Soon after the order for a National Military Draft in 1940, plans to build an expansive infantry training camp on seventy-thousand acres north of Paris, Texas accelerated. Bombs and declarations hastened deliberate and methodical construction of Camp Maxey and soldiers began arriving long before enough living and office structures were up to accommodate them.

A mish-mash of activated National Guard company and battalion size units from several states staffed a makeshift Infantry Division at Maxey. Only a few of the arriving companies had actual infantry training. Preparations to equip the division with weapons, train it, and bring it to full fighting strength of twenty-five-thousand officers, NCOs, and soldiers began immediately.

Eventually many of these units at Maxey shipped out to Great Britain to join tens of thousands staging for a military operation named *Overlord*.

Along with the Infantry Division, a Military Police Battalion of five-hundred men formed at Maxey with the mission to accompany the fighting unit to Europe. Unlike the Division, though, most individuals with the MP unit at least had some police training and experience.

Sergeant Willow 'Twig' Chestnutt was one of those military policemen. As a law enforcement officer, he had been classified II-A. Nevertheless, he answered the call from Uncle Sam and through social and political connections arranged to enlist as a Sergeant. His orders posted him to Camp Maxey. He expected to ship out when the order came down, and believed his unit would be a support element following the massive assaults on the European Continent.

"Oh, Twig, you're so impulsive. Last night, we decided to talk more about it before you volunteered, Sweetheart."

"I know, Resa, I know. Since Christmas, we've talked about me joining the Army. We've talked it to death. Every time we'd see a newsreel at the show, they put up the pictures of Pearl Harbor. Those images just kept eating away at me. I needed to do this, and you didn't object. You never said no. It was time for me to do it."

"Are you going to go to war, Daddy?"

"No, no, Tina, not right away, Sweetie. There's a lot that has to be done before we make the Japanese, Italians, and Germans stop fighting."

"What will you do, Twig? Will you be a sergeant in the infantry, like your guard unit?"

"No, Johnny brought the telegram to the cafe this morning. His recruiting headquarters gave approval to sign me up as a sergeant in the military police because I have a law enforcement certificate and work as a peace officer. I won't have to go to Camp Polk and go through boot camp. I report to a new place they're building north of Paris, Texas. It's called Camp Maxey."

"You're a Constable, Twig, not a policeman or deputy sheriff."

"I don't guess it makes that much difference, Resa. There's a war on, and the Army needs all the able-bodied men it can get. If a man has training, experience, and the right qualifications they ease the requirements. That's why I don't have to go through boot camp."

"When do you have to go to Paris, to this Camp

Maxey?"

"I have to be there Wednesday."

"WEDNESDAY! In four days?"

"I want you and Sweetie to go with me, Resa, so we got to get organized."

"I want to go, Daddy. I want to go. I've never been to Texas. Maybe I can see some cowboys and horses."

They sold small items at knock-down prices, traded clothing and jewelry for gas coupons, packed remaining meager belongings in the rumble seat of their Ford Coupe, and drove the 127 miles from Vivian, Louisiana to Paris where Teresa and Tina moved into an expensive boarding house run by Madame Estelle.

The next morning, Teresa and Tina drove the Ford back to the boarding house after saying goodbye to Twig at the Maxey main gate at Powderly.

To be close while Twig was learning to be a soldier and military policeman, they decided to absorb the steep rent for a furnished bedroom, closet, and shared hallway bath that included breakfast and supper. Tina was smart but not of school age, so leaving Vivian or arriving in Paris during school time was not an issue.

Teresa found a job in Tiny's Cafe a couple of blocks over from the boarding house. It was an easy walk for Tina and Teresa.

The minute Teresa and Tina walked through the door, Tiny Talbot decided right away to hire Teresa as a waitress. They had not yet said hello.

"My name is Teresa Chestnutt and this is Tina. We

just moved here from Louisiana to be near my husband.   He's in the Army at Camp Maxey.   I'm looking for a job.   I wonder if you might know where someone needs help."

"My name is Tonya Talbot.   Everybody calls me Tiny, of course.   I own the place.   Ever been a waitress?"

Teresa did not ask about wages.   Just having somewhere to go every day and having something to do was a blessing.   "Yes, I've done that before, Tonya . . . Tiny."

"Good.   Your shift is six days a week, Sundays off. You start at seven in the morning and finish at five, ten hours.   I pay forty cents an hour, and you keep all your tips.   What do you say, Teresa?"

"Thank you so much, Tiny.   I'll be your waitress. When do I start?"

Tiny, all three-hundred pounds of her, was accommodating and permitted Tina to help in the cafe. Tina thoroughly enjoyed being part of it.   She helped Wiley, the busboy, in a small way when he wiped tables with a wet towel, scraped scraps into the trash barrel in the kitchen, filled sugar, salt and peppershakers, and laid out knives, spoons, and forks wrapped in paper napkins.

For this, Tiny paid Tina ten cents a day, big money for a five-year-old.   The best part of the deal for Teresa and Tina was a free sandwich and drink at dinnertime.

Both of them loved Tiny, going to the cafe, and meeting customers.   The money was a big help.

One evening after supper at Madame Estelle's table, Tina made an announcement.   "Momma, Miss Tiny pays me ten cents a day. I think I'll pay you a nickel a day to help pay our rent. I'll save *my* nickels to buy a radio."

"Well, Sweetie, that is right nice of you to do that since we gave up our radio in Vivian. I'll make a deal with you. I know you miss listening to *Orphan Annie*, *Fibber McGee and Molly*, and *Abbott and Costello*, and I miss my mystery programs and all the great music shows, so I'll be a partner in the radio department. You keep your money and that way you'll be able to buy the radio sooner, and the sooner we can listen to our favorites. Okay?"

"No, Momma." Tina was determined. "I want to do my share."

On return from chores every day, Tina gave a nickel to Teresa and dropped her remaining nickel into an Ovaltine can Tiny provided. Teresa, in keeping with their partnership, frequently dropped Tina's Buffalo nickel as well as a couple of nickels and Mercury dimes of tip money into the primitive bank, too. Each time Twig came home on pass, he managed to add a nickel or dime to the growing radio fund.

As weeks passed, Teresa realized there were two sides to the rental war going on nine miles from a permanent and growing military installation. Hundreds arrived to apply for the abundant, great paying government and contract jobs. Of course, great pay permitted gouging by landlords of those renters already employed. Competition for space was fierce and the persuader was the highest bidder's dollars. Madame Estelle's boarding house was no different.

Teresa was upset by more than wrangling over rent

money. Seems that Madame Estelle's boarding house also was a thriving whorehouse, and even a blind man could see that the goings-on had gone on long enough. It was time to sever the contract and move.

"I don't know how to say this, Tiny, you've been so sweet to us and all."

"What's wrong, Teresa. I hope you're not going to tell me you're quitting."

Tears shimmered in Teresa's eyes as she nodded.

Tiny wrapped her fleshy arms around Teresa and held her close and tight. "Tell me what's wrong, Darlin. You and me can fix it." She stroked Teresa's hair with tenderness.

"We've got to move, Tiny."

"Why? What's wrong? Is somebody bothering you? Somebody bothering Tina?"

"No, no, nothing like that. Madame Estelle told me our rent's going up on the first of the month, from a dollar-eighty-five a day to two-sixty-five a day."

"That's almost double what you pay. You let me talk to her."

"Yes, it's a big jump, more than we can afford. But that's not the only problem."

With a thumb, Tiny flicked tears from Teresa's cheeks. She waited, peering into Teresa's eyes.

"There are . . ." Teresa started. "There are . . . prostitutes," she whispered.

Tiny's grin was wide. Her throaty laughter accompanied vigorous nods, her whole body shook. "I know, Honey, Lord, I know. A lot of our customers are working girls. You've seen them in here when they weren't *on duty*, without all the make-up. My place is sort of a neutral hangout for them, a place they can be themselves and relax. Delilah and Ginnie are the leaders, the organizers. They take care of the younger troopers."

"Now that you mention it, I recognized some faces. I never knew their names."

"Whether in Estelle's place or mine, they're the same person, they just dress differently. In here they relax, they're not on duty."

Teresa sniffed and swiped under her nose with the back of her hand. "I had my suspicions pretty early, but I thought we could tolerate the day and night goings-on. But I can't let Tina be in that kind of place."

Tiny's grin was still on her plump, cheeky face. She waggled her head from side to side. "I know you can't, Honey. Tina doesn't need to be around that sort of life. There ain't nothing we can do about what goes on at Estelle's. The Police Chief and Lamar County Sheriff are regulars at her place, so they ain't gonna bust down the door and close it up. It's a way of surviving. Can you find another place that's within your budget?"

"I looked. I wanted to stay here, work for you, you've been so kind to Tina and me. But, we have to move out of Paris. I checked with the three hotels and the other four boarding houses. They're all full. They have a waitlist. Anyway, even if there was a vacancy I don't think we could afford it. Everybody is raising their rent."

"Well, Honey, the hotels and other boarding houses are in it as deep as Estelle's. For them, it's about the money. There're thousands of soldiers and contractors out there at Maxey, not to mention the ones who work for the state and federal governments. What's here is for them, and for them it's all about pleasure and entertainment. With the war and build-up what we're facing here and over there is going to get worse, I think."

"I know you're right, Tiny. Sometimes I feel so anxious and so scared I think I'm going to scream."

"What about an apartment? I know a house would cost too much."

"Even if we could find one, an apartment is too expensive. And we don't have any furniture. Everything is out of reach now with all the people coming in to work at Camp Maxey."

"Okay, Darlin, we've got, let's see, five days till the end of the month. Let me make a couple of inquiries, I'll see what I can do. I'll take care of my two favorite girls. Okay?"

Twig was on a twenty-four-hour pass when Teresa told him about the development and their need to relocate. "It's a sign of the times, Resa, with the war and everything. We just don't have the money to pay the increase."

"It's not the money, Twig. It's . . . it's . . ."

"It's the Johns."

They looked at Tina. She sat on the floor at the foot of the bed, coins from her bank scattered on the worn carpet. She didn't look up from stacking pennies, nickels, and dimes.

"Where did you hear that, Sweetie?"

"Madame Estelle, Daddy. She said Johns were on

the street day and night with hands full of money waiting for a room."

Twig looked at Teresa and grinned.

Teresa shook her head. "Your daughter's ears have no trouble hearing what goes on, and if we don't move, her eyes are going to see more than they need to."

"My eyes are pretty good, Momma. I don't need glasses. Now, we only need one more dollar to buy our radio."

"Your eyes are beautiful, Sweetie. They sparkle like the stars." Twig pulled his wallet, withdrew the only money in it, and handed the lone one-dollar silver certificate to Tina.

"Thank you, Daddy."

"Okay, Resa. I know you're right. Where will you go?"

"Now Momma and me can buy the Philco radio we saw at the radio store for six dollars and ninety-five cents. We'll be able to listen to all our programs again."

"Six ninety-five? Half price?"

"It's an old, used radio, Twig. The man said somebody needed a loan and never came back for it."

"Will you go to the store with me, Daddy?"

"You bet I will, Sweetie. I bet the owner might give you a discount because you are such a smart, pretty little girl."

"The town is called Palomino. About 16 miles east, down the highway."

"Yeah, I remember. We passed through there on our way here."

"Tiny has a friend there, Miss Maybelle Winters.

They exchanged telegrams. Tiny said Miss Maybelle agreed to help find a place for us and maybe even give me a job."

"What kind of job?"

"Miss Maybelle has a cafe called Jeeps and owns the town newspaper. Maybe I could be a waitress or work at the *Palomino Press*."

"Palomino? That sounds like the town is named after a horse."

"Tiny said Palomino is a small community split down the center by a creek. On the east side of the water, Palomino is in Red River County and on the western side it's in Lamar County . . ."

"Ha. A town in two counties. I bet the two sheriffs feud when something happens — each one will say it's the others responsibility."

Teresa ignored Twig's interrupting supposition and continued. "She said some residents come to Paris and Camp Maxey to work. A few who live there are roughnecks for the oil rigs near a town she called Talco, and others work in the fields and cotton gins in Palomino. I like small towns, they're quiet. Like Vivian."

"Well, quiet is in the eye of the beholder. Vivian wasn't the quiet, quaint little town you remember it to be, Resa. Sometimes I had my hands full, you just didn't know what all went on." Twig shook his head. "I could tell you plenty of horror stories about some of the fine, upstanding, *charming* citizens."

"Well, I hope Palomino will be a sleepy little town where they roll up the sidewalks after sundown, where at night not much goes on. Certainly nothing like what goes on in Paris or here at Estelle's."

"Okay, but I can't go with you, can't help you move. The Colonel ordered my company on an assignment. We're going to be in the field for four or five weeks, maybe more. The engineer battalion built a huge holding pen with strands of concertina wire on top of a high, chicken-wire fence, guard towers, and spotlights, so instead of police duties, we're going to be training as prison guards. All the infantry units have to go through an escape and evasion program, and my company is going to handle those captured as if they were prisoners of war."

"That's okay, Twig. I knew you wouldn't be able to get away. Tina and I are big girls. We can do it on our own."

"When we go away, Daddy, will you come see us?"

"As often as I can, Sweetie. I'm going to miss my two Sweethearts."

THE INTRODUCTION
July 1942
Hitler orders capture of Stalingrad
Guadalcanal in Japanese hands

"When Teresa told Miss Ruby you'd be here on a weekend pass, I had the immediate thought to introduce you to some of the men in town, Sergeant Chestnutt. I'm glad you agreed to meet here at the store. We can walk down the street to Wilson's Domino Hall. We can have coffee and a piece of Henry's lemon pie, and talk a bit."

"Teresa told me this was an interview, to see if I fit in."

Nathaniel Dulfeine gave a friendly chuckle, and a grin spread across his face as he nodded. It was Saturday noon. They stood on the sidewalk in front of Dulfeine's Grocery and shook hands.

Twig thought the grocer presented himself with an affable, professional aura. His flowery red tie accented the starched white shirt with sleeves neatly folded across ample biceps. He stood erect but seemed taller than five-seven, which was the average height of the men in Palomino. His bright blue eyes were welcoming and followed Twig's moves. A full, manicured mustache could not hide that his nose had been broken. Twig noted Dulfeine was striking, rugged, a man's man.

"Your lady is right, of course. A couple of the boys wanted to get a good look at you. I'm not sure it's an interview. It's probably more for them to see if you deserve two great girls. We've all grown quite fond of Teresa and Tina in the couple of months they've been here. This is the first opportunity we've had to get you alone, among the menfolk. I can already assure you that you belong. A soldier in uniform is always welcome in Palomino."

"Well, I'm glad you asked me, Mr. Dulfeine. I'd like to interview some of the menfolk myself."

"I never had the chance to ask when you and your girls came into the store before. I want you to call me Nate. Come along, Sergeant Chestnutt, Wilson's is four doors down."

As Dulfeine and Chestnutt walked, they said howdy to the men, smiled and nodded respectfully to the women who traveled the sidewalk with purpose.

"When folks come to town," Dulfeine said, "they want to visit and socialize as well as shop and take care of business. It's difficult to decide which is more important. We try to do both in the store but sometimes we don't have as much time as it takes to listen to everybody who wants to talk, gossip mostly."

The hand-painted sign over the door announced **Wilson's Domeno Hall and Pies**. Twig smiled at the misspelling.

As they entered, Twig felt the coolness of the

rectangular-shaped room, both in temperature and welcome. Unlike a barbershop, this social hub was mostly all business when a game was underway. The competitors did talk between shuffles, but their purpose was to focus, plan, and make the bid or set an opponent.

The three blades on each ceiling fan swirled as fast as a P-40 Warhawk's propeller.

Four tables with four white-pine chairs at each table dominated the narrow parlor. Active players sat at two tables. They did not look up from their game. The four chairs at one table were empty, and only two chairs at the remaining table were in use.

Even at noontime, the playing area of the room needed the four incandescent, 60-watt bulbs because there were no windows.

A vacant, worn-out, leather couch with puncture marks dotting its arms and three cushions slumped along the right wall. Four brown, lonely, barstools stood along the left wall. At the back of the room, a black man stood behind a black cash register that sat atop the saloon-type bar. A closed door was on the left side of the back wall.

Two long walls were full of framed pictures of all sizes above the stools and couch. In a few of the black-and-whites, Twig could see men on horses. In one, six white men, one black man and one with a sombrero, sat on horses facing the camera. Here and there, between photographs, boxes of pads, yellow pencil stubs, and black-backed dominos rested on shelves.

"Hello, boys," Nate Dulfeine greeted the room. The

players did not respond.

He raised and shook a finger at the black man. "How you doing, Henry?"

Henry nodded but remained silent.

"Sergeant Chestnutt, this is Kingston Kline, our druggist and pharmacist, and Major Clay Monroe who owns most of the cotton fields around here and one of the gins.   Henry Wilson back there owns this establishment. It's our game room, pie shop, unofficial meeting place, and hideout from our women."

The two men stood, stepped forward to Twig. Kline extended his right hand in friendship. The Major extended his left, since he had no right hand.

Twig was comfortable with Kline's handshake, but felt awkward with the Major's left hand.

"I've seen you before," Twig acknowledged. "I was on pass, a couple of weeks ago. You were outside the grocery store when I came in with my wife, Teresa, and my daughter, Tina, to shop."

Kingston Kline was short and thin with a slim, humped, hooked nose. Wildly curled, brown hair wrapped around the sides of slick baldness on the front top of his head. For Twig, Kingston was the spitting image of Larry, the curly-haired character with The Three Stooges. From appearances, Twig judged Kingston was Jewish.

Major Monroe, on the other hand, stood with a statesman's stature. He was as tall as Twig's six-two and broad-shouldered. His black eyes sat deep in a face dime novel writers described as chiseled, and his contagious broad smile was magnetic. Groomed, neatly trimmed white hair peeked from under the sides of a clean, gray Panama hat.

Twig also had a second impression of Major Monroe and his image. Twig imagined he was looking at a rich owner of a cotton plantation, who ran the town, and who might be a politically active patron with deep pockets who could buy what he wanted, including people. Twig *was* impressed.

After introductions and small talk, Twig and Nate joined Major Monroe and Kingston at their table.

"Henry, please bring us all a piece of your lemon pie and coffee. Or, would you prefer a Dr. Pepper, Sergeant Chestnutt?"

"Coffee is fine, Nate. Thank you."

Major Monroe got right to the point of what was on his mind. "Teresa told me you were a Constable in Vivian before enlisting, Sergeant Chestnutt."

"I was the only law there for six years. Sam Boudreaux, the Caddo Parish Sheriff, wanted to make me one of his deputies but our Mayor said no. Alonzo didn't want to give control of Vivian to the Sheriff. Alonzo made sure he ran the town."

"We had a Constable, but he run off," Nate said.

"As a law man, Sergeant Chestnutt, and because of your age with a wife and child, you should've been exempt from military service," Kingston said.

He looked at each of them as he spoke. "Twig, please call me Twig. Yes, Sir, I was classified as Two-A, but when the Japs attacked Hawaii, I knew I had to join the Army. The Army recruiter for the Northern Louisiana Region, Sergeant Johnny Ziegler, was a friend." Twig looked at Kingston. "Johnny was Jewish, probably the only Jew in Vivian.

"I met him when he came down to our Armory. I was a Sergeant in a National Guard Infantry Company, and Johnny came by during drills trying to recruit guys. We hit it off. He'd drop by every couple of weeks, and we'd ride down to Oil City and eat ribs at a local smokehouse. He arranged for me to enlist as a Military Police Sergeant. I owe Johnny big time for the strings he pulled."

"Teresa told me your name is Willow, but I like your nickname," Major Monroe said. "Twig."

"Dad named me Willow, I'm a Junior in fact, but Momma gave me the nickname. 'Twig is sorta like a branch off the tree,' she used to say."

"Let's see, you've been on a couple of weekend passes . . ."

"Three, so far, Major."

"How do you like Palomino?"

"It's a lot like Vivian, mostly quiet. Palomino is bigger I think. I do have one burning question."

"What's that, Twig?"

"I've wondered about the town's name. When Teresa told me Palomino, I said it sounded like Palomino was named after a horse."

"It was, Twig," the Major said.

Sergeant Chestnutt waited for a more detailed answer but decided it wasn't coming without a prod.

"Okay, you can't leave it there, named after a horse. Where did it come from? How did it come about? What horse? Whose horse?"

"Delbert Porter," Kingston said.

"Porter named the town Palomino?"

"No, not really," the Major answered. "There were

31

eight cowboys who rode up this way with Captain Porter from South Texas, near Hebbronville. They named the town."

"Eight cowboys." Twig pointed toward the wall. "Those in that picture?"

"Okay, it's obvious you're interested, so we'll tell the story, tell what we know, what's been passed down, and what's in official documents and newspaper accounts in the library," Dulfeine said.

At that moment, Henry arrived with a tray of four servings of lemon pie. In short order, he returned with white ceramic cups of steaming coffee.

The four indulged in several gulping bites and slurps of hot liquid in chewing silence until the initial enjoyment waned. They picked at crumbs and settled in for the history lesson about to unfold.

"Delbert Porter was an eccentric, distinctive-looking man who sat a tall, prancing American Saddlebred," Nate said. "He paid a lot of money for the beautiful stallion he named Rufus."

The domino players had paused and turned toward the storytellers.

One of the players couldn't resist adding color to the story. "Rufus was proud and thought he should have a prettier name to go along with his stature and appearance, but had no voice in the matter. Rufus would have preferred the name, Hi Ho Silver."

They all chuckled and nodded knowingly as if Rufus had told them himself.

"Captain Porter came from the valley with his small herd, arriving at Pecan Creek on July Fourth, Eighteen-Seventy-Six," the Major said. "His great aim was to push safely through Indian Territory to the railhead in Wichita, Kansas. *Safely* was key — one never knew what could happen in the wilderness."

Another player chimed in. "Bandits, bootleggers, badasses, hawkers, real-estate agents, whores, and used horse traders were after his cowboys' wages. Rotgut whiskey was a problem, too."

The Major paused and took a swig of coffee. He looked in the direction of the players without speaking. His signal was clear to Twig — and apparent to the kibitzers. It was plain to everyone that the Major did not want outside participation in the telling of the birth of his town.

The players turned away, and the scraping and sliding and clacking of shuffling dominoes filled the room for a few seconds.

Dulfeine took the cue. "As they rode north, word circulated along the way that all tribes were on the warpath, wanting revenge and scalps because some crazy-ass Colonel attacked a million braves somewhere in Montana. Of course, we now know that was Custer. The most frightening report then was that all soldiers in the Colonel's outfit perished. Not a trooper or horse survived. Gossip was rampant. Since hearing that disturbing news, folks on dusty trails were cautious."

Kingston Kline picked up the telling. "The stop at Pecan Creek was for water and rest, but Captain Porter was also wary of venturing into warring tribes. Unfortunately, because of the stop, the grand scheme of selling his corn-fed livestock to The Great Cattle Co-Op of Waterbury, Connecticut for a bundle of money ended with a strike from a diamondback rattler."

Twig shook his shoulders. "Oh, Lord. I hate snakes, all kinds of snakes. Mr. Porter suffered a snake-bite?"

"No, Rufus did," Nate said. "Rufus did not welcome the insertion of venomous fangs in his left front pastern. Of course, Mr. Snake did not appreciate a 980-pound giant stepping on his tail. Thus, the snap of horseflesh was the incentive to move on. Instead, Rufus moved up on rear hooves, and Captain Porter moved down into the creek, flopped around, and drowned."

"Here, in this creek along Main Street?"

A player slammed a domino on the wooden tabletop. The sharp report sounded like a pistol shot. Twig turned his head with a quick jerk to look at the disruption. The demonstrative, aggressive display made an important set of a wild bid.

"I knew you held the five-ace, Samuel," the player said. "Held my double-barreled five to set you."

"Yep, the same one, Pecan Creek," Kingston resumed. "Anyway, the wranglers used sticks and rifle barrels to pull away the wad of nineteen angry water moccasins holding onto his face and throat after they pulled Boss Porter's lifeless body ashore. They killed many of the snakes with what they had in their hands, the rest slithered back into the creek. The boys chose a large grove of trees along the east bank of the creek because of shade. It took a full day and part of the evening to dig a hole large enough to bury them."

"They buried Mr. Porter in the hole with Rufus?"

"They did," Clay nodded. "Over snake-meat and beans that night, after planting him and Rufus, they talked about a name for their Captain's final resting place. While some dangled Delbert, others preferred Porter. Nobody wanted to name the place Rufus. Older cowhands decided to let their youngest one, Jeff Jeeps, pick the name. They didn't expect a significant contribution."

"They ate the snakes attached to Mr. Porter? The water moccasins? Good Lord."

"Yep, what was left of the nineteen," Nate answered.

"I've eaten a lot of wild game but never snake meat."

Dulfeine paused and sipped coffee.

Major Monroe picked up the tale. "The color of Delbert Porter's horse popped out of Jeeps' mouth and, without discussion or objection, every cowpoke around the campfire nodded his agreement. They were tired and sleepy, so it was an easy concession. Anyway, if an argument developed later, they could blame the name on the youngster. Nevertheless, they admitted it was a good choice."

"Mr. Porter had no relatives back where they came from," Kingston added. "The land they left was dry, wind-blown, worthless dirt, and the herders didn't feel like continuing the trek because it was a long ride to Wichita. Anyhow, they figured nobody from Waterbury was going to call."

"Following Mr. Porter's demise," Major Monroe said, "our eight founding fathers decided to divide the herd and settle down in their new community. They recognized that the soil was rich for farming and the grass was abundant for ranching."

Nate grinned as he presented the dénouement. "All the horses, foals, cows, calves, and bulls were happy, too, to be in Palomino."

"I knew Palomino was named after a horse," Twig said. "I knew it." He nodded and joined the warm, friendly, smiles. "Better than Rufus, I like the name Palomino."

Monroe pointed toward the wall full of photographs. "The eight hands who rode with Captain Porter are in that large rectangle picture up there, in the center of the shelves. The one you pointed at."

Twig rose from his chair and moved to the wall. He leaned forward, his nose inches from the faded, poorly focused, black and white portrait.

From his chair, Major Monroe guided Twig's inspection. "From the left is Merryfield Wilson, Henry's granddaddy. Next is Horace Thurgood. He had two boys, Hobart and Kermit. Kermit died awhile back. Henrietta, she goes by Henny, and Eliot are Hobart's kids. Both still live here. Next is Percy Chainlee, Miss Ruby's grandpa, then Bastion Albert, Bastion Albert the third and Kingston's wife, Dora's granddaddy, Nathaniel Dulfeine, Nate's granddaddy, Arthur Monroe, my grandpa, and Jeff Jeeps, Maybelle Winters' granddaddy. The man on the end, on the small pony, was Miguel Santos."

Twig turned away from the picture and waited.

"No kin of Miguel's here?"

The Major shook his head. "Miguel rode over to Paris and met a woman who was married. Maria Perez. Santiago, Maria's husband, was not happy about Miguel's advances and confronted Miguel on the street.

Miguel put a knife in Santiago's heart in the summer of Ninety-Six. Maria and Miguel fled to Mexico and settled in a little village called Linares."

"In Ninety-Six, Palomino incorporated, earned a local post office, and had a population of three-hundred-and-thirty-one. There were two churches, three general stores, an apothecary, a gristmill, two cotton gins, and several small businesses. It also supported a weekly paper called the *Palomino Press*," Kingston said. "The paper now belongs to Maybelle."

Sergeant Chestnutt returned to his chair.

"By the turn of the century, the population had increased to four-hundred-ninety-seven souls. The number of enterprises had blossomed to forty-six, including three physicians, a music teacher, a milliner, and a photographer. When the Palomino schoolhouse was finished, four teachers and sixty-two students moved in. Covered by rich, black soil, the surrounding area proved ideal for the production of cotton, corn, and abundant prairie grasses for the high-grade livestock, which was the consequence of Mr. Porter's small herd," Dulfeine added.

Henry approached. "Do you want more pie and coffee, Major?"

"Just coffee, Henry." The Major ordered for everyone.

"After a decade, the Paris and Mount Pleasant Railway put down fifty miles of track that ran on the outskirts of town. Yielding to the pressure from the townsfolk, the railroad also built a small station over here on the highway. This rail service provides transportation to Bogata, Pattonville, and Paris, and a connection in both hubs for travelers to St. Louis, Memphis, Shreveport, and Dallas. It was designated the Cotton Belt Line, for some unknown reason most folks ended up calling it The Katy. Rail-riding hobos often stopped in Palomino for a meal. None of them applied for a job in the mill or gins," the druggist said.

"They never stayed more than two nights," the Major said. "It wasn't in their best interest."

"After the First World War, the town's population grew to over eleven-hundred, and fifty-eight businesses supported the community. Later, the Great Depression and Dustbowl took its toll, and the population dwindled to seven-hundred-eleven. Two dozen of the minor merchants packed their goods, closed their shops, left the key in the door, and moved away," the grocer said. "December Seven, Forty-One, things changed again, and here we are, in another World War."

A wailing siren interrupted the silent pause.

"Fire call," one of the domino players yelled.

Everyone stood, two chairs toppled over.

The players rushed toward the front door, their dominos remained undisturbed, lined up, ready for play.

"We've got a voluntary fire department, Twig. We have to answer the call," Nate said. "I'm sorry, but you can't be part of it. No training, you might be injured."

In four seconds, the only two standing in *Wilson's Domeno Hall and Pies* were Twig and Henry Wilson.

EARLY WITHDRAWAL
January 1942
U-boats sink ships off American coast
Japan-Germany-Italy form Axis in Berlin

In time for their two dollar and eighty-five cent 1941 Christmas bonuses, the three older men and two thirteen-year-old boys, heads of households employed by the WPA (Works Projects Administration), completed the finishing touches on the Red River County State Bank in Bogata, Texas.

For four full, drawn out, months they had been able to obtain the hourly wages paid by the government. Now, supervised by their boss, the two teenagers climbed ladders that leaned against the shiny red bricks of the front outer wall. They slid the painted white sign with blue blocked lettering into the metal frame over the beveled green glass, double front doors. Job finished. It was three o'clock on Tuesday, December 30.

Standing there on the sidewalk, a few feet back from the small building, the men and boys admired their work. It was a nice building and blended in with older, similar structures.

To celebrate the occasion, Mr. Franklein Rosser, President of the bank, Miss Judy Jones, First Vice President and Chief Cashier, and Miss Myrtle Sherman, Second Vice President and Senior Teller served up five bottles of bubbly champagne brought all the way from Dallas. The adults looked the other way, pretending they did not see, while the youngsters gulped, savored, and swallowed the white wine.

A photographer from the *Bogata Bulletin* snapped abundant pictures, and a reporter took notes and acquired quotes to record this fantastic addition to the community.

"Our fine people waited a long time to have their own financial services," Mr. Rosser said. "I am proud of our achievement, what we've done here for our county citizens."

The scribe scribbled on her notepad.

"Now you be sure to spell my name correctly, Ina," the bank president said. "It's not Frank, it's Franklein, F-R-A-N-K-L-E-I-N, Rosser, R-O-S-S-E-R. Got it?"

"Yes, Sir, Mr. Rosser," Ina said. "Congratulations on your new bank. How much money you got in there, you think?"

Franklein Rosser grinned. "Well, now, Miss Nosey-Wosey, I bet you and all those Bonnies and Clydes and Johnny Dillingers would sure like to know."

"I think your bank customers would like to know that you've got your own money in the bank, Mr. Rosser," Ina said, "before they give theirs to you. I like to know there's enough in there for me when I come to take some of mine out. You know our recovery is still struggling after the Depression. There were a lot of folks who lost all their money when the little banks went out of business. Even some of the bank presidents took the money and ran."

Mr. Rosser nodded. "Yes, yes, Ina, I'm aware of what you're saying. But that's not going to happen here. Write that we have plenty of money in the bank for our customers and that I say we, at Red River County State Bank, will safeguard the funds of our valued depositors."

"Well, I hope your depositors have money to deposit. Otherwise, your bank might suffer the same fate as those who've shut their doors when people lost trust."

The *Bulletin* and the bank were closed Wednesday, New Year's Eve, and Thursday, January 1, 1942. The front-page, above the fold, feature story of Bogata's new enterprise did not appear until the morning of January 2, in a special edition. The three-penny, six-page sheet sold out in twenty-two minutes. Everybody was excited to come to town to see the bank, smell all the fresh paint and new money.

The event and convenience were talk of the county. Now Bogata and Red River County residents did not have to take a morning departure and afternoon return on the Katy railroad, or drive west on US Highway 271, to conduct their banking business in Paris or Palomino.

On the second day of 1942 and the first day of operation, at high noon Friday, two hours after Franklein Rosser opened the doors for business, three masked bandits walked in brandishing pistols as if they were performing a theatrical scene with James Cagney.

Two of the trio hollered, scared the shit out of everybody in the bank, and withdrew eight-hundred-seventy-five dollars, the grand total of all the pristine printed notes the bank president gave to the Chief Cashier to stash in the Senior Teller's station drawer slots.

In 240-seconds, the heist was complete. The robbers vanished with packs of one-dollar, two-dollar, five-dollar, and ten-dollar silver certificates, and several dozen twenty-dollar Federal Reserve Notes.

Standing in the space between the front doors and the teller cage, Red River County Deputy Sheriff Logan Amesa took charge of the investigation.

"I know everybody is excited to be a part of the first bank robbery in this establishment," Deputy Amesa said. "You'll have great stories to tell your grandkids. But I want to be the first to hear your story. So, one by one I want you to tell me what you saw and heard. I won't take long."

When the four patrons who were in the bank during the robbery revealed what they witnessed or remembered, their accounts did not correlate. Their descriptions of the bandits' height, weight, colors of clothing, shoes and socks, type and color of weapon, voice, or gender were off the chart. The only common thing was the red bandannas covering the culprits' mouths and noses. But he wrote each statement down in his official notepad anyway.

After the customers left, Deputy Amesa closed and locked the bank's doors to conduct his interviews with the three bank officers.

Miss Judy and Miss Myrtle were dedicated to their community and church. They were prompt for services every Sunday morning, studious during bible sessions Wednesday evenings, chaperones at youth dinners on Thursdays, and organizers of Saturday afternoon women's socials. They were busy-bees and lines of communication for the goings-on in Bogata. They paid attention.

"One was a woman, one was large, a farm hand, and the other might of been a teenager. He was a boy, small and short," Miss Judy said.

"That's right," Miss Myrtle confirmed.

"A woman?" Deputy Amesa questioned. "What makes you think it was a woman?"

"It was the way she walked and stood," Miss Judy said, "and held her pistol, close in, close to her body. A man will stand with his feet flat and legs apart when he holds a gun up for business. Like this. This one didn't. Her feet were close together, and she bent at the waist like she was choosing pears out of a basket."

"Okay. Did she speak, say anything?"

"Not a thing, Logan. The big one and the boy were the ones who talked," Miss Judy said.

"That's right," Miss Myrtle confirmed.

"Okay. What did the boy say?"

"He hollered, Logan, loud. Very loud," Miss Judy said. "Like he was scared to death, like he thought maybe we were all deaf. Lord enough, it was so quiet in the bank all of us could have heard a pin drop. He could have whispered, and we would have heard him."

"We were all scared to death, to say the least," Miss

Myrtle said. "At least I was. I've never been robbed in my life. I've never had a gun pointed at me."

"Okay. What did the boy holler, Miss Judy?"

"This is a stick-up, don't nobody move."

"Just like those gangsters when they rob a bank in the picture show," Miss Myrtle confirmed.

"What did the big one say?"

"'Fill this sack'," Miss Myrtle said. "He threw the sack at me like it was a dishrag. I pulled all the money out of the drawer and put it in the sack, like he said. The hole in the end of his gun looked like he was holding a shotgun. It was a big hole."

"How much money?"

"About fifteen thousand dollars, Deputy."

"Fifteen thousand dollars, Mr. Rosser? Fifteen thousand? That's a lot of money."

"We expected a lot of customers, Deputy Amesa. Good, honest, God-fearing, customers."

Franklein tugged at the sleeves of his brown suit before adjusting his green and white polka-dot bow tie. "It was fifteen thousand dollars of all denominations."

He jutted his chin and stretched his neck upward for emphasis.

Deputy Amesa looked at Miss Judy, who said nothing.

He looked at Miss Myrtle and waited for her to confirm the amount. She said nothing.

He looked at the bank president and waited.

Franklein Rosser nodded. "It was fifteen thousand dollars, Deputy. Fifteen thousand dollars. I counted it myself before I handed it over to our Chief Cashier who placed it in our Senior Teller's station drawer."

"What about their clothes? How were they dressed? From top to bottom. You go first, Miss Judy."

"Her suit and hat."

Deputy Amesa was a long time neighbor of Miss Judy and Miss Myrtle. As a boy, he had experienced their discipline when they caught him shooting his B-B gun at their wrens. Their justice was sharp with a swift backhand. He never forgot that and never, ever, mistook a wren for a sparrow again.

"What about her suit and hat?" the deputy asked.

"The woman wore a fedora, a black fedora, it looked new, very clean," Miss Myrtle said. "She wore a man's double-breasted, navy blue Sunday suit, a pink shirt, and red tie. There was a white silk handkerchief stuffed in the suit coat's pocket. I'll never forget all those colors."

"The pistol!" Miss Judy exclaimed. "My, Lord, it was a small, shiny pistol. It was silver. The pistol was silver, and she wore red leather gloves."

"That's good, Miss Judy, that's good," Amesa said. He nodded encouragement. "You said a pistol. Could it be a revolver?"

"It was a gun, Logan. Don't be so technical."

"Okay, Miss Judy. I understand. I was just trying to know the facts."

"Yes, I remember that shiny gun too. And her black eyes," Miss Myrtle added.

"You saw their faces?"

"No, Logan, red bandannas covered their mouth and nose. All I could see were eyes. And that little gun."

Deputy Logan Amesa did not attempt to steer either of them to address him as an officer of the law

45

investigating a serious crime. Had he tried to encourage the address of Deputy, his official title, they would have been hurt. So, instead of Deputy Amesa, he accepted Logan.

"And the big one?"

"Black hair, coal black," Miss Judy said. "Brylcreemed down, parted in the middle. Overalls too."

"Now, Miss Judy, were the overalls new looking, worn out, or what?"

"Not new, used, Logan, but only slightly faded."

"Will you and Miss Myrtle be okay? Do you need to see Doc Bledsoe?"

"Why?"

"Nerves?"

"No, Miss Myrtle and me don't need to see Doc Bledsoe. Franklein do you need to see Doc Bledsoe?"

"No, Miss Judy, I'm fine."

"What about the boy. How was he dressed?"

"He was a redhead, Logan, well not quite red, more sandy, I guess," Miss Myrtle said. "He wore a brown tweed newsboy cap and overalls. He had blue eyes. His gun was as big as the other boy's was. Just the woman had the small shiny gun."

"When they left the bank which way did they go?"

"To the right. We could hear two doors slam and the engine roar as they took off," the bank president said.

"Two doors slammed. You only heard two doors?"

"That's right, a two-door car. Or truck."

"Okay, I guess that about does it. Can you think of anything else to tell me?"

Franklein Rosser shrugged. "I know why people rob banks more than any other place, Deputy."

Logan tilted his head. "I think we all do, really, Mr. Rosser."

Miss Judy laughed. "For goodness sake, Franklein, everybody knows why. Banks have the money conveniently laid out in an open drawer for easy withdrawals."

"Mr. Rosser, I think it would be in your best interests to find somebody who can handle a pistol and hire them as an armed security guard. This time nobody was hurt. But you said all three had guns. The next time they may use them."

"Yes, of course. We need to do that. Do you have anyone in mind?"

"Yes, I do," Deputy Amesa said. "Deputy Walter Crawley. He's been a deputy sheriff all of his adult life, and he's retiring in April after a thirty-five year career. Between now and the time he retires I'm sure the sheriff would agree to place Deputy Crawley on the day shift with duty in the bank. After he retires, you could make a contract with him to be your security guard."

"Yes, of course. I know Walter," Rosser said.

"We all know Walter," Miss Judy said. "He'd be perfect with us."

"You boys did good. It was just as we planned it. Nobody got hurt, and that's a good thing. We had a good haul. It was easy work. I knew they'd be too cheap to have a security guard."

"When I tossed the sack at that old woman at the

teller window, her scream nearly scared me to death."

"Next time hand the sack over, M D. Don't throw it at anybody. She didn't know what was in the sack, that's why she screamed."

"Yes, Mam."

"Artemis, take the car back to Paris and park it someplace downtown. Park it at Mason's grocery on Main Street, in the back of the store."

"I got the car out of the Maxey parking lot. There's always a lot of cars, many are easy to wire up. I might bring it back there."

"No, you do what I tell you. It's better that you leave it in town instead of returning it where you borrowed it. That way you don't have to hitchhike, you'll already be in town and can walk to the station to take the train home. I don't want to see you until the first Sunday in February."

"What about my money?"

"You know the routine, Artemis. I've told you before I'll pay both of you later. Now, we'll meet on the first Sunday in February at the *Palace*, like we always do and I'll pay you. Last time I gave you money right away you spent all of it in three days and were back asking for more. When we started this project, I told you then what I would pay you each time. That's not changed. I'm not going to put up with your whining and crying and carrying-on about needing more money. If you're not satisfied, I'll find somebody else to drive the car."

"Well, I got expenses."

"We all have expenses, Artemis. I've got the show and the house to keep up. Don't tell me about expenses."

"How about giving me twenty dollars until then?"

"I'll give you ten. But that's all."

"Can I have ten dollars too?"

"Okay, M D, but that's all for the both of you until we meet."

"Ten dollars ain't much for a whole month."

"Well, that's all you're going to get for right now. Here, M D, you take the sack. I've put my gun in there with the money. Hide the sack in the usual place in the barn. I'll get it later and get the payments out. We'll meet during the show, sit in our regular seats, and when it's dark inside I'll slide your money through the space between backrests like always. Now go, both of you."

"Okay, Miss Ruby."

THE CONNECTION
June 1942
Eisenhower arrives in London
Japanese attack Midway

Teresa parked the coupe at an angle in a wide-open space in front of the *Palomino Press*.

On the two large, square, front plate-glass windows on either side of the newspaper's door, huge red-painted letters with black shadows announced the ***Best Weekly Newspaper of Lamar and Red River Counties***.

Below that acclamation, black lettering identified the proprietress as ***Maybelle Winters, Owner, Editor, Publisher — Est. 1896***.

A jolly jingle jangled when Teresa pushed on the door.

Tina looked up at the shiny silver bell. "That sounded like Jingle Bells, Momma. Just like Christmastime."

A voice acknowledged the ringing. "I'm in the back, be with you in a minute."

"Okay, thank you," Teresa answered. Teresa closed

50

the door gently to avoid jostling the bell, but it tinkled anyway.

"Hello, I'm Maybelle Winters. You must be Teresa. And you, young lady, must be Tina. I've been expecting you. Welcome to Palomino."

"Yes, we are Teresa and Tina, and thank you. We got away from Paris a little late. Tiny wanted me to come by her place before I left. Our goodbyes took a little longer than we planned."

"That girl can talk your ear off. She's got plenty to say, and we all listen when Tiny talks. She sent me a telegram that you were on your way. She had told me before all about you and Tina, and your husband at Maxey. I know Paris is getting out of hand. With Maxey and all the soldiers there, people in Paris want to make a lot of money before the war is over, over there."

Teresa smiled. "But the war just got started."

"Well, the starting is never the point of discussion because everybody believes it'll be over in a couple of months. When we went over there in Eighteen, we whipped them in six months and made them surrender. It's a mindset. If American boys are called on to do it again, it'll be over pretty quick."

"I sure hope so."

"I've arranged with Ruby for you to see the room she has in her big house, it's a mansion really, and she was agreeable for you to have a look. To be truthful, Ruby's house is the only place in town, and Tiny would've never sent you over here to us if there was no room available. We're not like Paris with a couple of big hotels and some apartments for rent. I think you'll be happy with what she has, and I think you'll find it affordable."

"That's so nice of you, Miss Winters. I feel a little overwhelmed by all the help. It was unexpected."

"Well, us girls have to keep it together, look out for each other. Our men don't think about what we need. Now, you call me Maybelle."

The bell clanged, a boy walked in and let the door slam shut.

"Pinky, I've told you a hundred times when you come and go to not let that door slam."

"Yes, Mam. I forgot. I didn't mean to. I'm sorry."

"Teresa, Miss Tina, this is Rayfield Paramore Pinkston, Jr., one of two paper carriers for the *Palomino Press*. The other is Waldo Sutherland. Pinky, Miss Teresa and Miss Tina are moving here from Paris. Be polite and say hello properly."

"Hello, Miss Teresa. Hello Miss Tina. Welcome to Palomino."

"Hello, Rayfield," Teresa said. She smiled at the handsome boy.

Five-year-old Tina fell in love at first sight. "My birthday is in two months. I'll be six-years-old. I'll start school and be in the first grade." Her wide, affectionate grin at Rayfield exposed two spaces where teeth had been.

Pinky still had plenty to learn about social manners and propriety. "When school starts in September I'll be in seventh grade. You got two teeth missing."

Tina jammed her lips together.

To the adults, the hurt was immediate and apparent.

"You've interrupted us, Pinky, what can I do for you?"

"I brought my route money, Miss Maybelle. Two customers haven't paid me for two months, so I'm a little short this month."

"Okay, put the money on the counter. We'll talk about collections next time you come in. I'm pretty busy right now. Is there anything else?"

"Yes, Mam. Stick Waldo is trying to steal my customers again. Mr. Arnold and Miss Young asked me who they should pay next month."

"Okay, I've told him before, but I'll speak to Waldo again. Anything else?"

"No, Mam. Oh, yes, Mam. Miss Ruby told me to start throwing an extra paper next week. I guess she is gonna have new people stay at her place."

"Yes, Pinky, that she is. I'll be sure to put another paper in your bundle so you can leave it at her house next Thursday. Now, say goodbye."

"Nice to meet you, Miss Teresa. Nice to meet you, Miss Tina. I think you're cute."

The gappy-toothed grin blossomed. Tina was dead in love, her adoration for Pinky absolute as she watched her new beau close the door.

Teresa picked up where they were before the interruption.

"Tiny was a sweetheart. She was like a sister to me and an aunt to Tina. I owe her a lot."

"Tiny said you were a great waitress at her place, that you brought in more customers the months you were there. She said she was going to have trouble finding someone to fill your shoes. She thinks a lot of you, Teresa, said you were special."

Teresa blushed and lowered her head. "I will miss Tiny. She treated me like I was one of her family."

Maybelle pointed.

Teresa turned thinking she would be looking at Pinky who had returned. She looked around the painted letters, out the window, expecting to see him on the sidewalk.

"Well, I own that cafe over there, across the street. It's called Jeeps, after my granddaddy. I need a dayshift cashier and waitress. Bobbie Jo is the manager, she does a great job but needs help. The girl I had, Mary Lou Keenan, ran off with our Constable. I'll pay the same as Tiny, forty cents an hour, you keep all your tips, and you and Tina can have a sandwich and drink for lunch, just like Tiny did. What do you say?"

Tears welled in Teresa's eyes. She grinned and nodded. "I say yes. Yes, Mam. My goodness, yes, indeed. I've been in Palomino for less than thirty minutes, met a wonderful new friend, got a job, a new boss, and about to get a place for us to live. How in the world can I ever repay your kindness?"

Teresa followed Miss Maybelle's directions to the expansive three-story mansion facing Clark Street at the corner of Evans Lane. Because a 1942 black Crown Imperial Chrysler filled the narrow driveway, she parked her Ford coupe parallel to the curb and looked out the window.

Miss Maybelle called it the Porter House and said it was the largest and tallest abode in Palomino. Looking at it, Teresa could see why.

The vivacious mother knocked at Ruby's front door.

Looking through the screen at the young woman and little girl, Ruby warmed to Teresa and Tina right away.

"Hello, Mrs. Bostick. I'm Teresa Chestnutt. Miss Maybelle called. You invited us to look at your vacant room."

Ruby smiled at the gorgeous, full-bodied lass in white shorts, a red Tee, and white, slip-on, canvass tennies. The young woman stood erect, poised holding the hand of her small, three-foot beauty. Both had hair, thick eyebrows, and sparkling eyes so black that carbon, coal, or ebony would be inadequate descriptors.

"Yes, of course, Dear." Ruby pushed open the screen door. "Please come in. My, my, what a pretty, little darling you have there. And you must be Tina. How old are you, Darling?"

Teresa's immediate impression of Ruby was of an image plastered under bold headlines on the front page of *The Paris News*. The only thing different was Hitler's mustache.

Tina cocked her head, shrugged both shoulders, and spread fingers and thumb of her right hand and one finger of her left hand. "I'm almost six-years-old. I'll be in first grade when school starts."

"My, my, almost six. You are a darling. Now, Tina, you and your mother come into the kitchen and have a seat. I'll see if I can find milk and cookies for you and coffee for your mother and me."

"My Daddy is a soljer. He's in the Army. He's in Camp Maxey. He lives in a barrett."

The table was not a dinette. Covered with a silk, embroidered cloth, the large mahogany structure could seat ten. The side, aligned, high-back chairs stood at attention ready for military inspection. The two end chairs were movie stand-ins for a throne. After presenting refreshments, Ruby sat at the commanding position with Ruby on her left and Tina on the right.

Tina focused on homemade chocolate chip goodies and a glass of cold milk. She ignored the conversation.

"My husband, Sergeant Willow Chestnutt, is a military policeman stationed at Camp Maxey. When he enlisted, we packed our belongings, our clothes and a few sundries, in our old car and left Vivian, Louisiana to be nearer to him. Tina and I rented a one-room-and-bath furnished apartment in Paris at Madame Estelle's boarding house."

"I know about Madame Estelle's boarding house."

"The clues were there very early, but I finally accepted I had to move because of Tina. I didn't want her exposed to all the goings-on that went on, day and night."

"I know."

"More than that, Madame Estelle raised the rent beyond what I could afford. I tried to find a place in Paris, but the available space was either too expensive or uninhabitable. There were too many people coming to Paris for the jobs at Camp Maxey. I had to move. Miss Tiny, I was a waitress in her cafe, Miss Tiny made the connection with Miss Maybelle and suggested I move to Palomino. That's our story."

"Your husband's name is Willow?"

"Yes, Mam. But everybody calls him Twig."

"He's with the Infantry Division?"

Teresa was impressed Ruby identified the type of Army unit. Most folks paid no attention. It was just *The Army* unless it was the bank to make a loan or a used car dealer to sell a clunker, on a weekly note, to soldiers.

"Twig is in the Military Police Battalion with the Infantry. He's a police sergeant."

"Well, eventually they'll all be shipping over to Germany."

Teresa caught her breath. She looked at Tina.

"I know there is a war, but I hadn't thought about them going over there."

Ruby paused. She had blurted a secret she had sworn to withhold. No explanation, backtracking, or crawfishing was going to withdraw what she revealed.

"Well, never mind. Now about the room. Maybelle may have told you there are nine-bedrooms and five-bathrooms in the Porter House. The second and the third floor of my home have four bedrooms on each floor, two on each side of the hall, with a shared bath. My bedroom and bath are on the ground floor, along with the kitchen, living room, dining room, and study."

"Is it possible you might have two rooms, one for me and my husband, the other for Tina?"

"I don't at the moment, I only have the one room on the third floor. If a room becomes available later I could rearrange things so you could have both rooms with a private bath."

"Okay, I understand."

"I rent my rooms fifteen dollars a month, about fifty cents a day. Rent is due in advance on the first day of each month. I don't require a deposit, but I would like to have a two-week notice when a tenant chooses to leave. You'll have to share a bathroom, but there are two locks on each door. The rent includes breakfast and supper. You'll have to take care of dinner for you and Tina."

Teresa did not hesitate with a counter offer. "Could you see your way to accept twelve a month?"

Ruby grinned.   She liked Teresa's spunk. "Thirteen."

"I accept, Mrs. Bostick. Thirteen it is."

"Don't you want to see the room first?"

"No, Mrs. Bostick. I see your home and how well you take care of it."

"First, Teresa, call me Ruby. Second, before we agree, I must tell you about the other tenants. They're all men renting rooms here.

"Otis Bassett and Ernest Blackmon have the two bedrooms on the left side of the third floor and they share a bathroom. Both work on an oil platform near Talco. They work in shifts, one works all night, the other is out on the rig all day so it turns out they have a little privacy.

"On the right side of the third floor is Pearson Keenan. Jimmy Madison occupied the other bedroom on the right side. He *was* our Constable. The room Jimmy had is the one that's available. You'll have to share the bathroom with Pearson.

"Edgar Kane has one bedroom on the left side of the second floor. Vincent Hager has the other bedroom and shares a bathroom with Edgar. They work in Major Monroe's cotton fields and gin.

58

"Jake Little has one bedroom on the right side of the second floor, Caleb Joiner has the other and shares a bathroom with Jake. Caleb works at Wolf Hunter's Gulf station there on Main Street and Jake runs the *Palomino Palace* for me."

"Palomino doesn't have a Constable anymore?"

"No, Jimmy ran off with Pearson's wife, Mary Lou, a couple of weeks ago, maybe it's three or four weeks now. Poor Pearson, he's a lost puppy since that happened. Pearson works for the city. He reads the gas and water meters. Keeps to himself, keeps his area clean. If he doesn't clean up the bathroom after, you let me know, and I'll take care of it. I run a tight ship with these boys. They know to mind their own knitting."

"My husband was the Constable in Vivian before he joined the Army."

"You don't say. We sure could use a Constable. We've got one character who defies the law. Eliot Thurgood. He's a mean son-of-a . . ."

Miss Ruby looked at Tina.

"Did you enjoy the milk and cookies, little Darling."

"I did, they were almost as good as Momma's."

Miss Ruby laughed and clapped her hands together. "I like honesty. Now, Teresa, now that you know about your neighbors, are you still interested? Will it be a problem for you and Tina to share a house with seven men?"

"No, Mam. I grew up with two older brothers. I've hiked, camped, hunted, and played rough and tumble tackle football with them. I think I can manage. I've seen and heard it all. I've probably used most of the words myself from time to time."

"Will it be a problem for your husband, Willow, for you to live in close quarters with seven men?"

"Twig will understand. Really, there's no choice. It's what we can afford, and it's near enough he can visit on weekend passes. Thank you, Miss Ruby, for taking Tina and me in."

Teresa pulled a worn, brown, man's wallet from the right pocket of her shorts, opened it, and removed four tens. She fanned the bills and laid the money on the tablecloth. "Here's the first three months' rent, in advance, Miss Ruby."

"Come on, let me show you around my home. I'll bring you to all the floors, and to your room. You can unpack, put your things away, and take a little rest before I make our supper. Tonight we'll have a beef stew with carrots and potatoes right out of my backyard garden."

"I want to bring in my new radio. We can listen to all our favorites again, Momma."

"We can play our radio, Miss Ruby?"

"Of course, Teresa. Welcome home."

THE SURRENDER
May 1943
Joseph Mengle becomes Chief Medical Officer in
Auschwitz
Japanese kill 30,000 Chinese in Changjiao massacre

Along with the defeated 16th Panzer Division, a decorated, battle-hardened unit of the demoralized Heeresgruppe Afrika (Army Group Africa) formerly commanded by Erwin Rommel, Sergeant Kraus Hopplendagger and the two remaining members of his beaten, depleted communications squad surrendered to British forces on May 12, 1943.

The weary and frightened Wehrmacht trio had not eaten or drunk for two days nor slept in three. Lost and cut off, in the blistering days and frigid nights they had walked in the desert without contact or hope. At daylight the fourth day, they stopped, slumped to ground, and dozed. There was no shade. All suffered cracked lips, swollen tongues, and bleary sight.

At 1000 hours, the driver of a British light armored tracked carrier spotted them, alerted his Corporal, pointed, closed the distance, and stopped. The infantry

61

non-commissioned officer of His Majesty's XXX Corps dismounted, approached, and gave his order.

"HANDS UP! *HANDE HOCH!* HANDS UP!"

Hopplendagger and his two men stood, crawled up from the ditch alongside the wind-blown, sandy trail, laid down their Mausers, raised their hands, and trudged toward the solitary Brit who kept his Bren aimed at them.

Wary and apprehensive, the three kept eyes on the machine pistol. They realized if the enemy soldier pulled the trigger, riddled them, and left them in the dirt to rot they would be a sumptuous meal for scorpions, snakes, and sand rats. They wondered if this would be their illustrious end to an inglorious surrender.

Exhausted, forlorn, and forgotten by their Field Marshal and Fuhrer, the abandoned members smiled at their captor and breathed a deep sigh of relief that it was over.

In the aftermath of the collapse and subsequent turmoil of the Afrika Korps — the men continued to call it that long after the Army Group was formed — Prime Minister Churchill asked President Roosevelt for help. Great Britain needed and wanted assistance and relief because there was no room or enough security forces in the Commonwealth to handle the tens upon tens of thousands of prisoners of war.

Farsighted advisors argued the prisoners had value for America's industry, businesses, ranchers, and farmers who needed labor to replace men going to the

Pacific and European theaters of war. Somebody had to gather crops, the advisors advised. Easily convinced, President Roosevelt tasked the United States Maritime Commission to assign Liberty ships taking supplies and troops to North Africa for Operation Torch to return to the east coast loaded to capacity with Italian and German POWs.

The Commission struck a sweetheart deal with Navy shipyard contractors who began configuring craft for this human cargo shuttle duty. Well paid, exempt union workers hastily constructed four Army field kitchens and fabricated four heads fore and aft on each designated ship. The standard operating procedure while afloat was prisoners with hoses attached to hydrants would flush the latrines and debris once a day from the deck.

As part of the negotiations, sleeping quarters, mess, and facilities above deck were improved and modernized for each vessel's Captain, first officer, second officer, cargo officer, navigator, communications officer, and thirty-four civilian seamen.

After nine days at the port in Tunis, Sergeant Hopplendagger, Corporal Edwin Becker, and Private Wilhem Weiss stood in line with the other captives for clearance and processing at the embarkation center. American and British military personnel sought to identify members of the *Allgemeine*, *Waffen*, *Totenkopfverbände*, and *Gestapo* SS before permitting prisoners to board the *Junior Glass*, one of the sixty Liberty ships in Convoy TT-43515-6NFV that was returning to America.

"What is going to happen to us?" Weiss asked.

"We are going to survive," Becker answered. "We are out of Africa and out of the war. *Danke Gott.*"

"No talking in line," an Army Sergeant commanded. He hefted his authority, a Thompson sub-machine gun.

Becker and Weiss looked at the soldier, military police armband, machine gun, and nodded compliance.

"State your rank and name," a processing clerk said in German.

"Corporal Edwin Becker," he reported. "First Communications Squad, Headquarters Company, Three-Thirty-Six Infantry, Tenth Panzer Division, Rommel's Afrika Korps," he added.

The clerk looked up. His face communicated danger. "You speak good English."

Becker pointed across his shoulder toward his companions. He swept his hand in a palm-up presentation in front of his chest. "We all do. My Sergeant lived in Illinois before the war and my Private went to school in England. We speak German, English, a little Tunisian Arabic, and a little French. How many languages do you speak, Corporal?"

"Remove your shirt, raise your left arm," the clerk ordered.

Becker complied, meeting the British Lance Corporal's unfriendly stare.

The clerk nodded and pointed with his pencil. "Move through that door and sit. No talking. In English or German, *verstehen?*"

"Yes, Corporal, I understand. *Auf wiedersehen.* Good day, my good man."

Weiss anticipated and removed his shirt before stepping up when Becker turned away. He raised his arm, bent it at the elbow, and placed his wrist atop his head to avoid any semblance of a Hitler salute. "Private Wilhem Weiss."

"Okay." The clerk nodded. "That door. Sit. No talking, in English or German."

Hopplendagger followed and raised his arm.

The three managed to stay close. Sitting in a huddle, they whispered.

"Why do they look under our left arm?" Weiss asked.

"To see who is a member of the SS," Sergeant Hopplendagger said.

Becker leaned close to Weiss. "Your blood group is tattooed under the left arm if you are in the SS."

"I am not in the SS," Weiss said. "I am in the Army, the Wehrmacht. I never even joined the Nazi party. Herr Hitler sent me a letter to report to the center in Oberursel in five days or I would be severely punished. All through training, nobody ever asked if I was in the Party. Five weeks later I was in Africa as a telephone wireman."

"Neither am I in the SS," Becker said. "My father enrolled me in the Hitler Youth, so I was in the Party. But I do not claim to be a Nazi."

"None of us are SS," Hopplendagger said. "If we were we would have a tattoo under our arm."

"The clerk did not ask to look on a hip," Becker said. "Some SS have the tattoo on a hip, I was told."

"Shhhhh," Hopplendagger cautioned. "Keep it down. If they split us up we will never get back together."

Weiss shrugged and held both hands out, palms up.

"Why do the SS have a tattoo?"

"Field medics check for a tattoo on the wounded. If there is a tattoo, the man is in the SS and the doctors would give him a blood transfusion before anybody else," Hopplendagger said. "Himmler says his men are elite and deserve special treatment. If the clerk sees it, whoever has a tattoo will not be going on this ship with us. These guys might just shoot him on the spot."

The American Sergeant's voice was loud and menacing.

"On your feet. Line up single file. When you pass through the door, say your full name and rank. Wait for a signal to proceed."

The Corporal on the Sergeant's left translated the instructions into German. A Private First Class on his right gave the same information in Italian.

The 587 prisoners obeyed and formed up, as trained and disciplined soldiers will do. They shuffled quietly, spoke name and rank as instructed. On the signal to move forward, they marched up the gangplank, and turned as directed. They accepted a life jacket from one Ordinary Seaman, an Army blanket from another (the Bo'sn of the *Junior Glass* pilfered six hundred blankets from an Army depot and stole an Army three-quarter-ton truck to haul them to the ship), and used the metal ladders to go below. Their sleeping quarters were the iron flooring in the cargo hold. There were no showers to wash or sinks to brush teeth.

It didn't matter.

None of the prisoners had a toothbrush.

At three bells on the forenoon watch of the fifth day of their voyage across the Atlantic to America, Hopplendagger, Becker, and Weiss were on deck at the stern for their two-hour respite for fresh, cold, salty air. Spray reached them as a fine mist when the bow cut through five-foot waves at eleven knots. They did not remove their life jacket once it was on. They wrapped the Army blankets around their shoulders for warmth and safekeeping. Standing tight for heat among the hundred other prisoners on break, they smoked American cigarettes issued by the ship's Purser.

"Now hear this." The ship's speakers came alive. "This is the Captain. This is the Captain speaking. We have received a signal that U-boats are approaching our convoy. All ship's crew and prisoners put on your life jacket. All ship's crew and prisoners put on your life jacket. Stand by."

The announcement caused a stirring of action, fear, and anxiety. All on deck turned to look when they heard a distant rumbling explosion. They watched rising black smoke billow toward the low gray clouds and form into a mushroom.

"One of our U-boats torpedoed a ship. We have no chance," Weiss said. "If one of our boats targets us, we will be blown out of the water."

"Our U-boats run in packs, wolf packs," Hopplendagger said. "A torpedo is sure to catch us."

For fifteen minutes, it was quiet.

They heard another blast and secondary explosions closer, within two miles. They watched roiling orange flames and black smoke swirl toward the cloud ceiling on the horizon.

"Two ships down," Hopplendagger whispered. "How many good men are lost? How many families are broken?"

The three shifted to look at a destroyer casting depth charges in rapid succession, two at a time. The sixth set struck home and thundered below the surface. They watched the water churn and erupt as black pieces of a U-boat catapulted out of the dark sea.

"*Gott segne unsere Seeleute,*" Weiss said.

"Yes, God bless our sailors," Becker said. "This war is a waste of lives."

"We are lucky to be prisoners and out of this madness," Weiss said.

"We will be lucky to escape these U-boats, Kraus," Becker said. "You know they smell blood."

The ships loudspeakers came alive again. "Now hear this. This is the Captain. This is the Captain speaking. I have cabled the International Red Cross and requested the German High Command notify the U-boats that we have German prisoners aboard ship. Stand by."

"A lot of good that will do," Hopplendagger said. "There must be fifty or sixty ships in this convoy. How will a U-boat commander know which one we are on?"

"We are doomed," Becker said. "The subs are here to kill ships. That is all they know or care about. A lot of help the Red Cross is going to give."

"First off," Hopplendagger said, "we are in the middle of the convoy. There are other ships on both sides. Second, escorts are the outer ring and those ships, the cruisers and destroyers, will keep the U-boats away from us. So, I think we are safe. We just need to enjoy the cruise, wherever we are going."

Becker and Weiss looked at Hopplendagger.

He shrugged and grinned. "What?"

Another thirty minutes passed, and it was time for their break to end. As they formed up at the ladders to begin their descent, a seaman spoke to no one in particular.

"This war is bitch. Somebody should've shot Corporal Adolf ten years ago."

A POW ahead of the trio responded in English, without fear of reprimand or reprisal. "They tried in Twenty-Nine, Thirty-Three, Thirty-Eight, Thirty-Nine, and Forty. You see no one has succeeded. So far."

Next morning, the three were on deck for their turn for morning fresh air.

"Now hear this." Once more, the ship's PA system blared. "This is the Captain. This is the Captain speaking. The International Red Cross sent a signal to us this morning. The German High Command acknowledged our message and said ships with prisoners must turn on their lights and keep the lights on day and night for identification. Our instructions are to leave this convoy. The five ships with prisoners will form up in a separate group and sail to Boston instead of Norfolk, Virginia. That is all."

The Wehrmacht communication squad's journey to America ended its sixteen days at sea as the *Junior Glass* maneuvered through Massachusetts Bay and tied up at a slip at Hanover Street Wharf. Upon disembarking, they marched in military formation, in step all the way for two miles, under armed guard, to the Boston South train station where they boarded a

Pullman car. They had no clue or choice of destination.

Settled in, they pulled Army blankets over their heads as the train pulled away from the station. Hopplendagger had managed to keep his squad together, from the time of capitulation in the desert, through the processing center, aboard ship, and now on a train headed west.

They heard the rumors. They would be slave labor, beaten, starved, and abused. The unknown they imagined was scary, yet they would prize the surprise that awaited them.

For the hundred soldiers, it was standing room only. They spoke in hushed tones. None of them knew for sure why they were there. Of course, rampant scuttlebutt was all about their impending shipment. They expected to be in Scotland for Christmas. They knew an invasion was the only way to defeat the Nazis. Members of the Military Police Battalion were fearlessly anxious to ride the bull in the Infantry Division's rodeo. The untested, garrison recruits saw the chests of fruit salad combat veterans sported. They were impressed. If one was not in the fight, the men reasoned, there would be no medals for bravery.

"ATTENTION!"

To a man, they assumed the position, clicked heels, and looked straight ahead.

"AT EASE, AT EASE," a voice boomed from the back of the room.

Sergeant Chestnutt cast his eyes.

"Stand at ease, Men. Stand at ease."

The voice belonged to Colonel Benicio Sardanna-Sanchez, Camp Maxey Provost Marshal. He moved swiftly through the soldiers and mounted the small classroom platform.

"Good morning, Men."

"GOOD MORNING, SIR!"

"I must tell you men the President agreed to accept prisoners of war coming to America from North Africa. In less than a week we will receive over five hundred POWs."

The Colonel paused. He waited until the shuffling settled and murmuring quieted.

"You know we were organized here to prepare and train to go with the Infantry Division and join the buildup in Europe. The situation changed and those in power decided to use Camp Maxey as a prisoner of war camp. It was a political decision the War Department could not overcome. Our senior commanders eventually surrendered to the Secretary's decision. That's why your company will remain at Maxey."

The Provost Marshal fed the political piece to deflect pressure and anger directed at the prisoners. It was human nature to vent, but soldiers in the room knew it was proper to keep their grumbling subdued.

"A few are Italians, most are Germans from Rommel's Afrika Korps. As all of you well know the Infantry Division and the MP battalion will ship out. Those of you here with me will be assigned to a special detachment and remain to handle prisoners, probably for the duration. Some of you will be happy to stay back. Others, like me, want to go over there to take care of business and be part of this war. I will tell you

71

now that reassignment out of Camp Maxey will be difficult. Nevertheless, I will endorse and recommend a transfer to a combat theater for any man who requests it. I make no other promises."

He paused again and scanned the group of military policemen.

"After this first batch of POWs we expect to receive between five hundred and eight hundred POWs a week. The final estimate we've been given could reach six to seven thousand.

"Our engineer battalion has started construction of a pen to keep that many incarcerated for the duration. But frankly, it will be sometime before we can have adequate space. We just don't have the room to house all of them at the present time.

"They'll live in tents until the division departs. Then they'll occupy vacated barracks.

"Now, I must tell you that you will move out of your barrack and live in tents like the prisoners."

The Colonel knew the response to that news would result in shouts of derision.

It did.

He folded his arms across his chest and waited. The room quieted.

"We are required by the Geneva Convention to house POWs in the same type of accommodations as their counterparts with equal rank. Moreover, the Convention provides that the POWs receive the same quantity and quality, or equivalent, rations as you. They will receive equal amenities. They will receive fair and humane treatment. You've heard about the camps over there. We will not run a concentration camp here."

Chestnutt shook his head.   He wanted to be a soldier, perhaps be on the front, in battle, to participate in the action.   He was not pleased to be part of those who remained.   He imagined he would not even be a policeman at Camp Maxey.   Here, he would be a security guard, a prison guard, impotent.

It was stressful.   He thought about submitting the paperwork right away, the minute this meeting was over, to go with the Battalion.   The Colonel said he would endorse and recommend requests for a transfer. Maybe his early request would receive consideration that is more favorable.   He could escape from a job he knew he would hate, rather than meekly surrender and be stuck behind a desk at Camp Maxey until the war was over.

Twig reached a plan, but he needed Teresa — to talk with her about what he wanted to do.

She was his strength; her counsel always wise.

THE AGREEMENT
August 1943
Patton slaps two soldiers
Burma becomes puppet state of Japanese Empire

Camp Maxey Deputy Commander, fifty-year-old Brigadier General Charles Pace, Jr., was a grossly overweight chain-smoker. He sat at the head of the gray-metal military conference table sucking on a Lucky Strike. Blue-gray smoke floated to the ceiling of the steel-roofed Quonset hut. On his right sat Colonel Benicio Sardanna-Sanchez, Provost Marshal, and on the Brigadier's left sat Colonel R. J. Jones, Camp Administrator and Chief of Finance.

"I'm General Charlie Pace." He flicked the cigarette's head toward a clear-glass ashtray. "General Evans asked me to convey his apologies for not meeting with you. I know you can appreciate our Commanding General is a very busy executive. Many internal and external demands require his time and attention, so he asked me to represent him as we finalize the agreement. He said he would try to pop in to say a brief hello. I know all of you have met and talked with Colonel Sanchez on a couple of occasions about taking on three German prisoners. I've met Mayor Shipp and Major Monroe."

General Pace looked to his left and nodded.

"This is Colonel Jones, our Personnel and Finance Chief. He handles the administration for all of our cadre and prisoners as well as the money business for the installation. Let's go round the table for introductions for Colonel Jones and me. Casey, please start off."

"I'm Casey Shipp, Mayor of Palomino. We welcome the opportunity to have prisoners in our community to work." Casey looked to his left.

"I'm Major Clay Monroe, Section One Representative. I own cotton fields and a gin, among other interests."

"I'm Martha Parker, Acting Representative of Palomino's Section Four. My husband is a Marine, resting and refitting in Australia after being in Guadalcanal. Our charter permits me to occupy his council seat while he serves. I'm aware of the shortage of labor, particularly this time of year, and the need for money in our town. Frankly, I'm concerned about German soldiers, the enemy, coming to live among us. Women and children in Palomino are vulnerable."

General Pace did not speak; he did not try to assuage her fears. He shifted his gaze.

"My name is Ruby Bostick. I represent Section Two of Palomino. I own the Porter House and the movie theater in town, the Palomino Palace." She looked at Wolf.

"I'm Wolf Hunter. I represent Section Three. I own

the Gulf station, the only gas station in town." He nodded completion.

"My name is Maybelle Winters. I'm the owner, editor, and publisher of the *Palomino Press*. We put out our paper every Thursday. Mayor Shipp invited me to attend and report on the meeting."

"Good, thank you," General Pace said. "Colonel Sanchez, you have the floor."

"Let me recount the background, mostly for Miss Winters. The United States Office of the Provost Marshal General has responsibility for tens of thousands of prisoners of war. Hundreds of POWs will continue to arrive in America every week. For the past few months, urgent construction is underway to build more than four-hundred POW camps. To reduce the expense of heating wooden barracks, most camps are in the south. Texas will have seventy camps. Camp Maxey is one of the largest, expected eventually to hold up to nine-thousand POWs."

The Provost Marshal paused.

Colonel Jones picked up the presentation. "We are bound to conform to the Geneva Conventions, to specific articles in the document for the treatment and care of prisoners. Our government hopes Germany will treat our boys as well as we treat theirs, but many look upon it as naive thinking. We've received two-thousand-ninety-two Africa Korps prisoners of war. We expect as many as five hundred late next week. You can imagine the troublesome public relations nightmare and population headache this many prisoners of war creates for Lamar County, in fact for all the surrounding counties. Relief, of sorts, presented itself with this new government program to permit selected and screened POWs to work in local communities."

General Pace snubbed his cigarette out and took over. "The prisoners will sort of be labor replacements for our men who are shipping to the Pacific Theater and staging in Great Britain to take on the Nazi Reich. We think they can do an adequate job with minimum training. There were agreement and endorsement for the program at the highest levels of our government in Washington, even by the President and Mrs. Roosevelt. The Secretary of Agriculture specifically mentioned your energetic and enthusiastic involvement, Major Monroe."

"Yes, I've had discussions with the Secretary and several members of our Congress. Are you a Democrat, General? Did you vote for our President?"

The tone of General Pace's voice could not conceal veiled disdain. "As a former soldier, Major Monroe, you're well aware military service members are not permitted to be in a political party and are forbidden to vote to choose their commander-in-chief. We depend on our Congressional representatives to be honest and sincere, our government of the people and for the people, to do the right thing for our nation. We hope they respond to the needs of their constituents and our country. I know faithful voters act in response to the particular requests of their favorite candidate during a campaign and at election time. They give time and money to help elect their boy."

"I am a Democrat, General Pace, I participate in party politics. I provide financial support for many who are or who seek to be congressmen and senators. On request, I stepped forward to help elect our President.

77

I did my best to convince my neighbors to get out the vote for him. I think many powerful people share my interests concerning our freedom and economy. President Roosevelt told me he appreciated my work and contributions." Clay Monroe did not take his eyes off the General. "I was a soldier in the first war, General. I attained the rank of Major and commanded a battalion of infantry soldiers in the Meuse-Argonne Forest. I faced the Germans. I left a hand there and carry shrapnel from that battle. With a war raging, you may have an altered view about how things work in our democracy, but I assure you we have the same goals. I have the ability to pursue them in a different way."

General Pace met Major Monroe's glare and did not blink.

Three seconds of pronounced silence felt like ten minutes to those seated at the table. No one moved or spoke. With an up close and personal perch, this exchange between two powerful men fascinated the onlookers. In a manner of speaking, each Palomino citizen felt proud the Major held his own.

Colonel Jones wiggled in his chair and placed his elbow on the table. He rolled a long yellow pencil with fingers of both hands as he spoke.

"If I may, General?"

"Yes, Colonel Jones, go ahead."

"As we've discussed before, when we sign the agreement, farmers and businesses will pay the government a dollar-fifty a day for each POW's labor. The government keeps seventy cents to pay for its POW program, the prisoner receives eighty cents of script he can use in the camp store. Prisoners have no money to buy goods and services in our economy.

"With this program, Miss Winters, fields and farms close by are easy to accommodate. Even a few businesses in Paris paid to have prisoners work in their storerooms or warehouses. Two car dealerships use prisoners as tool handlers and such, the prisoners can't work on cars and trucks. Fear of sabotage, of course. In the morning, POWs with an armed guard load onto deuce-and-a-half trucks, ride to work, and return to camp in the evening. Local owners in and around Paris are happy to have the labor.   "We've   learned, Major Monroe, that you have the ear of two Texas Democratic congressmen as well as the President. And like you, others a distance away from the camp wanted their piece of the cheap labor pie and complained — forcefully and loudly to those who needed monetary support and votes.

"However, there are issues we need to discuss before we finalize and sign the agreement."

"Are these three prisoners Nazis?" Martha asked.

"No, Mam, as far as we can determine. They've been through extensive screening with trained, professional interrogators."

"Do you think they're sympathizers?" Martha asked. "Like the American Nazis were in New York?"

"They answered no to those questions, Miss Parker," Colonel Jones said. "Their answer is all we have. It is almost impossible to determine what is in a man's head or heart."

"There are people in Texas who belong to that organization, Colonel, even close to home," Miss Ruby said.

They looked at Miss Ruby, puzzled by her use of present tense.

Casey opened his mouth, but before he could speak, Maybelle ventured into the silence.   "I think the Federation was struck a blow when Fritz Kuhn, its *Bundesfuhrer*, was convicted of embezzlement and imprisoned."

"Congressman Martin Dies and his committee were instrumental in denying the organization to operate freely after Germany declared war on us," Major Monroe said.   "Martin did a wonderful job and I supported his mission."

"Well, Major, we believe there are still people working with the Nazis in America, they've just gone underground," Colonel Sanchez said.   "Even though their membership dwindled, their need for funds to promote propaganda is alive and well."

"Those New York Nazis are about as bad as the KKK," Wolf Hunter said.   "We've got that problem close at hand, even in our town I think."

He awkwardly searched faces for reactions.   Wolf was surprised he spoke at all.   He lowered his eyes and bowed his head focusing on intertwining his fingers in his lap.

Colonel Jones waited for further interruptions before continuing.

"There are three important issues, well, there's a lot more than three, but the three of most concern are housing, food, and supervision."

"I believe we've got the housing and food covered, Colonel," Mayor Shipp said.   "We might be able to place all three at Miss Ruby's place."

Ruby Bostick smelled blood. While the Porter House had been mentioned during other meetings, a lucrative contract and a lot of money were about to be discussed. She knew how to play the game.

"I have a barn your prisoners can stay in. They'd need to bring Army cots and blankets with them. I can furnish a bucket and dipper for their water and a bucket for sanitary purposes."

The Palomino council sat dumbfounded, mouths agape. Only Maybelle Winters knew where this was going, she had been a classmate and watched Ruby wheel and deal on the school's grounds.

Before he spoke, Colonel Jones looked at General Pace.

"This is unsettling, Miss Bostick. Before, we talked about the prisoners living in your Porter House. The barn is out of the question. The prisoners must live where their guard lives, equal accommodations. Their sustenance must be the same rations as their guard or a variation of food they like that is equal in quality and quantity as their guard. These are mandates of the Conventions. We would not allow one of our soldiers to live in a barn."

"The barn is out, Miss Bostick," General Pace said.

Ruby looked at Maybelle and smiled. Maybelle took the cue. "What about the Porter House, Miss Ruby?"

"Of course, I've explained this before. If there were vacancies there'd be room in the Porter House, Miss Winters." Ruby looked at General Pace. "The Porter House has nine bedrooms and five baths, General. Right now, long-term, good paying tenants occupy all the rooms. But I'm sure during these difficult financial times, they can be persuaded to move out for the right amount of incentive."

Maybelle knew that Edgar Kane and Vincent Hagar had given notice; they were going into military service.

Major Monroe knew this. He said their absence created a serious vacuum in his cotton field and gin. This was part of the motivation for German prisoners to come to Palomino.

Only Ruby knew that Otis Bassett and Ernest Blackmon intended to move out of the Porter House, too. They told her their boss needed them to be closer to the rigs, to work double shifts because some hands answered the call to arms and joined the service.

Maybelle had published in the paper that oil field workers were exempt from serving, their job was to ensure the nation and military got oil.

Because they were exempt, the only way Otis and Ernest would leave the oilrig was by enlisting. Both preferred Talco, Texas rather than the enemy in the South Pacific or eventually in Europe. They worked double shifts with little sleep and stayed out of harm's way. Both knew their pay was ten times more than what an Army Private received.

Colonel Jones grabbed the worm Ruby dangled on her hook. "There is a need for three rooms, Miss Bostick, or, getting fewer prisoners, Major Monroe."

"Well, there is need on the farms and in the fields, Colonel. Of course, after the cotton is picked we'll need help in my gin. We all know our nation and the military need cotton."

"Yes, Major. Yes, of course." Colonel Jones realized there was little room to maneuver. "What incentive do you have in mind, Miss Bostick?"

Ruby was guarded, cautious. She didn't want to overplay her hand. ""I don't know, Colonel Jones. Maybe two hundred and fifty dollars for each man," Ruby answered.

"A thousand dollars is quite a bit of money, Miss Bostick," the Finance Chief said. He smiled, knowingly. "This money provided by the government would pass through your hands to your tenants?"

Ruby did not flinch. "It makes no difference to me, Colonel Jones. You could give me the cash and I could hand it over to each of my tenants, but I think a government check made out in the name of each of my tenants is preferable." She returned Colonel Jones's smile, knowingly. "Don't you?"

Colonel Jones held his smile. He paused longer than necessary before posing his question.

"What monthly rent would you expect for room and board, Miss Bostick?"

"I have a cook and housekeeper that come in every day. Ethel is very organized. Preparing and serving the meals will be no problem. And the laundry, of course. My rate is one-hundred-seventy-five dollars per month for each prisoner, breakfast, supper, and laundry included, Colonel Jones." Miss Ruby sat regally erect at the conference table.

The room was hushed. All from Palomino held their breath, waiting. The ball was in Colonel Jones' court. He was, after all, a government employee who had fiduciary responsibilities. They expected a low-ball counteroffer.

The opening of the conference room door drew

wide-eyed, surprised attention from everyone.

General Pace, Colonel Jones, Colonel Sanchez, and Major Monroe stood.

"Ladies and gentlemen, our commanding officer, General Evans," General Pace announced.

General Evans moved directly to Clay Monroe with open arms. They hugged and warmly patted each other's back.

"How are you, my friend?"

"I am well, Clay. It is good to see you."

After introductions, the four soldiers continued standing.

"Major Monroe and I were battalion commanders in the First Infantry Division in the Meuse-Argonne battle in France. He led the third battalion and I was the leader of the first. After action reports indicated that during that forty-seven day offensive, we lost an average of five-hundred-fifty men a day, KIA — and three times that wounded, every day. It was the largest and bloodiest battle America's ever been involved in. Had he not been severely wounded in the Meuse-Argonne he might still be serving — as a general officer."

This history was an admirable revelation for Clay Monroe's neighbors.

"We were about to reach a negotiated rent for our prisoners to live in Miss Bostick's Porter House, General."

"Good, R. J." General Evans looked at the civilians. "We got too many idle POWs here on the camp and not enough space. The Lamar County government is complaining, saying German POWs at other camps are living in a *Fritz Ritz*. Some German Generals do live in their own cottages. That is the way it is and can't be changed. We know families don't have enough to eat while the POWs enjoy the same quality and abundance of food our soldiers receive.

"Farmers and ranchers complain about a shortage of labor to tend the fields and livestock because our boys are over there. Mrs. Roosevelt and Secretary of Agriculture Brannan pressured the president to do something about it. So we're looking to place individuals, under military supervision, of course, to live and work in communities close to POW camps. I just wanted to pop in, say hello, and see my foxhole buddy. Thank you all for coming over here to talk with us."

General Evans gave no opportunity or invitation for others to speak. He theatrically looked at his watch, patted Clay Monroe's shoulder, and gave a mock salute.

"I am late for an urgent meeting. Please excuse me. I know you're in good hands with General Pace and my staff. I'm glad we could help by placing some of our prisoners to work in Palomino. You have my authority to conclude a deal today, General Pace, whatever it takes."

Unlike the others who shook his hand, Miss Ruby daintily touched the General's extended fingers. With a final nod, Evans marched from the room through the doorway trailed by his Aide-de-Camp.

The soldiers sat. Colonel Jones looked at General Pace who nodded.

"Okay, Miss Bostick. The Army will meet the two-hundred-fifty dollar incentive for each tenant who moves and pay one-hundred-seventy-five dollars per month room and board for each prisoner. Is there anything else?"

Mayor Shipp leaned forward and placed his arms on the table. He looked at General Pace.

"We have an idea about the guard, General. The council discussed and agreed to the suggestion I want to present. We would like Sergeant Willow Chestnutt to be the guard and supervisor of the POWs. He's a military policeman here at the camp. He was the constable in Vivian, Louisiana before joining the Army. He's an experienced lawman. More than that, his wife and daughter live in the Porter House. So he would live with his family, and the prisoners would have the same accommodations.   This meets the Conventions' requirements."

Colonel Sanchez grinned and nodded at General Pace before facing the Mayor. "Yes, Mr. Mayor, we're aware of Sergeant Chestnutt and his family's circumstances.   We were prepared to make that proposal to you."

Colonel Jones picked it up.   "The guard, the supervisor, Sergeant Chestnutt, will have an Army jeep to transport the prisoners to work and back and a trailer to haul gear and baggage. He will have coupons from a ration book to give to you, Mr. Hunter, for fuel and maintenance."

"There's one other thing we want your agreement to, General," the Mayor said.

"Yes, Mr. Mayor, I'm listening."

"The council voted unanimously to appoint Sergeant Chestnutt as the Constable of Palomino. We will pay him accordingly."

General Pace inhaled deeply and exhaled slowly. "I see. What do you think about that, Colonel Jones, Colonel Sanchez? Is there a conflict of interest?"

Colonel Jones nodded. "Technically, there may be, Sir. But you have the authority to make exceptions. The one concern is precedence. First and foremost, you must agree that Sergeant Chestnutt takes his instructions from his superior officer, Colonel Sanchez. If anything, anything mind you, is in contravention of his Army duties, the Army must come first."

General Pace nodded. "I agree. Mr. Mayor?"

Casey Shipp conducted an impromptu executive session of the Palomino council at the Army's conference table. "If I may, General? This proposal requires consensus vote by the Palomino council. All in favor of accepting the priority set by Colonel Jones please say aye."

The council voted unanimous acceptance.

"On behalf of Palomino, we accept that Sergeant Chestnutt's Army duties will come first."

"Good," General Pace said. "In that case, we agree Sergeant Chestnutt may be appointed as Constable of Palomino and share those duties and responsibilities with his Army mission. Now, I'll ameliorate that position. I will instruct Sergeant Chestnutt to be his own judge, and act accordingly when a conflict arises. I will authorize Sergeant Chestnutt to approve and sign invoices for purchases necessary to his duties and prisoner's needs."

"Merchants or owners must mail or hand-carry those approved and signed statements to my office," Colonel Jones said, "for processing and payment."

"I think the Army also should pay the same for the guard accommodations as the prisoners, room and board," Ruby said.

"But Sergeant Chestnutt's family lives in the Porter House," Colonel Jones countered.

"If they didn't the Army would have to pay for a guard to be with the prisoners," Ruby countered.

Snagged, Colonel Jones acquiesced. "Yes. Yes, of course, I see what you mean, Miss Bostick. Room and board also shall be paid for the guard."

"One-hundred-seventy-five dollars per month," Ruby said.

"Yes, of course, we agree," Colonel Jones said.

Colonel Sanchez cleared his throat.

"You have something else, Benny?" General Pace asked.

"Yes, something very important, Sir." He measured the visitors with an official gaze. "All of you must understand and accept that Sergeant Chestnutt will be armed with a pistol at all times and when he deems it necessary, he will carry a loaded shotgun and Carbine," Colonel Sanchez said. "His orders, as regards the prisoners, are to prevent escape. The pistol and shotgun are for close quarters, the Carbine for long-range targets. There will be no warning shot, he will shoot to kill."

"We acknowledge the caution, Colonel," Mayor Shipp said. "Thank you."

"If there is nothing else, our meeting is adjourned," the Deputy Commander declared and lit a cigarette.

The Brigadier placed the red Diamond matchbox on top of the green Lucky Strike pack and eyed them for a moment. He leaned forward and used a thumb to push two tips so the errant cigarettes slid back inside the pack. Then, with military precision, he carefully aligned the end and side edges of the box with the opened top and side edge of the pack.

Satisfied, General Pace sucked in strong nicotine and exhaled a long stream of gray, smoke.

THE SCREW-UP
November 1943
Himmler orders Gypsies to concentration camps
Battle of Tarawa begins

Now, on Monday, three days before Thanksgiving, Ruby Bostick and her gang were about to make another withdrawal, and the Red River County State Bank would encounter its first killing during a robbery.

"My Lord. Not again." Miss Myrtle was aghast, yet the pitch of her voice sounded irritated rather than alarmed.

"Mr. Rosser, they're here again," Miss Judy shouted. "It's unbelievable."

Franklein Rosser came out of his small windowless office and watched the three bank robbers split up and walk forward with their guns at the ready.

Waving his revolver from side-to-side he tried to look as menacing as he'd seen and say it just like he'd heard a dozen times at the *pitchursho*, but M D screwed it up.

"Don't yall make quick movies and reach for the roof and raise your arms up cause this is a bank robber-ry."

"Now, you three just better turn around and walk right back through that door before this affair goes any further," the bank president warned. "That way all you'll be guilty of is disturbing the peace." He held his left hand up, palm down with thumb extended, and swept his index and middle fingers with a dismissive motion at them. "Go on, now."

The two bewildered customers at the teller's window intending to make a deposit turned around and stared at M D, still clasping the few one-dollar silver certificates in their white-gloved hands.

"WHAT'D HE SAY, LOIS?" Imogene Akers asked.

"It's a robbery, Imogene. It's a robbery in the bank."

"SHRUBBERY? HE'S SELLING SHRUBBERY? IN THE BANK?"

"No, Imogene. The boy don't want us to move."

"WHERE WE GONNA MOVE TO, LOIS?"

"No, Imogene, we're not moving. Just be still and be quiet." Lois puckered her lips and placed a finger across Imogene's lips. "Shhhhhhh." She looked at M D.

"If that old woman yells again, I'll knock her in the head," Artemis blurted.

"You know Miss Akers is old. You know good-n-well she talks loud cause she's hard of hearing," Lois countermanded. "She doesn't know what's going on. She won't bother you, Artemis."

It sealed her fate the moment Lois spoke his name.

Puzzled, Artemis hesitated. Then he became afraid, before he fired.

The bullet struck Lois between her eyes. Dying, she

slumped onto the cool, varnished planks and lay on her side. Dark red blood streamed across her left eye and pooled under her temple and cheek. "Imogene . . ."

Imogene sure as hell heard the gunshot. Her shrieks rattled Artemis further, so he put two bullets into her face to shut her up. Only then did he hear M D and Miss Ruby screaming at him. He froze and stared at the bodies of the widowed sisters, Lois and Imogene Akers, who were his momma's friends and had been his next-door neighbors in Pattonville.

He was in that state when Walter Crawley came into view at the top of the stairs, his weapon drawn and firing.

Since their first run at the Red River County State Bank eighteen months ago, Miss Ruby and her gang had hit several banks, with middling success. In May 42, their take was eight-hundred-twenty-six dollars from the Clarksville, Texas bank, twenty-two miles from Palomino. October 42, their take was six-hundred-four dollars from the Idabel, Oklahoma bank thirty-six miles away. March 43, Mount Vernon, Texas, twenty-seven miles, their take was zero dollars — a sign in the door announced everybody had gone to Mr. Waskom's funeral. August 43, in a Mount Pleasant, Texas bank, Artemis jerked three dollars out of a bank customer's hand. When she realized he was stealing her egg money, the elderly woman screamed and fainted and scared M D who dropped the bag of bank cash on the floor in the rush to escape.

They returned to Red River County State Bank in

Bogata because last week, halfway to Hugo, Oklahoma, the car Artemis stole from the Camp Maxey parking lot had a flat. Miss Ruby was mad as hell. After mounting the spare, he turned around and drove them to the train station before parking the car in front of the Paris police station.

After each job, Ruby doled out meager spending money to her accomplices and turned over the remaining amount to Herr Higgins. The remaining money each time was never enough to satisfy Herr Higgins. He always demanded more. At each meeting with Herr Higgins, where she turned over most of the bank loot to fund his failed Bund, the uncomfortable pressure mounted. He always managed to let his threats about revealing her work with the American Nazi Federation slip into their conversation.

Since 1938, well before the war began, she had attended meetings with the Bund, but exposure of the association with him prevented her ending their contract with extreme prejudice. Miss Ruby had no objection to the Bund's purpose and goals; her regret was with Higgins and the risk of blackmail. She stood to lose the Palomino Palace and her granddaddy's prize, the Porter House.

Ruby's patience with Milton Douglas Draggert, a Palomino resident, and Artemis Canton who lived with his aunt in Pattonville, seven miles west of Palomino, had pretty well run its course. Before she recruited these two, Ruby's gang members didn't serve with her for more than a couple of robberies; she terminated their contract. But times were hard all around, so she extended their employment and kept M D and Artemis on the payroll, so to speak.

Arty was a smart aleck kid who smoked Picayune cigarettes. Ruby chose him to be their getaway driver because Arty knew how to steal a car and drive, but he was a careless car thief. When Ruby planned a job, Arty rode the Katy train to Paris and hitched-hiked to Camp Maxey where he chose a car from the large parking lot. Arty had his pick of vehicles because fourteen hundred people, military and civilian, worked at Camp Maxey. Many owners left keys in the ignition; other cars were easy to hotwire and start. Arty scouted for Fords, Hudson Super Sixes, and Packards. A black, four-door Packard was his favorite because everybody would remember the car and forget about them. But finding one in a government parking lot was difficult because most folks couldn't afford them during wartime. Usually, after a job was done, Arty drove to Paris, parked the car in front of Mason's Grocery, left the keys in it (unless he had wired it), and walked two blocks to the Katy train station.

Milton Douglas Draggert was Eliot Thurgood's nephew.

Along with a headshake and forlorn stare, folks in Palomino said, usually in a derogatory way, that M D, as he preferred, came from the same cut of linoleum.

At sixteen years, four months, and seventeen days, Henrietta Thurgood, Eliot's younger sister, married Drayton Draggert. Henny didn't love Drayton, in the romantic sense, but she did love the sex. And Drayton worked hard to please Henny, to give her as much as she wanted, whenever she wanted, which was often.

No, it was not for love nor money that she married

Drayton. It was because of her daddy, old man Thurgood.

Morning sickness gave it away when Henny fell into her Momma's arms bawling, confessing, and puking. Marietta told Hobart the news after his nose led him to the stench of vomit on her apron, which she could not wash out or hide with bleach or vinegar.

When Hobart learned from Marietta that Henny was knocked up, he swore he'd take his double-barreled Ranger shotgun he had bought at Sears, Roebuck and Company in Paris and put two loads of twelve-gauge, double-aught buckshot into Drayton's heart. It was a traditional shotgun wedding and talk of the town.

Marietta and Hobart Thurgood knew their son, Eliot, was a lost cause so they nicknamed their grandson, M D, in vain hopes and dreams that osmosis would prevail. Unfortunately, the gradual absorption of common sense they prayed for never materialized. M D proved early on he was like his uncle Eliot and, beyond any shadow of doubt, would never be a physician.

Although Palominoans would rather not use the specific words, most especially in mixed company, it was easy for men to acknowledge that M D would fuck it up, in a manner of speaking, if there were absolutely no chance in hell whatever-it-was could be.

So, as it turned out it was easy for these two, M D and Artemis, to screw up their last armed robbery of the Red River County State Bank in Bogata.

Walter Crawley had retired a year ago, on Friday, April 30, after thirty-eight years as a Red River County deputy sheriff.

Miss Judy had followed up on Deputy Amesa's recommendation and approached Walter about being the security guard for the bank.

He was a sheriff, he told her, not a guard.

Anyway, after the first robbery, Sheriff Blake occasionally posted Walter at the bank for security.

They belonged to the Bogata Church of Heavenly Saints, and she could see, as time passed, that Walter was bored. She had told him so, saying he needed to be out in the community. Miss Myrtle joined Miss Judy and together persuaded their church choir baritone to accept the job to protect them from marauding bandits, and Franklein Rosser. It took seven months of badgering before Walter finally signed on as their part-time bank guard.

Walter knew eighteen cents an hour wouldn't buy piss in a bucket. But he could wear a uniform and strap on his Colt .45, and that sealed the deal for him. Anyway, Miss Judy was right. He was bored. And since Lizzy, his beautiful bride for sixty-one years, had died suffering with a drowning bout with pneumonia, Walter was alone and lonely. He needed a place to go and to have something to do every day. Besides, he enjoyed saying hello and chewing the fat with the customers. Walter knew everyone who came through the doors. When a stranger entered, he became wary and vigilant.

Ruby explained the details and assignments of her plan a dozen times and repeated questions to measure fifteen-year-old M D and fourteen-year-old Artemis' understanding and comprehension. Ruby had doubts when neither accomplice could keep straight the time, location, and action, but thought she could manage. All she needed was the appearance of armed force they would provide.

The before and during went well enough, even though M D managed to screw up the wording. With the after came disaster, when Artemis shot the two women. It turned out to be a goddamn mess.

The 32 Ford Artemis stole from the parking lot at Camp Maxey failed as a getaway car. It ran out of gas at the railroad crossing west of town. Ruby was not happy and thought about putting a .22 bullet in the boy's temple right there on the tracks, even though Walter's Colt .45 had already done damage.

Back at the bank, while Doc Bledsoe and the ambulance crew took care of the bodies, Sergeant Stephan Stanton conducted his interview in Franklein Rosser's office.

"Now, Miss Myrtle, why do you say the robbers were the same ones as last year?"

"They looked the same, dressed the same, red bandannas and all. The woman wore a fedora, a black fedora, it looked new, very clean," Miss Myrtle said. "She wore a man's double-breasted, navy blue Sunday suit, a pink shirt, and red tie. There was a white silk handkerchief stuffed in the suit coat's pocket. I'll never forget all those colors. All of it just like last year."

"And the big one," Miss Judy said. "Black hair, coal black, Brylcreemed down, parted in the middle. Same overalls too, not new, used, only slightly faded."

"And the woman stood the same way with her gun," Miss Myrtle said.

"A man will stand with his feet flat and legs apart

when he holds a gun up for business. Like this," Miss Judy explained. "This one didn't. Her feet were close together, and she bent at the waist. Only this time she leaned forward more, like she was a hunchback or her back was hurt."

"Lois called the shorter one Artemis. I guess she knew him. That's when he shot her," Miss Myrtle said.

"Artemis?" Sergeant Stanton cocked his head. "Did you see his hair? Was it red?"

"Yes, he was a redhead kid, well not quite red, more sandy than red, I guess, Stephan," Miss Myrtle said. "Just like before, he wore a brown tweed newsboy cap and overalls. He had blue eyes. His gun was as big as the other boy's was. Just the woman had the small shiny gun."

"Artemis Canton? I might know that boy."

"You do?" Miss Myrtle asked.

"He was just a kid," Miss Judy said.

"Were all three of them kids?"

"No, just the one Walter shot. Artemis. He cried out with a whiny scream, like a kid does when he hits his finger with a hammer."

"Who shot Walter?"

"The other one. The taller one, the bigger one."

"Do you need to see Doc Bledsoe?"

"You know, Logan asked the same thing last time," Miss Myrtle said. "It's a shame what happened to him. He was such a good boy."

Sergeant Stanton nodded. "Deputy Amesa was a good man, a good family man. He was a good deputy."

"Did they ever catch the two boys who kidnapped him?" Miss Myrtle asked.

"Not yet, we're still looking for them."

"Miss Myrtle and me don't need to see the doctor, Stephan." Miss Judy spoke softly. "Those two poor women and Walter are the ones shot. They need Doc Bledsoe."

Stephan's voice was soft, filled with sorrow. "I'm afraid Miss Lois, Miss Imogene, and Mr. Crawley was killed, Miss Judy. The bullet went through Walter's heart."

"Oh, my goodness, what have we done, Myrtle?"

"What's wrong, Miss Judy? What did you do?" Sergeant Stanton asked, near a whisper. He watched tears shimmer in their eyes.

"We pressured Walter to take the part-time job," Miss Judy said.

"If we hadn't done that, Walter would be alive," Miss Myrtle said.

"I pestered him so much he finally took on the job of being the security guard for the bank. It didn't pay much. Eighteen cents an hour. But he loved coming down here in a neat uniform with his pistol on his hip," Miss Judy said.

"The taller one shot Walter," Miss Myrtle said. "The woman just stood there, probably in shock like the rest of us."

"Walter had to go pee a lot. He was coming down the stairs from the bathroom on the second floor," Miss Judy said. "He had prostrate issues."

"Prostrate?" Stephan questioned.

"Prostate," Miss Myrtle said. "He said Doc Bledsoe gave him a prescription, but he didn't like to take pills. Walter had never been sick a day in his life."

"When his Miss Lizzy died, the poor man lost his heart," Miss Judy said. "It hurt us to see him so depressed."

"Well, as a lawman Walter was strong, that's for sure. When I joined the department, I went through some of his tough physical training," Sergeant Stanton said. "Everybody admired Deputy Crawley. He was a crack shot, too."

Miss Judy shook her head. "For thirty-eight years, he stood against the meanest and deadliest in the county without even getting a scratch. We all thought being a bank guard was a soft job. Now he's dead. I am so sorry. I think it's my fault he was killed. God rest his soul, and please God, forgive me."

"Well, Miss Judy, you didn't kill Walter, that boy did. I'm surprised Artemis didn't go down when Deputy Crawley shot him with his .45."

"Well, he did. Dropped on the floor like a wet rag, he did. The taller one picked him up and carried him out on his back," Miss Myrtle said. "The woman just followed them out, still holding that little gun in her hand."

"We can't stay here in the rail shed, Miss Ruby. We gotta get Arty to a doctor. He's bleedin bad. That old man's bullet knocked a hole in Arty. It's a wonder it didn't blow out part of his back."

"It'll be dark in half an hour, M D. There's a handcart about a quarter mile up the track. They keep it in a little tin stall. I'll stay here with Artemis while you go get the handcart. Then you can come back down here in the dark so nobody sees, and we'll use the handcart to ride the rails up close to the Palomino station."

From the shed door, Ruby watched M D walk between the steel rails toward Palomino. When she thought he had gone far enough not to hear the .22's report, she squatted by Artemis and touched his arm.

"Is a doctor coming?"

"I'm afraid not, Artemis. I'm going to take care of things."

"I'm bad shot, Miss Ruby."

"I know you are, Artemis. If you hadn't of shot those two women, and if the deputy hadn't of shot you, and if M D hadn't of shot the deputy, we wouldn't be in this situation. It's a goddamn mess now, Boy, a complete screw-up."

"I need help, Miss Ruby."

"And if you had picked a car with gas in it, we'd be drinking wine and counting money by now, Artemis."

"Please help me, Miss Ruby."

"Well, Artemis, that's exactly what I'm gonna do. I'm gonna help you get out of your misery."

"Thank you, Mam. I need all the help I can get. I sure could use a drink of water."

Ruby placed the muzzle of her silver, caliber .22 revolver flush against Artemis' right temple and pulled the trigger.

As she suspected it would be, the pop was muffled.

THE ASSIGNMENT
August 1943
Sicily now controlled by Allies
PT-Boats block Japanese ships off Solomon Islands

Monday morning, Sergeant Chestnutt stood in the hallway anticipating First Sergeant Kinnison's beckon.

Scuttlebutt was rampant. Twig knew units of the Infantry Division had moved to Louisiana for further training. Rumors were wild, anecdotes lively, activity flourished on Maxey; the division was going to board ships in the Gulf, sail to Scotland, and gear up to storm the European mainland. Twig wanted to be part of it. His Platoon Sergeant tired of the constant pestering and arranged a meeting with Kinnison so Twig could make his wishes known about wanting an assignment.

While waiting, Twig replayed the scene when he approached Teresa with his plan Sunday afternoon. She had not been enthusiastic. He doubted she would be. Few wives wanted their husbands to go off and fight in the war. Thousands had already perished on islands in the South Pacific.

Twig had joined Tina playing hopscotch on the

pattern drawn in white chalk on Miss Ruby's sidewalk. Tina claimed Twig touched a line or put a toe down. They had laughed, giggled, and teased each other, enjoying the fun.

Afterwards, Teresa and Twig had sat hip to hip on the porch swing without swinging, his left arm around her shoulders, her right hand stroking, caressing his left thigh.

Tina rested on the top step. She seemed to pay no attention to their talk, tossing the small, red rubber ball and sweeping up one silver jack at a time.

"I'm glad you decided to talk with me about it, Twig," Teresa had said. "I know you want to be in this war, to do your part, but . . ."

"But, what?" Twig had spoken softly, encouragingly. "You've never held back on me, Resa. But, what? I want to hear what you have to say about it."

Teresa had shaken her head and smiled. "If I say stay at Camp Maxey where Tina and I will be able to see you, I know that's what you will do. But if I say that, it becomes my decision, not yours."

Twig had nodded but held back.

"You'll be safe for Tina and me, but you will not be happy as a guard. I want you to be happy, Twig. So, if you want an assignment overseas, Tina and I will support you."

Kinnison's summons broke Twig's reflection.

"CHESTNUTT!"

Twig stood in the doorway. "Yes, First Sergeant."

"Come in, Boy. I just got off the phone with the Company Commander. The Old Man wants you and me to meet him at the General's office right now. General Pace is waiting for you."

"Captain Morris and the General are waiting for us?"

"That's right, come on."

Kinnison moved down the hallway with long strides.

Twig followed, matching the pace. "What'd I do? What's going on?"

A clerk came through an office doorway into the hallway with folders in hand. He quickly retreated to avoid a bulldozing by Kinnison.

"Where you going, Top? I got the Morning Report for you to look at."

"Put em on my desk, Solomon, I'll look at em later. Me and Chestnutt are going to see General Pace. I'll be back in a few minutes. Goddamn paperwork."

Chestnutt's curiosity climbed. "Tell me what's going on, Top."

"The General has an assignment for you, Chestnutt."

Twig was stunned. Mouth agape, he hurried to stay on Kinnison's tail.

Kinnison pushed open the screen door and bounced down the barrack's eight wooden steps, two at a time. Out on the company street, the First Sergeant marched at quickstep. He did not slow or look over his shoulder as he spoke.

"What'd you want to see me about, Chestnutt?"

"An assignment." Twig grinned at his First Sergeant's back. "It can wait, Top."

After a filling breakfast of eggs, bacon, white toast,

and fig marmalade, they sat at the mess hall table sipping the last drops of black coffee from their mugs, the three of them.

"I like American food," Becker said. "I have gained weight since I come to America. I like American Army black coffee. I like America."

"I do too," Weiss said. "I want to stay in America after the war."

Sergeant Hopplendagger chuckled as he poked Edwin Becker's arm with a fist. "You like any food, Eddy."

"I do, Duke. I think my favorite American food is peanut butter on white bread. That is best to me."

"Do not like the bacon, Will?" Hopplendagger asked.

Will shook his head. "No, I have no taste for *Speck*."

"I never asked why you go by Duke. Where did that name come from?" Eddy asked.

"John Wayne," Sergeant Hopplendagger answered. "My schoolmates in Illinois said I look like John Wayne and in magazines, people called him Duke. So they called me Duke."

"I never thought about it, but you do look like John Wayne, in that picture *Stagecoach*. I like John Wayne. I like his cowboy pictures. Is he American royalty, like an England Duke?" Eddy Becker asked.

"No, I have not heard that. I do not think so."

"Well, how did he get the name Duke?" Weiss asked.

"Story goes his dog was named Duke. When he passed a fire station on his paper route in California, the firemen said 'there goes Big Duke and Little Duke'.

John Wayne was very big and tall. I like the name."

"I like John Wayne pictures, too," Weiss said.

"You know, Will, John Wayne is not his real name," Duke said.

"It is not?"

"No, it is Marion Mitchell Morrison," Duke said.

"HOPPLENDAGGER, BECKER, WEISS, ON YOUR FEET. I'VE BEEN LOOKING FOR YOU."

They quickly rose from the wooden benches and faced their barracks chief who called their names. They stood erect, attentive, but not at military attention.

"Yes, Corporal Shultz," Sergeant Hopplendagger answered.

"You three come with me. The Deputy Commanding General wants to see you."

The trio looked at each other.

"Now. Move it. Double time. Let's go. *Schnell*, *schnell*," Corporal Shultz ordered.

"Sergeant Chestnutt reporting to the General, as directed, Sir."

General Pace returned the salute. "Stand at ease." He gestured toward each person sitting along the right side of a conference table. "Sergeant Chestnutt, this is Colonel Jones, our Personnel Chief, Colonel Sanchez the Provost Marshal, and Mr. Casey Shipp, mayor of Palomino, whom I think you know."

Twig nodded toward to each individual but did not speak.

"Here, sit on that side of the table with Captain Morris and First Sergeant Kinnison."

Twig sat in the chair next to Kinnison, away from the General at the head of the table. The three military policemen looked across the table at Jones, Sanchez, and the mayor.

"How are things with you, Sergeant Chestnutt?" General Pace asked.

Taken aback, Twig nodded, shrugged ever so slightly. He felt uncomfortable with the General's informality. "Ah, fine, Sir. Just fine."

"Good," Pace nodded. "That's good. I understand you come from Louisiana. How do you like Texas?"

Twig nodded again. "Ah, fine, Sir. Just fine. What I've seen of it around Paris and Palomino where my family lives."

"Ah, yes, your wife and daughter. Teresa and Tina."

The General calling their names made Twig nervous. How could the General know their first names? he wondered. The Mayor, Twig thought, Mayor Shipp told him.

"Yes, Sir." Twig did a quick side-eye glance but only saw the right cheek of Kinnison's face. The First Sergeant focused his attention on General Pace. Twig brought his eyes back to the General's nose and nodded. "That's my family, Sir, Teresa and Tina."

"What we're about to discuss with you must be kept secret, Sergeant Chestnutt. Understand?"

"Yes, Sir. I understand, and it will be, Sir."

"Good."

General Pace nodded. Colonel Sanchez leaned forward and placed his arms on the table, looking directly at Twig.

"Sergeant Chestnutt, Colonel Jones, Captain Morris, and I reviewed your military record and performance. Your First Sergeant told us you are one of the top three non-commissioned officers in the company and among the top ten in the MP Battalion. We reached the conclusion that you can handle the unique and special assignment we want you to take. Colonel Jones and I made our recommendation to General Pace, which he approved."

The Provost Marshal leaned back.

Twig was impressed with the General and Colonel Sanchez' theatrics. As if it were a cue, Twig knew to look at the General when Sanchez relaxed in his chair.

"We are going to place you on temporary assignment off of Camp Maxey where you will supervise and be responsible for three prisoners. Your duty station will be in Palomino, Sergeant Chestnutt," the General said. "You'll live in Palomino and be with your wife and daughter." He smiled. "What do you think about that, Son?"

Twig felt wind fade from his sail. His heart skipped, his mouth was dry, it was difficult to swallow without his Adam's apple bobbing. He hoped to persuade Kinnison to help with an assignment, a transfer overseas to be in the war. Now, he knew that was not going to happen. Even if Kinnison went to bat for him, the General would not approve or sign the official order. He was stuck being a sentry. It didn't matter whether it would be at Maxey or Palomino because he would end up being an Army security guard for the duration. His life as a military policeman, he concluded, was never to be.

"If I have a choice, General, I'd rather not."

Corporal Oliver Schultz halted the column.

"Right, Face."

The trio conducted the movement with military precision.

"Stand At, Ease."

They assumed the position.

"Smoke if you got em. I'm going inside to report to the Sergeant Major that you're here. I'll have your ass if you break ranks and wander off. Hear me?"

Duke spoke for them. "We will wait here, Ollie. Unless good-looking Texas women come by and kidnap us."

Even with his beer-belly weight, Corporal Schultz jogged up the eight steps. He pulled open the left screen door and disappeared into the bowels of the Camp Maxey administrative headquarters building.

Passersby found it normal that three POWs stood in front of the Headquarters smoking. Often, POWs waited outside a building for a supervisor to march them to work. Nobody stopped to inquire why they were there or who they were waiting for. Many didn't care because they expected nine strands of barbed wire topped with rolls of concertina wire on eight-foot poles were sufficient deterrents to wandering off or attempting escape. Anyway, where were the prisoners going to go without being noticed? In a bustling din of activity, captors and captives went here and there, in and out of buildings, barracks, tents, or other Army structures.

Duke, Eddy, and Will waited as instructed. They had nothing to do, no appointments to keep. It was a good, safe, casual life they were experiencing, standing there smoking great tasting American Pall Mall cigarettes.

"Texas women. Some sure are pretty, others sure are plain," Weiss said. "Jane, the cashier in the canteen, smiled at me yesterday. I think she likes me. I wonder where we could get together for a little privacy."

"It has been awhile since I smiled," Eddy said. "Almost a year since I was with my *Schatz*."

"I bet your *Schatz* is smiling even in your absence." Will laughed, then grew silent.

Like the Three Stooges often did in a Saturday matinee movie scene, Duke, Eddy, and Will looked at each other and grinned.

"More than a year for me," Duke said. "I wish you would keep quiet about that. Now it is all I will think about."

The conference room door creaked.

"Yes, Tommy?" General Pace acknowledged the interruption.

A head appeared, the body shielded by the door.

"Corporal Schultz has the prisoners here, Sir."

"Yes, Tommy, thank you. Give us about ten minutes then come back in."

"Yessir." Tommy closed the door.

General Pace leaned forward. "That wasn't the answer I expected, Sergeant Chestnutt. I'm surprised, in fact. I can imagine how your Missus would react if she knew you'd rather not be with her and your daughter in Palomino."

In a brain flash, Twig decided not to reveal his discussion with Teresa and tell the General of her acquiescence. "I intended to request a transfer today to go overseas. I was waiting to talk with First Sergeant Kinnison about it when he brought me here. I want to be, need to be, part of this war, Sir. Sitting on a camp, or even staying in Palomino every day, is not my idea of being part of the war effort. I was exempt from military service. I'm a military police sergeant because I was the constable in Vivian, Louisiana and had an Army recruiter friend who pulled strings for me. I would prefer to be in the action over there, not in administration here in Texas on Camp Maxey or even in Palomino. Sir."

Twig shut his mouth. They stared at him. Ten seconds passed before General Pace spoke.

"That's a pretty severe indictment of all of us sitting here in a conference room instead of facing the enemy with bayonets poised, Son. I understand how you feel, believe me, I do, but we have an important job to do for our government, for our nation, here on Camp Maxey. If all the prisoners were penned where captured, imagine the impact on combat and support units that would have to secure them. There wouldn't be enough of our forces left to fight and win the war in the Pacific or European Theaters. Can you see that, Son?"

Trapped. "Yes, Sir. I can see that. Beg pardon, General, it doesn't change how I feel."

"Okay, I'll accept that. I need you to answer one question for me then."

Twig waited.

"If you receive an official, legitimate order from your superior officer, are you willing to carry it out in spite of how you feel about it?"

Twig did not hesitate. "Yes, Sir. I am and I will. I am a soldier."

"Okay, I accept that. I accept your word as a non-commissioned officer and as a man. Fair enough?"

"Yes, Sir."

"Good. Sergeant Chestnutt, your temporary duty assignment is to guard and supervise three German POWs. They will work as laborers in Palomino for the duration or until released. You will live with them. What do you say?"

"You're going to put Nazis in Palomino?"

General Pace patiently sighed. "Colonel Sanchez?"

"Well, we've singled out three who know each other, served together in the same signal company, and speak excellent English. One is a Sergeant, one is a Corporal, and the third is a Private. The Sergeant was the supervisor. They worked in a communications squad laying telephone wire and operating a portable switchboard, Sergeant Chestnutt," Colonel Sanchez said. "It is hard to know for sure, but best we can determine through tough interviews and intense interrogations they are not SS and they tell us they do not belong to the Nazi party. Only Becker admitted membership in the Hitler Youth."

"So, they're not Nazis?"

"We believe they are not, Sergeant Chestnutt. They

are only soldiers in the German Wehrmacht, as you are in the American Army."

"Satisfied? What do you say, Sergeant Chestnutt?" General Pace repeated.

"I will do my duty to the best of my ability, Sir."

"Good. Very good, Son."

All the while during the meeting, Casey Shipp was mesmerized to witness the inner workings of Army officers and soldiers. They were serious about their day-to-day jobs and duty to country. He was impressed.

"Now, Sergeant Chestnutt, Mayor Shipp has something to say about the matter. Casey."

"Thank you, General.

"Sergeant Chestnutt, on behalf of the Palomino town council who voted unanimously, I am authorized to offer you the position of Constable. We would like for you to accept."

Twig blinked.

After General Pace's gentle scolding, this development was perplexing. He blinked again and looked at the Brigadier.

Pace nodded and smiled.   "I think Sergeant Chestnutt is a bit overwhelmed. Son, we've discussed this in an executive session, so to speak, and I personally heard the unanimous vote for you by the Palomino council. I approved and later signed an official document for the record for the exception to policy concerning any potential conflict of interest. You will perform your Army duties and at the same time take care of law enforcement business in Palomino. There are caveats, though. You have dual reporting responsibilities. You will report to Mayor Shipp and the town council for Palomino affairs and report to Captain Morris and Colonel Sanchez. The Mayor and the Army agree your Army duties come first if there is any conflict. What do you say?"

"You'll have the best of both worlds, Sergeant Chestnutt. You'll serve your country and live with your family," Mayor Shipp said. "You'll be safe in Palomino, out of harm's way."

Twig tried to speak but only managed a perceptible nod.

"Good," General Pace said. "I'll take that as an affirmative."

Finally, Twig found words. "Yes, Sir, Mr. Shipp. I'd be honored to serve as the Constable for Palomino."

"TOMMY!"

The door popped open, and Tommy's head appeared.

"Tommy, bring them in."

THE KIDNAPPING
April 1942
Mussolini meets Hitler in Salzburg
Doolittle's pilots bomb Japan

Deputy Sheriff Logan Amesa arrived late, eighty-four minutes late. Serious about his work, it bothered him to be late for anything. He accepted, embraced responsibility. For Logan, there was never wrong in doing the right thing. He was special — folks depended on him. But his young wife and baby girl came first above all.

"I was worried about you, Logan. You're almost an hour and a half late for work, Son. You've never been late in your life," Deputy Walter Crawley said.

"Fay has the flu, Pop, and Lou is sick too."

"Well, that's not good for Fay to have the flu around your baby girl. Did she go see Doc Bledsoe?"

"Yeah, he said she had the flu. He told her to eat chicken soup, drink a lot of juice, use Vicks Salve, and stay in bed. Doc said she's young and she'd get over it in ten days. How is she going to stay in bed when she has a two-year-old to take care of? Little

115

Lou is a handful for a well woman."

"Damn flu is going around. Miss Judy and Miss Myrtle down at the bank have the sniffles. But they won't take time off. I tell them they gonna make everybody sick handling the money and doling it out."

"I thought you'd be on duty at the bank. Why aren't you over there?"

After the armed robbery of the Red River County State Bank a couple of months ago, the Sheriff, under pressure from the Mayor and vocal voters, agreed to occasionally place Walter in the bank for security. Franklein Rosser, the bank president, knew he had a good deal and felt confident there would be no repercussions or fuss when he refused to reimburse the county for Walter's pay.

It was easy duty for Deputy Crawley and made the citizens of Bogata feel safe. He enjoyed visiting with the customers. Everybody in town loved him and his wild tales of fighting crime. All said they hated he was going to retire but were glad he would be on duty as full-time security at the bank.

"Sheriff asked me to come to the office. Mavis is sick. He probably has the flu like Fay. Zack had to go out to one of the oil platforms in Talco to break up a argument between the driller and one of his roughnecks. I'm filling in. Just Minnie Belle and me are holding the fort."

"Where's the Sheriff?"

"Clarksville, at the County courthouse. Testifying at Pete Wayne's trial."

"The moonshiner?"

"That's the one."

"You ever drink any of his stuff?"

"Yeah, I've had a sip or two or three. He cooks some pretty good stuff, a little strong sometimes, though."

"Where's Sergeant Stanton, Pop?"

"Out at Aubrey's place. Aubrey said somebody stole two cows and Cricket, one of his foxhounds."

Aubrey Roach was eighty. He lived with three milk cows and a huge pack of pure-bred wolf and fox hounds on his place. Doc Bledsoe told Aubrey to stop driving his tractor around on the sixty-acres of prime timber for fear it would roll over. Aubrey had retorted if it did roll over and kill him it was alright because he was alone and lonely since his Wanda passed away. After that discussion with Doc Bledsoe, Aubrey added a codicil to his will — kill the cows, have a big bar-b-que, and let the dogs loose.

"Once a week Aubrey calls and says somebody stole a cow or one of them hounds. You know he's got twenty-six hounds," Logan said.

"Yeah, Stephan likes to go out there. He likes to see Aubrey's dogs. I didn't know he had so many."

"When we get out there he says he's miscounted, he only has three you know, and all his cows are present and the dog's come home. Then, we spend an hour listening to him carry on about this or that. You ask me, I think he calls and reports a crime just so we come out to his place. Since Miss Wanda died, he's out there by hisself. All he wants is somebody to talk to."

"Yeah, besides seein Aubrey's hounds, that might

117

be why Stephan likes to go."

"Does Sergeant Stanton like to hunt?"

"Not that I know of." Deputy Crawley shook his head and smiled. "He told me one time that he shot one of the wrens that nested at Miss Judy and Miss Myrtle's house. Mistook it for a sparrow. He thought they were going to scalp him."

"That was me, Pop. I'm the one who told you that story. I'm the one who killed their little wren. With my BB gun."

"That was you, Son?"

"Yeah, sure was. Miss Judy and Miss Myrtle were mad as hell. I think they still hold that against me."

"That was you, huh. I'da swore it was Stephan who done it."

"I was in the eighth grade, got my Red Ryder for my birthday. Right away, I was a game hunter stalking prey in the neighborhood."

"Uh huh."

"All that little brown bird was doing was just feeding babies in its nest. It was an easy shot. I raised my gun, squeezed the trigger, and . . ."

Deputy Crawley looked at Deputy Amesa, measured the young man, and nodded.

"You feel bad about it, do you?"

"Jesus, I sure do, Pop. Since I shot that little wren and watched it fall off the branch I've never wanted to kill another living thing, bird, fish, reptile, animal, or person. It even bothers me to see a dog, squirrel, fox, wolf, or possum run over and dead on the street."

The small office was quiet. Neither spoke for a

minute, which seemed the longest time.

"Look, Son, it's pretty quiet. I can take care of things. Why don't you go home and take care of your family."

Logan's voice was somber. The hurtful regret still evident for something he did more than a decade earlier, when he was a boy.

"You think it'd be alright, Pop?"

"Sure."

Logan stood and walked to the door. He stopped and turned. "If you need me, call me and I'll come right back. Okay?"

Before Walter spoke, the phone rang.

He leaned forward in his chair. He lifted the receiver off the hook and put it to his left ear.

Logan waited, watching Walter.

"Sheriff's office, Deputy Crawley. Hey, Jimmie, you keeping the County Seat safe? . . . A green Dodge, a thirty-six green Dodge sedan . . . license plate eight-nine-six, seven-one-eight . . . oh, shit, my pencil broke . . . uh-huh . . . a small, skinny kid . . . how old you think . . . yeah, I got it." Walter paused, listening. "Okay, thanks, Jimmie. We'll look for them."

Walter replaced the receiver. He opened his mouth to tell Logan about the call but the phone buzzed again.

"Sheriff's office, Deputy Crawley . . . hey, Billy Don . . . uh huh . . . green Dodge, a thirty-six green Dodge sedan, no kidding? . . . uh huh . . ." He attempted to make notes in his pad with the stubby, brown, broken pencil to no avail. "I see . . . a pack of cigarettes . . . a Baby Ruth candy bar . . . and . . . what else . . . oh, while he was pumping gas . . . they still there . . . oh, you holding them. I'll be right over . . . yes, Sir, Billy Don . . . I'm leaving right now, don't let them go."

"What is it, Pop?" Deputy Amesa asked.

"Deputy Dunn in Clarksville said a thirty-six green Dodge sedan was stole from a life insurance agent, for us to be on the lookout. License plate is, let's see, I didn't get it all wrote down, I think he said it was eight-six-seven, nine-eight-one, or one-eight-nine. Then Billy Don called said two boys in a green Dodge pulled up for gas and tried to steal a couple of items from the station. Billy Don and his mechanic are holding them in the bathroom."

"I'll go with you."

"No need, Son. I don't think there's a need for you to go. You go on and take care of Fay and baby Lou. It's just a petty theft thing, a pack of cigarettes and a candy bar. I'll bring them down here to get all the information. They'll pay a five-dollar fine and I'll let em go."

"But it's a green Dodge."

"Yeah. A thirty-six." Walter shrugged. "Probably a coincidence, green was a popular color for Dodge sedans in thirty-six. Luann and Darnell, over on Hudson Street, has one of them."

"Well, it's my job. It's the right thing for me to do to go with you, Pop. Let me go pee first, I'll meet you at the car."

Seventh graders Patricia Ann Parker and Rayfield Paramore Pinkston, Jr. sat side by side in Miss Ruby's barn smoking the two Old Gold cigarettes Patsy pinched from her mother's pack.

As she attempted to blow smoke circles, Patsy proposed the proposition to Pinky without his urging. Pinky didn't know why words, one word, escaped him when she asked if he wanted to look.

Patsy and Pinky were a twosome since second grade, most always together. He was instantly smitten when she kissed him on the lips during their third recess. After that, when one of them was in town, folks would ask where the other was. Everybody, including Patsy's mom Martha, and Pinky's mom Pauline, expected to see them together.

In Jeeps Cafe, Patsy sat on a stool with Pinky standing next to her as they drank an ice cream soda with two straws. Pinky always quit first, so Patsy had the last draw. Patsy rode her bicycle alongside Pinky on his paper route when he delivered Miss Winter's newspaper. In games, she chose him first, or the other way round. They were an item, a perfect pair.

Now, sitting together, their arms touching, she had asked her question. Of course, he wanted to look. At the moment, though, he just didn't know how to say yes.

Patsy looked at him and inquisitively tilted her head.

"Well, Pinky, do you?"

He had looked at Stick Waldo's pictures of fully naked women a kazillion times. Waldo had first flashed his seven, worn-out, black and white photos during sixth-grade homeroom when Ms. Barber was down at Principal Skaggs office. Waldo never needed encouragement to show the women posed in different positions in his Kodak photographs and he never rushed the display.

One lay on a couch, one held a baseball bat across a shoulder. Waldo would pause after the bat lady and say something like she hit a home run, didn't she?

Next in sequence was one who lay on a bed with a pillow under her butt, her hand in a prominent place, followed by the one sitting with her left leg draped over the arm of the chair.

Then, in order, came the one standing against a wall with her hands cupping both of her huge breasts and the one sitting on a girl's bicycle with a foot atop a raised pedal.

Waldo always saved for last the one sitting on a man's lap, his bare, hairy legs showing between hers. Waldo didn't have to suggest what the man was doing with the naked woman on his lap. She had the biggest grin of the seven.

All of them in Waldo's pictures faced the camera in an unabashed exposition of provocative frontal nudity. Nothing was left to the imagination, although Pinky and the other boys imagined wild and wooly what-ifs.

Pinky had never actually seen a naked woman, but he did not dismiss the fact that the ones in Waldo's pictures were pretty damn awesome. After about the fourth or fourteenth or fortieth viewing of Waldo's women, it was clear to Pinky his attention was always drawn to the four main attractions in each snapshot, notwithstanding whether a baseball bat, bicycle, armchair, or some other prop were present.

"Do you want to or not, Pinky?" Patricia Ann asked again, forceful persistence in her voice.

"Yes, Patsy. Yes, I do."

Patsy snubbed out the cigarette and hiked her dress. With thumbs in the waistband, she slid down her pink panties and pulled them over and off her Converse tennis shoes. She laid the panties aside and raised her dress again.

"See how thick and black the hair is?"

Oh, yeah, Pinky's eyes focused and zoomed in like telescopic binoculars.

He looked into Patsy's brown eyes and grinned. "That sure looks good."

"Do you want to touch it?"

He did, and did, and kept on doing it.

"Ummmm," Patsy whispered. "That feels nice. Right there. Yes, right there. I like that."

"I like it too, Patsy."

Patsy softly rubbed Pinky in the right spot and put her face close to his.

"Kiss me, Pinky."

He did, and kept doing gently, smoothly, rhythmically what Patsy liked.

"Take your blue jeans off." Patsy's voice was soft, almost a whisper. "It'll be better that way."

He did, and it was.

Patsy made it oh so much better for him there, on that special, memorable Friday afternoon, in Miss

Ruby's barn.

Artemis and M D sat on stools at the City Drugstore counter in Clarksville licking at their ice cream cones when the twins waltzed in.

Emma Lou and Ella Sue smiled and sat one stool down from the boys.

"I'd like a strawberry ice cream cone," Emma Lou ordered. She looked at Artemis. "One like he has."

Artemis grinned and pointed his cone at her. "Strawberry is the best. I like to use my tongue to feel the cold ridges and loosen bits of strawberry. The taste of fresh strawberry drives me wild. My tongue is very sensitive."

"I've got a chocolate ice cream cone," M D interjected, obviously oblivious to Artemis' attempt at creating a web of sexual attraction. "I can eat two of um at a time."

"I don't like chocolate, strawberry is my favorite," Emma Lou redirected. She smiled invitingly at the procurer. "I like to lick it from the bottom up with my tongue."

The soda fountain clerk handed the ice cream cone to Emma Lou and took her nickel.

"What flavor you like, little girl?" Artemis asked Ella Sue.

"I'm not a little girl," she snapped, "I'm almost sixteen. Let me have a Cherry Coke, please."

"Well, I'm sixteen, going on seventeen," Artemis lied. "What's your name strawberry lickin lover?"

"Emma Lou Hardy. What's yours?"

"Arty, this is my friend M D. What's your friend's name?"

"She's my sister, twin sister, Ella Sue."

"Twins?" M D questioned. "Yall don't look like no twins. You got brown hair and she's a blonde. You use Peroxide, Emma Sue?"

"It's Ella Sue. Hell, no," Ella Sue snapped. "I'm a natural blonde." She smiled and wiggled persuasively. "All over."

The soda fountain clerk set the glass on the counter and stuck a straw in the drink. He picked the nickel up from the countertop without a word and moved away to serve another customer.

"Well, we are twins," Emma Lou said. "We got all the good working parts, in all the right places. We're just not identical twins."

M D couldn't help himself. His drive for attention, and maybe an enjoyable wrestling match in the Roadside Inn down the road, propelled blurted thoughts. "You both sure are pretty girls. You look like growed up women, all over. Yall wanna go down to the Roadside Inn for a little bit?"

Artemis shook his head in disbelief. "Jesus, M D? You gotta be swave with women, Boy. Specially, good lookin women with all the right parts."

With his alluring invitation flattened, M D shifted gears and announced the brag he thought best, under the circumstances. "I rob banks. I robbed a bank three months ago."

Ella Sue blinked and arched her natural blonde eyebrows. "Are you like John Jillinder or that Clibe fella?"

"Naw, I'm better n nem. I wear a red bandanna so nobody can know who I am. It's my deguise."

Artemis' laugh was hesitant, nervous.

"Ah, go on now, M D, stop it," he chided. "Our new friends don't care about what you done. And they don't need to know."

His voice became stern.

"So be quiet about it."

"I ain't never robbed no bank," Ella Sue said. "What's it feel like?"

"Oh, it feels good. Top of the world, Baby," M D boasted. Even as tall and big as he was, in his mind he was James Cagney. He grinned, slid off the stool, and stepped up next to Ella Sue. "You wanna go with me now to rob one?"

Ella Sue called his bluff. "Sure, let me go pee first." She was off the stool in a flash, headed for the restroom.

Snagged, M D looked at Artemis for rescue.

"Okay, Emma Lou, you wanna go too?" Artemis' heart was not in it.

"Absolutely not. You both crazy as hell. And I sure as hell ain't gonna let Ella Sue go robbin no bank with two crazy idiots, neither. You gonna get yourself killed. We was ready to go to the Inn for some quick fun, but now that ain't gonna happen, neither."

Upon Ella Sue's return, Emma Lou grasped Ella Sue by the wrist and pulled her toward the door.

Ella Sue complained, but did not resist. "What happened? What'd you do?"

Artemis and M D watched the girls rush out of the

drugstore, turn right, and disappear.

"Well, you screwed that up, M D. More and more, I'm believing what folks been sayin all this time."

"What'd I do, Arty?"

"Emma Lou was ready to go to the Roadside Inn for a little roll in the hay. And now she ain't. That's what you did."

"Well, I don't think they twins, anyway."

"Jesus Christ, M D." Artemis shook his head for the fortieth time. "Come on, I'll drop you off at home and find a place in Paris to dump the green beast."

As they approached U.S. Highway 271, Artemis told M D he was going into Bogata first because they were running low on gas.

"The needle shows it's empty so there's no way we can make the twenty-five miles to Paris."

"Okay, I can get a pack of Chesterfields, too."

"Well, Boys, Deputy Amesa is going to ride with you and you'll follow me to the station to give information and pay a little fine for lifting things outta Billy Don's business that you didn't pay for. By the way, who owns your green Dodge?"

"My Uncle Sam," Artemis said. "He lives over there in Detroit. He let me borrow it so we could go to Talco to see some girls. We was on our way back and stopped for gas."

"Oh, I see," Deputy Crawley said.

"It's all a misunderstanding, Deputy. My friend just forgot to pay. When the gentleman accused him of theft, I apologized and offered to pay. But he was mad and locked us in the bathroom," Artemis said.

"I see," Deputy Crawley said. "Well, Son . . . what'd you say your name was . . . John . . . John Bennett . . . I've talked with Billy Don, the owner, and Buddy Teller, his mechanic, and they tell a different story. So, we'll all go down to the station, John, and you can put down your side of the story in writing."

His tone was flat, authoritative when Walter Crawley ordered John Bennett/Artemis Canton and Joe Jenkins/M D Draggert to get in Uncle Sam's 1936 green Dodge.

"Now listen to me, John Bennett. Deputy Amesa does not like wild rides so you just take it smooth and easy and he won't get carsick all over the back seat of Uncle Sam's nice car, you hear?"

"Yes, Sir, I understand, Sir, I'll be right on your bumper, Deputy," John Bennett/Artemis Canton said. It was feigned meekness.

Deputy Crawley held his speed at twenty. He turned left onto North Holt Street off U.S. Highway 271. He intended to park behind the station at the corner of Holt and Sycamore Street. They would avoid onlookers by entering through the back door. The moment Deputy Crawley turned, a school bus approached and Artemis paused. The school bus tuned right and followed Deputy Crawley, blocking his view.

Crawley expected the green Dodge to be behind the school bus because all he could see was the GMC emblem above the black grill.

As the bus turned behind Crawley, Artemis

gunned the Dodge, heading south on the highway.

"Hey, what are you doing? Stop the car," Deputy Logan Amesa yelled. "Stop this car. You hear me?"

Joe Jenkins/M D in the front passenger seat turned, rested the butt of his hand on the backrest, and pointed his .38 caliber revolver at Logan.

"Now, you be real quiet, Deputy, or I'll blow your brains out all over Uncle Sam's back seat."

THE RESIDENCY
August 1943
German and Italian forces evacuate Sicily
Lieutenant John F. Kennedy's PT boat rammed

General Pace returned Oliver Schultz' salute.

The General held out his hand. "Give me their personnel folders, Corporal, and have a seat. You prisoners stand easy."

Ollie handed the file over. Before sitting next to Twig, Schultz shifted his holster and heavy pistol so he wouldn't sit on them. They exchanged nods and smiles but did not speak.

Twig turned his eyes back to the prisoners.

Quiet breathing filled the silence as the General opened the folders one by one and read documents in each.

Sergeant Hopplendagger, Corporal Becker, and Private Weiss stood at a military posture of ease, their hands clasped against their buttocks. Each, in his own way, searched the room noting those who sat at the conference table. The man in the brown suit stuck out like the proverbial sore thumb among the military uniforms. They knew the insignia of the two bird colonels, recognizing only the Provost Marshal. They met Sergeant Chestnutt's gaze and indicated the slightest nod toward him.

"I'm General Pace, Deputy Commander of Camp Maxey." He placed the closed folders in column, left to right. "I've seen your pictures and read your files, so I know who you are. I know you speak excellent English. Based on interviews and interrogations, as well as your performance and behavior these past couple of months, you're here for me to decide if you are worthy to participate in a special program. Take a seat."

Becker and Weiss sat across from Chestnutt and Schultz. The only chair remaining was the one at the end of the table. Hopplendagger sat there, facing the Deputy Commander.

General Pace gestured open-handedly as he made introductions only by name. He leaned forward, placed his arms on the table, and picked up a yellow pencil. He rolled the pencil with fingers of both hands.

"You will be in a residency program. You will live in a home in a small town near the camp and work in cotton and vegetable fields and at other jobs as determined by your guard and supervisor, Sergeant Chestnutt. If you choose to participate in this residency program, you will obey Sergeant Chestnutt. He has written orders and authority from the Commanding General to shoot to kill. He will not fire a warning shot. Do you understand?"

Each answered yes, in English.

"Up to this point, the pay you received for your labor was used to purchase items in the canteen on Camp Maxey. Because you will no longer be in the camp, your wages of eighty cents a day will be in American currency, which you can use in town.

"You have the choice to participate in the residency program. If you decline, you will remain here in the camp and work in the fields, or other locations close by."

When Pace paused, Hopplendagger raised his hand.

"Yes?"

"May we ask questions, General?"

"Yes, you may. What is your question?"

"How will we move from the home to work? Will we march through town?"

"Sergeant Chestnutt has a jeep. He will drive you to the work and back to the residence."

"Will we be in Paris?"

"No, you'll be in Mayor Shipp's town. Palomino."

Hopplendagger closed his mouth.

Pace looked at Becker and Weiss.

Weiss blinked and kept his mouth closed.

Becker raised his hand.

The General did not address Becker or the others by name. "Yes?"

"Our countries are at war, General. We are soldiers. That is all we are. A soldier fights to survive, fights to win. On the battlefield, some are wounded others are killed. Families grieve the loss of their loved one. We are the enemy, prisoners of war here in America. There are hard feelings toward us, no doubt. If placed in a town to live and work, we have no protection or safeguards, no weapons to defend ourselves. You put us in danger. This is a violation of the Geneva Conventions."

Duke and Will, with their mouths ajar, looked at Eddy. They hung on his words, impressed.

Will was surprised his mouth moved and words escaped. "At a train stop on our way here, people of that town stood on the platform. They were waiting to board the train. We thought they were waiting for us. We were afraid of being attacked, beaten.

"A conductor told them we were German prisoners of war from the Afrika Korps. We watched many people gather into a group. We thought, uh oh, they are going to storm the train and attack us. Instead, they went away and minutes later returned with fruit, small sandwiches, and coffee. They greeted us with friendly smiles and gave us food. As the train pulled away, we could hear them say welcome to America. I cried with joy and relief. We are like you, General."

General Pace blinked.

"What do you know about the Conventions?" Pace looked at Corporal Becker when he fired the question.

"I do not know everything about them, General, but I have read about them. In school, my military history instructor lectured on the Conventions, and we discussed them. Palomino may not be like the place Private Weiss remembers. We could be in an unfriendly town. As prisoners, we depend on you, the American government, to protect us."

"Sergeant Chestnutt is your supervisor and guard. He will be under arms with a pistol at all times and with a shotgun and Carbine when he deems it necessary. He is your protector," Colonel Sanchez said.

Hopplendagger entered the discourse. "You said Sergeant Chestnutt would not fire a warning shot, General, that he has orders to shoot to kill. If we are attacked by the people in this town, in the mayor's town, will Sergeant Chestnutt also shoot to kill to protect us?"

"No, he will not." General Pace did not blink. "Do you have other questions?"

Silence again filled the room.

"Mayor Shipp," General Pace's voice was soft, "do you have anything for us?"

"Thank you, General." Casey scanned the faces of the prisoners. "Families in my town have men in the war, some in Africa and many in the Pacific." Casey looked at Corporal Becker. "As you suggested, some families have lost a loved one, a couple of our families have lost two. We have hard feelings toward Hitler and the SS. There are folks in my town who've never seen a German from Germany.   Some in Palomino enjoy a German heritage and probably have distant relatives there. There are people in my town who are Jewish.   We are well aware of Hitler's decrees about Jewry."

The mayor took a breath and continued.   "We agreed with the Army, with General Pace, to protect you while you live and work in Palomino. We will treat you as we hope our boys who are prisoners are treated. In addition to Sergeant Chestnutt's Army duties as your supervisor and guard, we also appointed him as our law enforcement officer. As Constable, he will have authority to arrest and detain Palomino citizens, as warranted, and place them in our jail, which we call *The Calaboose*. Do you have any questions of me?"

Colonel Sanchez waited several seconds before he spoke. "Mayor Shipp will handle the administration for your residency, including invoices and payments. You will take orders from Sergeant Chestnutt. Tomorrow morning you will transfer to Palomino. Your transport will be in front of your barrack at seven-hundred hours. You will put your personal belongings in your laundry bag and stow the bag in the trailer attached to Sergeant Chestnutt's jeep."

The General let the pause settle in before he invited Twig to speak.

"Sergeant Chestnutt, do you have anything you wish say?"

"Yes, Sir, I do. A soldier's duties when a prisoner of war is to escape, sabotage, or disrupt operations. I have supervised Sergeant Hopplendagger, Corporal Becker, and Private Weiss on several details. I have observed and talked with them. They know there is no place to hide in this flat country of Texas. On more than one occasion, they gave me their word and followed through. I do not believe they belong to the Nazi Party or support the Nazi regime. I believe they are worthy to participate in the residency program. I would trust them with my family."

The Deputy Commander nodded his approval and smiled. "Thank you, Sergeant Chestnutt. Well spoken."

He looked at the prisoners. "Do you choose to participate in the residency program?"

The trio answered affirmative, in English.

"How old were you when you knew you loved Daddy?"

"Sixteen."

"How old were you when you married Daddy?"

"Seventeen."

"How old was Daddy?"

"He was eighteen. Three weeks past his eighteenth birthday."

"How old were you when I was born?"

"Eighteen. Why are you asking these questions, Darling?"

"I was just wondering." Tina scooped up her jacks and rubber ball, placed them in the King Edward cigar box, closed the lid, and stood. She left the box on the top step and walked to where Teresa sat. She turned and plopped onto the porch swing, next to her mother. The swing swaggled sideways sharply.

Teresa pushed with her toes, the swing steadied, swayed back and forth.

"When did you know you wanted to marry Daddy?"

Teresa smiled. "When he asked your Grandma for permission to take me to the homecoming football game. He asked mother first, even before he asked me."

"And that made you love him enough to marry him?"

"Sort of. I had seen him and talked with him before."

"Where?"

"He worked at the gas station. I rode my blue and white bicycle down to the station one day because one of my tires needed air. He was confident, self-assured. He said he'd put air in the tire, and he said he'd patch it for free, so I let him do it. We talked while he fixed the tire. When I started to ride away, he smiled at me, said I was the prettiest girl he'd ever seen, and winked. He winked with his left eye. Then his smile turned into a grin. I had never seen a boy's eyes shine like your Daddy's."

Absent-mindedly, Teresa pushed more, and the swing swung.

"Once a week I would let just enough air out of a tire to still be able to ride to the station for him to fill it. I was crazy in love with your Daddy. I still am, Sweetie."

"I think I'm in love."

"Reeeely," Teresa let the word float out over her tongue. "Who are you in love with, Tina?"

"With Pinky."

"Uh huh. Our paperboy."

"His real name is Rayfield. I think that is a nice name. Rayfield. I think I loved him the first time I saw him, at Miss Maybelle's."

"Yes, I remember. Last year. You were five."

"I was almost six. He said I was cute."

"He also said you were missing teeth."

"I'm seven now, he'll like me better though when all my front teeth grow back."

"Here comes your beau now, Sweetie. Patsy is with him. I think she's his girlfriend."

"They always ride their bicycle together on his paper route."

"Why don't you go say hi?"

"Okay, but watch my cigar box. All my money is in there."

"I'll see that nobody runs off with your stuff. You better hurry."

Tina slid off the swing and bounded down the steps, waving.

Pinky and Patsy stopped and waited for Tina.

Pinky put his left foot down, the right foot on the pedal at twelve o'clock high.

"Hi, Cutie," Pinky said. "I haven't seen you since your birthday."

"Hi, Tina," Patsy greeted. "That's sure a pretty dress, red and blue flowers."

Pinky withdrew a triangle shaped newspaper from the canvas bag hanging off the handlebar. He handed it to Tina.

Tina looked at Patsy. "Are you Pinky's girlfriend?"

"I think I am, Tina, but why don't you ask him?"

"Is Patsy your girlfriend?"

"Yep, she sure is. Patsy is my special girlfriend."

"Are you going to marry her?"

Teresa smiled. She could hear the exchange. She felt good that Rayfield and Patricia Ann were so nice and friendly with her daughter. They had taken her to a Saturday matinee a couple of times, even invited her to a marshmallow cookout behind Patsy's house. She remembered Tina could never stop telling the ghost stories Pinky and Patsy had told that night. She couldn't remember all of the middle parts in the proper order, but she was dead-on with the endings.

Some afternoons when Pinky and Patsy came into the cafe and ordered an ice cream soda, Teresa would treat. She liked Pinky and Patsy, she thought in a way they reminded her of herself with Twig.

As she watched them, Teresa was happy they accepted Tina as a friend and would look after her. She knew Tina treasured Pinky and Patsy as her older friends. They would be there for her at the start of school. Second grade for Tina was a week away.

Pinky looked at Patsy and grinned.

"Yes, Cutie, I'm going to marry my girl."

Tina's face changed, and she bowed her head.

Right away, Patsy picked up on Tina's dejection.

"Tina, would you be Pinky's girlfriend, too? I think I need help with him."

Tina jerked her head up and beamed at Patsy.

Pinky didn't miss a beat. "Patsy is my senior girlfriend. Will you be my junior girlfriend, Tina?"

Tina's missing teeth accentuated her marvelous grin. "Yes, Pinky, I'll be your junior girlfriend if Patsy doesn't mind."

"We will be like the three musketeers at the *pitchursho*," Patsy said. "Deal?"

"Okay, I got to deliver my papers. I gotta go

now. See you later, girlfriend."

Tina watched them ride away, watched Pinky sling the folded papers, watched the copy of the *Palomino Press* sail into a yard. When they turned off her street, Tina ran up the sidewalk and bounded up the steps.

She handed over the newspaper to Teresa. "Pinky loves me, Momma. I'm Pinky's girlfriend."

"I heard, Sweetie. Congratulations."

"I've got two dollars and sixteen cents in my King Edward bank, Momma. How much do I need to buy a bicycle?"

"A bicycle?"

"We're the three mustard-tears, Momma. So I need a bicycle to go with Patsy and Pinky."

"I see." Teresa nodded and smiled at her daughter. "A bicycle. I bet you'd need one like I had."

"Yes, Momma. How much do you think a bicycle like the one you had will cost?"

"I think a new one will cost a lot more than you have in your bank, Sweetie."

"Well, I have my allowance and I get paid a little every time I do my chores at the cafe. And Miss Ruby gives me a dime sometimes when I do things she asks me to do."

"Let's see if there is an ad for a bicycle." Teresa opened the weekly edition of the newspaper.

Tina scanned the pages with her mother as Teresa turned them.

There were no bicycle ads, but Kline's Drugstore, in bold letters, issued a warning. *'DON'T WAIT,*

CHRISTMAS IS JUST AROUND THE CORNER'.

"You know what, Sweetie?"

"No, what?"

"I have an idea."

"What is your ideal?"

"Idea, Sweetie. My idea is, why don't we think about writing a letter?"

"To who?"

"Santa Claus, Sweetie. Maybe we could look in the Montgomery Ward catalog and pick out a bicycle. Then you could write your letter about what you found. Fore you know it Christmas will be here soon enough after your school starts."

"Yeah. That's a good ideal, Momma. Will you help me?"

"I sure will, Sweetie. And I bet Daddy will help, too."

"I want a blue and white bicycle, Momma, like you had when you loved Daddy."

THE ARRIVAL
August 1943
RAF bomb Peenemunde V-2 rocket facility
Japanese use chemical weapons against Chinese

The morning after their meeting at Camp Maxey, Miss Ruby heard five polite knocks at the front door.

"Somebody is at the door, Ethel."

"I'm goin, I'm goin."

Miss Ruby waited for a report. She drew a long inhale from her cigarette and exhaled smoke through her nose. She positioned an annoying bit of tobacco onto the tip of her tongue and placed her tongue between her lips. Instead of using a finger to remove the fragment, she stuck her tongue out between her lips, quickly pulled her tongue back in while at the same time blowing a puff of air to expel the grain of tobacco.

"There's a soldier boy out here, Miss Ruby," Ethel called out. "Where you at?"

"I'm on the back porch, Ethel. Bring him to me."

In a moment, the Porter House housekeeper and cook pushed open the screen door leading to the porch and stepped aside. Ethel wiped her hands with a dishtowel.

Miss Ruby did not turn her head to look at them, but she knew from a side-glance that somebody had joined Ethel on the porch.

"This here is Sergeant Miller, Miss Ruby." Ethel canted her head toward the neatly groomed youngster clad in an Army uniform. "He's from the Army camp over there."

Miss Ruby snubbed out her cigarette. She laid the matchbox on top of the gold pack of Philip Morris cigarettes. She remained in the rocking chair and turned to look at them — to her, Sergeant Miller appeared to be twelve or thirteen years old.

She spied the dark spots of perspiration under his armpits and smiled. His sweat, she thought, was from nervousness or the August heat.

"How do, Miss Ruby, I'm Sergeant Alvin Miller. I'm a top-secret courier. I came from Camp Maxey this morning to deliver a package from Colonel Jones."

"Thank you, Ethel."

"I'll be in the kitchen, Miss Ruby. I'm finishing up breakfast dishes. After that, I'll be upstairs." Ethel disappeared, easing the screen door closed.

Miss Ruby daintily extended her hand, palm and limp fingers pointing down.

Alvin shifted the leather case to his left hand and stepped forward.

He did not grasp her hand, instead held her fingers delicately. He bowed slightly as a commoner paying worship to the queen who sat on her throne.

143

She looked at the case, not the soldier.

"What do you bring me?"

Miss Ruby followed Sergeant Miller's hand as he opened the satchel and tilted it for her inspection.

She peered in at the banded bricks of fresh, unused denominations of ones, fives, tens, and twenties.

It was an unusual sight.

So strange that curious Lamar county folk walking the eight-mile stretch along both shoulders of US Highway 271 between the Camp Maxey main gate and Paris stopped and stared.

Town-folk moving up and down sidewalks in the city halted mid-stride, stood still and gawked.

It was not because an open Army jeep pulling a trailer attracted their attention — that was a common occurrence during these times. They gaped because of the four men in the vehicle. They stared because the two in the back seat and the one in the front passenger seat had a huge **P W** painted in white on the back of their blue denim shirts and along the outer seam of their trouser legs.

Too, they stared because the new olive-drab duty uniform sleeves of the chauffeur bore chevrons of an American Army sergeant.

"They get an eyeful, looking at us," Hopplendagger said. He followed Twig's instructions and did not turn his head to meet anyone's gaping gawk.

On departure from Maxey, Sergeant Chestnutt

had told them they were not to acknowledge or speak to anyone as they traveled to Palomino. "If there's any talking to be done, I'll do it."

Duke Hopplendagger sat in the passenger seat. Eddy Becker and Will Weiss sat in the back seat.

"They think we are devils," Duke said. "They are looking for our horns, our devil horns. We saw those looks in Boston when we marched from the ship to the train station. Remember?"

"Yes, in Boston they were chicken necking. Is that how you say it, Sergeant Twig, chicken necking?" Eddy asked.

"I think you mean rubbernecking. As people pass by something, like a car wreck, they turn their heads to look."

"Yes, rubbernecking. In Germany, we say *gummizug*. People turn and look. Rubbernecking."

Duke tittered but did not point. "Look at the little boy. He stands at attention and salutes. He will make a good soldier one day, for the next war."

Twig downshifted gears and slowed the jeep. He stopped to permit a car to back out from an angled parking space. As the car pulled away, Twig shifted to first gear, eased the clutch out, and followed at twelve miles per hour.

As the jeep moved forward, Duke smiled and nodded as he returned the tyke's salute. The boy's beaming grin communicated pure joy — for all of them. The youngster's mother, however, frowned and kept wary eyes fixed on the passers-by. Duke saw the mother waggle the small hand but could not hear her reprimand.

Twig kept his eyes moving from the two-door Chevrolet in front, to the yellow painted traffic light beyond. He tried telepathy, but the black coupe poked along. Twig did not want to stop on a street in the middle of Paris with a jeep load of POWs. He was not lucky.

The red light came on while the green light was on. There was no amber light. In two seconds, the green light went off. The driver ahead stopped. Twig downshifted, kept the clutch depressed, closed the gap, and braked to a halt. They sat, waiting. No one in the jeep spoke.

Somebody off to Twig's left yelled. "Those are prisoners."

"I see em. They've got P W painted on their backs," a voice behind the jeep proclaimed.

Twig decided they were too vulnerable stopped on the street, sitting high, exposed in the jeep, proverbial sitting ducks. He turned the steering wheel and eased the clutch out. He pulled around the car and drove slowly through the red light. He had not cleared the intersection when the police siren screamed.

Twig checked the driver side mirror and shook his head. "Damn."

He steered the jeep to stop behind cars parked in angled spaces in front of a store. A large sign above the front door announced *Mason's Grocery*.

The three prisoners turned to watch the patrolman approach.

"I want you to be quiet. I'll do the talking, understand?"

"*Jawohl*," Duke said.　He grinned when Twig looked at him.　"That means yes, Sergeant Chestnutt."

"I know what it means.　I've picked up a few words of German."

"*Du bist gefangen*," Eddy said.

"What does that mean?"

"You are caught," Will said and grinned.　"Our guard is caught doing a no-no."

"You run a red light, Son," the patrolman said.

"Yes, Sir, I sure did, and you caught me doin it," Twig said.　"I must tell you, Officer, I'm armed."

"What the hell does that mean, Boy?"

"I'm tryin to tell you I have a loaded pistol on my hip.　I'm an armed guard."

"You tryin to be a smart ass, Boy?"

"No, Sir."

It was then, as if slapped by a sap, the patrolman realized there were three in the jeep wearing blue denim military fatigue hats and blue denim shirt and pants.　The white P Ws were strikingly obvious.

"What are you doin with the prisoners in Paris, Boy?"

"Just passin through, Officer."

"I've a good mind to run you in, Boy.　You got a smart mouth."

"I'm guilty of running a red light, Officer.　Please give me a ticket and let me get out of the way."

From the direction of the grocery, a voice shouted.　"Them boys are prisoners.　They got P W painted all over their clothes."

The patrolman looked at the interrupting

observer. "You folks move along now. I've got this under control. Move along."

Twig inhaled deeply and looked at the policeman. "I'm a Military Police Sergeant in the United States Army, Officer. These three German prisoners of war are in my charge. We are on our way to another town to undertake a classified mission for Governor Stevenson and President Roosevelt."

"The Governor and the President, you say."

"Yes, Sir. They expect us to be at a certain place at a certain time. I'm sure my report will upset your Governor, and he'll call your chief to find out why we were delayed. So, please write the ticket and let us be on our way."

"You *are* a smart ass. I have to deal with all of you. Come into our town, break our laws, and get off scot-free. The ticket is two dollars, Boy. Or you can pay me five and there won't be no citation or record."

"*Ein Gauner.*" Duke smiled at the officer.

"I have no money," Twig said. "Payday is three days away. Please give me the ticket. I'll mail the money in to pay my fine."

"What'd *he* say?"

"That you're an honorable man and citizen and that you support those who are serving in the military during wartime," Twig answered.

"Oh, yeah? He said all that?"

"Yes, Sir, in a manner of speaking. I'm also a military intelligence interpreter."

"Put em in a concentration camp," someone across the street suggested. The voice was not loud.

It didn't have to be, the street was quiet.

Weiss, sitting on the left, looked left. People standing on the sidewalk across the street stood shoulder to shoulder as if watching a parade. Some were pointing, gesturing and talking, others only stared.

Becker, sitting on the right, looked right. Through the space between parked cars, he could see gawkers lined along the sidewalk. He felt uncomfortable.

"Put em in the ground," a woman's voice shouted.

As if on cue, Will looked right and Eddy looked left, searching for the woman. Their eyes met, fear shrouded their faces.

"They killed my boy," another woman cried.

The police officer and Twig surveyed the surroundings. They realized dozens of people had gathered to watch the proceedings. Now it was risky for them to stay in the middle of the street.

"We've got to move, Officer. This is dangerous. Look, everybody on the sidewalk is looking at us."

The patrolman nodded, acquiescing. "Okay. Be on your way, Boy. And don't run no more red lights in my town, you hear?"

"Thank you, Sir." Twig checked his mirror and pulled away.

"They're getting away, Thomas," someone yelled.

Twig checked his mirror again and was relieved no one followed. He shifted to fourth gear, and the jeep bumped along through busy streets. Trucks, cars, motorcycles, Army trucks, jeeps, and even wagons pulled by horses jockeyed for traveling space.

At one stop sign, Eddy opened up. "We did not kill that lady's boy, Sergeant Chestnutt."

"In North Africa," Will said, "we laid telephone wire and operated switchboards. I never fired my rifle, at anything or anybody."

"The desert is huge," Eddy offered. "Maybe he was in a battle somewhere."

"We're at war," Twig answered. "You and the Japs and the Dagos started this mess, another world war. There are a lot of boys dying on all sides. Imagine if you were driving three of Stalin's soldiers through one of your towns. What would German mommas cry out to the Soviets?"

Twig reached the town limit sign and pulled off the highway. "Stay put, I want to check the rope tie-downs for the canvas cover on the trailer. I thought I saw a loose corner flapping."

He was back in the driver's seat within thirty-seconds and started the engine. "What does *ein gauner* mean?"

"Crook.   Your   policeman   is   a   crook," Hopplendagger said.

Twig waited for traffic to clear before pulling onto the highway. He accelerated to a speed of thirty-five and maintained it. A mile down the road, a sign indicated eleven miles to Pattonville. After Pattonville, Twig knew, it was a little over seven miles to Palomino.

They rode in silence for several minutes before Will complained.

"I must *pinkeln*, Sergeant Chestnutt. Can you

stop alongside the road?"

Twig looked over his shoulder. "*Pinkeln*? Pee? Does that mean pee?"

"Yes," Duke affirmed.

"Can you wait about fifteen-twenty minutes, Weiss? I'll stop in Pattonville."

"I do not think so. What happened in town made me want to go. Now that I have said I must *pinkeln*, pee, I must pee. It is all I can think of."

"Okay, there's a clump of trees up ahead, I'll stop there."

Twig pulled over and directed everybody out. He turned off the engine and followed them to the trees. He chose a position to pee and keep watch on the three of them.

In the camp, he never paid much attention. Now, while they stood there, under horse-apple and paper-shell pecan trees alongside a Texas highway, taking a piss, Twig more closely took in their features. One had light colored hair, not quite blonde, and blue eyes — a square face and a lighter skin tone. A Hitler Aryan? Twig wondered. The other two had dark hair and dark eyes — darker skin too. An appearance similar to his Jewish friend in Vivian, Sergeant Johnny Zeigler, Twig remembered.

A blaring car horn startled the foursome.

Twig and the prisoners looked up toward the highway.

The 1942 cream-colored DeSoto parked behind the jeep's trailer had its nose pointed toward Paris. Two females crowded the driver's window, and two females filled the back passenger window of the four-door luxury sedan and peered down at the men.

"Wha-chall doin?" a girl's voice yelled. A flurry of girly giggles erupted.

A brunette in the back window laughed. She spoke loud enough even soldiers on KP at Maxey could hear. "They holdin onto somethin, Delilah. I wonder what it is."

Screaming giggles gushed again.

"Ginnie says yall are holdin somethin. Can we see what it is?" Delilah, the driver, asked.

They finished, stowed their equipment, and buttoned up.

The driver of the fast approaching semi-tractor towing a long trailer pulled down on and held his air horn cord, blaring at all of them as the truck roared past. The tractor and trailer were dark green — emblazoned in yellow on the driver's door and at the upper left corner of the trailer were *ETMF*. The driver waved at the four men walking toward a car full of women by thrusting his left arm out the window and extending the middle finger of his left hand.

As they approached the car, another trucker set down on his horn as his truck blew by the vehicles. This truck and trailer sported the letters *ABF*.

They stopped a dozen steps from the DeSoto. They felt windblasts of passing trucks and could see the car rock. Twig had not noticed, or paid attention to, all the trucks traveling east and west on the highway. Camp Maxey was busy shipping and receiving, he surmised.

"Hello, Ladies." Twig saluted.

"Are yall Army boys out there at the Camp?"

"Sort of," Twig nodded. "Where yall from?"

"Paris. We go to college, Paris Junior College."

"What are you studyin?"

"We're entertainers. We live in Miss Estelle's boarding house. We do a lot of entertaining there."

Twig grinned. "Mad . . . Miss Estelle's. I've heard about her place, her boarding house."

Duke, Eddy, and Will were inspecting and admiring the four pretty girls, who all seemed to be teenagers.

Ginnie stuck her right arm out of the car and pointed.

Eddy felt like Ginnie pointed at him.

"You're cute, soldier boy. What's your name?"

He did not hesitate. "Eddy."

"They have a dance out at the camp every Saturday night, Eddy. We all go out there to entertain the boys," Delilah said. "Will yall be there?"

Before Twig could answer, the girl behind Delilah made an announcement.

"Delilah, they're Germans. I *thought* I saw a P W. Look on the side of their pants. They're prisoners. They've escaped from Maxey. Daddy said if they escaped they're gonna ravage and rape all the women they can find."

The girl behind Ginnie shoved a silver revolver over Ginnie's shoulder and out the window. "I've got em covered, Delilah, take off."

Twig and the prisoners raised their hands, staring at the muzzle.

Delilah started the engine, ground the gears as

she shifted to first, and pressed the accelerator.

"Bye, Eddy," Ginnie yelled.

The DeSoto's rear wheels scattered grass and dirt as they spun searching for traction. A trucker's air horn blared as Delilah gunned the car and it swept out onto the highway in front of him.

Twig and his party watched the car scoot toward Paris.

"*Wunderschon*," Eddy said.

"The car or *das Madchen*?" Duke asked.

"Both are beautiful," Will answered. "I would like to go to the dance to bully-wooly with Ginnie."

"You saw who she talked to. Ginnie's my girl, Will."

"That'll be the day," Twig said. "Anyway, the music and dance is boogie-woogie, Will," Twig corrected.

"Yes, bully, boogie, boogie-woogie. I have heard that music. I think Ginnie can boogie-woogie well." Will was wistful. "I think she can."

"Okay, everybody back in the jeep. We need to get to Palomino before chow."

The layout had changed little after Delbert Porter's wranglers founded Palomino in 1876. The main part of town was in Lamar County and lay on the west side of Pecan Creek and Main Street. A smaller section of the community lay on the east side of the creek and was in Red River County. Great fussing and gnashing of teeth occurred at tax time each year when county appraisals arrived.

Comparison of property assessments were the talk of the town.

Two streets in town and the two-lane US Highway 271 shaped the western part of Palomino. On a map, this design with the three thoroughfares appeared like an odd triangle. The two high school mathematics teachers used the city's pathways to challenge residents and students' understanding whether the outline made an obtuse or scalene triangle. Most of the folks in town couldn't spell obtuse, scalene, or triangle and those who could never thought about the shape or didn't care.

Main Street was the base, the shortest side of the triangle. Main Street ran north off 271. The highway was the middle-length northwest-southeast leg. Clark Street was the longest side of the Scalene and ran due east from 271 to junction with Main Street on the north side of town.

Twig had two choices to enter Palomino. He worried about going the length of 271 and turning on Main Street. That course would take him through the middle of town, businesses on each side of the route. The experience in Paris of the threatening onlookers was a persuasive deterrent to using Main Street.

He decided to exit 271 at the Clark Street junction, west of town. Clark Street was better, he felt, because it was a direct path to the Porter House, which sat at the corner of Clark and Evans Lane.

He slowed, downshifted, and stuck out his left arm to signal his turn off 271. He stopped the jeep on the highway, waiting for two oncoming cars to pass. A semi-truck driver a quarter mile behind the jeep pulled the string, and the air horn bellowed.

Eddy and Will jerked around at the sound, Duke and Twig looked at the side mirrors.

Unsure the approaching truck could slow or stop in time Twig twisted the steering wheel left and gunned the jeep.

Hopplendagger, Weiss, and Becker grabbed hold of the frame to stay aboard in the sudden surge.

The jeep crossed the lane with only inches separating a new Cadillac's grill and the loaded trailer. The angry Caddy driver stood on his car horn for a quarter-mile.

The truck driver joined in adding his own displeasure with spouts from his horn.

Some citizens had anticipated Twig's shortest route to the Porter House. Up ahead, several men, women, and children of Palomino lined both sides of Clark Street. Some men held rifles, others hefted shotguns — all barrels pointed downward.

Sergeant Chestnutt resigned himself to troop the line in style. He held his speed at ten miles per hour and nodded at folks along both sides of the street.

Nobody acknowledged the occupants as the military vehicle passed by. Nobody smiled.

The prisoners sat at attention, hands along the top of their legs with heads up and eyes straight ahead. Tension was heavy in the late afternoon heat.

As he turned the jeep onto the Porter House driveway, Miss Ruby and Teresa rose from chairs on the front porch.

Tina stood on the top step. "DADDY'S HOME!"

They were the only ones in Palomino who smiled and waved a welcome.

THE DISCOVERY
November 1943
Italians bomb the Vatican
Japanese sub sinks USS *Corvina* near Truk

"Who found him, Stephan?"

"That guy there. Railroad maintenance man. Name's Poole, with an *e*. Jeremiah Poole. Lives in Bogata."

"Identification?"

"Artemis Canton. Goes by Arty. I know him as a petty criminal. Car thief. Lives in Pattonville. Lived there, anyway. Just a wild-ass kid. Fourteen or fifteen years old, Doc said."

"How'd he get down here, you think?"

"Probably from that abandoned car, Sheriff — member the one that had no gas, the one with blood in it? Somebody probably carried him from that to here."

"Been dead long?"

"Doc Bledsoe says a couple of days, maybe a day more."

"How'd he die?"

"Gunshots."

"Gunshots. *Gunshots*? More than one?"

"Yep. A forty-five and a smaller caliber, probably a twenty-two. I think the forty-five was Pop Crawley's hit. The small bullet was the kill shot. Right temple."

"So, you think this . . . you think Canton is one of the three who hit the bank before Thanksgiving."

"Believe so. A gasoline ration card with his name on it was in his billfold. A red bandanna was around his neck. And the ladies at the bank said Lois called out the name Artemis."

"A bank robber carryin identification, not very smart."

"Doc said the forty-five cut him pretty bad. Walter was always a good shot. Doc said the boy was so skinny it's a wonder the bullet didn't go all the way through and come out his back. The only thing Doc can figure is the bullet is stuck in a bone. There's dried blood spots along the track, so he was still alive when he was brought down here. Had to be in a lot of pain, I imagine. His accomplice must of dumped him here in the shed and took the handcar from that rail barn down there to make an escape."

"If the handcar was left on the tracks how come The Katy didn't hit it?"

"Poole said a few days ago the engineer saw it and stopped. He had the fireman put it off on a side rail up near Palomino. Poole went up there to bring it back here. Poole never looked in the shed until this morning, that's when he found the boy. The car's over there in the rail barn. Doc said it had dried blood too."

"So, the accomplice run off and left the boy?"

"Seems so. With a gut shot the boy was gonna die

anyway. So somebody didn't want him walking — well he wasn't going to walk in no hospital, that's for sure — they didn't want him in no hospital with a forty-five wad-cutter in his gut. So, somebody took matters into their own hands and popped him."

"It seems to me, if the handcar was left near Palomino then our bank robbers and killers are close by. Otherwise, the car would be in Paris or south of here, down toward Talco and the oil rigs. So, I think we need to go to Palomino and talk to Jimmy Madison and get him involved in this bank robbery and killin."

"You forgot, Sheriff. Jimmy's not there anymore. There's a new man in town, got there a month or two ago. Name's Chestnutt, Twig Chestnutt. He's an Army Sergeant, has three POWs in tow. The town appointed him Constable. He's doing double duty over there."

"Oh, that's right. I don't know how I could forget that with all the hullaballoo, for crissakes."

"It was in all the papers, even on the radio. Everybody made such a big deal about it. Some still argue and fuss about it."

"Well, why don't you drive over there tomorrow and have a talk with him. Tell him what we're dealing with, what we're looking for. Bring him into the picture and see if he can help. What do you think, Stephan?"

"Want me to take Sunday with me?"

Sadness transformed Sheriff Billy Blake's face, and he lowered his brown eyes. He swallowed and gave a half nod. He was a husky man with a huge chest and broad shoulders, and tall at six-two, but humble in manner. He pulled off his gray Stetson and pulled on his nose with a thumb and index finger. He brushed at his red tie as if to sweep lint away. He met Deputy Stanton's gaze and gave a slight smile.

Stephan realized the pause was intentional to give the Sheriff a few seconds to regain composure. He lowered his eyes to not embarrass his boss.

"Logan's been gone a year and a half, Stephan, and I still haven't gotten over it."

"I know, Sheriff. You treated him like a son. I know you miss him."

"I don't know why the agents up from Dallas couldn't find him or the two who took him. Billy Don gave them descriptions."

"Well, he didn't really give them much to go on, Sheriff. The Rangers did find the green Dodge in Mount Pleasant. Belonged to that life insurance agent in Clarksville."

"Even those boys didn't find the car, a citizen reported it. I don't think anybody, Rangers or those two boys from Dallas, were even interested in looking for the car, kidnappers, or Logan."

"We'll find Logan, Billy, and bring him home for Fay and Lou, his baby girl."

Sheriff Blake put his hat on and adjusted it. He took a deep breath.

"Before I go to Pattonville, I'll call Dudley in Paris and tell him I'm going to be in his county making some inquiries. He might want to send one of his deputies out to be with me. Maybe Canton has family there. Maybe they can tell us who he run with. Somebody ought to know something about this boy and his family."

"Sheriff Dudley will want to help, I think."

"Yeah, I think so, too. Well, Stephan, I guess before you go talk to the Palomino Constable, maybe talk to the bank folks and arrange for them to come to the hospital to give a positive identification of this Canton boy, to have another piece of evidence to connect him to the robbery."

"Okay, Sheriff. Ah . . ."

"What? I can see it in your face, Stephan, what's on your mind?"

"A memorial. For Walter."

Billy Blake shook his head from right to left, twice. He licked his lips before he spoke.

"I don't know. I'd sure like to do it, but the mayor is always complaining about not having money for this or that."

Deputy Stephan Stanton shrugged and lifted his hands. "If the town won't pay for it I'm sure Franklein will. After all, Walter was part of the bank. The bank president ought to do something."

"Franklein is tighter than a bent piece of bob wire, you know that, Stephan. I doubt he would fork over even a dollar bill for a memorial. He probably wouldn't even pay for a plaque to put up on a wall in the bank to recognize Walter."

"I'll make a five dollar donation to get it started, Billy. I'll talk with Aubrey, I know he'll want to donate."

"Well then, I'll kick in five dollars, too. I'll pin the mayor and the town council. We'll get it done."

Doc Bledsoe approached. "Well, Sheriff, we've done all we can here. The boys are going to bring the body to the hospital. I'll do the official autopsy. After that, I'll notify Zellman and have him pick up the body. His funeral home can prepare the boy for burial and notify next of kin they have him."

"That's fine, Doc. Stephan is going to talk with Miss Myrtle and Miss Judy, ask them if they'll look at the boy. We think that will give us another positive piece the boy was part of the robbery before Thanksgiving. We'll do that once Abraham has prepared the boy."

"I'll tell Zellman your plan once I release the body."

"Stephan and David Sunday, our new deputy, are going to Palomino tomorrow to talk with their new Constable. His name is Chestnutt."

"I've read about him in the paper. He's got three German prisoners of war over there. They pick cotton, work in the gin. It's been on the radio. Folks are talking about it, some are asking why we don't have prisoners working around here, Sheriff. It's cheap labor."

Blake smiled. He avoided Doc Bledsoe's prod. "We think because the handcar was left near Palomino the accomplice might be local. Maybe Chestnutt can make inquiries and help us discover who it is. I'll drive over to Pattonville to see if I can find out who the boy's relatives are and who he run with. If I find somebody, I'll notify Abraham Zellman. Then he'll have a next of kin to give the boy to and talk with about getting paid."

"You better call Dudley before you go walking around and talking to people in Lamar County, Sheriff."

"I will, Doc. Me and Dudley have a good working relationship. Well, most of the time, anyway."

Doc Bledsoe pulled a piece of paper from his shirt pocket and handed it to Sheriff Blake. "I almost forgot this. Found it in his pocket."

Billy Blake unfolded the small sheet and looked. "Herr Higgins? Who's Herr Higgins?"

"Never heard of him. Never heard the name, the words Herr Higgins remind me what I've read in the paper and seen in the *pitchursho* news. Herr Hitler."

Pinky felt safe in their stall hideout in the only original barn still standing within the town limits of Palomino.

Always observant and curious, he had not noticed it when he first settled into concealed idleness, which was strange.

Imitating his Saturday matinee private eye, Sam Spade, he flicked the white head of the matchstick with a thumbnail and flamed the tip of the fag. He had shaken the fire out and slid the burnt match stem back into its strike anywhere, red box before relaxing and inhaling the soothing vapor of addictive, unfiltered nicotine.

On the third drag of the pilfered Chesterfield, slipped out of his Momma's pack, beginning eighth-grader Rayfield Paramore Pinkston, Jr. spotted the flop-eared top of a five-pound flour sack.

Now, he sat in their secret spot, smoking serenely, staring at the small, crumpled, soft-fabric bundle. Somebody had stuffed it behind a ragged, cracked-leather horse collar hanging from a nail, and the bulky contents caused it to sag from its seclusion. The little sack was clean, store-shelf fresh looking, but opened. As if a light switch flared a bulb, he recognized the paper nametag sewn into the top seam and the daisy pattern. It had the same design and colors of a shirt his mother had made and was saving for him to wear for the Christmas cakewalk at the school gym Saturday night. Paula Pinkston wanted her son to appear nice. She knew Mr. Stan Stern, the only portrait and newspaper photographer in Palomino, took pictures at school and community events. She hoped Pinky's picture would be in the newspaper so she could send it to his dad.

Pinky finished the smoke and gingerly snuffed it out on a bare, wall stud. Careful not to leave evidence of his presence, of the extinguished cigarette, or of a fire ignited in a tinderbox of worn, aged, desert-dry planks, he field stripped the butt and scattered tobacco remnants along the grubby floorboard. He rolled the paper, pressed it between his thumb and forefinger three times, and flipped away the tiny ball. He had learned all this by watching Sergeant Twig Chestnutt do it.

He stood, shoved the box of matches into his blue jean pocket, pulled the weighty bag down, and peered in. His gasp was telling — he looked up and around, searching to see if anyone was near.

His pulse quickened when he thought he saw movement through the spaces between boards of the warped, timbered wall. In haste, he twisted the top into a bunch, gripped it, and rushed out through the opening where huge double doors once hung.

At the same time he saw Patsy, she saw him. He froze, knowing it was useless to turn away. He knew she would want to know why he had not asked her to go with him to the barn. He also knew he couldn't hide the sack. He should have known better. She was in love with him. She did not like to be without him. She had told him so, many times.

And he was in love with Patsy. Oh, yeah, he *was* in love with her.

Patricia Ann coasted toward him on her blue bicycle. Billowing from the rush of air, the bottom of her flower print dress hiked above her knees exposing white socks and black, high-top Converse tennis shoes. She braked when she came alongside him.

"I've been looking for you, Pinky."

"I figured as much. Why're you looking for me?"

"Because. You know why. After I helped you fold papers for your paper route yesterday, you promised to meet me at Jeeps at one o'clock. You said you'd buy me a chocolate sundae with a cherry on top, and a Grapette."

"Oh, yeah. I forgot."

"I figured as much. That's why I was looking for you."

"Well, I can't right now, I have to take care of something."

"Where'd you get that?"

"This? This old flour sack? I just found it."

"Where at?"

"There, in Miss Ruby's barn."

"How come you didn't tell me you were going to that old woman's barn? You know that's our secret place."

"I was hiding."

"I bet you were in there smoking."

"No, no. I was hiding."

"Who from?"

"Stick Waldo."

"Why were you hiding from Stick?"

"He said he was gonna beat me up."

"Oh, yeah? What'd you do to Waldo?"

"I didn't do nothing to Waldo."

"Well, if he wanted to beat you up you had to do something, Pinky."

"He keeps tryin to steal my customers. When I tell Miss Maybelle about it, she yells at him to quit. Then he comes looking for me for squealin on him."

"So? Why don't you punch him in the nose or kick his leg?"

"If I do that he'll knock my teeth out."

"Well, if you don't do it he'll keep on until he puts you out of business. He's a mean bully. I'll talk to him, man to man."

"You ain't no man, Patsy."

"I may not be but I can sock him in the throat. Then, by God, he'll leave you alone."

Pinky knew Patsy could do it, would do it. He had seen her in action.

"Whatcha got there?"

"Just a sack."

"You said that already. I see it's a sack, Pinky, it's a Pillsbury flour sack. My momma makes dresses and shirts out of Pillsbury sacks. Your momma makes your shirts out of Pillsbury sacks. My momma made this dress out of one of those sacks. What's in *that* sack?"

"If I tell you, you gotta keep it a secret."

"It ain't gonna be no secret for long, Pinky. You took a sack out of Miss Ruby's barn. The beatin and thrashin you gonna get from Miss Ruby when she finds out you stole the sack out of her barn is gonna be the talk of the town. And Twig will put you in *The Calaboose* for bein a robber."

"It was hid behind a horse collar but it slipped out because of the heavy stuff in it. I was gonna put it back, but then I looked in it. I think she saw me."

"Well, if she saw you, she's gonna come lookin for you when she finds out her sack is gone. You better go in right now and put it back."

"Okay, I will. Can I trust you, Patsy?"

"Good Lord, Pinky. If we're gonna be married for life and have a bunch of kids you got to trust me."

"Okay, but you got to swear and cross your heart and hope to die, and spit on the ground you won't tell nobody what I found in Miss Ruby's barn if I let you look."

And eighth-grader Patricia Ann Parker did just that. Afterwards, she pushed her bicycle to the barn and leaned it against the wall, then followed Pinky through the opening. They sat side by side, in their secret spot.

"Now, tell me what's in Miss Ruby's sack."

"Money."

"Aw, go on. What's in the sack?"

"And a gun. It's a shiny, silver gun with a white handle. Just like the Lone Ranger's guns."

"No lie? A real gun?"

"No lie, Patsy. And a lot of money. Probably a hundred million dollars."

"Let me look at the money and the gun."

Pinky opened the sack, and Patsy peered in.

She reached in and withdrew the shiny .22 caliber

revolver.

"Good Lord."

Patricia Ann Parker was disappointed. She turned the small revolver over from side to side and hefted it in her palm. She was not impressed.

"This ain't like the Lone Ranger's guns. It's puny."

Just like a cowboy in a Saturday matinee, Patsy aimed and verbally fired the gun, letting it recoil in her hand.

Patsy pointed the gun at Pinky. "This is a stick-up. Give me a kiss."

Pinky leaned into her and kissed her lips.

"Let me see the money."

Pinky opened the sack again.

Patsy shifted the revolver to her left hand and reached into the sack with her right. She withdrew a grip full of loose bills. Four ten-dollar bills slipped from her grasp and floated to the floor.

"You weren't lying. There must be a hundred million dollars in that sack. I wonder where it come from?"

"I bet it was a bank robbery."

"Miss Ruby? A bank robber? Nah, not Miss Ruby."

"Who then?"

Patsy looked at Pinky. Her expression was a big question mark.

"Her housekeeper?" Pinky asked.

"Miss Ethel? Nah, Miss Ethel is a good person. So is Julius, Miss Ethel's husband. Julius is Miss Ruby's yardman, handyman, and driver. Neither one of them would rob a bank. They'd be too scared."

"Maybe we better tell Twig about the money and

gun?"

"Okay. Let's go up to Pecan Park. The deputy sheriff is over there now."

"Twig Chestnutt is the Constable, he ain't a Sheriff."

"I know that, Pinky. Two Red River County deputies from Bogata is at the park with *Constable* Chestnutt and his Germans."

"What they doin in the park with the Germans?"

"I was at the cafe waitin for you when the deputies came in askin for Twig. Mrs. Chestnutt said he was at the park pickin up trash."

"Okay, you can hold the sack. I'll pedal, you sit on the seat. We'll go up to the park and give him the sack and gun."

"Where's your bicycle, Pinky?"

"I left it at home. I came over here to smoke a cigarette."

"I knew it. I knew you were smoking and didn't ask me. Give me one."

"I don't have no more. I brought just one from my momma's pack."

"Well, what we have to do is buy a pack and stash it here so we don't have to worry about taking a cigarette when we need a smoke."

"Okay, come on, we'll go on your bicycle and bring the sack to the Constable."

"Maybe we better leave the gun and sack full of money here, and just tell him about it. If we take it out of the barn we're stealing it."

Patsy picked up the four tens, aligned them with the others in her hand and returned the money and revolver to the sack.

"If we leave it here, somebody might take it. We should bring it all to Twig."

"It might be Miss Ruby's hiding place, for her property and has nothing to do with robbing banks. If we take it out of the barn, we'll be crooks, Pinky. You'd be arrested for bein a criminal."

"Well, you would be one too, Miss Smarty Pants."

"We'll leave it and ride over to the park."

Pinky surrendered. Then a plan bloomed in his mind.

"After the park, maybe we can go to our special place?" Pinky ventured.

Patsy smiled, her eyes shined. "Our kissing place?"

Pinky thought the isolation might be conducive to snatching a few wonderful kisses from his girl, too. "Yes, down to the shed where the Major's cotton scales are."

With the suggestion to go to their love nest, the importance of the contents of the flour sack to Patricia Ann took a back seat to the possibilities she imagined might take place with Rayfield behind the closed door of the Major's shed. Patsy's smile turned into a grin. The thought of swapping a few kisses with her boy pleased her, too. "Okay, let's go to the shed. That'll give us a little privacy."

"Yeah, and maybe I can show you somethin else too."

Patsy's grin widened. Her eyes seemed ablaze. "I bet you can. I might even have a surprise for you."

Pinky was encouraged. He leaned toward her and Patsy met him halfway. Their lips touched, and she put her arms around his neck. They held the sweet kiss for several seconds before she pulled away.

Patsy stood and straightened her dress. "Okay, put the sack back and let's go."

She walked to the opening and waited.

In haste, Pinky thought he hung the sack back on the same nail where he discovered it. His anticipation was far greater than his attention to detail.

Outside, he held her bicycle steady as Patsy mounted for their ride to blissful secrecy. "I wonder what they talkin about at the park?" he asked.

"Maybe they're talking about the Christmas cakewalk. What are you gonna bring for the cakewalk?"

Pinky placed his left foot on the pedal, shoved the bicycle forward, lifted his right leg through the open space, gained a footing on the right pedal, and propelled them from the barn toward Clark Street.

"My momma is gonna bake a chocolate cake. She always bakes cakes and stuff for things at school."

At Clark Street, he steered right. Because it was an uphill trek to the park, he stood and pumped on the pedals all the way.

As Pinky chauffeured Patsy up to Pecan Park to tell Twig what they found, the dried stud surrendered the rusty nail which Pinky attached the sack to behind the horse collar.

The heavy sack dropped to the barn floor. The weight of the revolver pulled the sack and its contents over into the space between wall and flooring, where it rested out of sight.

Patsy had pedaled past as he walked toward the Porter House. Patsy rode her bicycle directly to the barn. Pinky came out with the sack, M D stopped in his tracks. Fear filled his throat.

He stood there on the sidewalk, watching them talk. In a few moments, Patsy pushed her bicycle forward, leaned it against a barn wall, and followed Pinky into the barn.

M D had seen them in the barn before, knew they smoked there. He decided to keep his distance.

In a few minutes, M D saw them come out of the barn. Pinky held the sack while they talked. Then, Pinky went back into the barn, stayed a few seconds, and came out again without the sack. They got on Patsy's bicycle and Pinky pedaled up the street.

Now, as they rode away, he was unsure about what to do. He knew Miss Ruby would be mad to learn Patricia Ann and Rayfield discovered the goods. He was worried, afraid. Her anger might boil hot, her murderous rage directed at him.

She had trusted him to stow the sack securely, with the money and gun in it. Put it in the usual hiding place, Miss Ruby said, where it can't be found. We'll wait awhile before dividing up the money, she had told him.

He had dutifully obeyed and stuffed the sack behind the horse collar that hung from a big nail, next to the leather whip she had used on him and Artemis a couple of times.

As M D stood there watching them wheel away, he decided his first action would be to retrieve the sack and its contents and find a different hiding place. But he knew that wouldn't be enough for Miss Ruby. That's the way she was, it wouldn't be enough.

Maybe now was the time for him to just take it all.

M D nodded. That would really stir the pot.

So, before she would make him pay for his carelessness, his second and final action would be to end the relationship. He would take care of Miss Ruby.

He rushed into the barn and panicked upon the discovery that the sack was not on the big nail. It was nowhere in sight.

Now, M D knew she wouldn't hesitate.

She was capable of taking care of him the way she took care of Arty after the bank guard shot him.

He knew he was in big trouble.

From the barn, M D walked the two miles to the Katy train station for a ride to Paris.

Halfway to the station, he decided Pinky hid the sack.

THE ADJUSTMENT
August 1943
Axis forces withdraw from Sicily
Allies occupy New Georgia

After introductions of the prisoners to Miss Ruby, Teresa, and Tina in the driveway, the arrivals retrieved their bags from the trailer and followed Ruby as she conducted a sweeping orientation of the first floor of the Porter House and led them up the staircase.

Miss Ruby made a special allowance since the Army was paying enormous rent for eight rooms. She gave Tina a bedroom by herself on the left side of the second floor. Tina shared the bathroom with her mother and daddy who had the other bedroom.

She had helped Teresa and Tina move from the third floor to the two bedrooms on the second floor vacated by Edgar and Vincent when they joined the Navy. Tina was excited she would have her own room, and Teresa was excited she would share a bed with Twig without Tina in their room.

Of course, the money Colonel Jones sent to Miss Ruby to pay her tenants to move never lined Edgar or

Vincent's pockets. Otis and Ernest had moved to Talco weeks before. None knew she received money for them, and Miss Ruby did not mention the incentive.

Duke and Eddy chose the bedrooms on the left side of the third floor where Otis and Ernest had lived. They would share the bathroom.

Will took the bedroom on the right side of the third floor vacated by Teresa and Tina. Will would share the bathroom with Pearson.

Caleb and Jake occupied the two bedrooms on the right side of the second floor and shared that bathroom.

When Duke, Eddy, and Will brought their belongings into their rooms, Ruby gave instructions. "Freshen up, wash your face and hands. Ethel will serve supper in an hour. Don't be late."

Ethel had worked tirelessly preparing the bedrooms, cleaning the bathrooms, and preparing the special, evening meal for the German prisoners. She had never seen a German and wondered what they looked like, what they smelled like. Oh, she'd seen pictures of Germans and German soldiers in Miss Maybelle's newspaper and watched them in the newsreel at the *pitchursho*. She was anxious and apprehensive and expressed those feelings to Julius.

Julius warned Ethel to keep her nose out of white-folk business. "You take care of the house, the cooking, and Miss Ruby," Julius commanded. "You leave them people to themselves." Julius warned her three times, but he knew his wife, knew she'd poke her nose in where it didn't belong regardless of his order.

After name introductions to the three tenants, the ten residents sat at the grand table with Ruby at one end, Twig the other.

Ruby organized the seating — nearest on her left sat Pearson, then Will, Eddy, and Duke and on her right was Caleb, Jake, Teresa, and Tina.

No sooner had they adjusted their chairs, Julius and Ethel appeared. Julius carried the water pitcher and a tray of bread. Ethel held the bowl of her special stew with two kitchen mittens. Julius placed the bread nearer Twig. Ethel set the hot bowl on a platter in front of Ruby. The dinner plates were stacked between Ruby and the bowl of stew.

"I'll dish the stew and pass it down," Miss Ruby said. She lifted a plate from the stack. "We'll start with Miss Tina. As the meal passes down one side, Twig, please pass the bread up the other side."

The serving went smoothly with seemingly practiced precision.

They consumed supper with sparse, quiet talk. Ethel gathered the dishes as Julius made the rounds with coffee.

"I have a couple of rules for the Porter House," Miss Ruby said. The room grew still and silent. "The kitchen is closed at nine o'clock, no late night raids on the icebox. The exception is for Jake because he comes in late after closing the *Palace*. Be courteous to other tenants, no bathing after ten o'clock and no loud radio, music, or talking after ten. No smoking in the house, but you can smoke on the front or back porch or in the yard. You can sit out on the porches as long as you wish." She paused and nodded at Twig. "As long as

Sergeant Chestnutt permits it."

Twig smiled and nodded at Miss Ruby.

She continued. "Clean up the bathroom after yourselves. Put your laundry in the bag outside your door Monday morning before you leave the house. Ethel will collect the bags and return your clean clothes Wednesday morning. Once a week, on Thursday, we exchange bed sheets. Breakfast is at six except on Sundays and then it's at eight. Does anyone have a question?" In turn, she looked at Will, Eddy, and Duke.

They said nothing.

"I know this particular situation in the Porter House, as well as in Palomino, will be an adjustment. I do hope everything works out for the best. Anything to add, Sergeant Chestnutt?"

"Thank you, Miss Ruby. I will go over my instructions with Will, Eddy, and Duke at another time, but for your purposes, our workday begins at breakfast at six and we'll be out of the house by seven."

Miss Ruby addressed her question to Twig as she looked and nodded at the three prisoners. "I think all of us would like to hear more about them, their background? Do you mind?"

"It's okay with me, I'll leave it up to the individual, Miss Ruby. Will, you begin if you'd like to tell us about yourself."

"My name is Wilhelm Weiss. I go by Will. I am eighteen years old. My hometown is Oberursel, near Frankfurt. My father is a banker, and my mother is a seamstress. I have one brother and one sister who are younger. I went to school in Stratford, north of London, for four years where my father worked in a bank. I completed A-Levels there two months before we returned to Germany.

"A year later Herr Hitler sent a letter ordering me to report to an Army barrack or face imprisonment. I was a Private and worked as a telephone wireman and switchboard operator. I never fired my rifle at a British or American soldier. I never hurt anyone.

"After capture in North Africa, we arrived by ship in Boston weeks later. A train ride brought us here, to Camp Maxey I mean. When I arrived at Camp Maxey, a toothbrush, toothpaste, razor, shave cream, and soap were on my bed with a blanket, pillow, and clean sheets. At that moment, I knew I wanted to live in America for the rest of my life. My hobby is tinkering with radios.

"Besides German and English, I speak a little French and Arabic."

Will surveyed the faces, anticipating questions. After a few seconds, he looked at Eddy.

"My name is Edwin Becker. I go by Eddy. I am nineteen. My hometown is Wiesbaden, south of Frankfurt. My father drowned in a boating accident on Lake Michigan. He worked at a Pabst brewery in Milwaukee.

"On our return to Wiesbaden, the government offered my mother a job with the civil service. I have no brothers or sisters. I was a Corporal in our communications squad. I like America too and hope to live here after the war. My hobby is dancing, mainly the polka and the waltz."

Duke waited for questions before he spoke.

"My name is Kraus Hopplendagger. I go by Duke. I

am twenty-one years old. My hometown in Germany is Berlin. My father was a doctor. When I was fourteen, he received a fellowship to study epilepsy at Northwestern University. We lived in Evanston, Illinois. We lived there four years.

"After my high school classes, I would ride a city bus up to the radio school. Dr. Anthony was a professor there. He often came to our house to play bridge. My voice was masculine, mature, even when I was a teenager. He gave me speech lessons and let me read sports over the school radio. I did that for three years.

"We returned in late 1940. Months later, the same day I finished communications school in Berlin, the Gestapo killed my father. They accused him of spying for America.

"My hobby is listening to radio shows and news broadcasts and practicing saying what I hear. I want to work in broadcasting in America after the war."

The pause was long.

Twig cleared his throat before he spoke. "I think it would be nice if we knew a little about your other tenants, Miss Ruby."

"Yes, of course. Caleb, would you like to tell us about yourself?"

"My name is Caleb Joiner. My friends call me C J. I am twenty-seven years old. I live in the Porter House with Miss Ruby. I work at the Gulf station for Mr. Hunter."

"Caleb was in third grade when he quit school," Miss Ruby said, her voice almost a whisper. "A tractor turned over and crushed his Daddy. Caleb went to work to help support his Momma and two brothers and two sisters. He could not pass the test to enter military service, but he can take a car or truck engine apart and put it back together in no time."

"I work on cars and trucks, change oil, and fix flats," Caleb added. "I like to fix things with my hands."

Miss Ruby looked at Jake and nodded.

"My name is Jake Little. I'm twenty-six. I manage Miss Ruby's theater, the *Palomino Palace*. I'm also the projectionist and accountant for the house." Jake scanned the faces of the three prisoners. "I've seen all the newsreels about what Germany is doing in Europe, and one of the disturbing things I saw was the report about concentration camps where thousands of people are imprisoned. Hitler and Himmler need to be shot. Were you part of these camps?"

Duke spoke for them. "No, Jake, we were not. It is as disturbing to us as it is to you and the people of America."

"We are soldiers, just like Sergeant Chestnutt," Will said. "We were drafted into service and sent to North Africa after training. We had nothing to do with those camps."

"But you had to know about the roundups and the persecution of the Jews in Germany," Twig challenged.

Again, Duke spoke for his squad members. "Yes, we knew about that, it was well publicized. But we were not part of it."

"It is sad and horrible what Hitler and the Nazis are doing," Will said. "The world will punish Germany for a long time after the war. Germany cannot win the war against America. We know that."

They fell silent.

"Pearson, tell us about you," Miss Ruby invited.

"I am Pearson Keenan. I am twenty-five. I was rejected for military service because of flatfeet. I work for Mayor Shipp and read gas and water meters. Sundays I go to church and sometimes go fishing.

"Sergeant Chestnutt, how can you protect our community against three enemy soldiers? They can overwhelm you, take your weapon, and kill citizens of Palomino."

Duke, Eddy, and Will looked from Pearson to Twig.

Twig nodded. "Yes, that is possible, Pearson. I can tell you that I will die trying to not let that happen. They know there is no place to hide. The people of Palomino would find and kill them without mercy.

"Besides, all three were released to me to work in Palomino because of their good behavior. I know them. They worked on details at Camp Maxey for me. I listened to their stories. I believe they want to remain in America after the war. I'm confident *we're* safe. The problem, of course, is keeping them safe from the people here in town."

Ethel came back into the room with Julius. Will followed them with his eyes as they moved behind Teresa and Tina. When they approached the back of his chair, Will rose and faced Ethel who stopped in front of him.

"I am sorry," Will said. "I have never seen a black person. I do not think there are people from Africa in Germany."

The room was still. All eyes were on Will.

"I've never seen a German," Ethel said. "The only

reason black people are in America is because our ancestors came here as slaves."

Will nodded. "Yes, I read about that in school. I am sorry." He hesitantly reached up with fingers extended. "My name is Will."

Ethel watched his hand and lifted her arm toward his fingers. "My name is Ethel."

Will touched Ethel's arm and smiled. He caressed her forearm with light strokes.

Ethel placed her right hand on Will's cheek and smiled.

"Your skin feels like mine," Will said.

Ethel nodded and tenderly patted Will's cheek.

"My skin may be darker, Mr. Will, and we may come from different worlds, but we both are God's children, my chil."

There were three loud knocks at the front door.

"Julius?"

"Yessum, I'm goin, Miss Ruby."

No one spoke, all heads turned toward the front room. In a moment, Julius appeared followed by Casey Shipp.

"It's the Mayor, Miss Ruby."

"Come in, Casey. We've just finished supper and are learning about one another."

"I didn't get a chance to tell about me," Tina said.

"Well, my goodness, you sure didn't, Miss Tina," Miss Ruby acknowledged. "You go right ahead, Sweetheart. We're listening."

"My name is Tina Chestnutt. I live here with my mommy and daddy. I am seven years old. I will be in second grade when school starts. My daddy is in the

Army and my mommy works at Jeeps Cafe. I help my mommy sometimes and Miss Bobbie Jo pays me ten cents."

"That was very good, Sweetie," Teresa said. "You are a smart young lady."

"Thank you, Miss Tina," Miss Ruby said. "Now, Casey, what can we do for you?"

"I came by to tell Sergeant Chestnutt to come to my office at nine Saturday morning. At that time, in that place, he will take the oath of office and officially assume the duties of Constable of Palomino."

The four of them sat on the back porch, smoking.

"Here is the order of march," Twig said. "Reveille is at five every workday morning. Breakfast at six. In the jeep at seven for departure to our work areas. We work Monday through Friday at tasks assigned by the Mayor or Major Monroe. Saturday mornings you will do chores I chose. Saturday afternoon beginning at one and Sundays are free of work unless a special requirement arises. Saturday afternoons we will go into town and shop, eat ice cream at Jeeps Cafe with Teresa and Tina, and mingle. If you wish to go to church on Sunday, we all go.

"There is concern about you three being in town, you heard that expressed. Make no mistake about it, your safety is in my hands. I will protect you the best I can, but you must always be alert for danger. If you attempt to escape, I will not tell you to halt or fire a warning shot. Once a month we will go to Camp Maxey. What are your questions?"

"Can we go to the dance?" Eddy asked. "I would like to see my girl, Ginnie."

THE MEETING
November 1943
June 1944 invasion of Europe decided in Tehran
America shocked by heavy losses on Tarawa

Tuesday morning, the last day of November, Lamar County Sheriff Jim Dudley drove his squad car the twelve miles east from Paris, and Red River County Sheriff Billy Blake drove the twelve miles west from Bogata. They arrived within thirty-seven seconds of each other at the Pattonville Feed Store.

Besides facial features, the only other discernible difference between the two sheriffs was their Stetson. Both were six-two, broad-shouldered, and shapely fit. They wore khaki trousers, white shirts, and red ties. Their gun belts and holsters were custom made by Farley Hogg; their shiny Colt .45s were Remington. Billy's wool hat was gray. Jim's was a white felt.

They grinned, shook hands, and patted each other on the shoulder.

"Good to see, you, Billy. Let's go in and have a cup of Baker Mill's coffee. He has a table we can sit at and work out a plan."

"We need to meet sometime, Jim, where we don't have to talk business."

"Times have changed with this war, Billy. A lot of people have gone plumb crazy with meanness and greed."

They waited until Baker moved away.

"I know, Jim. You'd think this boy would've got him a good payin job with the government instead of robbin a bank. We believe he was with the same gang who robbed the bank in Bogata last year. The difference between the two robberies was my former Deputy, Walter Crawley. Walter retired and went on with the bank part-time as the security. He shot the Canton boy, a forty-five Colt gut-shot. But Walter's bullet didn't kill the boy, a temple shot did. Doc Bledsoe thought it was a twenty-two. Anyway, we found the boy in a Katy maintenance shed. We think the other two robbers took a handcar from a rail barn and left it on the tracks up toward Palomino. So, I figured whoever was with him, who might of killed him, are in or near Palomino. I've sent Stephan and my new deputy, David Sunday, over there to talk with the new constable."

"Chestnutt."

"Yeah, Twig Chestnutt."

"He's an Army military policeman out of Maxey."

"Yeah, that's right, Jim."

"It was all in the papers and on the radio. Big hullabaloo about it."

"It was. He brought three German prisoners to Palomino to work in the fields and gin. They live someplace in town."

"We even got prisoners who work in Paris, but they

go back to Maxey at night. Think he can help? You think Chestnutt can help?"

"Well, we don't have a choice. He's the only lawman in Palomino."

"Well, Palomino is split between my county and yours, Billy. Pecan Creek divides the town almost equally into two parts. How do you want to handle it?"

"Since my boys from Bogata are closer why don't I take it and see it through."

"Suits me, Billy. But I'm just a phone call away if you need help. Okay?"

"Good, I'm glad we can work together on Palomino."

They fell silent and sipped the strong, hot coffee.

Sheriff Dudley pulled a pack of Camels from his shirt pocket. When Sheriff Blake declined the offer of a cigarette, Sheriff Dudley pulled one from the pack and stuck it between his lips. Replacing the pack, he slipped a matchstick from the pocket and flared it with a thumbnail. He eyed Billy through the flame before shaking the fire off the stem.

"What have you heard from the agents in Dallas about Logan?"

Billy Blake drew in a deep breath as his face saddened. He shook his head with slight movement, avoiding Jim's gaze. "We've heard nothing in the past six or seven months. The case is cold. With the war, everybody is now worried about spies and espionage. Nobody is thinking about finding Logan's kidnappers and killers."

"Well, Billy, we still make inquiries. Logan Amesa is one of us, he's not forgotten in Lamar County, I assure you."

Billy looked at Jim and nodded. "Thanks, Jim. We appreciate that. I'll tell Fay about your continued interest in finding Logan so we can bring him home."

"Okay, Billy. Now, about this Canton boy. The only information I have about family is an aunt here in Pattonville. His ma is locked up down there in the state house at Rusk. She killed her oldest boy and managed to get a pickax in the back of her old man. Didn't kill him, but he caught pneumonia in the hospital and died. Artemis was six or eight, opinions vary, when his ma was put away. One of his daddy's sisters took him in. We think she still lives across the tracks about four miles down on One-Ninety-Six. It's a tenant farm, four-room house, no running water, and an outhouse."

"Why don't we take both cars, Jim. I'll follow you. We'll meet with his aunt. I'll tell her where he is and how she can contact Fellman's to arrange a funeral."

"Maybe she can tell us who he run with."

"I was hoping the same thing, Jim."

"Let's get after it then."

The two lawmen stood. Sheriff Dudley reached into his trouser pocket and withdrew a Walking Liberty coin. "Hey, Baker, thanks for the coffee. I'm leaving a half-dollar on the table."

As they moved to the door, Jim spoke again. "Maybe we could even talk the aunt into letting us have a look around her place, conduct a search where the boy slept."

"You know, I think it would be great if we found evidence linking him to the first bank robbery. We might even discover who his accomplices were."

There was no driveway to speak of. There was only a worn path off the asphalt farm road onto the front yard.

When Sheriff Dudley knocked, a small woman, no more than four-feet tall, shuffled into view. She stood behind the screen door, her shoulders covered with a gray shawl, her hands wrapped in a raggedy dishtowel.

"I'm Sheriff Dudley.   This here is Sheriff Blake. We're looking for a lady named Maude Sims, Mam. Are you Mrs. Sims?"

"I don't have the money, Sheriff."

"Beg pardon?"

"I don't have the money."

"Are you Mrs. Sims, Mam?"

"Yes, but I don't have the money from the bank."

Jim glanced at Billy before he looked back at her and spoke. "What money are you talking about, Mrs. Sims? What money, from which bank?"

"The rent money. I know I'm two months behind. I told Mr. Ferrell I'd have the rent money when my boy got back from the bank. He said he'd get the money from the bank so I could pay Mr. Ferrell. I'm sorry, Sheriff. But he never brought the money. It's been over a week, almost two, since he went off to get it."

"You mean Artemis?"

Maude gasped. "You know my boy?"

He did not take off his hat in solemn gesture, but the Lamar County Sheriff's voice was soft and compassionate when he spoke. "Mrs. Sims, may we come in? We need to talk a bit, Mam, and have a look around, if you don't mind. You could be a big help to us, and we do have something to tell you about your boy, Artemis."

Red River County Deputy Sheriff Stephan Stanton and Deputy David Sunday drove west the seven miles from Bogata to visit Constable Twig Chestnutt in Palomino. Stephan steered the cruiser down Main Street searching for a parking slot. Up ahead a pickup was backing out, so Stephan slowed. He pulled in, in front of Jeeps Cafe.

"Let's start here, Dave. We can get a cup of coffee and ask about where we might find Constable Chestnutt."

"The last time I was in Palomino was three years ago. I was a senior in high school and we played the Palomino Prairie Dogs here for Homecoming. You know their mascot is a prairie dog. At halftime, their six cheerleaders run from an end zone to mid-field with prairie dogs on leashes. They stopped and faced their home team crowd while the school band played their school song. Somehow, they got the prairie dogs to sit up while the band played. I'd never seen a prairie dog on a leash, and I'd never seen one sit in front of a bleacher full of yelling, clapping, crazy people. It was a sight."

"Yeah, I came to that game, Dave. The Prairie Dogs whipped us good. Forty-two to six or something like that."

"Yeah, it was not our night. They made four touchdowns alone on two of George Ellis's interceptions and my two fumbles. It was a bad night for Bogata football."

When they entered, they paused to survey the surroundings and search for a suitable, safe place to sit because customers filled the cafe. They had one choice, stools at the counter.

The waitress approached, her smile illuminating.

"Welcome to Jeeps." She placed a menu in front of Dave and Stephan, set napkin-wrapped silverware alongside the menu. "My name is Teresa. Would you like coffee or iced tea?"

"Coffee for both of us," Stephan ordered.

"Be right back. Cream and sugar is on the counter. I'll give you a little time to look at our menu and come back to take your order after I pour the coffee."

"Wow," Dave whispered. "She's gorgeous. I wonder if she's married? Maybe I could ask her for a date?"

Both ordered and enjoyed the sixty cent, blue-plate special of meatloaf, black-eyed peas, and mashed potatoes with brown gravy. They sipped coffee and waited. When Teresa appeared to remove their dishes, Stephan asked about Twig.

"I'm Deputy Stanton, and this is Deputy Sunday. We work with Red River County Sheriff Billy Blake. Could you tell us, Miss, where we might find Constable Chestnutt or his office?"

For a few seconds before she spoke, Teresa measured the two sitting at the counter and sensed no danger.

"Ordinarily he might be out in one of the cotton fields. But since it rained last night and the fields are muddy, he's up at the park."

"Where's the park, Miss?"

"At the junction of Two-Seventy-One and Clark Street." Teresa pointed. "From the cafe, go that way on Main, turn left on Clark, and that will take you up to the highway. The park is on the left at the highway."

"Will the German prisoners be with him?"

Her anxiety rose with Stephan's question. Teresa felt warm blood flood her neck. "What is this about?"

Sunday's officiousness rose, he lifted his elbows off the counter and sat up. "It's about county biz . . ."

"We'd just like to meet him and tell him we're just a phone call away if he needs us, Miss," Stephan said. "That's all."

"He's my husband."

"I see. Your reaction to my question about the prisoners is understandable. I did not mean to upset you, Mrs. Chestnutt."

A rotund, short woman waddled up, wiping her hands with a towel, and stood by Teresa. "What's goin on, Teresa? These cowboys with their big heads . . . I mean hats . . . and shiny guns givin you trouble?"

"I be damn." Stephan's laugher was loud. "Sweetness, Bobbie Jo." He stood and reached out with both arms across the counter for a hug. "You're just as beautiful as ever."

Bobbie Jo hugged Stephan and patted his back. As he sat, she pointed at him and laughed. "When he was younger, this boy was a looker. Junior Class President and voted most handsome. All of us wallflowers wanted a piece of him. Then, in our senior year, June won his heart and broke all of ours. How is your Sweetheart?"

"Love of my life, Bobbie Jo. She's a momma, you know. We got twin girls, Sharon and Shelia, three years old come January."

Along with the few remaining customers, Teresa and Sunday became an audience for another few minutes as Stephan and Bobbie Jo reminisced. Then, Teresa spoke.

"Deputy Stanton and Deputy Sunday are here to meet Twig, Bobbie Jo, and tell him they're just a phone call away if he needs help." Teresa's jab did not go unnoticed.

"Really?" Bobbie Jo glared at Stephan. "That sounds like a bunch of you know what, Stephan. What's goin on? Why did you drive all the way over here just to meet our Constable and scare Teresa?"

Sunday's youthfulness smothered discretion. "We're here on confidential county police business."

Stanton looked at him and smiled. "Thank you, Dave. I think we'd better leave these ladies to their business and go take care of ours. We'll be on our way to the park." He stood, touched the brim of his Stetson, and nodded ever so slightly. "Ladies. Come on, Dave."

In the car, Stephan counseled his partner. "Practice humility, Dave. Be a nice person to nice people. Don't act like the universe exists because of your presence. Folks will warm to you. If they feel comfortable with you they'll have confidence that you know what you're doin about bein a deputy sheriff." He turned the key, started the engine, shifted to reverse, eased the clutch out, and let the car move backward out of the slot. "Otherwise, every time you open your mouth, you'll confirm their opinion that you are a real asshole."

At Clark Street, Stephan turned left and headed for the park.

Before the rain came, Twig removed the equipment from the trailer and had the prisoners mount the metal frame on the jeep and attach the canvas to it. This provided a roof and rear cover for passengers. At that moment, he decided to leave the doors and back side panels off.

The four of them sat together at one of the four picnic tables in the park. The prisoners had picked up all the trash and placed it in the nearest fifty-five-gallon barrel that served as a trashcan. They heard the car approaching and watched it turn into the park's parking lot and stop next to the jeep.

The prisoners became wary when two large men with pistols in holsters got out of the car and walked toward them.

"Cowboys, Twig. Look at the cowboy hats," Eddy said.

"They look just like John Wayne, Duke," Will whispered.

"We have visitors, Twig."

"I see em, Duke. Way they're dressed, I think they might be county sheriffs."

"That is police?" Will wondered.

"Yes." Twig slid off the bench and waited. "Stay where you are," Twig instructed. "And be quiet."

"Sergeant, ah, Constable Chestnutt, how you do? I'm Red River County Deputy Sheriff Stephan Stanton.

This is Deputy David Sunday."

In turn, Twig shook their extended hands. "Call me Twig."

Stephan nodded toward the prisoners. "I heard talk about your double duty, read about you in the newspaper, heard a lot about the program on the radio. But this is my first time to see German prisoners of war. Do they speak any American?"

"Yes, Stephan, would you and Dave like to meet them?"

After introductions and brief explanations by the prisoners of the work they did for Palomino, Stephan spoke of their business. "Twig, David and I need to speak with you privately about an investigation we're working on." He looked at the prisoners then pointed at the farthest table. "Could we move over there, to that table?"

"Sure." Before moving to the table, Twig nodded at the prisoners. "Stay where you are."

"We found a boy shot dead in a railroad maintenance shed near Bogata. He was one of three people who robbed one of our banks a few days before Thanksgiving."

Twig nodded, interested. "I guess our paper, the *Palomino Press*, will print the story this week. The paper is only distributed on Thursdays."

"Well, the man who found the boy in the shed also reported a handcar out of the rail barn was left on the tracks close to Palomino."

"That means maybe the other two are in Palomino," Deputy Sunday concluded.

Twig looked into Sunday's eyes and did not blink.

"You don't say, Deputy?"

Stephan intervened in the developing friction with a soft voice. "Well, we think that's a possibility. You see, we believe the getaway car ran out of gas. Somebody, maybe the two somebody's, carried the boy to the shed."

"So, he wasn't dead, wasn't killed during the robbery?"

"No. A former sheriff's deputy was security at the bank and shot the boy with his service revolver, a Colt forty-five. It was a gut-shot, but Doc Bledsoe — Doc acts as our medical examiner — said the large caliber bullet was not the kill shot."

"So, somebody carried him to the shed and killed him there?"

"A somebody put a small caliber, maybe a twenty-two, flush against the boy's head and popped him."

"That was the kill-shot," Sunday added.

"Then, we believe, they used the handcar to leave Bogata," Stephan continued. "I can't imagine two people pumping a handcar *through* Bogata to escape south to Mount Pleasant."

"Yes, I see," Twig said. "So, they came this way."

"Yes, and that's why we came over here because we want you to help," Sunday said.

Twig nodded.

"The boy's name is Artemis Canton. He was a petty criminal, stealing from stores, shoplifting, breaking and entering mostly, but he also was a good car thief. My sheriff, Billy Blake, is in Pattonville with Lamar County Sheriff Jim Dudley to try to find next of kin. Artemis is at Zellman's funeral home in Bogata."

"How can I help?"

"Well, I guess the first thing is the eyes and ears. If talk begins to float around town about Artemis, and I suspect it will when your newspaper prints the story on Thursday, who he might of run with would be important." Stephan withdrew a business card from his shirt pocket. "Our phone number is on this card. Ask for me or the Sheriff."

"You can ask for me, too," Deputy Sunday inserted. "I'm part of this investigation."

Stephan sighed. "We need your help. We have a strong suspicion that at least one, maybe both, of the remaining robbers live in or near Palomino."

Twig took the card and stuffed it in his shirt pocket. As he did, movement on Clark Street, beyond the jeep and sheriff's car, attracted his attention. He canted his head for a better look.

Stephan and Dave turned their heads, too.

Pinky had stopped the bicycle and was standing with both feet on the street. Patsy's head and shoulders were visible.

"It's two of our kids," Twig said. "Rayfield Pinkston, Pinky, and Patricia Ann Paramore, Patsy. They're good kids, always together."

"What do you think they want?" Dave asked. "Why'd they stop in the street and just stare?"

"I dunno," Twig drawled, "but I think your car, guns, and Stetsons gave them some pause."

Deputy Stanton turned and waved a signal for them to approach.

Instead of the youngsters approaching on the bicycle, they watched Pinky mount, pedal a bit, and turn back toward town.

Twig waved when he saw Patsy turn her head and look at the police and prisoners gathered in park. "Something scared them off from coming up to us. I'll talk to them later."

Stephan stuck out his hand and Twig shook it.

"Thank you, Constable Chestnutt, for helping us. We'll be on our way back to Bogata. I know the Sheriff will want to fill Dave and me in about any next of kin for Artemis."

Dave stuck his hand out and Twig shook it. "Thank you, Constable Chestnutt. I look forward to working with you."

The two deputies took several steps toward their car before Stephan stopped and turned. Dave stopped and turned too. Stephan signaled with his fingers and Twig approached.

"About a year and a half ago one of our deputies was kidnapped by two boys in a green Dodge. The Dodge was found in Mount Pleasant, but we never found Logan, Logan Amesa. It's pretty clear the kidnappers killed him and dumped his body."

Twig nodded as he listened.

"There's something I'd like you to consider."

"Okay, I'm listening, Stephan."

"If we get a lead on where to look for Logan, would you consider you and your prisoners joining our search party? Eight more good eyes and four more noses could be a big help."

Twig nodded. "Yes, absolutely. You can count on the four of us, Stephan."

THE CONFRONTATION
September 1943
Eisenhower announces surrender of Italy
Australians capture Lae, New Guinea

The Mayor's office was small, and with five members of the town council, three German prisoners of war, Teresa, Tina, and Twig, it was crowded.

Saturday morning, a week before Tina started first grade, the swearing-in and orientation had been ceremonial, the pinning of the official badge brief.

Mayor Shipp held a key up. "This is to *The Calaboose*."

Twig took the key. "I've seen the Palomino jailhouse. Not much to it."

"It's a ten-by-ten wooden building with no facilities. If someone is in *The Calaboose*, somebody has to be near. It's a council requirement."

Casey and the representatives, as well as the prisoners, congratulated Twig and shook his hand. Teresa and Tina hugged and kissed his cheek.

"Congratulations, Constable Chestnutt," Teresa said. Her smile transmitted tremendous pride in her husband.

Twig grinned. "Thank you, Mrs. Chestnutt. I will do my best to serve and protect our community."

"That sure is a shiny badge, Daddy," Tina said.

"Well, we better let you take care of town business," Teresa said. "Tina and I have some shopping to do at the grocery store, and then we'll go home." She kissed Twig again, smiled and nodded her goodbyes. Hand-in-hand Teresa and Tina left the Mayor's office.

The representatives said their good-lucks and goodbyes and departed.

"Why don't we have a cup of Henry's coffee and a slice of lemon pie," Casey said.

Twig looked at his charges. "Let's go to Henry Wilson's domino hall for coffee and pie to celebrate this occasion."

Before they turned to walk the few doors down to Henry's place, a commotion up the sidewalk attracted attention.

A man held Nate Dulfeine in a chokehold.

Twig instinctively reacted, and quick-stepped toward the fracas. Casey, Duke, Eddy, and Will trotted behind.

Twig ordered the release of the grip. "Free Mr. Dulfeine, Sir."

"Get Lost," the man said. "This is private business."

"Release your grip," Twig demanded, "or I'll take you down." His voice was stern.

"I said get lost," the man repeated.

Twig stepped behind, wrapped his arm around the man's throat and squeezed. The man gagged, released his hold on Nate, and shuffled back as Twig applied more pressure.

Duke and Eddy stepped forward raising their hands

toward the man to assist Twig.

"Step back, Duke, Eddy. Both of you step back," Twig said. He brought the man down to the sidewalk and knelt at his head. He released his chokehold and stood.

The man rolled over and propped himself up onto his knees, holding his throat. He looked up at Twig.

Twig placed his hand under the man's armpit and lifted.

It was then that Twig saw Teresa and Tina standing in the grocery doorway. They had witnessed the attack and rescue. Twig motioned with his head at Teresa, fear clouding her face, to take Tina back inside. Little Tina's eyes were large and round with fright.

The man wobbled to his feet and faced Twig. He was a head taller than the Palomino Constable and weighed fifty pounds more.

The few on-lookers applauded.

"I'll kill you for this," the man growled, "and your bunch of goose-steppin Krauts." He pushed his way past all of them — Dulfeine, the prisoners, bystanders, and on-lookers.

"Are you alright, Mr. Dulfeine? That chokehold he had on your throat was hard for me to break loose."

"Yes, Twig. Thank you for coming to my rescue."

"What started this mess?"

"He started cussing me out in the store. He accused me of adding a heavy thumb on the scale for a pound of ground meat. I told him to leave the meat and to leave my store. I followed him out while he was cussing the whole time. When we got on the sidewalk he grabbed me."

"That man had the wildest look in his eyes. Pure evil."

"That man is Eliot Thurgood, Twig. He's crazy mean."

"Ruby mentioned the name when I was going through orientation with the town council. The way council members talked, I imagined him to be a king-sized man. He must be six-five or six. He's broad-shouldered and strong."

"You should take his threat seriously, Twig. He is a mean-ass son-of-a-bitch."

"Oh, I don't think he'll try to kill me. He was just embarrassed I intervened. He's going to have some bruises tomorrow. I was pretty rough with him. He's going to have to pay a fine for disturbing the peace.

"If you'll make an official complaint for assault, I'll ask one of the Lamar county judges to come over to conduct court. I could confine him for a few days until the judge can come."

"I can't. I'm afraid to, Twig. There's something you need to know about Thurgood."

"Major Monroe told a little about him. He works at the Major's gin as a roustabout."

"He's more than that, Twig. You remember the pictures and names in Henry's domino hall? Thurgood's granddaddy was one of the original cowboys who settled in Palomino. Horace Thurgood found a woman in Paris and brought her back here to raise a family."

"I remember that Horace was Thurgood's grandpa."

"Yes, that's right. Horace's son, Kermit, built the cotton gin. When Eliot was eight, he fell from a ladder in the gin. He was in a coma for six weeks. He had a hairline fracture of his skull. He suffered severe head trauma. Doc Burns did all he could, but Eliot was never normal after he woke up. When he was ten, Eliot set his puppy on fire and beat it to death with a baseball bat."

"Yeah, I saw something in his face, in his eyes, that took me aback. It was a wild, evil look."

"Well, it is. He is evil. When Eliot was 15, Kermit was beating the boy with a whip in the gin. For some infraction — we never knew exactly what happened or why Kermit beat Eliot."

"Whip? You mean with a real whip? A leather horsewhip?"

"Yes. Eliot swore he was going to kill Kermit for the beating. All the workers in the gin saw it and heard Eliot say it."

"He was going to kill his uncle?"

"Yeah. And a week later Kermit was dead. One of his workers found him on the gin floor. He'd been shot through his mouth. With a .22 rifle. And Kermit kept the .22 at the gin to kill rats, squirrels, and possums. Eliot still keeps that gun at the gin."

"Eliot shot his uncle?"

"Well, it couldn't be proved. We didn't have no law here, then. Sheriffs didn't have enough deputies to cover the county, so we was on our own. Nobody ever came to investigate. Doc Burns listed the death as suspicious only because Kermit could've put the rifle in his mouth and shot himself. The gun was on the ground beside Kermit's body."

"But folks didn't buy that? Didn't think it was suicide?"

"No. We all thought Eliot killed Kermit. Then, maybe because he believed he got away with murder, Eliot turned into the town bully. Everybody began watching their P's and Q's when Eliot was around. We still do. It's gut-churning fear. We're all cowed. Jimmy Madison was afraid of Eliot and steered clear of him.

"We thought you could be our savior from Thurgood."

"Well, this little run-in with him puts me on notice for sure, Mr. Dulfeine."

"It does, Twig. And that's why you have to take Thurgood's threat to kill you as most serious. And you have to know, too, that your family is now in danger."

Twig looked at Duke, Eddy, and Will. He sought solace.

Duke grinned. "Constable Chestnutt, me and my boys will protect you and Miss Teresa and Miss Tina from this mean man in Palomino. Do not worry, Twig."

The Monday following Labor Day, Tina's first day in second grade at the Palomino Elementary School did not start out well. She found herself bullied and pestered and called names she didn't understand.

Her daddy was the town Constable who brought three prisoners to Palomino. All the kids in town heard from their parents over the weeks before school started how threatening and evil these Germans might or could be.

As she walked alone from school the quarter mile along Powell Street to Clark Street and the Porter House, Tina cried all the way. She kept her head down in shame dreading facing her mother because of what the kids in her class said. Even at recess, they continued until she ran to the restroom. Miss Barber and Principal Skaggs found her hiding there and escorted her to the classroom.

She didn't go into the house where she knew Ethel waited for her with two chocolate chip cookies and a glass of Borden's chocolate milk. Instead, she sat on the top step of the front porch and held her head in her hands. She felt unclean, unwanted, dispirited.

"Goodness gracious, chil. I've waited for you in the kitchen. I been worried to death. Where you been? Come inside for your cookies and glass of cold milk."

Tina shook her head. She did not look up.

Ethel pushed open the screen door. "What's wrong? You sick?"

Tina shook her head again. She laid her arms across her knees and placed her forehead on her arms.

Ethel stood behind her. "Why is your head down, little girl? What's wrong?"

Tina did not speak nor look up.

Ethel sat beside Tina and wrapped her arm around Tina's shoulders. "Tell *me*," Ethel whispered.

Tears streamed down Tina's red cheeks as she looked at Ethel. "Everybody was mean to me on my first day at school. Everybody says I live with germs. They say I love germs." Her bottom lip quivered. "I don't know what germs look like. I couldn't find any germs on my clothes or hands."

Ethel smiled and pulled Tina close. "You ain't got no germs, Miss Tina, believe me. Lordamercy."

"They say I live with germs, I'm a germ lover,

206

everybody says it. I can't go back to school. I might give kids my germs."

"Tell me the words they said."

"*Tina lives with germs. Tina is a germ lover. Tina lives with germs. Tina is a germ lover. Tina lives with germs.* They wouldn't stop."

Ethel nodded and with both thumbs wiped despair from the child's face. "You know what?"

"No, what?"

"I bet they said you live with *Germans*. You think? I bet the kids said *German lover* instead of *germ* lover. I hear that same meanness, chil, but there is one word that is different. When my Luther was jumped on at his school, I told him to sock that bully in the nose and that would end it. But *you* are a lady, so you listen to me. If there's another naggin at school by one of them bullies you tell em to stop it, walk away, then you get your friends to be with you, Master Rayfield and Miss Patricia Ann. The three of you will scare away them bullies, they'll leave you alone."

"Like the three mustard-tears?"

"Exactly. Okay?"

"Okay." Tina grinned. "Did it work?"

"Did what work?"

"Your Luther, did he sock em and they stopped?"

"Well, it did. But you are a lady so you don't go around sockin noses, you hear?"

"Are you a germ lover, Miss Ethel?"

Ethel let out a mighty laugh and hugged Tina tightly.

"I am a Miss Tina lover, chil. Now come in the house, let me clean your dirty face fore you momma

207

gets home, and we'll have cookies and milk."

There, sitting on the top step, Tina hugged Ethel as tight as possible. She looked at Ethel's beaming face, at Ethel's warm, motherly smile and bright black eyes and felt soothed before burying her face in Ethel's bosom. "I love you, Miss Ethel."

"I know you do, truly. I love you too, Miss Tina, like you was my own."

Martin Church brought his tractor and trailer to Major Monroe's cotton field each morning. In late afternoon, the final pickers brought their bags to Martin for weighing.

Martin deftly looped the strap around the end of the bag to form a sling. Then he and the picker hefted the bag, and Martin placed the sling/strap onto the scale hook. Dallas Church, Martin's youngest daughter, recorded the weight on the picker's sheet in her notebook.

Martin and the picker unhooked the bag and tossed it over the trailer's high railing to Preacher Adams.

Preacher was, indeed, a properly recognized ordained minister by legitimate officials of the northeast Texas Baptist convention. He performed weddings, baptisms, and funerals in and around Palomino and often the Palomino Baptist church elders invited Preacher to conduct a Sunday sermon. Preacher was a huge black man who had worked in Major Monroe's fields for decades. Many believed Preacher was near seventy, but he was never able to confirm his age because he did not know when or where he was born.

Preacher shook each bag violently, so all the cotton spilled into the trailer. At day's end, Martin drove his tractor and trailer at six-miles-an-hour down Main Street to the gin.

Preacher stood proudly atop the heap of white, enjoying the slow parade through town. When folks standing on the sidewalks on both sides of Main Street waved and shouted, "Hello, Preacher", he bowed and nodded and waved like a conquering hero.

At the gin, a pipe vacuumed everything — bolls, seed, leaves, stems, and anything else out of the trailer. Gin operators processed these particles through an ancient process of combing until only the cotton fiber remained. Separated seeds were stored for new plantings.

Once Preacher cleared the trailer, Martin pulled it aside and left it at the gin until next morning. During harvest, tractors and trailers left unattended in fields faced the same fate as stolen cattle — rustlers would drive them away from this part of cotton country.

Odessa Church, Martin's oldest daughter, earned a little spending money by serving as water bearer for hands in Major Monroe's cotton field. She was twenty and a second-year student at Paris Junior College.

Odessa had been a member of the famed bevy of beautiful, full-bodied, young women called Rangerettes but was serving a suspension for what stoic school administrators called inappropriate Christian behavior. Odessa's chastisement was for what normal hot-blooded teenage boys and girls did in the back seats of Packard's and Hudson Super Sixes. Because the Rangerette staff matrons probably behaved in similar fashion when young, they did not dismiss Odessa.

When Odessa saw Duke the first day in the field, with his shirt off, she was smitten. It didn't take long, though, for Major Monroe, Martin, Preacher, and Twig to warn Duke that if he wore no covering his skin would burn. Duke heeded their advice and slipped his blue denim shirt back on.

When Duke saw Odessa, he could not take his eyes off her inviting beauty and body. She matched images he remembered of blonde, blue-eyed girls in *Glamour of Hollywood*, the magazine his mother bought when they lived in Illinois and the young girls in Hitler's *Bund Deutscher Madel* or *BDM*.

Odessa's revealing, worn, thin, cotton dress that buttoned down the front excited his imagination and fantasy when she stood straddled-legged between him and the morning sun. After all, he had not been with a woman for over a year. The sight of her intensified his sexual appetite and made his desire for her strong.

He noted, focused on, the two top buttons Odessa strategically and tactically left unbuttoned so admirers could enjoy her unmistakable, pleasurable, fullness.

He smiled at her as he took the empty sack from Martin. She smiled too and slightly canted her head. He looked back and was pleased to see she was watching him walk the quarter-mile to the end of the row, just short of the distant woods' tree line.

Duke, Eddy, and Will stayed abreast, walking in their own rows for three full lengths, picking cotton. They were halfway down their fourth row when they saw Odessa approaching with a pail of water and dipper.

They stopped, straightened, and moaned. Will and Eddy looked at each other and grinned.

"*Mein Gott.   Mein rucken schmerzt,*" Eddy complained.

"Mine, too," Will said. "My back *and* my fingers hurt."

Duke laughed and groaned. "I laugh because we are spoiled soldiers. Look at the other people in this field. They work two times faster than we do and pick more cotton without crying and without stopping. They do this hard work because it is their way of life. They earn money picking cotton every day. They may not like it, but they do it. The children do it because it is an adventure. It is fun for them. We are *heulsuse*, crybabies."

Each of them pulled on their canvass shoulder strap and hefted their full, seven-foot, cotton sack to relieve the strain and pressure on their back.

"When I wore warm, comfortable shirts and underwear, I never thought about cotton," Weiss said. "Look at me, picking the wonderful fluff somewhere in the middle of America."

"In Texas," Eddy added. "When I watched cowboy westerns at the cinema, I never thought I will be in Texas."

Will plucked fingers' full of cotton from a boll and held it out to Eddy. "Maybe I will wear a shirt made from this stem when the war is over."

He shoved the clumps into his bag.

"She is coming up your row with water, Duke. I

211

think she is a pretty girl. She looks like a German model with blonde hair and blue eyes," Will said.

"She has the full shape, too," Eddy said. "I could not take my eyes off of her. All I could think of was what it would be like to be with her."

"I think she likes me," Duke said. "She smiled at me this morning before we started."

They looked beyond Odessa at their guard.

Twig stood forty yards away, at the beginning of their rows. The butt of the Carbine propped on his left hip.

"Is Twig watching her coming in our row?" Will asked.

"No, I do not think so. It looks like he is reading something," Duke said.

"I need a big drink of water," Eddy said. "My tongue is thick and dry."

Duke watched Odessa, his eyes unwavering as she stopped at arm's length from him.

"Here is water," she said. "My name is Odessa Church."

"Water, please," Eddy said.

Odessa lifted the heavy water container up over the three-foot, fully blossomed cotton stalks. Eddy took it, set the bucket on the ground, and lifted a dipper full of cool water to his lips.

"My name is Kraus, but I go by Duke. The thirsty one is Eddy, and Will is in the other row. Your pretty name goes well with the pretty girl, Odessa." Duke gripped the shoulder strap with his right hand chest high. His left hand gripped the top of the sack.

Odessa stepped closer and reached out with her

fingers to touch Duke's right hand.

Duke felt the sensation sweep through his body, the soft touch of a beautiful girl's fingers sent chills along his spine. He did not move. His eyes remained fixed on her smile. She did not blink.

"I've never touched a German. I've never *seen* a German. I think you're cute, Duke."

When Odessa raised her hand to Duke's, Eddy stared, the dipper inches from his open mouth. Two rows over, Will closed his gaping mouth and stopped breathing.

Eddy and Will watched Duke raise his left hand and extend the fingers to stroke Odessa's right cheek. Both made quick glances to see if Twig was looking their way.

"I have never touched an American girl as beautiful as you are, Odessa," Duke said. "Your skin is so soft and smooth."

Odessa's touch was more satisfying to Duke than his thirst for water.

She wanted more time with Duke. "Your touch is stimulating."

"Water, Will?" Eddy asked in the silence and a bit too loudly.

The spell broken, Duke and Odessa dropped their hands, and Odessa took two steps back.

Will took the dipper from Eddy and gulped the refreshing liquid.

"Water, Duke?" Will asked. He handed the dipper to Eddy who filled it and passed it over the row to Duke.

As he drank, Duke met Odessa's gaze.

"You sound like an American when you talk,"

Odessa said.

"I lived and went to high school in Illinois before the war," Duke said. "After the war, I want to live in America."

Twig's voice reached them as he approached behind Odessa. "Is everything okay here, Odessa?"

She turned to look over her shoulder. "Everything is fine, we were just getting to know each other, Constable Chestnutt. I learned Will, Eddy, and Duke's names but I would like to know more. Would it be alright if I came by the Porter House some evening to visit?"

Twig was surprised, unsure how to respond. General Pace, Colonel Sanchez, Mayor Shipp, nor Major Monroe ever gave guidance on social requests. "Yes," Twig heard himself say, "I guess it'd be alright some evening."

Odessa looked back at Duke. "Okay. I better take water to other hands."

With that, Eddy handed the pail over. Odessa took the dipper from Duke and cut through the rows walking to nearby cotton pickers.

The four of them watched Odessa move away.

"Like me and my Ginnie, Twig," Eddy said, "Duke has a girl friend."

THE FRIENDSHIP
September 1943
Mussolini rescued by German SS troops
Incarcerated Japanese-Americans removed from
Tule Lake Center

Twig decided the oath of office ceremony and confrontation with Eliot Thurgood was enough excitement for a Saturday morning. He reached out for Teresa's hand.

"Come, let's all go over to Jeeps for hamburgers and ice cream."

Teresa took his hand. The relief brought a smile to her face. "I think a hamburger and a chocolate sundae are what we need." With her other hand, she reached out for Tina's hand. "Would you like that, Sweetie?"

Duke smiled and nodded at Tina. "Miss Tina, your daddy is a hero just like in the cinema."

Holding her mother's hand, Tina looked up at Duke. "What's a sinaman?"

Teresa laughed. The tension flowed from her body. "Cinema, Sweetie. Duke said cinema. It means *pitchursho*."

Duke grinned. "Yes, *pit-chur-sho*." He raised eyebrows for reassurance of correct pronunciation.

Teresa grinned and nodded. "Yes, that's good. You say it almost like a Texan."

Duke rubbed his hands together. He was pleased.

"It has been a long time since I ate a cafe hamburger," Eddy said. "I sure would like to try one at the Jeeps."

Twig acknowledged Saturday shoppers as he led his family and contingent a dozen steps up the sidewalk. In the street, measuring the slow approach of traffic, they weaved and trotted between vehicles.

Bobbie Jo spied them as they entered. "Wait a minute, Teresa, let me pull two tables together."

Eddy and Will stepped forward and lifted the table Bobbie Jo grasped.

"Here, move it here. Put these two together," she instructed.

They did.

After the table was in place, Twig and Duke rearranged the chairs.

But like most supervisors, Bobbie Jo touched and twisted and scooted the tables and the chairs so they were neatly aligned and balanced, and reset the salt and pepper shakers and napkin holders.

"Good," Bobbie Jo said, satisfied. "Now, all yall have a seat and relax. Dallas will bring water and menus in hot minute, okay?"

At the mention of her name, Will searched the cafe for Dallas. He had become taken with Odessa's younger sister when they were in the field, had watched and admired her at arm's length. He had even found courage to mumble brief fragments to her a couple of times as she wrote the weight of his cotton in her book. He had enjoyed her smile at his weak joke.

After that, each time he brought his cotton sack for weighing, he thought about speaking up and telling Dallas she was more gorgeous than Odessa. The nearness of Martin, her daddy, influenced the massive degree of caution and restraint Will felt he needed to be safe.

Dallas Church was eighteen, a high school senior who would graduate in June 1944. Like her sister Odessa, Dallas was a blonde, blue-eyed, full-figured beauty. She noted Will's nervous infatuation — she was as drawn to him as he was to her. While waiting for the weighing and the dumping of cotton from his sack into the trailer, he stood close enough so she could hear his incoherent whispers. She acknowledged his sweet nothings with a smile. When Will took his empty sack from Preacher and turned away, she followed him with her eyes as he returned to the field and strolled up a new row. She thought he was cute and enjoyed his attention. She was attracted to eighteen-year-old Will, and there in Major Monroe's cotton field began thinking about how to arrange some private, cuddly time with the handsome, German prisoner of war.

She kept her gaze on Will as she approached with a tray of six glasses of water, six red, vinyl-covered menus, and six sets of napkin-wrapped silverware.

"Hello, Mrs. Chestnutt, Miss Tina, Constable." Dallas nodded individually at Duke and Eddy before speaking to her secret admirer. "Hello, Will."

Following the revelation that Dallas knew and called Will's name in public, Tina broke the four seconds of silence.

"Hi, Miss Dallas. I choose a cheeseburger with mayonnaise, please. No onions. And a Grapette with a straw."

Dallas laughed. "No onions, Sweetie? You got a new boyfriend you plan on giving kisses to?"

Tina laughed with the others, but she lowered her eyes as shyness filled her cheeks with redness.

"My boyfriend is Pinky. I'm his junior girlfriend. Patsy is his senior girlfriend. We haven't kissed yet." She looked up and grinned. "Onions make me belch."

This time everyone respected Tina's honesty and kept quiet.

Dallas went around the tables and wrote down the choices. Twig and Teresa ordered cheeseburgers, potato chips, and Dr. Peppers. Duke and Eddy wanted a hamburger, French fries, and a Coke. Everyone's mind was made up, the process moved quickly.

Will could not take his eyes off Dallas. He followed every move she made from customer to customer. At last, she stood next to him with pad and yellow pencil poised.

"What would you like, Will?"

Again, the table grew quiet. The adults looked at Dallas, at Will, and back at Dallas. They waited with anticipation. They were surprised and pleased Dallas spoke Will's name, but more than that, they detected in her voice the unmistakable tone in which she said it — alluring. It was obvious to the four of them that Dallas had a beau.

Will smiled up at Dallas as she peered down, pad ready. Will wanted to rise from the chair, take Dallas in his arms, and smother her with passionate kisses. His thoughts were *I would like for you to be my wife*, but the words out of his mouth were "I choose like Miss Tina, Dallas. But a Coca-Cola instead of Grape. And no onions."

"Okay, I've got everyone's order, I'll be back with your drinks in a couple of minutes. By the way, the music machine is working now in case you'd like to drop a nickel or dime in."

"Oh, I'm glad Bobbie Jo got it fixed," Teresa said. "A lot of people complained during the week about not having music with their dinner."

"Pearson fixed it before yall came in. Took him ten minutes," Dallas said. "All that was wrong was a loose wire in the plug. He took it apart with his pocketknife, fixed the wire, and wrapped tape around it. Bobbie Jo said he could have a free sandwich, drink, and dessert. Be right back."

Teresa opened her purse and withdrew a quarter. "Come with me, Tina, let's play some music."

Teresa dropped the coin in. They talked about the tunes they liked before deciding. Finally, Tina pressed the lighted buttons for their choices: *I've Got Spurs That Jingle, Jangle, Jingle; That Old Black Magic; Deep In The Heart of Texas; I've Got a Gal in Kalamazoo*; and *Chattanooga Choo Choo*.

The other patrons did not mind that Tina and Teresa sang along with each song. The music and mood were contagious.

They waited for the jukebox to load the third record.

219

When the needle hit the groove, they sang,
> *The stars at night*
> *are big and bright,*

and Tina and Teresa tapped the tabletop four times before loudly covering Gene Autry with . . .
> *DEEP IN THE HEART OF TEXAS.*

Then,
> *The prairie sky,*
> *is wide and high,*

BANG-BANG-BANG-BANG,
> *DEEP IN THE HEART OF TEXAS.*

Teresa's nod at Duke, Eddy, and Will commanded them to join in. While the trio did not know the verses, they easily picked up the table banging and chorus.
> *The sage in bloom,*
> *is like perfume,*

BANG-BANG-BANG-BANG,
> *DEEP IN THE HEART OF TEXAS.*

Twig joined in.
> *Reminds me of,*
> *the one I love,*

BANG-BANG-BANG-BANG,
> *DEEP IN THE HEART OF TEXAS.*

They heard Bobbie Jo and Dallas.
> *The coyotes wail,*
> *along the trail,*

BANG-BANG-BANG-BANG,
> *DEEP IN THE HEART OF TEXAS.*

Suddenly, caught up in the camaraderie, all the diners added their voices.
> *The rabbits rush,*
> *around the brush,*

BANG-BANG-BANG-BANG,
   DEEP IN THE HEART OF TEXAS.
A siren wailed, muted by the music and singers.
   The cowboys cry,
   Ki-yip-pee-yi,
BANG-BANG-BANG-BANG,
   DEEP IN THE HEART OF TEXAS.
The siren wound up and grew louder, shriller.

Teresa and Tina continued singing, unaware of the fire call.

Twig and the patrons stood, listening.

Eddy's smile faded, and he closed his mouth when Twig rose.

Dallas was halfway to the tables with both hands and arms full of plates with burgers when Eddy shoved his chair back and stood.

Unaware, Duke followed, then Will.

Gene and Tina were oblivious to the calamity. Teresa's eyes were pinned on her husband, her mouth open in apprehension.

   The doggies bawl,
   and bawl and bawl,
Only Tina slammed her palms on the table.
Plop-Plop-Plop-Plop,
   Deep in the heart of Texas.
"Fire call," Bobbie Jo shouted.

"There's a fire," Twig shouted. "Let's go help."

Twig, prisoners, and patrons quick-stepped through the door.

Only then did Tina realize there was serious interruption to the fun.

Out on the sidewalk, they saw the smoke and flickers of orange and red up the street at the Ice House. In an instant, Twig decided it was nearer to run to the Ice House rather than go the other way to the jeep and drive the block up. He led the way to the fight on foot.

The volunteer firefighters dutifully took up their tasks. Three men unloaded the hose off the truck, and two women dragged the end of it to the hydrant. A young woman with a huge wrench unscrewed the bolt on the water cap. The two women with the hose connected it to the hydrant as a third woman with a different wrench twisted the nut on top of the hydrant to open the valve. The men hefted the hose, aimed the spray of water at the flames, and inched forward.

"They're inside," someone shouted.

"Who's inside?"

"Martin Church and Preacher Adams. They're inside."

"Anybody else?"

"No, Stanley got out. He's here. He sounded the alarm."

Twig saw slight movement on the floor through the doorway, beyond the flames and roiling smoke. "I see em. They're down on the floor. Can they get out back?"

"No," Stanley shouted. "Backdoor is locked, and I've got the key."

"Step aside, Constable," a burly man said. "This is for trained folks to handle."

Twig stood erect and pinned the volunteer with a glare. "Training is not going to save them, going in and bringing them out will."

"Yes, Twig?" Will answered, thinking Twig called his name.

Twig gave directions to the volunteer. "As I move forward keep water on me, even as I go through the door and get on the floor. If you keep me wet, I can get to them and bring them out."

With that, Twig scrambled toward the door.

Duke, Eddy, and Will followed on his heels.

As instructed, the volunteer kept the spray of water on them.

Through the doorway, Twig lay down and started his military low crawl toward the figures he could see through smoke.

The trio was on his heels, assumed the same low crawl position, and followed him in.

There were no flames near when they reached them, so they were able to stand and lift Martin and Preacher to their feet. Twig and Will propped Martin across Duke's shoulders and Preacher across Eddy's shoulders.

The water stream was now in their face, so they lowered their heads and dashed into the spray.

They stumbled from the building, overwhelmed by smoke inhalation. Duke burdened by Martin's weight and Eddy by Preacher's enormous bulk sank to their knees and fell faced down in the soaked grass. Martin lay across Duke's back, both gasping for oxygen. When Eddy fell, Preacher rolled over and off and laid face up.

The siren had drawn Odessa from Wilburt's to the sidewalk. She jumped into her daddy's pickup parked in front of the store. She arrived as Duke fell to the ground with Martin on top of him. She left the truck's door open as she ran to her father.

Teresa, Tina, Bobbie Jo, and Dallas had followed the men out the door of Jeeps cafe and watched the activity from the sidewalk.

When Teresa saw Twig rush into the building, she screamed. "NO."

She stepped into the street, turned to her daughter and smiled. "Tina, Sweetie, stay here with Miss Bobbie Jo." Then she turned and ran for Twig.

When Dallas saw Duke stumble from the building with Martin across his back and Will alongside holding her father's shoulders, she screamed, "DADDY," and jumped off the sidewalk. She ran up the street, fearful her daddy was dead.

Will could not get a breath, his eyes burned, and then suddenly someone was picking him up. He felt cool water pour over him.

The fireman with the hose doused all of them, the refreshing water chilling their skin, clearing the way for fresh air to fill their lungs.

Volunteers hurried forward, still under the water spray, and brought the rescued and rescuers to safety, farther away from the dying fire.

When Martin gained his footing and senses, he nodded at Duke and Will. "Thank you, boys. You saved my life."

Odessa held Duke's face in her hands and kissed his cheeks before kissing him full on his lips.

Dallas helped Will to his feet, hugged and held him close before kissing him on his lips, longer than necessary for just a thank-you.

One person began clapping, then two, then twelve, until it sounded like all of the citizens and visitors in Lamar County and Red River County were applauding. Yelps and whistles voiced approval to the saviors.

Odessa and Dallas held their father as they guided him to the truck.

Teresa stepped forward and hugged Will, Eddy, Duke, and Twig in turn. "You are my crazy heroes. Thank God, you're safe."

Preacher Adams stood alone.

"Preacher, you're soaked. Walk with us down the street to the jeep, and I'll drive you home."

"Okay, Mr. Twig, thank you, Sir."

At the jeep, Twig asked Duke to cram in the back with Will and Eddy. "You sit up front with me, Preacher. That way, you can give me directions."

From Main Street, Twig drove to 271 and turned right, toward Paris. A little more than half a mile, he turned left off 271 onto FM 1503. Preacher told him to stop at the creek.

He pointed. "My place is up the creek there a bit, Mr. Twig. I can walk to it from here."

Twig dismounted and walked around the front of the jeep. Duke, Will, and Eddy dismounted too. Twig looked up the creek. Among the trees along the bank, he saw a faded, white-brown, plank shanty. From its appearance and location, he knew there was no electricity or running water in Preacher Adams' home.

Preacher stuck his hand out to Eddy and lowered his head. "Thank you, Mr. Eddy, you saved my life. I have a debt I can never pay."

Eddy gripped the calloused fingers and palm, but

said nothing as he shook Preacher's hand. Then he released Preacher's hand and wrapped his arms around the large black man in a warm embrace.

Surprised, Preacher raised his hands and hesitated before hugging Eddy and patting his back.

The two stood together for four seconds before separating.

Preacher stepped back and turned to extend his hand to Will, Duke, and, lastly, to Twig. "Thank you all. I am blessed by the Lord our Savior you were present today to save Mr. Church and me."

"You are a good man, Preacher Adams." Twig palmed a ten-dollar note into Preacher's hand when he grasped it in a handshake. "You will need a new shirt and overalls. I will speak to Mr. Wilburt on Monday. When the store is open, the clothes and boots you choose will all be paid for."

They stood for a minute watching Preacher walk to his home.

"Okay, mount up. Let's go to the house. We've had too much fun for one day."

"I think we made new friends today," Eddy said. "Did you see the pretty girls kissing your prisoners, Constable Twig?"

"I did. And a lot of other people of Palomino saw it too." He started the engine and shifted to first gear. "The three of you must stay vigilant and be very careful, you hear?"

Days later, on her return to school, Tina made Miss Ethel's proposal to Pinky and Patsy. Without hesitation, they agreed to join forces with her as protectors.

Within minutes of that discussion, Tina witnessed first-hand how the strategy and tactics of handling bullies could fail and succeed.

Waldo approached, grabbed Pinky's shirt in a menacing grip, and pinned him to the down plank of a playground seesaw.

"I told you I'd break your neck if you didn't pay me a quarter every week. Now, you told on me again to Miss Maybelle."

To the rescue, Tina spoke first. "You're a bully. You leave him alone."

"Get lost, Shrimp, or you'll be next."

Since reasoning, the first course of action, didn't work, Tina kicked at Waldo's shin but missed. She gathered her feet to kick again but lost balance.

Waldo shoved Tina away with his free hand. "I said get lost, Shrimp, or you'll be next on my pain plan."

Tina stumbled back but then made a fist ready for attack although she knew she wasn't tall enough to reach his nose. Before she could strike, a hand came from nowhere and snatched Waldo's collar, jerking him away from Pinky.

Waldo released Pinky's shirt and turned to face his aggressor.

It was a balled-up, female fist that she planted square on his nose. It was not, nor intended to be, a glancing blow. It was not a slap, nor a push. Nope, she brought her arm back and with a catapult-forced, straight-shot, horizontal trajectory, and level as an arrow, jabbed and busted Waldo's nose.

Waldo screamed and clasped the injured organ. As

227

tears welled, he shook his head and dropped to his knees.

His fingers muffled cries of pain and embarrassment. "You broke my nose, Patsy. You broke my nose." He withdrew his hands and spied the thin streak of snot and blood. He swiped a finger under his swelling, bulbous snout and then wiped the finger on his overalls. "I'm going to bleed to death. You broke my nose."

"And next time, I'll box both your ears, too, if you bother Pinky ever again. You hear me?"

Waldo did not answer.

Patsy clasped fingers-full on Waldo's curly tuft of hair and raised his head. She put her face close to his. "Answer me, Slug. You hear me?"

"Yes, Patsy. I'm going to tell on you. You can't beat me up."

"Teachers and Principal Skaggs don't like bullies, Waldo, and that's exactly what you are. You tell on me, and they'll know why I socked you in the nose. And, oh, yeah, Waldo. Everybody in town will know a girl kicked your butt."

The trio stood over him as Waldo sat on the ground and cried. A moment of sorrow swept through Patsy as she heard Waldo's moans.

Maybe his nose is broke, Patsy thought. Then the site of Twig locking the door on *The Calaboose* flashed in her mind's eye.

Mrs. Barber approached and broke Patsy's trance.

"What's wrong, Waldo? Are you hurt?" She looked at the bystanders who tried to appear innocently sad. "What happened?"

"He . . ." Tina began.

"We don't know for sure, Mrs. Barber," Patsy interjected. "Maybe Waldo can tell you."

Mrs. Barber put both hands under Waldo's armpits and lifted him to his feet. She pulled a tissue from her blouse pocket and dabbed at his nose. "What happened, Waldo? Why do you have a red, bloody nose?"

Waldo looked at the three mustard-tears and grinned. "I got hit by the seesaw, Mrs. Barber. I wadn't payin attention and it jumped up and hit me in the nose. My three friends came to help."

"Well, alright, then. Come on, I'll bring you to Nurse Crabbe's office so she can doctor your nose."

Waldo smiled. "Okay, Mrs. Barber, then can I come back to be with my friends?"

"If Nurse Crabbe says it's alright and there's enough time left for recess, Waldo, I guess you can."

Tina glanced at Pinky and Patsy before she smiled and spoke to Waldo. "Your three friends will watch for you, Waldo."

THE LINK
December 1943
Rommel appointed Chief Planner for expected Allied offensive
Chinese troops have some success in Burma against Japanese

Aubrey's pack of hounds would not come to the call of his hunter's horn. They paused when he blew it three times, but resumed barking and howling when his horn quieted.

He could identify Bugger's throaty ruffs, Red's howl, and Cricket's snappy yapping, and knew they were telling him they had treed or run to ground something important and were imploring him to come. On other hunts, he heard their summons and knew the hounds would not come to the call of his horn.

He drove his truck and dog trailer down the trail along the Sulphur River, stopping and listening, until he thought he was near the hounds. From the sound of their unique voices, Aubrey thought he was 60 to 90 yards from them. But it was midnight, and he was tired.

More than that, there were dangerous swamps on both sides of the river. And at 80, he was not physically able to crash through thick underbrush with only a flashlight to get to the dogs. He knew he'd have to sit in his truck until daylight before going into the woods, or go home now and return later.

In the past, when the hounds would not come in, he left the trailer open for them as a homeport. When he returned in early morning, some were asleep in the trailer while others lay on the ground nearby. So, now, he unhitched the trailer, lowered and set the tongue prop, and pinned open the trailer door.

He sat in the truck for half a minute or more, listening, before he started the engine and switched on the headlights. A startled deer jumped up from a resting position in the middle of the pathway and stared into the light before legging into the darkness. Two jackrabbits scurried toward the truck's lights before veering off into the tall grass along the shoulder of the trail.

He turned his pickup around on the sandy logger's road and drove home.

"Where did you say you found it?" Deputy Sunday asked.

"I told you, boy. You need to open your ears and listen instead of runnin your mouth all the time. Where's Stephan? I want to talk to Deputy Stanton. He's got more sense than you do. He pays attention."

"I told you he was out of the office for a minute. I'm the deputy on duty here. Now you be respectful of the law, old man, you hear?"

Deputy David Sunday remained seated. Aubrey stood his ground in front of the deputy's wooden desk.

They glared at each other, defiant, intractable.

"I told you one of my hounds brought it in. Down there on the loggers trail along the Sulphur River."

"That's south of here, almost to Talco."

"Good God, boy, you are a piece of work."

They turned to look toward the creaking as the office door opened.

"Hello, Aubrey," Deputy Stanton greeted. "You're in town mighty early of a mornin."

"I come in to report what my hounds found, Stephan. I think it's important."

"I saw your truck and trailer out there on the street. Comin in from a hunt?"

"I was out last night. I had to leave em in the woods. They wouldn't answer my horn, wouldn't come in. Went back this mornin to get em."

"He brought this in," Sunday said. He held a piece of tattered, weather-beaten, faded cloth.

Aubrey pointed at the fabric. "That piece was hooked on the metal buckle of Red's leather collar when I returned this morning. I got all my hounds loaded and drove right here with it."

Sunday handed it over when Stephan reached out.

Deputy Stanton inspected it, turned it over and over, back and forth.

"He said he was down on the loggers road along the Sulphur River," Sunday said in the silence.

"That's right, Stephan. You know where it is?"

"Sure, Aubrey, down Two-Seventy-One, near Talco."

232

"I was across the river, just across the bridge, off on the right side."

"You were on the other side, south of the bridge?"

"Yeah, there's a trail that meanders alongside the river. Fox and wolves come down to the river at night to hunt and drink. I've hunted down there before."

"Well, across the bridge is Franklin County," Stephan said. He handed the piece of cloth to Sunday. "What do you think this is, Dave?"

Sunday turned it over and over, flipped it back and forth as Stanton had. "It's a piece of cloth," Sunday deduced. He looked at Stephan and raised his eyebrows.

"What kind of cloth, you think?" Stephan tested.

"Old cloth. Tattered, worn, and weather faded cloth," Sunday said and looked at Stephan for approval.

"I think it's cotton, Dave. I think it might be from a white cotton shirt. I think it is the right top of a shoulder, where the sleeve was, because of the thread line. I think there is blood spatter on it too. Aubrey, you think you can find the spot where you left the trailer for the dogs?"

"Well, it was dark, but I think so. It's about a half mile in off the highway. Are you gonna go down there?"

"Yes. But since it's in Franklin County, we'll need permission. Dave, call Sheriff Gregg over in Mount Vernon. See if he can send a couple of boys to meet us tomorrow, on his side of the bridge. I think we need to have a look because of what I believe is blood on a piece of a cotton shirt."

Deputy Sunday opened the desk drawer and

withdrew a Big Chief tablet. He licked a finger and thumb and flipped sheets before pointing at a page with his middle finger.

"You don't need the number, Dave, just tell Betty to ring Sheriff Gregg's office. She has the number."

Sunday rose and went to the wall phone. He lifted the receiver off the hook and placed it to his ear. He grasped the ringer handle, wound it three times, and waited. He leaned into the extended mouthpiece. "Betty, this is Deputy David Sunday. Connect me with Franklin County Sheriff Jeff Gregg — okay, *okay*, Betty, *pulleese*."

"Aubrey, why don't you go on home now and take care of your hounds. They must be hungry."

"Okay, Stephan. Do you think what I brought you is important?"

Stephan's face was somber as he nodded. "Yes, I think it is very important. I'm afraid of what it might lead us to, though. We've looked for over a year, and one of your hounds just happened to get a piece of a shirt hooked on its collar."

"It was Red. It was on his collar. What were you looking for, for so long?"

Dave Sunday replaced the receiver on the hook. "Sheriff Gregg and two of his deputies are sick, mumps and measles of all things. Deputy Freeman said they're too shorthanded at the moment for anybody to meet us at the bridge tomorrow. But he said if we wanted to go there on our own it would be okay. He'd just make an entry in the record that we was there with Sheriff Gregg's permission and authority."

"What are you thinking, Stephan?"

"I'm thinking your hound, Red, may have given us a link to help find Logan. Dave, have Betty track down Constable Chestnutt and give him the message to call me. We're gonna need him and his prisoners to come help us search the woods."

Sheriff Dudley parked the car in front of the cafe. He waved back and nodded to pedestrians who paused on the sidewalk in front of his car and greeted him. He sat there for several minutes reflecting on the visit with Artemis' aunt. As the folks moved along, he replayed the conversation with Maude Sims in his mind.

Maude had invited them in and listened as Sheriff Blake told her about the bank robbery.

"We believe there were more robberies than the two in Bogata. But witnesses said it was the same three doing the robberies at that bank."

Maude had shaken her head at that news.

She had been unemotional when Billy told her about finding Artemis in the Katy railroad shed, dead with two gunshot wounds. "Your boy killed two ladies in the bank. You may know them, the Akers sisters, Imogene and Lois. Lois called Artemis' name before he killed both of them. Right there in the bank."

Sheriff Blake had paused when Maude shook her head again.

He continued when she had said nothing, had not acknowledged she knew the sisters. "After your boy shot Lois and Imogene, he was shot first by the bank security guard. It was the second shot that killed him. That was done by one of his gang members, we believe."

Maude confessed that she had not intervened when she learned Artemis was running with a bad crowd. The one particular boy was a lout, she said. "I never knew his name, only saw him once. Brylcreemed hair, parted down the middle, dumb as a turkey. I knew he was no good."

Billy had ventured the name on the piece of paper found in Artemis' pocket.

Maude once more shook her head but quickly cocked it. "Who?" she had asked.

"Higgins," Billy had repeated. "A Herr Higgins."

"He lives someplace in Paris," Maude had said. "Artemis said he drove a car for him sometime."

Maude had taken Billy's card and looked on the back at the scribbles as he pointed out Zellman's phone number and address.

She returned from the bedroom with a blurry snapshot of Artemis. He was standing by a 1939 gray, four-door Plymouth. She had pointed out the car was the one Artemis said he drove for Higgins.

In reply to their attempt to push for more information about Higgins, she mentioned a boarding house in Paris. She could not remember why the boarding house was in her mind nor could she be sure there was a connection between Artemis, the boarding house, and Herr Higgins. Responding to their question, Maude had said she didn't think the boy she had seen once was Higgins. "No," she had said. "The way Artemis had described the man, Higgins was probably forty or fifty years old."

At last, as the two sheriffs stood to leave, tears

came to Maude's eyes.   But it wasn't because of sadness at the loss of her nephew, they learned. She was crying because Maude said she did not know how she would pay for Artemis' funeral or where she could have him buried. "I just don't have the money."

Both sheriffs had heard that lament before. They had become immune to it and felt no obligation to pass a few dollars to Maude. Anyway, they didn't own enough money to help all the families who needed funds to bury a loved one.

Now, sitting there in his car, Jim withdrew the photo from his shirt pocket and stared at the grinning youngster. What drives a kid to do bad things? Jim wondered — this boy was a car thief and petty criminal, how in the world could he end up in a gang of bank robbers and kill two innocent people in cold blood, two people who he knew as next-door neighbors?

He returned the picture to his pocket.

After closing the car door, he marched the few steps into the cafe and took a seat on a stool at the counter.

"Hello, Jim," Tiny greeted. "Jody, would you take care of serving these folks' meals? I'll take care of the sheriff."

"Where's the other girl?"

"What other girl?"

"The black-haired lass. She had a little girl that was in here sometimes."

"You mean Teresa? And Tina, her little girl?"

"Yeah, I guess so."

"Christ, Jim, that was a year ago, maybe even a year and a half ago. It's been that long since you've been in here?"

"I guess so, Tiny. I been kinda busy with the soldiers and everybody wanting to take their money. So, Jody is new?"

Tiny laughed. "No, Jim, she's been here since January, a whole year."

"Okay, Tiny, get me a cup of coffee, I need to talk with you. I need information about a case I'm working on with Sheriff Billy Blake over in Red River County."

Tiny set a mug and spoon in front of the sheriff. After she put the coffee pot on the stove, she walked around the counter and sat on the stool next to him.

He pulled the photograph out of his pocket. "Know this boy?"

Tiny took the photo and stared. She swiped a finger across the image as if that would make it clearer. Then she nodded. "In the past two or three months I seen him in here. He was a regular at Estelle's, brought Ilene in here for a meal a time or two, I think."

"Eileen? How do you spell her name?"

"I-l-e-n-e. Ilene Smith. I'm not sure Smith is her real name."

"She's one of Estelle's girls?"

"Yes, a cute redhead. Naive as all get out. She come down from Arthur City."

"How you know he was a regular?"

Tiny canted her head. "Good Lord, Jim, you oughta know what intuition is."

Sheriff Dudley grinned. "Yeah, I know."

"What's his name? What's the boy's name?"

"Artemis. Artemis Canton."

"My goodness, I do remember that name. Ilene called his name. It's a peculiar name, Artemis. Wad he do? Why you lookin for him?"

"He killed two women doin a bank robbery in Bogata last month."

"Oh, my. I remember about the bank robbery, and the two sisters from Pattonville. Read about it in *The Paris News*. But Artemis' name wasn't in the story."

"I'm not lookin for him. He's been found, dead. Bank guard shot him and one of his gang killed him with a bullet in his temple. I'm tryin to find a link, to connect who the other two robbers are and which one killed him."

"I only saw him when he was in here with Ilene. Maybe she can help?"

"You ever hear the name Herr Higgins?"

"Of course, everybody has."

Jim quizzically looked at Tiny.

"What?"

"I've never heard of him."

"No lie, Jim?"

He shook his head. "No, no lie."

"He's the one that went round town askin for support for his *Bund*."

"What bundle?"

"Not bundle, Jim, *Bund*. It's a German American organization — or was. The guy who run it, Fritz somebody, got sent to prison, years ago. Everybody who belonged to it went underground, except for creeps like Higgins."

"Ah, the Federation, the German American Federation. They supported the Nazi Party."

"That's the one."

"I'd forgotten about that. So, this Higgins is a

Nazi?"

"Well, he was, or at least sympathetic to Hitler's Germany. Who knows now? I'm sure you remember reading in the paper about the Forty-Two Christmas declaration condemning Nazism that was signed by Babe Ruth and a bunch of other people. That and Congress made em disband the *Bund*."

"If there's no longer the *Bund*, what's Higgins doin?"

"My guess is he's shakin down people cause they contributed money and carried a membership card. Now they're afraid of being exposed."

"Blackmail."

"Yep, through and through."

"Thanks, Tiny. You're good people. Evertime I've come to you, you've helped me. I'm goin over to Estelle's to see if she and Ilene can connect the other two to Artemis. I'll ask about Herr Higgins. I might need to have an official conversation with him about his dealings in the county."

"You need to come by more often."

Sheriff Dudley smiled. "I will, Tiny. Now, how can I help you?"

Tiny took a breath. "Talk to Chief Tarleton. Estelle's girls are complainin about some of his new youngsters on the force. They're workin girls, and there's money to be made with all the farm boys out there at Maxey comin into town for relaxation and learnin the pearls of wisdom. The only time the girls need police is when they can't handle the bad ones or the rowdy ones."

"What should I say?"

"Ask him to put out the word to help, not harass the

girls."

"Okay. Anything else?"

"No, Jim. I worry about you and your deputies. There are some mean bastards in Lamar County. You take care, you hear?"

Sheriff Dudley left the car parked in front of Tiny's cafe and walked to the boarding house.

In its heyday, it had been a three-star hotel. The few cowboys still driving small herds of skinny cows from Mexico and south Texas to the railhead in Sedalia, Missouri fifty years ago had stopped and rented a room for a bath, shave, and home-cooked meal. For ten years after the crash in 29, it served as a flophouse for the down-and-out.

Out of the blue, Estelle Kerns blew into town and bought it at a knockdown price when the hotel was in a knocked down state of disrepair. She renovated the 16 rooms, divided the grand lobby into a sitting area and dining area, and replaced the outdated and stained indoor plumbing. The plain, white, rectangular sign with black lettering above the double front doors proclaimed *Estelle's Boarding House*, Estelle Kerns, Proprietress.

With the war heating up in Europe, and particularly following the disaster at Pearl Harbor, military activity at Camp Maxey increased. The young male population out there, and in Paris, doubled, then tripled in a matter of months. These boys and men found it difficult to find satisfying recreation and relaxing entertainment in the Bible sector of northeast Texas.

Delilah and Ginnie were the first to take up residence and employment at the boarding house. These two entertainers persuaded Estelle to establish a new, enterprising business. The energetic soldiers and construction workers were thrilled. Paris turned a blind eye, money had trumped over religiosity.

"Ilene's not here anymore, Jim. She went home a week or so ago," Estelle said.

"What about this guy Higgins?"

"Herr Higgins? Yeah, he lived here for awhile."

"What do you mean, 'lived here'?"

'He's dead, been dead a week or so, Sheriff."

"What happened?"

"Somebody put a bullet in his temple. One of my cleaning women found him. He was fully dressed, lying on top of his bed."

"Who shot him?"

"Dunno. Anybody could have. We have all kinds comin in here at all hours, day and night, you know. Anyway, he was askin people for money after his Nazi business dried up. Probably blackmailin a lot of folks here in town and the county. I'm surprised you never heard of him or picked him up. Don't you talk to Chief Tarleton?"

Dudley ignored the implication. "Well, Estelle, I can't know everbody and their business in the county unless somebody tells me or complains."

"He was a mean rascal. Nobody liked him. He even beat on a couple of my girls and Chief Tarleton beat on him, too, one night right here in the sitting room."

"Nobody heard the shot?"

"Guess not. Radios playin, talkin, yellin, drunks

singin, and all the normal carryin on here."

"Nobody heard a gunshot in a closed room?"

"It was a large caliber, a thirty-eight, maybe, Doc Kramer said. Nobody heard the pop because a pillow muffled the shot. Pillow with powder burns was by his head, Doc said. He was probably drugged. Damn good riddance if you ask me."

Sheriff Dudley pulled the picture from his pocket. "Did you ever see this boy?"

She took the photograph and examined it. "Yeah," she shook the picture. "I seen this boy here before. He come to visit Ilene a time or two. Never knew his name. He acted like a snot-nosed kid. I remember he come one time with an older boy. They wanted to see Higgins, but he was gone."

"Gone? You mean dead?"

"No, no. They come askin for him sometime early last month."

"I see. Did you talk to them?"

"Just to say hi, can I help is all. Gave them Higgins room number. They went up but came back down pretty quick. They said 'he's not home' or something like that."

"So, a month ago, before Higgins was found dead, you told the boys Higgins' room number?"

Estelle waited. "Why you lookin for the boy?"

"Bank robber. Killed two women. I'm tryin to connect his partners."

"He won't tell you, Sheriff?"

"No, Estelle, the boy's dead."

"No lie?"

"No lie. What'd this other boy look like?"

"A bit older. Dressed funny."

"What do you mean dressed funny? Christ, Estelle, don't you ever listen to the detectives on the radio or pay attention at the *pitchursho*? I'm conducting an investigation, and I got to ask every damn question to get the information you have?"

"Well, Jim, you don't have to get huffy about it. I didn't know I'd be interrogated."

"Okay, what'd you mean dressed funny?"

"Overalls instead of a pants and shirt."

Estelle paused and met Jim's gaze.

"Well, go on."

"I was waitin for the interrogation to continue."

Sheriff Dudley lowered his head and shook it ever so slightly.

"Okay, okay. The overalls were faded but clean. I remember the boy's hair. Coal black hair, parted down the middle. Looked like he used a lot of Brylcreem. He didn't act like he was too smart, though."

Jim Dudley blinked.

Estelle grinned. "How'd I do with interrogatin?"

THE CAKEWALK
December 1943
General Eisenhower appointed Supreme Allied
Commander Europe
U.S. Troops land on Arawe Peninsula of New Britain
in the Solomon Islands

The annual cotton, watermelon, corn, and beet harvests were complete. The contingent was in Paris to help Bastion Albert bring his final load of produce to market.

Once their work with Bastion was finished, Twig drove up to Camp Maxey to check in with Captain Morris and First Sergeant Kinnison and let them see his prisoners.

The four guards at the front gate and four at the security gate checked Twig's identification before allowing passage into the barricaded compound. The three prisoners sat with hands in full view on top of their thighs and stared straight ahead. They kept their mouths shut and barely breathed through their noses.

Twig parked the jeep in front of his company's headquarters building. All dismounted and climbed the steps.

Kinnison invited them into his small office. Duke, Will, and Eddy stood with their backs pasted against the wall just inside the office door.

"This place is not the same since the division left," Twig said.

"They're in Scotland now," First Sergeant Kinnison said. He looked at the three prisoners. "It'll be over, over there soon enough."

Will, Duke, and Eddy said nothing, made no movement.

"These boys saved a couple of men from a fire, Top."

"You don't say?"

"A couple of months ago the ice house in Palomino caught fire and we happened to be close at hand. Two men, Mr. Martin Church and Preacher Adams, a black man, inhaled too much smoke and fell on the floor. We went in and brought them out to safety."

Kinnison pointed at the trio with his yellow pencil. "That's a good report on your behavior. I'll have that recorded in your personnel files."

"People in town were grateful these three saved the lives of two of their citizens. We seem to be treated a little differently. Friendly, maybe, I think." He looked at the three of them. "Think so?"

"Maybe," Duke answered.

"Okay, go to the mailroom, see if yall got any mail from home. You can go to the camp store to buy items you need, and then come back here," Twig said. "Be back here in twenty minutes."

As they left, Twig sat in the chair in front of

Kinnison's desk.

"I need some advice, First Sergeant."

"Go ahead, Twig."

"It's about romance."

"Really? You been foolin around? You in trouble with your wife?"

"No, no, it's not about me, Top, it's about these boys."

"Your German prisoners? Romance, you say? What's going on?"

Twig explained the encounter between Duke and Odessa in the field. He described the exchange between Will and Dallas in Jeeps Cafe, and how things progressed between them.

"Who is Odessa and Dallas?"

"Mr. Church's girls. Odessa is the oldest, nineteen or twenty, and Dallas is the youngest, eighteen, I think, same age as Will."

"Hmmmmm."

"Yeah. That was the beginning. Then after the rescue of Mr. Church, both girls held the boy's faces and kissed them square on the lips. In front of a lot of people. When everybody saw the kissing, they applauded."

"That seems innocent enough, in public."

"Now, they may also have been applauding because their men were saved. Hard to tell."

"I see. Unusual, though, about the girls kissin prisoners."

"Well, the first time in the field Odessa had asked if she could come by the Porter House some evening and visit Duke. Since I'd not had any guidance, I said okay.

247

Well, it wadn't just one visit, she came two or three times a week. Later on, Dallas came to visit. We was all pleased, especially Will."

"That's fraternization, Twig."

Sergeant Chestnutt closed his mouth.

"I think that look on your face tells me there's more to this story."

"They spent some time together, Top."

"I'm afraid to ask any questions. Go on."

"At first, they'd sit on the back porch and talk. After the first couple of times, Duke, and later, Will, ask permission to sit out on the back steps."

"And you let em."

Twig nodded. "Well, they were in view, when we sat on the back porch too."

"And there's more?"

Twig nodded again. "At first, it was just Duke and Odessa walking out to one of the trees in the backyard. Will and Dallas always stayed close at hand."

"In the dark, you couldn't see em? Out there at the tree?"

"Yeah, well, Duke's gained my fullest trust, First Sergeant. I didn't think anything about any of them being out of sight, so to speak. He wadn't gonna run away, try to escape. And the girl's were sweet on Duke and Will. It was young love, you see?"

"Oh, shit. What I see is dangerous fraternization, Sergeant Chestnutt. You may have violated a Army regulation."

"Which one, Top?"

"I dunno, but there's probbly one or more."

Twig blinked.

"There's *more*?"

"I didn't tell Duke he couldn't go when he and Odessa went out to the barn a few times."

"Oh, Christ."

"The barn is about ten yards or so from the back of the house. There was enough light from town and the back porch. I could see where they went. I thought it was okay to let them have a little privacy. I mean, I think they're in love, Top."

"Love my ass. You're crazy as a bed-bug if you don't know what Duke was after."

Twig shrugged. "Well, Odessa was after the same thing, Top, believe me. That girl knows what she wants, and she wanted Duke."

"Christalmighty, Twig. Kraus Hopplendagger is a German prisoner of war. Can you imagine *The Paris News* front-page headline announcing a romance between a prisoner of war and a local girl? We'd all be at the main gate fightin off the lynch mob."

"Well, the reason I raised it with you is to ask what I should do?"

"I think you done enough already, Twig. You need to tell em to cease and desist, to stop the fraternizing, to quit foolin around."

First Sergeant Kinnison paused and pulled on his nose. He scratched his right eyebrow with a thumb before absentmindedly pulling on the thick black hairs. Finally, he made a decision.

"Christalmighty, we gonna have to tell the Captain right now. The Captain will need to tell Colonel Sanchez, who'll need to tell General Pace, who'll have a goddamn fit."

Kinnison rose from his chair and stepped to the Company Commander's closed door. He tapped it lightly with a knuckle.

Carsey Belew was able to read her magazines between the pluggings and unpluggings of her Palomino telephone switchboard and relished listening in on juicy, gossipy conversations. She was the unofficial news lifeline of the town. Everybody knew it and tolerated it. But Carsey would always respect privacy when anyone prefaced their connection request with 'this is private' when they had something private to talk about.

Between interruptions, she scanned every photograph in *Life*, *Look*, and *The Saturday Evening Post*, but read over and over the lustful stories in *True Romance* and *True Confessions*. If hard pressed to name favorites, Carsey would say *True Detective* and *Master Detective*.

The buzzer startled her. She folded the magazine over but held her place with a finger. She pulled the cord up and plugged it into the receptacle.

"Palomino switchboard operator."

"Carsey, this is Betty, ring Deputy Chestnutt for me. Deputy Sunday wants me to give him a message to call."

"He's a Constable, Betty, he's not a Deputy."

"Well, ring Constable Chestnutt for me. I have a message for him."

"He's not here."

"Where's he at?"

"He went to Paris with Bastion. They took a load of produce to market."

"Well, okay. I need to give him the message to call Deputy Sunday as soon as possible."

"What's going on?"

Betty hesitated. She knew if she shared her suspicion, Carsey would broadcast it throughout her circles. On the other hand, if she didn't tell Carsey, then Carsey would withhold secrets.

"Promise not to tell?" It was a natural, reflexive query but Betty knew it was a useless question if there ever was one.

Carsey could not, would not promise. And she knew that Betty knew she knew she wouldn't. "How long we been friends, Betty? Thirty years, thirty-five? Why you ask me such a question?"

"You know I had to ask you, Carsey."

"Yeah, I know, Darlin. Now, tell me, what's going on?"

"Well, Deputy Sunday asked a deputy sheriff in Franklin County if someone could meet them at the bridge, on the south side of the Sulphur River. The answer was too many were out sick, but it was okay to go ahead. Then Deputy Sunday asked me to track down Deputy . . . Constable Chestnutt. Right after that, Deputy Stanton told Sheriff Blake he was going to organize a search party along the Sulphur River in Franklin County and was going to ask Deputy . . . Constable Chestnutt to bring his prisoners over to help."

"What are they lookin for?"

"I dunno."

"What do you mean, you dunno?"

"Stephan said 'Betty, stop listening', and I said I wasn't listening."

"Well, that gave it away."

There were a few seconds of silence. "I know, I wasn't thinking. So I unplugged the cord."

"So, we don't know what they gonna search for."

"Maybe I'll call Sheriff Dudley's office to see if they can find Constable Chestnutt and tell him Deputy Sunday wants to talk to him."

"Well, Betty, when you hear something be sure and fill me in."

After disconnecting, Betty rang the Lamar County Sheriff's office, and the Sheriff himself answered the phone.

"I'm Betty Crane, the switchboard operator in Bogata, and I have an urgent, official message from Deputy Sheriff David Sunday for Constable Chestnutt who is at the Farmer's Market. Will you help me, Sheriff Dudley?"

"I'll do my best, Betty."

"Deputy Sunday wants Constable Chestnutt and his prisoners to come to Bogata to help in a search along the Sulphur River."

"What are they searchin for?"

"I don't know, Sheriff, Deputy Sunday just asked me to get ahold of Constable Chestnutt and have him call."

"Okay, you say Chestnutt is at Farmer's Market?"

"He and his prisoners are with Bastion Alberts who brought a load of produce."

"Okay, I'll see he gets the message to call Deputy Sunday in Bogata. Anything else?"

"No, Sheriff, nothing else but I think this is pretty

important because Deputy Sunday wanted Franklin County sheriffs involved and Deputy Stanton called Sheriff Blake and told him about it."

"Okay, Betty, now I think I understand better the urgency of the situation. Sheriff Blake and Sheriff Gregg need help, and I'm the messenger."

"Thank you, Sheriff. I'll call Deputy Sunday and tell him you're personally going to Farmer's Market to give the message to Constable Chestnutt."

Jim Dudley hung up, told his secretary where he was going, drove his car the four blocks, and parked in front of the front door of the Farmer's Market office. In four minutes he found Bastion, learned that Twig and the prisoners had been gone an hour, got back into his car, and headed north to Camp Maxey.

They stood in General Pace's office. Colonel Sanchez opened the meeting, his voice soft.

"There is a serious situation that we needed to bring to your attention, Sir."

General Pace lit a Lucky Strike and leaned back in his chair. He exhaled a stream of gray smoke. "I have to admit I'm curious, Benny. When you told me it was urgent and wanted to bring Captain Morris, First Sergeant Kinnison, and Sergeant Chestnutt with you to this meeting, my first thought was Chestnutt lost one of his prisoners."

Benny Sanchez and Captain Morris sat in comfortable chairs in front of the huge, official desk. The General had not invited Kinnison and Twig to sit. They stood in the center of Pace's office, behind their two officers, at a relaxed parade rest position.

"Well, Sir, it is about the prisoners. I'm afraid a romance developed with one of the . . . two of the local girls . . . and prisoners Hopplendagger and Weiss."

General Pace blinked and cocked his head.

Watching, Twig thought the General stopped breathing.

"What?"

Colonel Sanchez did not quickly jump in to repeat. He inhaled deeply.

He let the words flow out with his exhale, "A romance, Sir, of sorts."

"What?" This time Pace leaned forward and snubbed out his cigarette in the amber glass ashtray that was overflowing with butts. "What do you mean a romance?" He rose from his chair, placed balled fists on top of his desk to prop his body, and jutted his chin at Twig.

"What does he mean 'a romance', Sergeant Chestnutt?"

Twig came to attention. "Yes, Sir." Twig swallowed with difficulty. His heartbeats pounded in his neck and ears. "It's an unusual story, Sir."

"Well, Son, make it usual for me. What the hell is a German prisoner of war doing fraternizing with a local girl . . ." Pace looked at Sanchez. "Two POWs and two local girls? For Chrissakes, explain to me how in the world you let this happen?"

Fraternizing. That's what First Sergeant Kinnison mentioned, Twig remembered. Fraternizing. Even the word sounded dangerous, ominous. Twig found his voice. "I think I'm sort of responsible for . . ."

"Sort of?" General Pace's voice now sounded official — like the change of police officers' voices Twig had heard during tense situations.

Twig kept his voice soft. He spoke quietly. "Yes, Sir, General Pace, please let me tell how all this came about."

General Pace nodded. "Okay, Sergeant, I'm listening." He sat and lit another cigarette.

In three minutes, Twig summarized how Odessa approached Duke in the field, requested to visit, and eventually was permitted private time at the Porter House. He thought it best, at the moment, to hold back the couple of trips to the barn. He also told about how the two teenagers, Dallas and Will, seemed to be a special pair.

There was silence. Twig held his breath, prepared for the worst. He expected the wrath of the Deputy Commanding General.

General Pace looked at Colonel Sanchez. "This is a court-martial offense. Permitting German prisoners of war to fraternize with the local populace is a court-martial offense, Benny. With two girls, for Chrissakes. Can you imagine the public relations nightmare this can cause? The people of Paris will be in an uproar. Hell, the people of America will be in an uproar about this. What the hell are we going to do about this Benny?" He looked at Twig. "Do we need to court-martial Chestnutt?"

"It is a sensitive problem, General. I think Sergeant Chestnutt used poor judgment, but I don't believe his motives were intended to be harmful to the Army or the war effort. I do not support preferring charges against

Chestnutt. That would serve no purpose. Anyway, the court-martial and punishment would produce major headlines resulting in a nightmare of publicity."

Twig felt relief upon hearing Colonel Sanchez' support.

The General extinguished his cigarette in the ashtray.

"On the other hand, Sir, you have the authority to relieve Chestnutt of his duty in Palomino, bring him back to Maxey, bust him to Private, and forfeit his pay for six months."

Twig's heart sank. He knew he was in deep shit. He knew Teresa would be heartbroken. He knew *he* would be heartbroken. If the General took the action Colonel Sanchez said he could, Will, Eddy, and Duke would be heartbroken too. Not to mention Odessa and Dallas.

Twig shook his head. What the hell was he thinking? He knew, he really knew, for the first time in his life that he was about to be humiliated.

"Well, that's probably the course we need to take, Benny. You got anything to add, Captain Morris?"

"I do, Sir. I support Sergeant Chestnutt. I do not believe a court-martial is in order, nor do I believe the non-judicial punishment mentioned by Colonel Sanchez is appropriate. When he was here in the compound, he was an outstanding soldier and non-commissioned officer. I depended on him, I gave him many missions, and he always accomplished them to my great satisfaction. I have no doubt he has performed in an exceptional manner in the months he's been in Palomino. He may have used poor judgment, Sir, but who among us have not."

When he saw Pace flinch and straighten, Morris immediately wished he could take those last few words back, but it was done.

"I think Sergeant Chestnutt might be idealistic, Sir," Morris continued, "and that caused a lapse in his assessment of the circumstances."

Pace raised his eyebrows. "First Sergeant? You have anything to say about this?"

Kinnison came to attention. "Yes, Sir. I support Sergeant Chestnutt. I agree with Captain Morris. No court-martial. There was a fire in the icehouse in Palomino and Twig . . . Sergeant Chestnutt . . . and his prisoners saved two men from burning to death. No punishment, Sir."

A loud rap on the door preceded the General's Aide-de-Camp opening it.

"Yes, Tommy?"

"I'm sorry to interrupt, Sir, but Colonel Jones and Lamar County Sheriff Jim Dudley wish to speak with you about an urgent matter."

"Yes, of course, show them in." General Pace, Colonel Sanchez, and Captain Morris stood. When Pace walked around his desk, Kinnison and Chestnutt moved out of his way and pasted their backs to the wall.

After greetings, Colonel Jones spoke. "Sheriff Dudley came to my office seeking Sergeant Chestnutt whom he was told was here on Maxey. He brings an urgent message from the Red River and Franklin County Sheriffs' offices for the Sergeant."

"Very well, Sheriff Dudley, you're very fortunate. He's right here, may I introduce Sergeant Twig

257

Chestnutt."

They shook hands.

"I went to Farmers Market first, Twig, was told you were here. The urgency of the message and call for assistance from two county sheriffs prompted me to come looking for you. Deputy David Sunday wants you to call him. The Sheriffs need your help, Constable Chestnutt. They want you to come with your prisoners to Bogata as soon as possible to help in a search along the Sulphur River."

Dudley rendered an informal salute for General Pace. "Thank you, General. I apologize for interrupting your meeting. I've done my job passing the message, so I'll be on my way, Sir."

"Well thank you for coming in, Sheriff."

Jim Dudley stopped in the doorway and turned back to Twig. He withdrew the photograph from his pocket and reached out with it to Twig. "This is a picture of Artemis Canton. Please give it to Deputy Sunday or Deputy Stanton when you get to Bogata. Canton was part of a gang. They robbed the Red River County State Bank in Bogata a week or so before Thanksgiving and he was shot by the bank security guard. We believe he was killed later by one of his gang members."

Twig looked at the picture before placing it in his shirt pocket. He took Dudley's handshake again.

"Good luck, Constable Chestnutt."

As Dudley turned to leave, General Pace asked Colonel Jones to remain.

The Aide closed the door.

The officers sat, and the two enlisted soldiers

assumed a military posture of at ease with their hands behind their backs.

"We have a situation with Chestnutt, R. J.," the General began and looked at Twig. "I asked you to stay because this falls under your administrative office. It seems that Sergeant Chestnutt has . . ."

The office door popped open.

"Yes, Tommy?"

"Congressman Martin Dies is on the phone for you, Sir."

Pace picked up the phone and listened.

"Hello, Congressman. Charlie Pace. How can I help you, Sir?

"Yes, Sir, I understand, Congressman. Yes, Sir. You don't say? The Chief of Staff and the Provost Marshal. And the President himself? Major Monroe. Yes, yes, I know Major Monroe. Newspapers and radio picked up the story. Yes, Sir. Well, thank you very much, Congressman. We take our duty with prisoners of war very seriously. Thank you, Congressman. We appreciate your support and your good words, Sir."

General Pace hung up.

"That was the Texas Democratic Congressman, Martin Dies, Jr.

"Major Monroe, who is a staunch Democrat and supporter of the President, told Congressman Dies about the rescue of Martin Church and the black man, Preacher Adams in Palomino. The Congressman told the Army Chief of Staff, who told the Provost Marshal General in Washington. Major Monroe also managed to tell the President.

"It seems, Sergeant Chestnutt, you and your

prisoners are well-known heroes in our nation's capital.

"Sergeant Chestnutt, you are hereby verbally reprimanded for a lapse in judgment to permit fraternization of your German prisoners of war with the local populace."

Twig and Kinnison grinned like happy possums.

With a sweep of his hand, General Pace dismissed Sergeant Chestnutt. "Now, Constable, get on with the mission Sheriff Dudley handed you."

Twig snapped to attention.

General Pace returned Sergeant Chestnutt's salute. "And take care of yourself, Twig, and your prisoners."

The sweet, enticing aroma of Ethel's four cakes in the oven wafted through the kitchen doorway onto the screened-in back porch of the Porter House. She had four more cakes sitting on the counter, ready for baking.

"That is a good smell, Miss Ethel," Tina said. "What is it?"

"I'm baking cakes for the cakewalk at school tonight."

"That's going to be a lot of fun. I've never been to a cakewalk."

"What-cha got there in that box with the pretty red ribbon?"

"It's a present. I need to hide it until Christmas. Do you know where I can hide it?"

"How about in the closet, out there on the back porch? I keeps my canning jars in there. Nobody else ever looks in there. Just a bunch of junk."

A large box on the closet floor seemed ideal for stashing the present. Tina removed the lid and saw a black Fedora nestled in the box. It looked new.

She lifted the hat out, placed it on her head, and set her present in the bottom of the box.

Tina turned toward the sound of the screen door opening.

"Where did you get that hat?" Ruby's voice was stern.

Fear was in Tina's voice. "In the box, Miss Ruby." She had never seen that look on Miss Ruby's face. It frightened her, made her want to run upstairs and hide.

"Well, little Miss Nosey Wosey, put it back and put the lid back on top of the box. And stay out of that closet. You hear me?"

"Yes, Mam. I'm sorry, Miss Ruby."

Tina removed the hat and gingerly placed it on top of her present on the bottom of the box. She put the lid in place and stood frozen in place just inside the closet.

Ruby blocked her path to safety, Tina had no escape.

Ethel heard it all and called from the kitchen.

"If you're done puttin your present away, Miss Tina, come help me with my cakes."

THE DANCE
December 1943
Edward R. Murrow broadcasts nighttime bombing raid
on Berlin
American Marines land on Cape Gloucester, New
Britain

When the First Sergeant and Twig came into Kinnison's office, the prisoners were sitting on the floor talking. Each had a small paper sack that held their purchases.

"Okay, go out in the hall," Twig instructed, "I need to make a phone call before we return to Palomino."

Without a word, they gathered up and went through the door.

Twig picked up the phone on Kinnison's desk and went through the convoluted process with the Camp Maxey operator for making a long distance call.

The First Sergeant waited a few seconds after Twig hung up. The silence got the better of him. "What?" Kinnison asked. "What do they want?"

"That was Minnie Belle, the secretary. She said none of the deputies was in the office, but she told me his message. Deputy Stanton wants us to meet him at the sheriff's office in the morning. He needs us to help with a search party. It'll be him, Deputy David Sunday, a deputy named Mavis Raymond, and the four of us."

"What are you gonna look for?"

"She didn't say, I didn't ask. Before, when Deputy Stanton came to Palomino he had asked if I would help if they needed us. We were picking up trash at Pecan Park when he and Sunday came over. They told about three people doing a bank robbery and the killin of Artemis Canton, a boy who was part of the gang — it was a picture of the boy that Sheriff Dudley gave me. A handcar was on the train tracks halfway between Bogata and Palomino, and that made them think maybe the other two came to Palomino. He asked me to be eyes and ears once the story was published in the *Palomino Press* about the robbery and Artemis."

"Was it?"

"Was what, Top?"

"The paper, was the story published in the paper?"

"I guess it was, on Thursday. The paper comes out once a week, on Thursdays. So if it wasn't in the paper a couple of days ago, then it'll be in next Thursday's paper."

"The ninth, on Thursday the ninth."

They fell silent.

"Yeah, the ninth," Twig acknowledged. "Two years and two days after Pearl Harbor."

"Are you gonna go straight to Bogata from here?"

"No. We'll go back to Palomino. There's a cakewalk at the school tonight. I promised to take Teresa and Tina. And the boys. I thought everybody'd get a kick out of going and get a little relaxation. We'll get up early in the morning and drive over to Bogata."

"You better bring your boys to the supply room to pick up backpacks, field jacket liners, and gloves. And flashlights, with extra batteries."

Kinnison picked up the phone. "Supply." He paused. "Burl, this is Kinnison. I'm sending Sergeant Chestnutt over to you to draw some field supplies. You give him what he wants. What? No. I said no, Burl. I sure as hell ain't gonna bother the Captain about signin no requisitions. You give Chestnutt what he wants, he'll sign for everything. Give him a machete, and give him a couple of cases of those new C-rations if he wants those too, you hear?"

Kinnison hung up and grinned. "It gives me a great deal of pleasure to screw around with Sergeant Braddock. He is a great supply sergeant, but he's always wrapped around the axle about needin signed requisitions."

"Thanks, Top. That's a good idea to get supplies. It has turned cooler in the past couple of days. I hadn't thought about liners for our field jackets."

"Well, it's gonna get colder. It is December, you know. Even in Texas it can get cold as a witch's tit in summer."

"The gloves and flashlights will be handy too. I didn't think about working in the woods where there might be little sunlight."

"Ask Braddock for tent poles. He has some five-foot poles that have metal spikes on the end. They'll make good walking sticks for the woods and are strong enough you can turn stuff over with the spikes, or lift stuff up to look under.

"And get a bunch of tent pegs. You can use tent pegs to mark places or stuff on the ground as you walk through the woods. Any you put down, just leave em there. Don't worry about bringing tent pegs back.

"Oh, and ask Braddock for ponchos. On the other hand, if you wear a damn poncho, you'll sweat from the body heat it creates. Well, either way you'll get wet. But ponchos can help as a cover, too, if you need it.

"And rope. Get three coils of half-inch rope, twelve feet long. Your boys can wrap the strand around their necks. Rope always can come in handy in the woods.

"Oh, and get the new shovels. They're called entrenching tools. It has a strong wooden handle and a folding spade. It's really something else. The spade folds up against the handle so it can be carried on the backpack, unfolded half way so it can be used as a pick, and out all the way to be used as a shovel. Everybody went crazy when they were issued, it was like the kids got a new Christmas present. The infantry guys was digging up Maxey, playing with them."

"Okay, anything else?"

"Do you have a water can and gas can?"

"No, they were not on the jeep when I drew it from the motor pool. I didn't think to ask for cans."

"Okay, get them from Burl. And keep the five-gallon gas can full. You never know when you'll need it or when you can help somebody else with gas."

"Right. Anything else?"

"Yes. This fraternizing business. There's gonna be a lot of publicity about this. The Paris paper, probably the Dallas and Fort Worth papers, and maybe even some big newspapers are gonna want a story about you and the prisoners. It'll be a goddamned dance you're gonna have to do with reporters and photographers, so the thing I will tell you, my straight-up advice, is to keep your mouth shut and don't let any of your boys say a word neither. Refer all questions to the Camp Maxey Public Affairs Office. You hear me?"

"Yes, First Sergeant. Loud and clear."

"The only reason the General didn't bust you to Private is because of that Congressman's phone call. You probably have that Major to thank, too, for saving your butt."

"Major Monroe."

"Yes, Major Monroe. Is he a real major or somebody like the plantation owners we see at the *pitchursho* who call theirselves Colonel?"

"Yes, Top, I think he's both. He owns cotton fields and a gin, and he was in the First War. Some of the men told me the Major is a decorated hero. He's disabled, you know. He lost his right hand."

"Obviously he's a big wig in politics too, calling the President, for cryin out loud. Okay, that's it, be on your way. What's the cakewalk for?"

"To raise a little money for school supplies and maintenance, and to buy some presents for kids whose momma and daddy don't have money for Christmas. Some of the money buys food for families, too."

"What's wrong, Sweetie? Are you alright?"
"Miss Ruby is mad at me, Momma."
"Why? Tell me what happened."

"I was hiding a present in a box in the closet, and she saw me do it."

"And that made you scared? Because she saw you hide the present?"

Tina hesitantly shook her head.

"It's okay, Tina. You can tell me about it. Tell me what you did."

"I put the hat on."

"The hat. There was a hat in the box where you put the present?"

Tina nodded.

"Is that all, Sweetie? You wore the hat?"

"I didn't get it dirty or anything, Momma. My hair is clean."

"I know it is, Sweetie. Whose hat is it?"

Tina shrugged and stuck her bottom lip out. "I dunno. It was just a hat."

"Did Miss Ruby see you with the hat on?"

Tina cast her eyes down, her bottom lip still pushed out. Her nod was a slight movement.

"Was it Miss Ruby's hat?"

Tina's small shoulders arched and lowered in an exaggerated shrug. "I dunno, but she told me to put it in the box."

"Did Miss Ruby see you put it back?"

Tina lowered her head further and nodded. "Miss Ruby told me to leave it alone and stay out of the closet."

"Which closet? Miss Ruby's closet? The closet in your room?"

"On the back porch."

"I see, the storage closet."

Tina looked up at her mother. "I told Miss Ruby I was sorry. My present is still in the box."

"You left the present in the box because Miss Ruby told you to leave the box alone."

"I couldn't get out of the closet."

"Why not?"

"Miss Ruby was standing in the door."

"When did she move to let you pass?"

"When Miss Ethel called for me to come in the kitchen and help with her cakes."

"Was Miss Ethel there, when Miss Ruby told you to put the hat in the box?"

"She was in the kitchen with her cakes."

Teresa reached out with both arms and Tina moved into the embrace. "Let's you and me go downstairs and apologize to Miss Ruby for touching her belongings."

"I told her I was sorry, Momma."

"I know you did, Sweetie. But this way, with you and me, Miss Ruby will know you've told me about the hat, and together we can tell her again that we're sorry."

Hand in hand, they went down to the kitchen.

"She's not here, Miss Teresa," Ethel said.

"We came down to say we're sorry for Tina going into the storage closet, opening the box, and wearing the hat that was in the box."

"Yes, I heard. I didn't know Miss Ruby had secrets in there. I goes in because I put my canning jars in that closet. I'm the one told Miss Tina to put her present in the closet. I didn't know Miss Ruby didn't want nobody to go in there."

"We need to get Tina's present out of the box. Can

we go get it?"

"It ain't there. Miss Ruby had Julius move it into her bedroom closet. And I wouldn't go in there if I was you."

"Where is Miss Ruby? I'll ask her to bring Tina's present out."

"She went to the school to bring my cakes for the dance tonight."

"A dance? I thought it was a cakewalk?"

"Same thing, cept at the schoolhouse this is how white folk do it."

"I didn't know the cakewalk was a dance. All the cakewalks I've been in were in a circle on the floor, usually in the school gym."

Ethel chuckled and wiped her hands on her red-and-white checkered apron. "The cakewalk began a long time ago, Miss Teresa. My granmama told she and her man dressed up on Saturday nights to do the dance on the plantation."

"Your grandmomma was a slave?"

"In Georgia. Some says the dance came up from the Seminole Indians in Florida but I don't know about that."

"Your grandmomma did cakewalks?"

"Yessum. But she said way back when, it started out as a cake-line walk. The people would put a bucket of water on their head and walk the line. Who could walk the best and not spill the water won the prize.

"Granmama said the plantation workers watched how the white folk dressed up and danced at parties in the big house, like they was from across the ocean, like what we see at the *pitchursho*, paradin in a grand march, dainty, and such. The ladies in their long dresses goin one way and the mens with their long coats goin the other, and meetin up again and linkin arms to strut down the middle. So my people started to act like them. Instead of walkin a line with a bucket, they danced in a circle.

"Granmama said they would sweep the yard real clean and set benches for the party. Men would come with their banjos and fiddles for the music. The women wore long, ruffled dresses with hoops and their men had on high hats and long split-tailed coats they got from the owners. When the owners come to the party to watch the fun, they gave a prize to the fanciest dressed couple who strutted best."

"The prize. A cake?"

"That was it. That was how the cakewalk started, way back when."

Julius came into the kitchen with a handful of radishes.

"Hello Miss Teresa. Hello Miss Tina."

"We was just talkin about the cakewalk, Julius," Ethel said. "Put your radishes down and let's show Miss Teresa and Miss Tina how to do the cakewalk."

"Here? There ain't no room, and there ain't no music."

"Well, we'll make our own room, and we'll make our own music." She linked arms with Julius, kicked her foot high, and started the dance with a familiar song.

Camptown ladies sing this song,
Doo-Dah! Doo-Dah!

Ethel and Julius swaggered with high-steps around Teresa and Tina.

Camptown race-track five miles long,
Oh, doo-dah day!

Around the large kitchen table, through the kitchen door into the dining room,

I come down there with my hat caved in,
Doo-Dah! Doo-Dah!

Around the majestic dining table, back through the door, around the kitchen table,

I go back home with a pocket full of tin,
Oh, doo-dah day!

And around Teresa and Tina again.

This time, Teresa linked her arm with Tina's, they joined in, kicking, and high-stepping following Ethel and Julius' strutting dance steps. The four of them loudly sang the chorus,

Goin to run all night!

Through the door into the dining room,

Goin to run all day!

Around the majestic dining table,

I'll bet my money on the bob-tail nag,

Back through the door, around the kitchen table,

Somebody bet on the bay.

They stopped, gasping for air.

"That was fun," Tina cried. "Let's do it again."

And they did.

They arrived at the Porter House with enough time to put the supplies in the trailer and go upstairs to clean up for supper and the dance.

Ruby had not returned home.

While still at the table, after the sumptuous meal of

Ethel's basic potato and carrot stew, Twig decided they should walk to the school.

"There's gonna be a lot of cars and trucks parked on the street at the schoolhouse. If we drive the car and jeep, they just add to the congestion. It's only a couple of blocks anyway."

Ethel and Julius collected dishes from the table.

"Are you going to the cakewalk, Miss Ethel?" Will asked.

Ethel and Julius paused.

"No, Mr. Will, we can't go to the cakewalk."

"I thought everyone would be going to have some fun."

Twig spoke. "Miss Ethel and Julius were not invited to the cakewalk, Will. It's . . . it's . . ."

"Um hummm." Ethel's disdain was evident. "It's for white folk only." With her head, she motioned for Julius to follow her out of the dining room.

"Okay, let's get our coats to keep warm from the chill of night air and meet at the front door in five minutes."

On time, they walked out into the evening. Even though it was casual, Twig wore his pistol and placed the prisoners behind them for the quarter mile stroll. Tina walked between Teresa and Twig holding their hands.

"We learned how to dance the cakewalk, Daddy."

"Really? I didn't know there was a dance to it. I thought you just moved around in a circle until the music stopped."

"Ethel and Julius showed us how to dance the cakewalk," Teresa said. "Ethel said her grandmomma did the dance on the plantation."

"Her grandmomma was a slave?" Twig asked.

"In Georgia."

"We sang doo-dah doo-dah and danced the cakewalk in the kitchen and dining room, Daddy. It was a lot of fun. I want to do it again in the school."

As they approached the crossing, Twig could see a group of a dozen or so men standing along the sidewalk leading to the school's entrance. His instincts kicked in. "Stop for a minute."

He spoke to the prisoners in military terms. "There is a security line up ahead. As we advance, I want you to close it up and stay tight as a group. Don't say anything or make any kind of movement. Don't even cough or sneeze. Understand?"

Duke spoke for them. "We understand, Sergeant Chestnutt."

Twig led his family and the group across the street and up the sidewalk. They turned to pass the gang of men who blocked entry into the school.

The men did not move out of the way. They did not even step aside in gallant courtesy for a lady and her daughter to pass.

"Evening, Miss Teresa. Evening, Constable."

"Good evening, Sam. How's Miss Elvira?" Twig inquired.

"She's fine, inside helping get set up. We was all wonderin if you was goin to bring along your Germans?"

"Well, you see I did. I thought it would be good for these boys to experience a little of small-town American life."

"Are you sure they'll be safe?" a voice asked.

"Are we sure we'll be safe?" another voice snorted.

"I'm surprised there is concern among you," Twig said. "These boys have been living and working in Palomino for six months, and you act like you don't know them yet?"

"Come this way, Mrs. Chestnutt, Miss Tina." Caleb Joiner came from behind and pushed through the cluster of men. He held out his hands to Teresa and Tina.

Pearson Keenan pushed through as well. "C J and me live with these fine folks. You boys make room for this family and their guests to pass."

The bunch moved to the edges of the sidewalk, allowing ample space for the three to stay abreast.

"Thank you C J," Teresa said. She and Tina took his hands and passed the gauntlet unfazed.

Twig waited. When his wife and daughter had gone into the building, he looked at Sam and spoke.

"That was uncalled for, Sam." Twig scanned the men on both sides. His voice was flat, firm, authoritarian. "If any of you have a problem with me and my prisoners we'll deal with it like men should. You leave my wife and daughter out of it."

He paused, waiting for anyone of them to make a noise.

"We'll handle it as it comes. You hear me?"

To a man, each looked down, cowed.

Twig felt Duke, Will, and Eddy touching his back and arms they were standing so close.

Pearson spoke. "Okay, you boys come in the schoolhouse and see how Palomino turns on an

274

American cakewalk."

Twig moved forward, his prisoners glued to his body. "Thanks, Pearson, you lead the way."

Sam raised a hand to pause Twig. Twig stopped.

"You're right, Constable. Please tell Miss Teresa and your daughter we're sorry."

"I'll tell em, Sam."

"We can handle the other matters at another time."

"You say when and where, Sam," Twig answered.

With that exchange, they followed Pearson into the school gym. Inside, Twig thanked Pearson for his assistance.

Pearson dismissed it. "Some folks still haven't accepted the situation, Twig. Your boys made a big impression when they went into the fire and brought out Martin and Preacher Adams. There's always one or two holdouts. They'll come around, though. Miss Henrietta and Miss Maybelle want your attention, Twig. Have fun."

Henny and Maybelle smiled and greeted Twig.

"Welcome Constable. Yall can put your coats over there. Teresa said you'd pay the entry fee for everybody," Henny said.

"That'll be a dollar a person," Maybelle said. "Six dollars, please."

"I didn't know we had to pay to get in. I thought we had to pay for a cake if we won."

"We do it a little different," Henny said. "The cakes and pies and punch are donated by the community. The money we collect at the door is used for Christmas."

"That way, it's all fair and square," Maybelle said.

She collected Twig's six silver certificates and put them in a blue, metal box.

"Yall have fun now. And good luck," Henny said.

Twig surveyed the gathering. He guessed there were two hundred people in the huge room and noted that Ruby and the Major were absent. Wolf and his family were there but C J and Pearson had disappeared.

Twig saw Martha Parker and Pauline Pinkston. He searched for Patsy and Pinky, knew they'd be together somewhere, but couldn't see them.

The raised basketball backboard permitted an unhindered view of the stage where a four-member band played a soft tune. There was an accordion, saxophone, guitar, and drums. A Sousaphone and a clarinet stood in a stand.

The two half-courts held two giant circles marked by tape. The outer band of tape on the circles was blue; the inner band, red. Each circle held 24 squares, and white tape formed a number in each square.

Clusters of women and clusters of men on the gym floor and in the bleachers on both sides chatted and laughed. Younger boys and girls stood in separate groups, peering at each other from a safe distance giggling, talking. Older boys and girls stood together, mingling, courting.

On the floor at the base of the stage was a length of tables covered by maroon cloths. On top of the tablecloths was a pot with pieces of paper as well as dozens of cakes, pastries, and pies.

On either end were eight or more large pitchers and stacks of small paper cups. Attendants poured liquid from the pitchers. Next to the tables, large trashcans stood on the floor.

Mayor Shipp took the stage. "Welcome, folks, to Palomino's annual cakewalk to support families at Christmastime. I'm going to turn the program over to our Mistress of Ceremonies, Mrs. Martha Parker."

"Welcome. Are you ready to get started?"

The applauding response was lively, energetic.

"Are we gonna have fun?"

The wild hooting and whistling was boisterous.

"Here's the rules. On Dora Kline's signal, a couple will stand on a square. When the music starts, couples will do their cakewalk dance around the circle until the music stops. Dora will draw a number from the pot. The couple on the number drawn may choose a cake, a pastry, or a pie as their prize. Once a couple wins, they may not participate in another cakewalk. Our band tonight is the Brown Family Band from Paris. It's all yours, Dora."

Teresa, Tina, Twig, and his prisoners sat in the bleachers and watched the merriment. They kept time with their hands and feet, enjoying the relaxed, fun atmosphere. Upon completion of the fourth go-round, Tina said she was ready to do their dance.

"Come on, Momma. Let's show them what we learned from Miss Ethel."

On Dora's signal, they went to a square and struck a pose. When the music started, Teresa and Tina strutted, swaggered, high-stepped, and kicked for two rounds around the oversized circle. The band got into the rhythm and excitement of Teresa and Tina's performance and played longer than usual.

The number called was not theirs.

Teresa rushed to the bleachers and pulled Eddy out. "Come on, you see how we do it."

Tina pulled on Twig. "Come on, Daddy, do a cakewalk dance with me."

Odessa and Dallas came for Duke and Will.

The band played, they all strutted and swaggered and high-stepped and kicked and had a ball.

But none of them won a prize.

When the program was over, there was thunderous applause, whooping, and shrill whistling with joy. It took several minutes to get close enough to retrieve their coats.

When they left the gym, nobody blocked their path.

Odessa and Dallas walked with them, holding hands with their beaus. Twig did not intervene. Eddy walked behind everybody.

At the steps of the Porter House, their girlfriends said goodnight without kisses and walked away.

"Okay, guys. Remember, breakfast at six, on the road at seven. It'll still be dark when we start out on our way to Bogata. Dress warm."

Later, with Tina put to bed and the lights out, Teresa put her arms around Twig. He turned to her and adjusted his pillow.

"I had fun tonight," she said.

"I know. I'm glad. I did too. It's funny how simple little things can make it all better sometimes."

"I like how you strutted and swaggered."

"I've always been a pretty good dancer."

"I know. I like how you move when you dance with me," she said. "I've missed dancing with you. We haven't danced in a while you know."

Twig moved closer, wrapped his arms around and held her in his embrace.

Teresa pulled him in tight. She kissed him. And kissed him again.

"I've been so busy, Resa, it's hard to think about other important things."

"What are you thinking about now?" she whispered.

"I'm thinking about the same thing you're thinking about."

"Well, do you want to do more than think about it?"

"Oh, yeah," Twig whispered and kissed her. "I sure do, Mrs. Chestnutt."

"I was hoping you would."

THE SEARCH
December 1943
US Army VIII Corps and XV Corps arrive in the
European Theater
Six US carriers and nine cruisers attack Kwajalein,
Marshall Islands

After a filling Saturday morning breakfast of Ethel's pancakes, molasses, link sausages, and hot coffee, Twig and the prisoners stood in darkness while smoking on the front porch.   Low clouds and a light rain confronted them.

"We will be wet, Twig," Duke said. "The ponchos are in the trailer, under the tarp."

"You did not put on the sides," Eddy said. "Wind will blow the rain on us."

"It is too late now," Will said. "We will be wet."

Twig chuckled. "Yes, my little darlings, it's too late to worry about it. You tender sweethearts will not melt in a little rain. Come on, let's go."

They did not trot or run across the depth of the front yard to the jeep parked along the curb. Instead, braving the small drops of moisture, with military discipline they marched in single file behind Twig to the vehicle.

Chill of the winter morning air nipped them as Twig started the engine, turned on the headlights, turned on the windshield wipers, shifted to first gear, eased the clutch out, and drove slowly away.

He turned right and cruised along Main Street. Lights were on in some stores, and in Jeeps. Twig saw Bobbie Jo moving about in the cafe and thought about Teresa. He knew she would probably leave Tina at the house with Ethel and drive their coupe to work.

At the 271 stop sign, Twig waited for several trailer-trucks heading in both directions to pass.

"Where do all the trucks come from, Twig?"

"Ones from the east are coming from the railhead in Marshall, from the T and P shops, going to Maxey. Trucks from the west, from Paris and Maxey, are going back to Marshall for another load."

"What is T and P?" Will asked.

"Texas and Pacific railroad. The shops in Marshall build and repair railroad cars. It is a big operation, a lot of people work in the shops."

"Some trucks have *A-B-F* letters, and some have *E-T-M-F* letters. What do the letters mean?" Will asked.

"They're abbreviations for the truck company's name, Will. *A-B-F* stands for Arkansas Best Freight, and *E-T-M-F* stands for East Texas Motor Freight. They are regional carriers."

"Since we come to Palomino," Eddy said, "I see many trucks with these names when we are in the cotton fields and vegetable fields and the park."

Twig pulled out onto the highway, turned left

toward Bogata, and accelerated to forty. Spray increased on both windshields, and the wipers struggled to keep the glass clean and clear. A truck's headlights behind the jeep switched from low to high beam. The reflection in the driver side mirror blinded Twig. The truck's air horn blared, the driver impatient that the jeep was poking along down a busy road.

Duke looked in his front seat passenger side mirror.

"He is in a hurry, Twig."

A distant truck's rapidly approaching headlights impaired Twig's vision. He squinted and peered at the right shoulder of the highway to avoid the glare. The truck swooshed past. Its blowing spray from huge tires swashing Twig, and Will on the back seat.

There was room ahead for the truck behind the jeep to pass and when the tractor with its long trailer came alongside, the driver pulled his cord. The air horn blared again to signal his displeasure.

Twig let the truck expand distance between them before increasing speed to forty-five. He held that pace for the six miles until he reached the gas station at the 271 and County Road 37 junction.

He pulled onto the Cities Service apron and parked between a Red River County Sheriff sedan and a battered pickup with a trailer full of dogs hooked to it.

Aubrey's hounds welcomed the military party with howls, woofs, and whines.

Twig and the prisoners dismounted.

"Eddy, unstrap the gas can and water can. Duke, take the gas can and put four gallons of regular in it. Will, see that faucet, there, by the empty Coke cases . . . fill the water can."

Twig stood in the sprinkling mist and waited for them to take care of their chores.

With cans filled and placed back on the carriages, Eddy reattached the straps.

They followed Twig into the gas station. The store was small, its space filled by two shelves of goods, a red, double lid, Coca-Cola cold drink icebox, and a counter with a cash register. Deputy Stanton greeted and welcomed them. Sunday only nodded, the other three men stared.

"This is Constable Chestnutt, and his German prisoners, Duke, Will, and Eddy. You know Deputy Sunday, Twig, and these three gentlemen are Deputy Mavis Raymond, Aubrey Roach, and Billy Don Owens, owner of this business. Mr. Roach's hounds found a piece of fabric that led us to decide to conduct this search."

There were cautious how-dos and uncomfortable but civilized handshakes.

"I read about you in the paper, Constable," Mavis said. "You're an Army Sergeant doing double duty. My uncle Grady was a platoon sergeant in a tank company with Patton in North Africa. Now, he's somewhere in Sicily or Italy, or somewhere over there."

Twig smiled. "These boys were with Rommel over there, in the Afrika Korps." He looked at Billy Don. "I need to pay for four gallons of regular gas and five gallons of water we put in our Army cans."

"The gas is forty-eight cents, twelve cents a gallon. Let's say two-bits for the water, Constable."

Twig handed over three quarters to Billy Don.

The proprietor jammed them into his overalls'

pocket and made no motion to give the change.

"I've never seen a German, let alone a German prisoner," Aubrey stated.

Twig gave up expecting Billy Don to give him two pennies. He looked at Aubrey and chuckled in an attempt to mitigate potential hostility. "Mr. Roach, these boys are under my supervision. I know them, they have worked for me, I would trust them to care for my wife and daughter."

"They fought in the war against our boys. Did they hurt or kill some of our boys, Constable?" Billy Don asked.

"We . . ." Duke began but stopped when Twig raised his hand.

"They are soldiers just like our boys are, Mr. Owens. They served the will of their government at war just as our boys do. They tell me they never fired their rifle, never hurt or killed anyone. I believe them, and I ask that all of you believe them.

"Here, in Texas, today, they are prisoners of war. When this mess is over, they want to live in America as citizens. We came to help the deputies conduct a search, but if anyone would rather we not be of help then speak up now and we'll get in our jeep and go back to Palomino."

Twig looked at each man's face in the silence.

Deputy Stanton spoke.   "I asked Constable Chestnutt for help, and I want him and Eddy and Will and Duke to help us. So this is an official search, it is an official request by Red River County Sheriff Billy Blake, and the Sheriff's Office, for their help. So, like Constable Chestnutt said, if anybody has a problem with this, then speak up now."

With that summation, there were shuffling of feet and lowering of heads.   No one spoke for a few seconds.

"Okay, good.   Now, here's what we're going to do. We're going to drive south on Two-Seventy-One.   We'll cross the Sulphur River bridge, turn right off the highway onto a trail.   Once everybody is off the highway, we'll stop and let Aubrey with his hounds get in front.   He'll lead us to the spot where he parked on the trail when he was hunting, where one of his dogs brought in the fabric snagged on its collar.

"At the spot on the trail, we'll set up a command post.   Aubrey will lead us into the woods to about where he thinks his hounds treed something, which may be the spot where the fabric was.   At that point is where our careful search begins."

"What are we searching for, Deputy Stanton?" Twig asked.

"Deputy Logan Amesa's body, Twig.   Logan was kidnapped by two boys here at Billy Don's station. Logan was in their car with them following Deputy Crawley to the office.   They sped away down Two-Seventy-One when a school bus blocked Deputy Crawley from following them.   Logan's been missing for a year and a half, the fabric may be from his shirt.   Our search is to determine if that's where Logan is."

"Oh," Twig blurted.   "Sheriff Dudley gave me a photograph for you."   He unbuttoned his shirt pocket and withdrew the picture.

Stanton peered at it.   "That's Artemis Canton, a petty thief and bank robber.   Deputy Crawley shot him during the robbery before Thanksgiving, but one of his gang killed him with a shot to his temple."

Stephan handed the photograph to Sunday who looked at it briefly before handing it to Mavis. Mavis handed it to Aubrey who handed it to Billy Don.

"My God, Stephan," Billy Don gasped. "Good Lord Almighty."

"What is it, Billy Don?" Stephan Stanton asked.

"This is one of the boys. He told Walter his name was John something. I can't remember the last name."

"What do you mean? Artemis was John?"

"Yeah, and the other boy, the big boy, was Sam something. No. Wait a minute. Sam. It was Sam, it was Uncle Sam's car, the green Dodge. The other boy, the big boy's name was . . . I can't remember his name, it's been so long. But I'll think of it for sure."

"That's okay, Billy Don. Artemis was John, and I bet Uncle Sam was a play on words."

"A play?"

"Uncle Sam, the government," Deputy Sunday said. "They used fake names, Billy Don."

"Oh, yeah, I see. Well, this boy, John, he pumped the gas and the bigger boy was tryin to steal a candy bar and cigarettes. Me and Buddy, my mechanic, locked them in the restroom until Logan and Pop Crawley could get here. Logan got in the car with them to follow Pop to the office. This boy, this John, is one of the kidnappers, Stephan. Good Lord Almighty. He's one of the boys who killed Logan."

When they came down for breakfast, Teresa asked

Ethel if Miss Ruby was up and about.

"They gone off to Paris, left early this mornin. Miss Ruby say she got important bidness and need to go. I'm worried about it cause Julius don't drive too good in the dark, and in the rain. He don't drive too good noways."

Teresa and Tina sat in their place at the large kitchen table.

"I wonder if it would be alright if you let me go get Tina's present out of the box? You could go with me and watch?"

Ethel thought about it. Doubt tilted her head. "I dunno Miss Teresa. I knows Miss Tina has a right to her present, but Miss Ruby had Julius move it to her closet so nobody would get in that box again."

Teresa nodded, understanding Ethel's reluctance.

Tina spoke. "How can I get my present out if I can't get in the box? What is so secret in a hat box, anyway?"

Teresa looked from Tina to Ethel. "I thought it would be okay, Miss Ethel, but I understand your caution. It would sort of be like we were sneaking around behind Miss Ruby's back, going through her things."

"Yessum."

Teresa thought Ethel's response was encouraging, so she continued. "I would tell Miss Ruby what we've done when she returns. I would take all the blame and say to Miss Ruby that we needed to get Tina's present out of the box and thought it would be okay, that I didn't think she would mind us going into the closet for five seconds."

"Yessum."

"What do you think about it?"

"I think we would be in big trouble. I been with Miss Ruby goin on fourteen years, since the crash mind, you, and I sure would hate to lose my job, and Julius' job, too. It scares me to death to think how Miss Ruby would do if she knew we went in her closet."

Jake and Pearson came down the stairs. They were talking about the annual Christmas lights displayed by Paris residents. They were ignorant of interrupting Teresa's attempt to persuade Ethel. Both men cordially greeted the women and Tina.

"What did you ask Santa Claus to bring you for Christmas, Miss Tina?" Jake asked.

"A bicycle. A blue and white bicycle. My Momma had one, and I want one with the same color. I wrote him a letter a long time ago so he could have time to find the right one."

Jake looked at Teresa and nodded. "I see, a blue and white one."

Pearson spoke. "Have you ever ridden a bicycle, Miss Tina?"

"No, but it looks easy. Anyway, I'm a fast learner. I knew my alphabet when I was three, and I could count to a hundred."

C J came down the stairs and joined them at the table. "Mornin, everybody."

"I will bring coffee first and make your breakfast," Ethel said.

"What were you saying about Christmas lights, Jake?" Teresa asked.

"There are a few neighborhoods in Paris that go all

out with Christmas lights. They put up their displays and lights a couple of weeks before Christmas."

"A lot of people from the surrounding counties make the pilgrimage every year just to look," C J said. "They did last year too since there's no blackout."

"Excuse me, Momma."

"Yes, Sweetie, go ahead but don't be long. Miss Ethel will bring your breakfast in a minute."

For several seconds, Tina stood in the doorway, listening. She waited to see if anyone was watching her.

"I'd like to go see the Christmas lights," Teresa said. "I need to know that other people love Christmastime as much as I do. I'll ask Twig to take us. Maybe we could all go in a convoy and be together. We could eat at Tiny's where I used to work and then see the lights."

"There's one house that always has Santa in his sleigh with all the reindeer on the roof. They have all color of lights outside."

"Santa's reindeer. Let's see, there was Vixen and Dancer and Dasher . . ."

"And Prancer and Blixen," C J added.

"No, C J, it's Blitzen, Blitzen," Jake corrected.

"Yes, Blitzen," C J said.

"And Cupid and Comet," Teresa said.

"And Rudolf the red-nosed reindeer," Pearson said.

"There's one more," Jake said. He shook his head. "There's one more reindeer, we only said eight. Santa had nine."

"Where's Constable Chestnutt and the prisoners," C J asked, oblivious to Jake's dilemma.

"They left early this morning. To Bogata. They're

going to help the sheriff's deputies hunt for something."

"Hunt? You mean like hunt for wolves and fox?" Pearson asked.

"No, no, they're going to do a search, a search instead of a hunt."

"Are they searching for somebody?" Jake asked.

Teresa shook her head. "Twig didn't tell me, and I didn't ask."

Ethel came in with the pot and made the rounds pouring coffee.

The table was quiet as they focused on adding cream and sugar to the brew in their cups.

"Donner," Jake shouted.

Ethel recoiled.

"The ninth reindeer is Donner." Jake beamed with pride.

"That's the one," Pearson confirmed.

Tina made her move and went into Miss Ruby's master bedroom. The closet door was easy to spot, and Tina opened it.

On the floor on the left side of the closet were six boxes and on the right were four, all sitting under hanging clothing. Tina couldn't remember what the hat box looked like where she had placed the present. She pushed aside the navy blue Sunday suit that had a white silk handkerchief in the coat pocket and removed the lid of the nearest box, searching for her present. That box contained a pillow with fancy embroidery from the *1939 World's Fair*. The next three boxes held shoes and belts. The fifth box was the right one. She lifted up the black fedora then plucked the gift-wrapped box out of the hatbox and put it on the floor. Tina replaced the hat but couldn't remember which lid was for which box. She picked up lids, laid them on boxes, picked up the present, and closed the closet door. She heard her mother's call as she rushed upstairs to stow her box in her own closet.

"Tina? Tina, come for your breakfast. Hurry, before it gets cold."

Dora and Maybelle were at the counter, talking about Curtis' promotion and assignment to the aircraft carrier CV9, USS *Essex*.

"I want to write a story for the paper, Dora, and print Lieutenant Kline's picture on the front page."

"He was promoted to a junior grade Lieutenant, Maybelle. He said a real Lieutenant wears two silver bars instead of one like he wears now."

"Yes, that's good clarification for the story. The only picture I have is the one Stan made for Curtis' senior yearbook. Don't you have a picture of Curtis in uniform?"

"I do, I've got some right here, I received them Thursday. The envelope was postmarked November sixth." Dora stepped away and picked up a white envelope off a back shelf. "It took four weeks for his letter and pictures to get to Palomino from somewhere in the Pacific Ocean." She came back, handing a photograph to Dora. "This is a picture of him standing by his airplane on the deck of the ship."

Maybelle looked at the photograph. "You can barely see Curtis, Dora. Whoever made this picture wanted the whole airplane in it, so Curtis looks like a midget

he's so far away. I can't even see his face good.
That's a funny looking airplane. What kind is it? What
does it do?"

"I don't know, but I have more pictures he sent with
the airplane." Dora opened the envelope.

"In this one, he's sitting on the big tire."

"Well, that's a better one. I can crop it so we only
see him in the paper, but the whole image is a little
blurry. Let me see all of them, there may be a better
one that's close up and clear with a sharper image."

"That will be so nice to have a story in the paper
about my boy."

Outside, headlights of a parking black sedan shone
through the front windows of Kline's Drugstore. The
two occupants sat for a few moments before opening
their doors. They mounted the sidewalk, walked to the
door, and pushed it open, jingling an alert bell.

Dora spoke as she looked up.

"Hello, welcome to Kline's Pharmacy."

The appearance of a tall Naval Lieutenant and a
First Class Petty Officer standing just inside the closed
door struck Dora with a rush of anxious panic.

"Oh, my."

Maybelle looked up from the photograph. She
recognized fear on Dora's face and turned toward
where Dora stared.

"Kingston." Dora called without turning her head.
"Kingston, Darling, come up front." Her voice was
hushed, quiet.

Maybelle knew, could feel, the need. She walked
around the end of the counter and put her arm around
Dora's waist.

"Kingston?" Dora's raised voice communicated urgency.

Kingston came out from the enclosed room of the secured pharmacy.

"Yes, Dora, what is it, Dear?"

Kingston stopped at the end of the counter and stared at the sailors.

The Lieutenant stepped forward, with the Petty Officer alongside.

"I'm Lieutenant Gene Pattman, this is Petty Officer Douglas. Are you Mr. and Mrs. Kingston Kline?"

"No," Dora said with a hesitant, nervous shake of her head. "No, no, oh, no, no, oh please, no, please no," she whispered.

"Yes, we are," Kingston said. "Please, is our boy dead?"

Lieutenant Pattman and CPO Douglas removed their cover and moved to within a foot from the counter.

"On behalf of our President and Secretary Knox, it is my duty to report to you that your son, Lieutenant, Junior Grade, Curtis Aaron Kline, is missing at sea and presumed dead."

Maybelle felt Dora's body go limp. She squeezed Dora's waist and grabbed her shoulder to hold her up. Kingston put his hands on the counter for support.

Kingston's hope shrouded denial. "Then my boy is not dead. He's somewhere in the water."

Maybelle couldn't resist. "I'm Maybelle Winters, Lieutenant Pattman, a close friend of the family and owner of our newspaper, the *Palomino Press*. As a reporter . . ."

"Maybelle, please," Kingston reprimanded.

"Lieutenant? What can you tell us?"

"Our information is sketchy, but it is our duty to tell you as much as we know. Lieutenant Kline was flying his PBY, a search aircraft, off the carrier Essex. During his reconnaissance off the Gilbert Islands, he first reported enemy contact by a Zero. His second call was a Mayday. He reported his intent to try to land in the sea and gave coordinates. Rescue planes could not find his aircraft, markers, him, or any of his four-man crew. Search missions ceased upon the beginning of the battle of Tarawa. I'm sorry. Lieutenant Kline is presumed dead, killed in action. Please accept condolences from a grateful nation."

Dora screamed.

Maybelle gathered Dora in her arms and tried to soothe her with soft whispers.

"Oh, sweet Dora. I've got you, I've got you, Dora."

Mayor Shipp and Nate Dulfeine rushed in.

Maybelle looked at them and shook her head.

The Mayor spoke to the sailors, who stood still.

"We saw the car," Shipp said, "and heard Dora's screaming."

Kingston sank to his knees, wailing. "My boy is gone. Oh, Lord, my boy is gone."

The Mayor and Nate went to Kingston and knelt with him in his sorrow. Nate wrapped his arms around his friend.

They listened to Kingston's prayer.

"*Say not in grief 'he is no more' but in thankfulness that he was.*"

When he wept, they all whispered Amen.

THE RECONCILIATION
December 1943
General Eisenhower named head of Overlord, the
invasion of Normandy
Japanese employ poison gas in an attack on the
Chinese city of Changteh

The rain had stopped as they entered the city limits, well before Julius parked the majestic Crown Imperial between a 1936 Chevrolet coupe on his left and a 1940 four-door Plymouth on his right.

He often parked in the same space when he drove Miss Ruby here. The last time was a couple of weeks before Thanksgiving. Julius liked this parking spot in front of Madame Estelle's Boarding House because he could watch all the comings and goings.

He noted some women went into the boarding house with men close behind; others went in holding hands with young soldiers.

He had more fingers on one hand than the number of women who went into the office next door. He had never seen a man go in. Painted lettering above the door and on the large pane of glass that occupied the front half of the building's facade announced **B. D. Baldwin, Esquire, Attorney-At-Law & Premier Bail Bondsman**.

Julius rolled down his window.

A young boy and young girl, teenagers, sat in the coupe.

Two bloodhounds sat in Plymouth with their long, wide, red tongues hanging out — one sat on the front seat, the other on the back seat.

Both cars' windows were open halfway.

The hounds' big heads, with their large black noses, were stuck out. They had watched, scented, and listened to the couple in the coupe arguing.

The hounds woofed at Julius, upset he blocked their view from the entertaining pair.

Julius was immediately amused to hear two white kids fussing at each other, but he did not turn his head toward them.

"You're a spineless snake," the girl said.

"I am not," the boy answered.

"If you don't stand up to daddy, J W, I caint marry you," she said.

"If I *do* stand up to your daddy, Wynona, he'll beat me so bad you won't have nothin to marry. Your old man is gonna be mean crazy when you tell him."

"*I'm* not gonna tell him. *We're* gonna tell him," she corrected.

"Well, I got to think about it."

"Well, I'm gonna be showin in a couple of weeks, so you better hurry up thinkin about it."

"Well, I'll marry you, Wynona. We'll find a preacher to do it. *Then* I'll tell your daddy. Maybe he won't kill me when I'm his son-in-law."

"Open the door and let me out, Julius," Miss Ruby said.

"Yessum."

When Julius opened his door, the girl in the coupe turned to look at him.

"What are you lookin at?" she accused.

Julius nodded, but said nothing. He gripped his lips to keep from smiling.

He opened the back door of the Chrysler for Miss Ruby.

"Let's go, J W," the girl ordered.

J W started the coupe's engine.

Miss Ruby dismounted and circled around behind her car to the sidewalk.

"Let's go, J W, *now*," the girl demanded.

"I gotta wait till he closes the door, Wynona, for Chrissakes. Why don't you hush?"

Julius shut the door and got back in behind the steering wheel.

J W backed the Chevy into the street.

"Now, go on," Wynona directed. She glanced at the Chrysler.

In his driver side mirror, Julius could see the girl still staring, her mouth still moving. He grinned.

From the sidewalk, Miss Ruby gave instructions. "You stay in the car. I'll be back in a few minutes."

"Yessum."

He watched her open one side of the double glass doors and walk into the boarding house.

The grand lobby was empty, quiet. Stale cigarette and cigar smoke could not hide a prevalent and powerful musty smell.

At the front desk, Ruby spoke to the concierge.

"I'd like to see Miss Estelle, Craig."

"Yes, Miss Ruby. She's upstairs with Eunice, one of our new maids. She'll be down in just a minute." Craig pointed to his left. "You can wait in her office if you like."

Even though there were two armchairs placed in front of Estelle's desk, Ruby sat on the small sofa alongside a wall. She inspected the space and noted Estelle's habitual tidiness. Books neatly aligned on top of the wooden three-drawer file cabinet stood at military attention. A glass ashtray and a single manila folder lay in the center of Estelle's Louis XIV's apricot desk. Her riding crop laid parallel to the top left edge, although Estelle had never been on a horse.

Autographed pictures of mostly men in varied portrait poses adorned the wall behind the desk as well as the sidewalls. Prominent were Clyde "Red" Julian Foley, James "Jimmy" Clarence Wakely, Orvon "Gene" Grover Autry, and a teenaged-looking Hiram "Hank" Williams. Ruby had met Red and Jimmy and liked them both.

As she sat there scanning the photographs, Ruby wondered whether the country music artists had stayed or only been entertained in the boarding house. She knew each of the singers and their bands had performed at least once at Camp Maxey.

She heard Estelle and two other women talking as they approached the office. She remained seated on the sofa.

Estelle came through the door followed by young

girls.

"Here you are, Ruby. Craig said you were waiting." Estelle reached her arms out for a hug.

Ruby rose and embraced Estelle.

Estelle stood back and gestured. "Ruby, this is Delilah Wheeler and Ginnie Tyler. They're my senior staff."

Delilah stuck out her hand. "I'm glad to meet you, Mrs. Bostick. I've heard a lot about you."

Ruby shook Delilah's hand and smiled at the attempt of cordiality.

Ginnie extended her hand. "I've been to Palomino and your theater, Mrs. Bostick. I'm pleased to meet you."

Ruby nodded at Ginnie's sincerity.

"It is my pleasure to meet Miss Estelle's senior staff."

"Why don't you two give us a few minutes," Estelle said. "When we've concluded our business, you can come in, and we'll talk about your plan to entertain out at the camp."

After Delilah closed the door, Ruby sat again on the sofa.

Estelle sat behind her desk and opened the middle drawer.

"Delilah and Ginnie are good girls, Ruby, they are really popular. You'd like em if you got to know em."

"Ginnie seemed sincere, but I don't know about that Delilah."

"Both are good earners, and they're not boozers."

She withdrew a pack of Chesterfield cigarettes, slipped one out, stuck it between bright red lips, and lit it.

Ruby pulled an Old Gold from the pack in her purse and flamed the cigarette. She rose from the sofa but left her purse there. She stood by one of the armchairs and flicked ashes into the ashtray on the desk.

"Would you like a cognac, Ruby?"

"Yes, that would be nice."

Estelle brought out a Hennessy quart and two glasses from the bottom drawer of the file cabinet. She poured the brandy and set the uncapped bottle aside. Estelle handed the drink to Ruby. They toasted by touching the lips of their glasses, then sipped ceremoniously before they sat down.

"What brings you to town so early in the morning?"

"I'm looking for one of my associates. I thought he might have checked in here."

"Which one? Moe, Larry, or Curly?"

Ruby laughed. "You were always a card, Estelle."

"We were a good pair twenty years ago, Ruby. We were like sisters. Whatever happened to those good ole times?"

"Well, Benjamin was one of the things that happened." Ruby canted her head and smiled. "And two years, four months, and twenty-six days in the Bexar County jail."

"I'm sorry, Ruby. I've said I'm sorry a thousand times, and it's still not enough is it?"

"It is, Estelle, I just can't resist reminding you. It's part of the fun."

"Do you miss Benny?"

"Sometimes, but I get over it."

"Well, I don't. I loved Benny."

"I know you did. And in his own wild way, he loved you too."

They fell silent, sipped brandy, and smoked. Finally, Estelle snubbed out her cigarette and leaned forward.

"Who are you looking for?"

Ruby put out her own smoke and rubbed her fingers over the ashtray. She leaned back in the chair.

"M D Draggert. If he's here, he probably registered as Milton."

Estelle snorted.   "Yep, Milton *was* here, until Thursday. Jim Dudley checked him out but didn't pay Milton's overdue rent."

"Why did the Sheriff pick him up instead of the Chief?"

"No room in the inn. City jail is a whirlwind rotation of gamblers, panhandlers, and soldiers, not to mention the out-of-towners coming in to make a dollar. Day and night goings-on were an administrative nightmare, so the Chief made an agreement with the Sheriff to hold thieves and criminals."

"How much does M D owe?"

"Ten days at three-twenty-five a day."

Ruby rose from the chair and lifted her purse off the sofa. She withdrew three tens and handed them toward Estelle. "I don't have any ones, will thirty do?"

"Of course." The Madame took the money and folded it into her brassiere, above her left breast. "Your Milton has sticky fingers."

Ruby smiled. "Yes, I believe he does. That's one of the reasons I'm looking for him."

"Story goes he lifted a couple of packs of cigarettes and four Baby-Ruth candy bars from a shelf over at

301

Mason's Grocery. It was so out in the open the cashier and two customers saw him do it. When the cashier called him on it, he ran out of the store and right up to his room here. He's not a smart kid, got shit for brains."

Ruby nodded. "He's lacking in that regard, runs in the family."

"When Jim came looking and described him from witness accounts, the boy was easy to identify. Big boy with black, Brylcreemed hair, and overalls. Did he take something from you?"

"Yes. I believe he has. That's why I'm looking for him. I'd like to get it back."

"The Sheriff asked Mason what he wanted to do. The grocer said the boy needed to pay for the merchandise, stay a week in jail, and pay a fine. If I know Jim Dudley, he don't want to spend county money to feed the boy three meals a day for seven days. Are you gonna bail him out?"

"I suppose so. I'll get the lawyer to handle it so I can avoid direct involvement. I need to see Brainard anyway on other business he's handling for me."

Estelle took a deep breath and stood.

Ruby put her purse under her left arm and stuck her hand out for a handshake.

Instead, Estelle came around the desk and wrapped her arms around Ruby.

"I love you, Ruby."

"I know you do."

Estelle kissed Ruby on the lips and held the embrace.

Ruby put her right arm around Estelle and held the

kiss.

They separated, moved close again, and kissed before Ruby turned toward the door. "Goodbye, Essey."

"Bye, Love."

Ruby walked past Delilah and Ginnie, who were sitting together on a divan in the lobby. "Good day, Ladies."

"Oh, Miss Ruby," Ginnie said, "I hear you've got German prisoners in Palomino?"

"Yes, we do. Three of them."

"Is one of them named Eddy?"

Ruby paused. "Why, yes. How would you know that Ginnie?"

"I think they were on the way when we met them. They were on the side of the highway taking a leak. Delilah stopped, and we talked a bit. I thought Eddy was cute. Would you tell him Ginnie said hi."

"I will, Ginnie. I'll tell him for you."

Outside, Ruby motioned to Julius.

He got out but stayed on the street by the car. "Yessum?"

"I've got business here with Mr. Baldwin, then I'll get us some sandwiches for dinner. We'll have to wait awhile, I think, because I'm expecting to bring somebody with us in the car back to Palomino. Are you alright?"

"Yessum, nobody been botherin me."

"Okay, get back in the car. This may take thirty minutes. Then we'll eat."

"Yessum."

Ruby turned on her heels and went to the lawyer's

door.

Julius returned to the Chrysler and watched Miss Ruby as she paused a moment before going through the door.

"Hello, Miss Ruby."

"Hello, Jane, is Mr. Baldwin in?"

"Ruby," Baldwin called from his office. "Come in here and give me a hug."

Ruby went into his office and let him hug her.

B. D. Baldwin was cigarette thin and sported a black pencil mustache on his gaunt face. Several long strands of hair lay across his crown. He adjusted wire-framed glasses and grinned. "I was just thinking about you, Ruby. The codicil is all done. All we need is your signature and the signature of two witnesses."

Ruby held up her hand, turned, and went out the office door. She signaled for Julius.

When he joined her on the sidewalk, she spoke. "There is a document in the lawyer's office I want you to be a witness to. All you have to do is put your mark or signature on the paper in the place Mr. Baldwin will point out. Will you do that?"

"Yessum."

Julius followed Ruby inside. "I'm ready to sign, and I've brought Julius, my witness. Jane can be the other witness."

Formalities done and notary stamp applied, Julius went back to the car.

"If you'll excuse us, Jane, I'd like to talk with Brainard."

"Yes, Mam. I'll put your copy of the documents in an envelope for you. When you're ready, they'll be on

304

my desk."

Jane closed the door.

Ruby sat in the cane-bottomed straight chair in front of Baldwin's desk.

"What do you want me to do, Ruby?"

She opened her purse and withdrew two twenties. She leaned forward and placed the money on his desk.

"There's a boy in Jim's jail. He owes a little money for minor stuff he stole at Mason's and a small fine. Get him out and bring him to me. I'll take him back to Palomino."

"You mean now?"

"Why would I mean some other time, Brainard? I'm here now, I don't want to come back another time to pick up the boy. Take the money, pay the grocer, pay the fine, and bring the boy to me, here, in your office. You can keep the change."

"It's almost dinnertime, Ruby. It may take awhile to get Jim to let the boy out."

"I'll wait, Brainard. Now go get it done."

"What's the boy's name?"

"M D Draggert. He may be in jail under the name Milton."

"What'd he take from Mason's?"

"Two packs of Chesterfield cigarettes and four Baby-Ruth candy bars. Forty cents of merchandise. Pay Mason a dollar and the Jew'll be happy."

"My goodness, Ruby. You know they're killin em."

"Who?"

"The Jews."

"What are you talking about?"

"The Germans are sending thousands of Jews to

concentration camps and death camps, Ruby. You've seen the papers, the newsreels. Hitler's government even bragged about opening Dachau ten years ago."

Ruby stared at him.

"Why do you call Mason a Jew? You know he's a Baptist."

"He acts like a Jew, raising his prices."

"He can't raise his prices. There's rationing. The government controls the prices. And if he did raise prices his customers would turn him in."

"Look, Brainard, I came here to finish the codicil and get the boy. So, are you going to do what I pay you to do or not?"

Baldwin scooped up the two twenties. "I'll do what I can. Come back to my office in a couple of hours."

Ruby went to the car. Julius dismounted and opened the back door for her.

"We'll drive the couple of blocks over to Tiny's. We'll get a sandwich and drink for dinner."

Traffic was light, and Julius was lucky once more. A parking slot was open ten steps from the cafe door.

Julius opened the car door for Ruby. When she got out, he touched her arm.

Aware, she looked at him. "What is it?"

"I gots to go, Miss Ruby."

"Number one or number two?"

Julius smiled. "Just number one."

Ruby pointed. "See the alley. Walk around to the back door, I'll tell Tiny. She'll let you in to use the bathroom."

"Yessum."

Julius locked the car and headed for the alley.

Ruby entered the cafe and went directly to Tiny.

She laid two dollars on the counter. "I need to use the men's restroom."

Tiny grinned. "Really, Ruby?"

She shoved the money forward. "It's for Julius, my chauffeur. He's colored. He needs to go real bad."

"Number one or number two?"

"One. He's at the back door now."

"Okay."

"And we want to eat dinner in your kitchen."

Tiny agreed. "Okay, go bring him in. I'll stop anybody who wants to go to the bathroom while he's in there. You keep your money, Ruby."

Relieved, Julius stood at the back door as instructed while Ruby ordered their dinner. When the sandwiches were prepared, she opened the screen door and motioned him inside. They sat side-by-side eating a hamburger and drinking cold drinks. The cook and waitress ignored them.

Tiny came in and leaned on the table.

"How are my two girls doin, Ruby? I sure miss em."

"Teresa and Tina are doing just fine, Tiny. I really like them, especially Tina. She's full of energy and mischief. Sometimes she reminds me of me when I was her age. You know, I look at Tina and think about the possibility if she were kin, like a granddaughter. How would I treat a favorite granddaughter?"

"She *is* special. How are Twig's Germans faring in Palomino? Are they still alive?"

Ruby chuckled. "They get by. As time goes along, most people in Palomino seem to accept the Germans a little more every day. They all want to live in America when the war is over. I think two of them have girlfriends already."

"Girl friends or *girlfriends?*"

"Girlfriends. They found love with Martin Church's oldest girls, Odessa and Dallas. Even Ginnie at Estelle's asked me to tell Eddy hi for her."

"Well, after all, there ain't a lot of young men around anymore. A girl's gotta latch onto whatever's handy."

Ruby laughed. "They may be latching onto it alright."

Julius felt embarrassed sitting there listening to Ruby and Tiny go on about white folks messing around. He stood and wiped his mouth with a napkin.

"Excuse me, Miss Ruby, Miss Tiny. I'll go on back to the car now."

"I'll be along in a minute," Ruby said.

"Thank you, Miss Tiny, for using your bathroom. The hamburger and the Coca-Cola was a good one."

"You're welcome, Julius. I'm glad you liked Mae's cooking."

After Julius left, Tiny whispered. "He is a good man, Ruby. I hope you treat him well."

"I do, Tiny. I treat Julius and his wife, Ethel, like family." Ruby stared blankly and nodded. She lowered her head, her voice almost a whisper. "Julius and Ethel are the only family I have now. And Teresa and little Tina."

"Uh huh."

Ruby stood. "I'm going to the ladies room and then I'll go to Brainard's office. He's taking care of a little business for me."

Tiny stepped forward and hugged Ruby.

"Don't squeeze too hard, Tiny, you'll make me pee in my pants."

Julius got out of the car and opened the door when he saw Ruby come out of the cafe.

Before she got in, he spoke softly to her. "Thank you, Miss Ruby."

She patted his arm. "You're welcome, Julius. Let's go back to the lawyer's office."

Julius drove down the street and made left turns at the end of each block to get back to Brainard's office. The parking slot was still open and he pulled into it.

Brainard and M D were standing in front of Jane's desk when Ruby entered.

"Here's your boy, Ruby."

"Okay, Brainard, thank you."

"Mason accepted the dollar for the cigarettes and candy. Sheriff Dudley assessed a five dollar fine."

"Okay, Brainard. Thank you."

"When I told your boy here you were the one who paid everything and was waitin for him in my office, he didn't want to come."

"Is that right?"

"But Sheriff said he had to go, he wasn't goin to let him stay in jail."

"I know why you want me," M D said.

"Good, M D, that'll make it easier. You know there's something we need to talk about when we get back."

"I didn't tell the Sheriff about anything."

Ruby set her jaw and eyed the potential danger standing tall over her. She glanced at Baldwin to see his reaction to the statement and was satisfied the lawyer had no clue what M D was talking about.

"Well, you did the right thing, M D. Now, come on with me. I'll take you home. Your momma is probably worried sick you been gone so long."

"Don't forget the envelope on Jane's desk."

Julius saw them coming up the sidewalk, got out, and opened the back door.

"You ride up front," Ruby said.

M D got in the passenger seat as instructed.

"Let's go home, Julius."

"Yessum."

Julius knew there was something bad between the passenger and Miss Ruby.

He knew his boss and sneaked several glances at her face in the rear view mirror during the seventeen-mile drive from the office of B. D. Baldwin to the driveway of the Porter House.

The trip was in stone cold, deadly, silence.

THE PRESENT
December 1943
German bomb hits Allied cargo ship carrying
Mustard gas, 83 dead
Japanese destroyer sunk by American submarine
near Okinawa

Thick, gray Stratus clouds produced a light drizzle, which looked like fog that hadn't touched the ground. From Billy Don's Cities Service station, a sprinkle stayed with the small party for six miles. As they came closer to their destination the rain stopped, yet the dark, low veil remained.

Deputy Stanton drove; David Sunday rode in the passenger seat with Deputy Mavis Raymond in the back. Aubrey followed the sheriff's sedan in his pickup with his hounds in the trailer. Twig and his prisoners in the jeep, trailer loaded with gear, brought up the rear of the little convoy.

At the south end of the Sulphur River Bridge, two signs announced US Highway 271 South and entry into Franklin County. Stephan turned right and eased down the rough, bumpy trail for a couple of hundred feet. He stopped the car and rolled down his window.

On Stephan's signal, Aubrey pulled around and took the lead. The three vehicles moved forward again for another half mile, maybe more, before Aubrey stopped and got out of his truck.

Aubrey pumped a balled fist pointing with his index finger toward the ground as he spoke. "This is about where I left the trailer. Right here. I think. Right here."

Stephan rolled up the window, shut down the engine, and turned off the car's headlights. Deputies and soldiers dismounted their vehicles, and the seven of them gathered in a cluster. They looked at Aubrey, waiting.

Aubrey stared back.

The hounds were restless and stirred in the confined space. One whined, anxious for the hunt, another panted. Black noses stuck through small squares of the rabbit wire walls of the trailer, sniffing and scenting, seeking release.

Dave Sunday snorted. "Well, old man, you got to give us more information than just jabbing at the dirt."

"This is the spot, right here. This is where I left the trailer."

"Good Lord, Aubrey, we're not here to look at where your hounds come home," Sunday said. "We here to make a . . ."

"Thanks, Dave." Stephan's voice was soft, measured. "Aubrey, can you give us an idea where you think the hounds treed?"

Aubrey pointed to the woods. "I'd say about fifty to sixty yards in there, maybe more."

"Okay, half the length of a football field?" Stephan looked at the tree line and shook his head.

He shifted so he could see the search party's faces. "We're looking for Logan Amesa, looking for any clue or evidence, for anything unusual that will tell us where he is if he's here.

"But I can't believe those two boys who kidnapped him would walk him fifty to sixty yards into the woods to kill him."

He looked at the woods again. "My guess is, if he's here, he won't be more than ten or fifteen yards into the woods."

No one spoke. Even the dogs grew quiet. The prisoners watched an experienced Texas law enforcement officer at work and were impressed.

"Okay, here's the plan," Stephan continued, "we'll stay abreast, at arm's length, and move slowly. Each forward step is a measured advance. When a tree or obstacle prevents straight-line progress, others will pause until we overcome the interference."

Stephan scanned their faces. "Any questions?"

"No questions," Twig said. "I need to get stuff out of the trailer before we start."

"Okay, go ahead. We have stuff in the trunk to get too. Aubrey, why don't you release the hounds? Maybe they'll go back to the place they found during the night and bark."

"Okay, Stephan. I only brought my best three — Bugger, Red, and Cricket."

"We'll be lucky if they find the place again," Sunday said.

"Well, they're the ones who told me they found

something," Aubrey retorted.

"Well, they ain't bloodhounds, Aubrey, they're foxhounds."

Aubrey opened the trailer door, and the dogs bailed. Two scampered through the tree line; the larger animal paused, sniffed the left front wheel of the sheriff's sedan, raised a leg, and peed for sixteen seconds.

Deputy Raymond laughed. "That hound needed to pee in the worst way. No tellin how long he's been holdin it."

"That's Bugger. Just makin his mark," Aubrey said. "That boy'll piss on anything and everything. You better watch your leg, Sunday."

"Dogs won't mess their house, it's nature," Raymond said. "But when they're penned up too long, they just can't hold it anymore. They go when they gotta go, house or not."

The soldiers went about military business without speaking. Eddy and Will untied the ropes holding the trailer tarp in place. Duke threw back the covering. They selectively withdrew gear. They pulled out web belts with canteens full of water attached and wrapped them around their waists. Each put gloves on, grabbed a flashlight (automatically operating the on-off switch and looked into the light), and hooked it onto the web belt. Each one of them took a backpack, expertly attached an entrenching tool, and slipped the pack on. They each took five tent pegs, individually stuffing them behind the web belt. Next, they pulled a strand of rope and put it around their necks. Finally, each man took one of the five-foot, wooden tent poles with spikes.

Duke dragged the tarp back into place, and he and

Twig retied the restraints.

In a cluster again, Stephan spoke to Twig.

"It looks like you boys are loaded for bear."

Twig smiled. "We're soldiers, Stephan."

"Well, those flashlights and long poles will be a big help. I'm not so sure about the other stuff."

"Tent pegs can mark things on the ground, and we might need rope," Duke said.

It seemed thunder cracked when Duke spoke. Bodies shifted away, and all eyes turned on him.

Duke shrugged. "I am trying to help."

Stephan put a hand on the old man's shoulder.

"Aubrey, your job is to stay here with the vehicles. If your hounds return give me three short blasts on your horn."

"Which one?"

"Which one what?"

"My truck horn or my hunter's horn?"

Stephan grinned. "Use your hunter's horn if the dogs return. Three long blasts on your truck horn for anything else, okay?"

"Yes, Stephan. That's good. Two different signals. Hunter's horn for hounds, truck horn for anything else. Got it."

Stephan spoke to the team. "If you get separated, come back to the trail and rally here at Aubrey's truck. Any questions?"

Stephan stepped to the edge of the trail and faced south. He held out his right arm. "Dave, you'll be on my right, Mavis on Dave's right. Twig, I want you to anchor the right flank so put your boys between you and Mavis."

Without a word, Duke pointed for Will to be on Twig's left, Eddy on Will's left, and he took the space between Mavis and Eddy.

Now, they were lined up facing south on the edge of the narrow pathway.

Stephan accepted the formation and order of march. "Okay, let's start."

The line had taken no more than six steps into the woods when the dogs alerted.

"That's Bugger and Red, Stephan," Aubrey called out. "They're in one place, they're not trailing or chasing. They've found something and are calling for me to come to them."

Stephan resisted the temptation to rush. to the beckoning call of the hounds.

"Stay the line," he said. "Maintain your place and maintain the pace. If they're not running game, they'll wait for us with whatever they've found."

But the searchers did not reach the dogs. Thirteen feet off the trail and another twelve feet into the woods, Eddy saw a glint in a heap of brush from Duke's flashlight.

"Stop," Eddy said. "Stop. I saw something bright from Duke's flashlight, it was a shine, how do you say — glint? A glint? It is in the bush in front of me."

"Okay, halt here," Stephan commanded. "Everybody stay put." He moved to Eddy. "Point where you saw it, I will go near, and you guide me to the spot."

Deputy Amesa lay on his back. His sheriff's badge over the left shirt pocket had reflected the lamp's beam.

316

Brush and broken tree limbs, heaped over him, covered his decayed remains.

Logan's shirtsleeves and trouser legs were gone, disintegrated or torn from his body, dragged away by animals, or used by birds to feather a nest. Remnants of his red tie and the front chest of his once white shirt were visible. His saddle-tan leather belt and weave holster were still in place on the waistband of his khaki pants but were rotted gray-black with decomposition. His Colt .44 was gone, as well as bullets he kept in the belt loops.

For more than an hour, they worked tediously with Twig's machete to trim dead branches and with their entrenching tools to clear undergrowth without disturbing the skeleton.

"Okay, stop for a minute," Stephan said. Without moving, he peered at Logan.

"We're going to need something to put his body on to carry him."

"Ponchos," Twig said. "I've got ponchos in the trailer." He looked at Duke.

Duke and Eddy went to the trailer. They returned with all four ponchos within a couple of minutes.

The prisoners realized they witnessed deep sorrow on Stephan's face. Each of them felt uncomfortable, vulnerable. They knew their presence in the midst of a devastating loss was perilous. They kept quiet and did not move.

"Dave, you and Twig establish a perimeter. Say ten to fifteen feet out. Mark it with your tent pegs and rope, Twig. Search for anything. Search within the circumference."

"What about the hounds?" Mavis asked. "Maybe they found something important?"

"Nothing is more important than Logan," Sunday said. "We brought the dogs to find him but they run off chasin rabbits or something."

Stephan pointed at Deputy Raymond. "Mavis, go tell Aubrey we've found Logan. Then, take the car, go to the office. Call Sheriff Blake and tell him we've found Logan, and notify Sheriff Gregg's office. Bring Doc Bledsoe here. He'll have to perform medical examiner duties at a crime scene, and Doc needs to call Zellman to come down here with a hearse for Logan."

They roped off the area while Stephan knelt on the soaked ground. With his pocketknife, he cut the thin fabric and took Logan's badge. He gingerly opened the shirt pocket and removed Logan's small notebook.

He left the wristwatch alone, but delicately slipped Logan's gold wedding band off the bone and put it, along with the badge, in his pocket.

He opened the notebook and read Logan's note of reminder silently.

Fay and Lou are sick, ask Doc Bledsoe for medicine. I love my wife and baby girl. Tell them. Tell them of my love.

He turned the page.

green dodge. uncle sam. 2 boys.

lic. 8-9-6-7-1-8.

cigarettes, baby ruth candy bars.

John Bennett, short, 5-5, 5-6, reddish hair, green eyes, smartass.

Joe Jenkins, big boy, 6 feet, 6-2, overalls, black eyes, black brillcream hair parted in the middle.

The prisoners, with Dave and Twig, watched and waited.

Stephan looked at them. "I took Logan's wedding ring and badge," he said. "I intend to give them to Fay."

The driver of the Montgomery Ward truck parallel parked behind cars in front of Dulfeine's grocery. He opened the back doors, hopped up into the bay, and pushed the wide, elongated cardboard box to the tailgate's edge. He jumped down, efficiently slid the box out, and grasped it under his arm. He slammed the doors, fastened the latch, mounted the sidewalk, and quick-stepped into the store.

"I have a delivery for Mrs. Teresa Chestnutt."

"Here, young man," Margie Dulfeine called. "I'm Mrs. Dulfeine. Bring the box up the stairs, back there, and leave it along the back wall, under the window. I'll sign for Mrs. Chestnutt."

Once delivery was complete, the driver went on his way.

During this time, it was normal for folks to wonder why a young man was not in uniform. Margie was no exception, but she held her tongue – even though she was dying to ask him why he was able to drive a delivery truck for a national department store instead of carrying a rifle somewhere over there. Exemptions, she mused, real and purchased, were handed out like peppermint sticks. Margie knew there were some who avoided the call to arms, but many more who served their country's need, like Curtis Kline.

Nate came through the door.

"Where did you run off to?" Margie asked. "One minute you and Casey are in here talking, the next second you're gone?"

"Did you not hear Dora screaming?"

"Dora was screaming? Good Lord, what happened?"

"Navy men came to tell them Curtis is missing at sea and presumed dead. His plane crashed into the ocean — or he was shot down, they're not sure. Search planes couldn't find him or his crew, so they finally stopped looking because of more pressing business."

Tears welled in Margie's eyes. "Oh, my goodness."

"I think it would be a good idea if you went to Dora. Maybelle was there, thank goodness, to help her, to hold her. Casey and me heard her screams and went there to see what was wrong. Kingston was in bad shape, too. The Navy Lieutenant told us about Curtis. Months ago, I told Kingston that Curtis would be okay, and now he's not. I feel so bad for them. Curtis was a good boy, a good son."

"I'll go to Dora. She'll need her friends. By the way, the Montgomery Ward truck driver brought Teresa's present. I had the boy bring it upstairs. I told him to put it under the window on the back wall." Margie couldn't help herself. "The truck driver is safe driving around the county delivering presents for Christmas."

"So?"

"He's about the same age as Curtis."

Julius stopped the Chrysler in the driveway and opened the door for Miss Ruby.

M D got out and came around the back of the car to face her.

"Go wait on the back porch," she told him. "I'll be there in a minute. We need to talk about important matters, you hear?"

"Yes, Miss Ruby."

She watched him walk alongside the house and turn the corner.

She spoke to Julius. "Take the car." She handed a dollar bill to Julius. "Go to Henry's and buy two lemon pies for supper."

Julius took the money. "Yessum. Will you need the car later, Miss Ruby?"

"No. Now, go on."

Ruby went in the kitchen and spoke to Ethel. "I sent Julius to Henry's for lemon pie tonight. As soon as I put my purse and hat away, I'll be talking with a visitor on the back porch."

"Mr. Twig and his Germans ain't come home. They may not be back for supper. Miss Teresa and Miss Tina been workin at the cafe but they should be home any minute now."

The moment Ethel said the words, they heard Tina and Teresa come in and close the front door.

"Well, they're home," Ethel said.

"In a minute I'll be on the back porch."

"Yessum."

Ruby tossed her purse on her bed and opened the closet door. Her mouth went slack standing there with one hand on her hat, the other fiddling with the hatpin.

Arms raised, she froze and stared at the six skewed box lids.

She withdrew the pin, removed the hat, reinserted the pin, and placed the hat on top of a shelf. Ruby knelt. She touched the lids but did not move them.

"ETHEL. ETHEL."

From the kitchen. "Yes, Miss Ruby. I'm here. I'm here, Lordamercy."

Ethel appeared at Ruby's doorway but did not enter her bedroom. "Yessum?"

Ruby's strident voice softened, she controlled her anger. "What were you looking for?"

"Mam?"

"What were you looking for? In the boxes? In my closet? What were you looking for?"

"I didn't look for nothin in your closet, Miss Ruby. I ain't been in there since you asked me to."

"Well, somebody has. Come in here. Look in my closet. Look at all the lids moved around."

Ethel grasped her apron, stretched her neck, and cautiously ventured into Miss Ruby's boudoir. She sidestepped to be able to peer into the closet but did not approach it. When she saw the lids, she gasped. "Oh my, oh my."

"When I left this morning all the lids were in place, on the right boxes. Now look at that. Somebody has opened every box and scattered the lids. Who's been in here?"

"I swear, Miss Ruby, I ain't been in your closet in a long time. There ain't nothin in there that I needs to be goin . . ."

"Tina."

Ruby didn't shout, but Ethel jumped anyway.

"Tina, that little rascal." Ruby stared through Ethel.

Seconds passed before Ruby waved her hand for Ethel to clear the way. She rushed around her housekeeper and marched up the stairs to Teresa's door. Ruby inhaled deeply before tapping softly on the wooden panel.

"Teresa? Teresa? It's Ruby. May I speak with you?"

Teresa opened the door. Her smile faded from the cold blankness covering Ruby's face. "Yes, Miss Ruby?"

"I'm sorry, Darling. I wonder if I could speak with Tina?"

Wary, Teresa canted her head. "Is something wrong?"

Ruby struggled to show patience. She inhaled deeply before speaking. "When I got home just now, I found someone had gone through the boxes on my closet floor. All six boxes. All of the lids were out of place so it was obvious someone had opened them. Ethel told me she did not disturb the boxes, and I know you would never go into my bedroom closet without permission."

"Yes, I see. Of course. I must tell you that I did ask Ethel this morning if you were up and about. When she said you had left early on business, I asked if I could bring Tina in your closet so she could get her present out of the box. Ethel said no, so we did not go in there."

"Ethel did not, you did not, so I'm wondering if I may speak with Tina to ask if she did? Do you mind?" Ruby's question was a blunt demand.

For a second, Teresa hesitated. Her thought was to question Tina privately, whether she had gone into Ruby's box. But since this seemed an urgent matter of their landlord's protocol, Teresa relented. After all, she was aware Ruby had admonished Tina to stay out of a box in the back porch storage closet, which Ethel had said Julius moved to Ruby's bedroom closet. Anyway, Teresa did not think Ruby was threatening Tina, accusing her of an invasion. She just wanted to ask a question.

Teresa pushed open the door, stepped aside, and invited Ruby in.

"Tina's in her room, we can go through the bathroom."

Teresa closed the door and led the way.

Tina's bathroom door was open, and they could see her standing at the foot of her bed.

In a low, animated voice, Tina was talking to the present that sat regally on the bedspread.

"Tina?"

Startled, Tina brought both hands to her chest, jumped, and squealed.

"I'm sorry, Sweetie, I didn't mean to frighten you."

Tina gathered herself and faced her mother and Miss Ruby.

"I was just practicing, Momma."

"Tina, Miss Ruby wants to ask you about something."

Ruby controlled herself and spoke to the child in a civil tone. "Tina, Sweetheart. You remember the box in the closet on the back porch? The one your present was in?"

"Yes, Mam."

"I was wondering about the box, about the present, Sweetheart?"

Tina turned and lifted the gift-wrapped box off the bed. "I was just practicing. I was going to put it under the tree, but since we don't have a tree . . ."

Tina moved to Ruby and reached out with the present. "Merry Christmas, Miss Ruby. This present is for you because you have been so nice to me and my momma and my daddy and Will and Eddy and Duke and everybody and I wanted . . . I wanted . . ."

Tina forgot the rest of her speech. She presented the gift with outstretched arms. "This present is for you, Miss Ruby. I put my school picture in a frame so you can look at me and remember me."

Both Teresa and Ruby sucked wind.

Ruby took the small box, wrapped with a red ribbon, from the child's hands. "Oh, my Lord," she whispered. "Sweet Jesus."

Teresa watched tears well in Ruby's eyes and became embarrassed for her. "Tina, that is so nice of you to give Miss Ruby her present."

Ruby sniffed and wiped her nose with the back of her hand. "Thank you, Tina." Ruby looked at Teresa. "Now I know I've done the right thing . . . a nice present."

"I don't mind if you want to open it now, Miss Ruby. Christmas is not too far away, anyway."

Teresa held out her hands for the ribbon and paper Ruby pulled away.

Ruby pinched and lifted the lid. Teresa took that too.

325

Ruby withdrew the frame.

She held it so Teresa could see the picture.

They smiled at a beaming face with bright sparkling eyes that reflected the school photographer's lighting, and the huge grin exposing new front teeth beginning to fill in gaps.

SECRETS
December 1943
German infantry exterminate most of the men and
boys in Kalavryta, Greece
Thanksgiving comes late; Christmas comes early for
Marines on Tarawa

Eddy heard her soft voice and felt warm fingers
around his wrist.

"Pulse was normal," she said, "but now it's slightly
elevated."

"That's because you're holding onto his hand,
Jeannie. Nurses in hospitals have that effect on men.
Young men, anyway."

He turned his head toward the voices.

"He moved. I think he's waking, Kitty."

"That's a good sign. I'll let Doctor Bledsoe know."

"Tell Deputy Stanton too. He's in the waiting room
with the others."

Eddy smacked his lips and swiped his tongue across
them to create moisture and wipe away dryness. He
opened his eyes and grimaced from the excruciating,
searing agony of pain that creased his forehead when

he shifted them upward searching for the sources of voices.

She was dressed in white. Her eyes were blue. Her hair was blonde. To him, she looked as beautiful as girls he remembered in Wiesbaden.

She brought a cup with a straw up to his mouth.

"Here, drink some water."

Eddy clasped the straw with his lips and pulled in the liquid. He did not move his head, but opened his mouth to release the straw.

"My name is Jeannie."

"Gin . . . Gin . . . Ginnie? My Ginnie?"

"No, Jeannie. It's Jean. With a J. Jeannie."

"My head hurts. My ears ring."

"Yes, I know. You've been hurt. Kitty has gone for Doctor Bledsoe. He'll explain things for you."

"My friends? My friends are here?"

"Yes. Wait until the doctor . . . oh, here he is now."

"Hello, young man, I see you're still with us. How do we feel?"

Eddy blinked. "We?"

Doc chuckled. "Good. That's good. Yes, how do *you* feel? Any pain, headache, numbness, ringing in your ears?"

"Yes, my head hurts, and my ears ring."

Doc Bledsoe sat on the edge of Eddy's bed. He pulled a slim penlight out of his shirt pocket and adjusted his head mirror. He grasped Eddy's chin with his fingers and shined a beam of light in Eddy's left eye, then the right one, peering through the hole in the center of the mirror.

Doc's face was so close Eddy could smell pipe

tobacco.

Doc breathed through stuffed up nostrils. "Hummmmm . . . good dilation . . . uh huh . . . good skin color, skin feels normal."

Eddy tried to withdraw his head from the vise, but Doc held on tight.   "The light is bright," Eddy complained.

Doc turned off the light and raised the head mirror. He turned his head away and sneezed, twice.

"God bless you," Jeannie said.

"Thank you.

"You've had a bad knock on your head, young man. That's why your head hurts, and you hear ringing." Doc stuck the penlight back into his shirt pocket. "With aspirin, that'll go away soon enough, I think. I stitched the split in your scalp.   That's why a bandage is wrapped around your head. We're going to keep you here in the hospital for observation, for a day or so. Do you have any questions?"

Eddy blinked. He had a thousand questions but he couldn't think which one to ask first.

Jeannie spoke. "He drank a cup full of water a few minutes ago."

"Good, that's good," Doc said. "Has he been to the bathroom?"

"No, he just woke up, that's why Kitty came for you. He asked for his friends."

Doc patted Eddy's shoulder.   "Your friends and Deputy Stanton are in the waiting room. I think it'll be alright if they visit for a couple of minutes. Okay, Jeannie, I'll be in my office. Bring his friends in. Just for a couple of minutes though."

"Yes, Doctor."

Doc Bledsoe and Jeannie disappeared.

Eddy smacked his lips again. He turned his head slowly to see his surroundings. With mouth open in a huge yawn, a bolt of pain shot up his neck through the top of his head. The ringing in his ears rushed louder. He grunted and moaned from the throbbing pressure in his temples. He heard Jeannie's voice but did not move to look her way. Then he heard Twig's voice before he appeared at the bedside.

Twig touched Eddy's arm. "I'm glad you're awake. We were worried about you."

Duke appeared next to Twig. Then Will came into view. "You are lucky, Eddy," Will said.

Twig saw the question in Eddy's face and eyes. "Did the Doctor tell you what happened?"

"No."

Deputy Stanton appeared on the other side of the bed. "Well, Eddy, Doc Bledsoe thinks you're going to be okay. He wants to keep you for a day or so for observation. Just in case."

Eddy looked at Twig.

Twig shrugged. "Deputy Sunday hit you in the head with an entrenching tool."

"He didn't mean to hit you, Eddy. It was an accident," Stephan said. He nodded his head to reinforce the affirmative. "It was an accident. Deputy Sunday feels bad about what happened."

"Deputy Sunday was using the shovel as a pick," Twig said. "He was spiking and digging around . . . so . . . so we could put ponchos . . ." His voice trailed off.

"The deputy on the ground?" Eddy asked. "We

were going to put ponchos under to pick him up."

"Yes. So you remember that. That's good," Twig said. "Deputy Sunday was swinging down and up hard and fast, with a lot of force, to cut the ground."

"I was bringing ponchos and tent poles."

"The back-swing hit you, Eddy," Duke said. "A bloody gash."

"You are lucky the spike end of the shovel did not hit your head," Will said.

"We were shocked," Stephan said. "Dave thought he killed you. He was very shaken by what happened."

"When Doctor Bledsoe arrived with the hearse, we put you in it. Doc took care of you first, brought you here to the Bogata hospital," Stephan said. "Then he returned with the hearse for Deputy Amesa."

"You've been here about six, seven hours," Twig said. "We were in the waiting room for an hour or so. After we finished in the woods."

Jeannie approached. "I'm sorry to interrupt, but Doctor Bledsoe said only a couple of minutes, and it's been almost five."

"Okay, boys, say goodbye for now," Twig said. "Eddy, I have no choice but to leave you here, without supervision. You have to give me your word. It's all I can ask. It's all I have."

"Yes, Sergeant Chestnutt," Eddy said. "It is all I can give you. You have my word as a soldier, I will not try to escape, and I will not hurt anyone."

"Thank you, Eddy. I will come back tomorrow morning."

"We'll look in on him for you, Twig," Stephan said. "He'll be taken good care of."

Jeannie watched them walk away.

"Can I bring you anything?"

"Water. I would like water," Eddy said. "Pretty please?"

Jeannie smiled. "Pretty please is an American expression, maybe even a Texas expression."

"I lived in America before the war. Near Milwaukee. My father worked at the Pabst brewery. He was fishing on Lake Michigan. A speedboat rammed his boat. He was hurt and fell in the water. He drowned. My mother and I returned to Germany before the war. I was called to serve in the Wehrmacht."

Jeannie touched his shoulder. "I'm sorry about your daddy."

"You are very beautiful, Jeannie. I guess all the Texas boys tell you that."

"I have heard it before, but it sounds sweet coming from you."

Jeannie stared at Eddy, and he met her gaze. Their eyes were locked for the longest time before he spoke.

"I would like water, pretty please, and I would like to hold your hand, Jeannie."

She was holding his hand when they came in. A gentleman, Pinky had pulled the door open so Patsy could enter first.

She did not speak, but her slight nod was enough thanks to please Pinky. She released his hand and led the way to the counter stools.

Teresa picked up a coffee pot and spoke. "Hello,

Patsy. Hi, Pinky. Is it still chilly outside?"

"Yes, Mam," they said in unison.

Patsy sat before Pinky straddled a stool and slid into place.

"What can I get you?"

"We were looking for Mr. Twig," Patsy said.

"Oh. Okay. Let me serve this coffee, I'll be right back."

Teresa moved away and went to a table behind them to pour coffee for customers.

Pinky leaned in close to Patsy and whispered. "Are you sure you want to do this?"

She replied in a whisper without looking at him. "Yes. Now we talked about this. Don't you go start crawfishin on me, you hear? We're in this together."

"What if we tell and he goes and asks questions? That's the first thing he's gonna do, you know that Patsy. And when he asks the first person about it, their answer is gonna be a question, 'who told you'? And then he'll tell our names."

"Twig would never reveal his sources. I'm sure he's listened to Treacher Tracer on the radio and heard how detectives say that."

"Shhhh, she's coming back."

They watched Teresa move around the end of the counter, place the pot on the stove, and come to stand in front of them.

"Why are you looking for Constable Chestnutt?"

"Could we please have a ice cream soda? Two straws, please?" Pinky ordered.

Teresa smiled. "Oh, of course. Coming right up."

In a whisper. "Why did you do that? Why didn't

you tell her?"

"Because, Patsy, I'm not sure now. We could be in big trouble."

They fell silent and watched Teresa make the order. In a few seconds, she placed the tall, flare-topped glass in front of Patsy and stuck two straws in the ice cream.

"Why are you looking for Constable Chestnutt?"

"We have a secret to tell him," Patsy said. She looked at Pinky.

Teresa smiled again. "Oh, I see. A secret for the police?"

Patsy blinked. "Maybe."

"Well, he's not here. He's in Bogata working on another police matter."

The children leaned forward, wrapped lips around their straws, and drew in Coca-Cola with bits of vanilla ice cream.

"Will you tell him we have a secret to tell him, Miss Teresa?" Pinky ventured.

"Yes, I will. As soon as he comes home. Should he come to your houses or will you come to the Porter House?"

"No, no, no." Pinky's response was rapid fire. "We'll wait."

Teresa's interest in their dilemma turned to concern from the quickness and tone of Pinky's "nos".

She placed her arms on the counter and leaned in close to Patsy.

"Okay. What's wrong? What's going on?"

Patsy's bravado waned. She liked Teresa, liked her spunk, liked how she stood bold.

334

"Pinky found a sack in Miss Ruby's barn."

Pinky gulped and skewered Patsy with his glaring stare.

Teresa penned Pinky with her black eyes.

"A sack?"

Patsy looked at her future husband, tilted her head, and narrowed her eyes.

Pinky wilted. "It was full of money and a gun," he whispered. "But I didn't take it." He looked at Patsy then back to Teresa. "We didn't take the sack, and we didn't take any of the money. I left it in the barn. And we didn't take the gun."

Teresa nodded. She leaned closer and whispered. "I see. What kind of sack?"

"A flour sack," Patsy whispered.

"Oh, Teresa?" a customer called. "Could we have some more coffee, please?"

Teresa straightened. "Both of you stay put," she whispered. Then, "I'll bring it over right away, Ben. More cream?"

"No, just coffee."

Teresa lifted the pot up and moved away.

"Well, you spilled your guts. Why didn't you just say it was a sack with things in it?"

"Cause. The next thing she'd of asked was what was the things in the sack? Anyway, you started this mess. You told her I found the sack."

The cafe door opened and Nate Dulfeine came in. He greeted the customers by name. He sat on the stool next to Pinky and greeted both the children by name too.

"Kind of a chilly day for an ice cream soda," he

said.

Teresa came back and picked a mug off the shelf. She poured until Dulfeine waved his hand.

"I'll put a fresh pot on, be just a minute." She turned away and became busy filling the eight-cup pot with water. She scooped coffee out of the red Hills Bros Coffee tin and dumped it into the percolator basket.

Nate spoke to her back. "Kingston and Dora's boy, Curtis, is missing at sea. The Navy just came to tell them. They're heartbroken."

Teresa turned to look at him. "That is so terrible. I am so sorry for them." She finished making the coffee and put the stainless steel pot on the stove. "This war . . ."

"Not so long ago I told Kingston his boy would be alright. Now, I feel terrible I said anything."

Teresa faced him and touched his hand. "They know you meant well."

Dulfeine turned to Pinky and Patsy. "What are you two up to?"

They sat up and looked at Teresa.

"They've been telling me about their Christmas plans."

Both sighed with relief. Patsy adored Teresa.

"Oh, I almost forgot why I came over. A Montgomery Ward driver brought your package awhile ago. Margie had him put it upstairs. Where is Twig?"

"He's in Bogata. He's helping the deputy sheriffs over there."

"Well, ask him to let me know when he wants to

assemble it. If it's after we've closed the store, I'll come down and let him in. I'd think an hour or two for him to put the pieces together."

"Thank you, Nate. I'll tell him. He and the boys should be back this evening. I hope by tonight, anyway."

Dulfeine got off the stool and pulled a quarter from his pocket. "Give the change to Tina. Where is she?"

"In the kitchen. Bobbie Jo is letting her help make cornbread."

"Okay, tell Twig to let me know. He's only got a couple of days before . . ."

"He'll come see you."

Dulfeine left. Teresa leaned in close again.

"What did you do with the sack?"

"I put it back on the nail, where I found it."

"Did anybody see you?"

Pinky shook his head. "I don't think so." Then he paused before adding a qualifier. "Maybe."

"What do you mean, maybe?"

"Maybe. I saw something moving, through the cracks between the boards. Maybe."

"What did you do then?"

As most his age might, Pinky withheld details. He did not reveal that he left the barn with sack in hand, met Patsy, went back into the barn, and they played with the gun and money. Instead, he made a long story short.

"That's when Patsy came."

Teresa turned attention to Patsy. "What did you do then?"

Patsy was cornered. It flashed through her mind to lie, but it was not her nature to do so. "We took some of the money out of the bag to look at it."

"And the gun," Pinky said.

"But we put it all back."

"And then?"

"We got on my bicycle, and Pinky pedaled us up close to the park where Mr. Twig and the Germans were. We were gonna tell him then about the sack."

"Why didn't you go all the way?"

"The sheriffs were there," Pinky said. "They were busy talking. So I turned around and left."

"Okay. So a flour sack with money and a gun in it is hanging on a nail in Miss Ruby's barn."

"Yes, Mam."

"Don't you think the sack and the things in it belong to Miss Ruby? That those things are her property."

"I told Pinky if we took it, we'd be stealin and Miss Ruby would be mad and we'd be put in jail."

"Well, that's right. You did the right thing by putting it back. What were you doin in Miss Ruby's barn anyway?"

They looked at each other.

Teresa saw their faces turn red and realized she had crossed a personal, intimate boundary in her interrogation.

"Okay," Teresa filled the silence, easing the embarrassment. "That's okay. Who else did you tell about your secret? Your mothers?"

They shook their heads.

"Okay. I'll tell Constable Chestnutt you want to

talk with him. He'll listen and decide what to do.
Now, don't tell anyone else until you talk to Constable
Chestnutt, okay?"

"Yes, Mam."

From the table, Ben spoke. "There sure is a lot of
whispering goin on over there. What's all the secrets
about?"

"We're just talking about secret Christmas gifts,
Ben. You and Phillip want more coffee?"

It was late on this winter day. Clouds diffused
fading light. Darkness came soon.

Miss Ruby had put Tina's present away before
going to the back porch. When she came through
the door, the chairs were empty. M D was not where
she had told him to wait.

She peered through the porch screen, focusing on
the barn. She nodded, knowingly. The big fish has
gone for the money, she thought, now is the time to
set the hook.

She went back to her bedroom, to the nightstand
beside her bed. She opened the drawer and
withdrew her new seven-inch, bullet-style, Ray-O-
Vac, copper-plated flashlight. She knew the two
batteries were fresh, but pressed the button to check
the light anyway. She turned it off, admired the
smallness in her hand, and laid it on the quilted
bedspread.

Miss Ruby reached back into the open drawer and
lifted out Arty's revolver. She pressed the cylinder
release and inspected the inserts. One cylinder insert

was empty, the other five held cartridges. But Ruby forgot Artemis had fired the gun three times in the bank, once at Lois and twice at Imogene. She rolled the cylinder. When the blank insert was on top, she closed the cylinder and jiggled to set it into the locking notch.

From her closet, Miss Ruby pulled down a cashmere shawl and draped it around her shoulders. She picked up the flashlight and tucked the gun into the knitted tips of the cream-colored fashion accessory.

"Ethel?"

"Yessum?"

"I thought I saw something out at the barn. I'm going out there to look. Somebody may be out there trying to steal tools or stuff."

"Do you want me and Julius to go with you, Miss Ruby?"

"No, I have the flashlight. I have all I need. That should scare them away. I'll be back in a minute."

"Yessum."

THE NEWS
December 1943
Trains 47, 50, 58, and 63 depart with French Jews to
Germany
Chicago Bears win NFL championship

As told, he went around the house. He crossed the yard and stood at the back steps for a couple of minutes. He looked through the windows for activity but didn't see Ethel or Julius moving around. He opened the screen door and went to a rocking chair on the back porch. He sat and rocked, waiting, thinking, imagining, planning — resolving. He knew her, knew she was upset. He imagined her reaction when she had probably gone to the barn searching for the sack and its contents. He knew he was in dangerous trouble. M D knew what Miss Ruby was capable of doing — she had done it to Arty. But he was not going to let that happen. He would take action first.

When Miss Ruby did not immediately appear, M D decided it best to leave. He rose from the comfortable chair, eased open and closed the screen door to keep it from screeching, and escaped, running fast past the

341

barn and through Ina Riley's backyard. He headed to the place where he could get help. He knew his Uncle Eliot would know what to do.

When Ruby discovered M D was not on the back porch, she suspected he had gone to the barn to take the sack and its contents. Days ago, she had gone looking for it. When she couldn't find it hanging on the nail behind the collar, she suspected he had hidden it or taken it outright.

She decided she'd had enough of the boy and would terminate his contract. The moment she took the gun and flashlight out of the bedside table drawer, she determined it would be a fight to the finish between them. She was witness to M D's demonstration that he would kill. His later bragging about shooting the bank security guard and the thrill he told her he felt when he shot Higgins were the evidence for her. She wanted Higgins to stop the extortion. That's why she sent M D and Artemis to Paris. Ruby wanted the boys to persuade Higgins, to convince him to leave her alone. Instead, M D killed Higgins in Estelle's boarding house.

Ruby had no doubt M D was a dangerous threat. She reckoned, erroneously, that he had spilled his guts and implicated her with the bank robberies and Artemis to the Sheriff in Paris. She knew damn well the town would be better off if the lazy, worthless creature was no longer around. She was prepared to make it so, even if M D gave up the sack with the money and her .22 caliber revolver.

As she walked through the kitchen toward the back porch with the flashlight in hand, and the gun concealed in her shawl, she declined Ethel's offer to go to the barn. By going alone, there would be no witness to what she knew she had to do. And the barn was the perfect place to take care of business once and for all. It would be easy to explain the circumstances. She went out to investigate something suspicious, defended herself from an attack, and killed the molester.

Ruby walked across the backyard with the light off. She lifted away the cashmere tips concealing Artemis' .38 and held the gun down alongside her leg. She slowed her pace and crept closer. She paused at the barn door, listening, peering into the darkness.

"Milton?"

The only sounds she could hear was her heart thumping, her breathing, and a dog's bark several houses up the street.

"Milton? Are you in there? I know you're scared, Milton, but it's alright. I'll take care of everything. You can trust me, Milton. We've worked together for a long time." She paused. "Answer me, now, so I know where you are."

She waited for twenty seconds, listening. The chill in the night air was too frigid for crickets to chatter or barn rats to scamper about.

"Okay, Milton, I'm coming in. We need to talk. I don't have a gun for my protection, so I need to get my gun out of the sack. Milton? I'm coming in."

Ruby passed through the open doorway. She stopped five steps inside and turned on the flashlight. She followed the beam as it swept across the ladder, the hayloft, walls, and stables. She momentarily held the light where the important nail protruded, the one supporting the ragged, cracked-leather horse collar.

The one that should have the flour sack hanging from it. She lowered the light to her shoes and the worn boards of the barn flooring under her feet.

The floor was dirty now, not clean and sparkling as she remembered — where her daddy held wonderful dances when she was a little girl. The vision of fun and merriment rushed into her senses as she held the beam steady and could hear the fiddle, banjo, and guitar and the whoops of the young enjoying a barn dance. She had danced too, standing on top of her daddy's skinned and scarred brogans as he swept her into a fantasyland.

She walked to a wooden crate and sat. She laid the gun beside her thigh and turned off the flashlight. Ruby withdrew an Old Gold pack and box of matches from her dress pocket, shook the pack, felt for a cigarette, and pulled it out. She dragged a match along the crate and flared the tip of the butt, inhaling the satisfying nicotine. She puckered her lips and blew out the flame. Then with her thumb and middle finger, she flipped the match stem toward the enclosed horse stall.

In the darkness, she pondered and planned her next move as she smoked her cigarette.

They arrived late, well after supper. The drive through Main Street was quiet, lighted by illumination through a few storefront windows and three street lamps.

"In America, all the places we see at night have lights. In Germany, it is all black-out," Duke said. "No lights at night so English and American bombers do not see us."

"The town is deserted," Will said. "I have never see Main Street so empty."

"You've never seen Main Street this late at night, Will. When the *pitchursho* is over, everybody goes home," Twig said. "After eight o'clock, all small Texas and Louisiana towns roll up the sidewalks."

"They roll up sidewalks?" Will asked.

"It's a manner of speaking."

"The sidewalk is concrete, Twig, how is it rolled up?"

Twig and Duke laughed.

"They have a doo-hickey that can make concrete soft," Twig said. "And when the concrete turns soft, the doo-hickey rolls it up."

"A doo-hippy?"

"Hickey, Will, not hippy. A *doo-hickey*."

"I have never seen one of those," Will said. "A doo-hickey."

Duke looked at Twig. "Twig has never seen a doo-hickey, Will. He is pulling your leg."

"I do not feel it, Duke."

"Feel what?"

"Twig pull my leg."

Twig and Duke roared with loud laughter.

"It is a joke, Will. Just a joke," Twig said. "Doo-hickey and pullin your leg are expressions, jokes."

Approaching the Porter House, the jeep's headlights shone on Dallas and Odessa sitting on the porch, their feet on the top step. Twig parked alongside the curb and shut off the jeep's lights and engine.

Odessa and Dallas rose and descended the steps.

They stood there, on the sidewalk, waiting.

In faint light from a street lamp a hundred feet up the street, Twig could see Duke's face. "Why is Odessa here?"

"Dallas, too," Will said. A smile was in his voice.

Duke did not look at Twig, only shook his head. "I do not know why she is here, Twig."

Twig gave his instructions. "Okay, here's what we're going to do. Will, you and Duke unhook the trailer from the jeep, put the stand down, and set the brake. Take your flashlights so you can see what you're doing. Take the water can off, empty it in the street, put it back on the rack, and attach the straps.

"I'll take the gas can. I'll bring the gas to the barn. If I leave the gas can on the jeep, I'm afraid somebody will help himself to free gas. That'll give you two a few minutes to find out what's going on. But no fraternizing, you hear?"

When Twig unhooked the straps holding the gas can, he felt moisture. He shined a light on the top of the can and discovered the boys had not screwed the lid in place properly. During movement, with bumps and turns of the jeep, gas had sloshed out and drenched the sides of the can. Now he had gas residue on his hand. He tried to attach the cap but something was wrong. The threads on the can's mouth and lid were stripped. Somebody, Twig thought, a German somebody, screwed up the gas can. He knew Teresa would complain of the smell once he came inside the house. Not much he could do about it now, Twig deduced. He picked up the can and headed to the barn.

Once chores were done, with flashlights still on, Duke and Will walked toward their girls.

Odessa reached for Duke's hand. "Let's sit in the jeep, Duke. We need to talk."

Dallas took Will's hand. "We can sit on the steps."

Neither girl asked about Eddy.

On the steps, Will turned off the flashlight.

Dallas whispered. "Odessa needed to speak with Duke in private."

Will was unconcerned about their privacy. "That is okay. We are alone too. We can sit and talk until Twig comes back."

Duke sat behind the steering wheel, Odessa in the passenger seat.

Duke turned off his flashlight. "This is a surprise, you waiting in the dark."

Odessa was quiet for several seconds. "I need to tell you something."

Duke held his tongue, watching her. The dim light was enough he could see her face, see that she was looking down at her hands in her lap.

Then, Duke heard Odessa catch her breath and realized she was sobbing.

"Odessa. Odessa? Why are you crying? What is wrong?"

"I'm in trouble."

"Trouble? What kind of trouble?"

"Family trouble."

"Did someone hurt you? Did someone say something about us?"

"No, no. It's not that. It's not that kind of trouble. Not yet, anyway."

Duke got out and walked around to Odessa. "*Schatz*, what is wrong? You have to stop crying. Will and Dallas will hear you. Tell me what is wrong."

He reached into the jeep, put his arms around her, and pulled her close. With her face against his chest, he kissed the top of her head and stroked her hair.

Odessa sniffled, caught her breath, and swiped her runny nose. She straightened up and wiped her eyes and cheeks with both hands.

Duke pulled a blue bandanna from his denim pocket and handed it to her.

"Here, this is pretty clean. Wipe your eyes, take a deep breath. It will be alright. We will be alright. I like holding you in my arms."

Soothed by the closeness, Odessa's voice was almost a whisper. "I've always wondered why you speak good English. You sound just like we do. You don't talk like a German at all. You don't sound like the ones in the *pitchursho* who try to act like Germans with a accent."

"Ah, you do not remember I told you. I lived in America before the war."

"Oh, oh, yes, I remember that. In the cotton field, the first time, when I brought water."

"My father was a doctor. When I was fifteen, he received a fellowship to study epilepsy at Northwestern University. We lived in Illinois."

"Illinois. Like Chicago?"

"Yes, in Evanston. It is north of Chicago. We lived there three years. After my high school classes, I would ride a city bus up to the radio school. Doctor Anthony was a professor there. He often came to our

348

house to play bridge. He gave me speech lessons and let me read sports over the school radio. I did that for the three years we lived there. My voice was masculine, mature, even when I was a teenager."

"You said your father *was* a doctor?"

"He died the same day I finished communications training in Berlin. The Gestapo killed my father. They accused him of spying for America."

"My daddy may kill me."

"Why? You must tell me what is wrong. Why are you so upset?"

"I was sick, puking all the time. I missed my period two months in a row. I went to see Doctor Burns. He did a blood and urine test. He said I am with child. I swore him to secrecy, but I don't trust him. I'm afraid he'll tell momma. Or my daddy. We're going to have a baby, Duke."

"So, that is the trouble? That is what this crying is all about? I am smiling, Odessa."

She looked at him. "I can see that you are. Why are you smiling?"

"Because I am happy. I am happy for you, Odessa. You are going to be a mama. And, I am happy for me. I am going to be a papa. A dad. A daddy, as you say. We are going to be a family. We are going to have a baby."

"But the war. You're a prisoner of war. Some here still see you as the enemy."

"The war will end. They will release me when the war is over. I did no wrong. I was not part of Himmler's gang. I will not be on trial for war crimes. I will be a free man when the Allies are victorious."

"But you will be shipped back to Germany. Then what are we going to do?"

"Now. Here is what we are going to do now. Here is what I want you to do. Tomorrow, *Ja*, go look for Preacher Adams. Find him. Twig said he is a real preacher."

"But . . . but, he's a . . . he's not one of us."

"He is a human being, Odessa. The color of his skin is not important."

"What do you want me to say to him?"

"Ask him if he will marry us."

"He can do that?"

"Yes. He is a Baptist preacher, ordained. In the eyes of God, Preacher Adams can marry us. After what we did at the Ice House, I am sure he will be happy to do it. It is one of his gifted blessings."

"What if he says yes?"

"Then, you decide a day and time for our wedding to take place."

"Where?"

"Here."

"Here? Here, in the Porter House?"

Yes, in the Porter House. In the big city of Palomino, Texas. I am so happy, Odessa. I will make you my bride, *meine Braut*."

"What will I tell my momma and daddy?"

"Tell them they will have a new son-in-law. Tell them they are going to have an *Enkelkind*, a grandchild. Tell them they are going to be a *Grossmutter*, an *Oma*, and a *Grossvater*, an *Opa*, a grandma and grandpa. Tell them they are going to be as happy as we are."

"I love you, Duke."

"I love you, Odessa. My Sweetheart. Come into my arms, *mein Schatz*."

Odessa got out of the jeep and stepped into Duke's open arms.

They kissed. He held her in a loving, heartfelt embrace.

"Your sweet kisses make me feel safe. I will go tell Momma and Daddy the news."

"Tomorrow, find Preacher Adams."

Ruby saw the light beam approaching the barn. She moved from the crate to the stall. She stood concealed, peering between the horizontal slats.

Head down, Twig trailed the light beam covering the ground in front and followed it into the barn. Eight steps inside, gas can in hand, he paused. He raised the flashlight up.

A lingering wall of blue-gray smoke from Ruby's cigarette hung in the air. He inhaled the sharp freshness of burnt tobacco before a drift of a slight breeze slowly wisped it passed him.

He swept the light from side to side and stepped farther into the barn. He stopped next to a wooden crate. Distracted by the presence of cigarette smoke, he raised his head, following the light. Without looking down, he absentmindedly set the gas can on a corner of the box.

Twig wondered aloud. "Pinky?"

He grabbed at the can as it slid off his leg. Three pounds of steel and twenty-four pounds of fuel slammed down on the planks.

"SHIT."

Gasoline streamed from the cap, the sharp scent of the spilling fuel evident. He jerked the can upright and left it sitting on the floor. A wide rivulet flowed along the floor.

"Hello, Twig, it's Ruby." She moved out of the stall.

"Holy shit."

Twig swung his light up from the river of fuel to light her face. Then he lowered the beam to her knees.

"You startled me, Miss Ruby. What are you doing in the barn this late?"

"I thought I saw someone fooling around out here. I came to have a look."

"Well, I came in the barn to stow my can of gas so nobody would take it off the jeep."

"We don't do that in Palomino, Twig."

"Do what?"

"We leave our doors unlocked day and night. About the only time there are locked doors, is when somebody goes away for a week. Like a vacation."

Ruby turned on her flashlight and aimed it at the gas can. "The smell is pretty strong, seems you spilled some of your gas."

"Yeah, I did. I thought I put it on the box, but it fell off and turned over. The lid was not screwed on right or the gasket is worn out." He chuckled. "The boards are soaked now, so don't throw a cigarette or match on the floor."

She turned off her flashlight. "Well, I was just about to go back to the house."

Twig stepped aside to let Ruby pass. "I'll follow you out. I need to stop by the backyard faucet to rinse the fuel off of my hands."

Before either one of them advanced toward the doorway, Twig saw two silhouettes in the yard approaching the barn.

"Duke and Will are coming to check on me. They were unhooking the trailer from the jeep."

Twig raised his light.

Ruby gasped and stepped back.

Eliot and M D raised their hands to shield their eyes. A stogie was between Eliot's fingers of his left hand — he held a shotgun along his leg with his right hand. A cigarette hung from M D's bulging lips, a gun was in his right hand.

"We came to get M D's goods," Eliot stated. He advanced to the doorway with M D by his side.

Ruby retreated. Twig stood his ground. "Stop where you are, Mr. Thurgood."

"Get out of the way, Constable. This ain't none of your business."

"I think it might be since you come along on private property in the dead of night carrying weapons."

"Ruby has things that belong to M D, and he asked me to come help cause he knew she wouldn't hand them over."

"Is that right, Miss Ruby?"

"No, Constable. M D stole my property out of my barn. He has things that belong to me."

M D pulled the cigarette from his mouth with his left thumb and fingers and exhaled smoke.

"Now, that ain't true. I put the sack where it's supposed to be hanging and it ain't there. Uncle Eliot and me come to find it."

Twig felt like he was watching ping-pong, going from one face to another.

"If you didn't take it, who did?"

"You did, old woman."

Ruby bristled.

"You know damn well I wouldn't be out here looking for you and the sack if I took it."

Twig caught his breath upon hearing that confession. Ruby had told him she was in the barn looking for an intruder.

Now, these back and forth accusations and revelations about a sack that three people would be looking for in the night became interesting and intriguing to the Constable of Palomino. As the town's law enforcement officer and investigator, he knew to keep his mouth shut and ears open.

Eliot spoke. "Well, I think that's a lie. Why would you be out here this late if you wasn't picking up the sack? M D told me what yall have done."

Twig slipped in a question. "What do you mean?"

Nobody spoke for several seconds.

"Bank robbery," M D said. He raised his gun and pointed at Ruby. "She robbed banks."

"Killing," Ruby retorted. She looked at Twig and pointed at M D. "He killed a bank security guard and a man in Paris."

"You lyin bitch," M D screamed. "You shot Arty and left him to die in a rail shed."

Duke and Will approached behind Eliot and M D.

"Hey, Twig, we are worried you have been back here so long," Duke said.

Surprised, Eliot swung around to face the voice.

The presence of the two prisoners infuriated him. He raised the shotgun.

Ruby raised her gun and fired.

The .38 slug struck Eliot between his shoulders at the base of his neck. He jerked from the impact, raised both arms, and fired the shotgun into the air. As he fell, his cigar crashed onto the barn floor.

Soldiers reacting to gunfire, Duke and Will hit the ground in a military prone position and rolled.

"God," Twig shouted. The blast shocked him. Stunned, he recoiled and drew his service pistol.

She turned her gun toward M D.

Before she could pull the trigger, M D fired two shots from Deputy Amesa's .44 and struck Ruby in the face and neck.

She dropped to the floor like a sack of flour.

M D aimed at Twig and pulled the trigger.

Twig fired his .45 as M D's bullet zipped past his ear.

M D fell forward, his cigarette landing on the gasoline saturated planks.

Fuel on the floor instantly flared and acted like a fuse. Flames ran up the side of the gas can. The fire and pressure exploded the container and spewed burning gasoline.

Shrapnel from the gas can pierced Twig's thigh and side. He dropped to a knee and grimaced. The heat was worse than the pain and a great motivator.

Twig staggered to his feet, grabbed Ruby's arms, and shuffled backwards, pulling her toward the doorway.

Duke and Will dashed into the barn. Duke took hold

of Eliot's ankles and Will grabbed M D's, and they dragged them out.

The three bodies and the three soldiers lay on the ground, safely away from the fire.

Ethel, Julius, Teresa, Tina, Odessa, and Dallas ran to them.

The fire department siren screamed and wailed, again and again, summoning the Palomino volunteers.

Duke grunted, turned to look at Twig.

"Palomino is not like our towns in Germany."

Teresa knelt beside Twig and laid her hand on his shoulder. From the glow of the burning barn, she could see blood spots from shrapnel punctures.

"You're hurt, Sweetheart."

Twig nodded and raised his hand to hers. He coughed from smoke inhalation.

"Palomino is a nice town, Duke. Some of the people in the town are not so nice."

Julius and Ethel looked at the burning barn and at the people on the ground.

"My, my, goodness sakes, Lordamercy," Julius proclaimed. "Madness. It's jist all madness, I say."

"White folk," Ethel mused.

The flames appeared to lick and slash across her shining black eyes as she stared at the crumbling structure.

"Um hummm, white folk."

THE BICYCLE
Christmas 1943
Chaplain Wuebbens arranges a burlesque show for
crew of USS *North Carolina*
LIFE magazine features a wife awaiting return of her
American bomber pilot

Six minutes before the military trio from Camp Maxey arrived at the hospital, Teresa asked Duke and Will to come with her to Dulfeine's so they could help assemble Tina's bicycle.

"Mr. Dulfeine said he would let us come in the store and go upstairs. He said he had tools we could use," Teresa said.

"We will bring it to the Porter House?" Duke asked.

"Tonight, after Tina has gone to bed. We still wait for Santa Claus to come on Christmas Eve."

"*Sankt Nikolaus* will roll the bicycle to the house later," Will said. "Miss Tina will be happy to have her bicycle."

They were walking the couple of blocks to the back door of the store as the Army sedan parked in front of the six-bed hospital.

The three soldiers dismounted and entered the all-white, H-shaped building.

"Hello, Nurse. I'm Colonel Sanchez."

"Yes, Colonel. I'm Linda Thomas, Ward Nurse. How may I help you?"

"I was told you have a patient by the name of Sergeant Willow Chestnutt."

"Willow?" She smiled. "You mean Twig. Constable Chestnutt. Yes, he's here. He sustained injuries from an explosion."

Her smile turned into a blank stare as she looked at the other two soldiers standing with the Colonel.

"Yes, of course," Sanchez said. "This is Captain Morris, Consta . . . Sergeant Chestnutt's Company Commander and First Sergeant Kinnison, his, ah, Sergeant Chestnutt's First Sergeant."

Linda maintained her expression, acknowledging the introductions.

"Mayor Shipp called me. We came from Camp Maxey to see Sergeant Chestnutt, to talk to him."

"I see." Nurse Thomas shuffled papers out of view below the counter. "I'm sorry, Colonel, but Doctor Burns has given no instructions for visitors outside of his family and, of course, Duke and Will."

"Duke and Will?"

"His Germans."

Colonel Sanchez partially turned to glare at Kinnison.

Kinnison snapped to. "Yes, Sir. Duke is prisoner Kraus Hopplendagger and Will, Sir, is prisoner Wilhelm Weiss."

Sanchez turned back to Thomas. "Where is the

other prisoner?"

Nurse Thomas raised her eyebrows and shrugged.

He looked at Morris. "What is the other prisoner's name?"

Kinnison jumped in. "Becker, Sir. Prisoner Edwin Becker."

Sanchez looked at Thomas. "Where is Becker?"

Her stare told Sanchez who was in charge within the Palomino Hospital. After a professional pause, she spoke. "I am sorry you have misplaced one of your prisoners, Colonel. I do not know where your Mr. Becker is, but I can tell you he is not here in the hospital."

Sanchez took a breath and reined in his impatience. He softened the tone of his voice. "I'm sorry, Nurse Thomas. Mayor Shipp called about the . . . about . . . about the accident. We're here on official business. It's important that I be able to talk with Sergeant Chestnutt. It's about secret military matters."

"Ah, secret military matters. I see." She pointed. "If the three of you will have a seat over there in the waiting room, I'll ask Doctor Burns if it is okay for you to visit Sergeant Chestnutt."

"Well, call him right away, Nurse, it's urgent."

"Go. There. Please have a seat, Colonel."

The trio moved away from the nurse station. Since Colonel Sanchez did not take a seat in the sparse room, Morris and Kinnison remained standing too.

"Nurse Thomas likes to be in charge, ordering people around." He glared at his subordinates. "Duke and Will? German prisoners of war are taking American names?"

"Some have, Sir," Captain Morris said.

Sanchez frowned. "Isn't that obvious, Captain?" His frustration and impatience mounted. "Where is the Doctor?"

"Right here, Colonel." Doc Burns was a short, thin man with a Hollywood-styled pencil mustache. He was fifty-seven years old but appeared to be thirty. He removed his wire-framed glass and placed each lens in his open mouth. After exhaling on them, he wiped off the haze with the broad tip of his necktie. "Nurse Thomas said you needed to talk with Constable Chestnutt about military secrets?"

Sanchez was amused to eye such a small man. His assessment, however, was mistaken. Smallness was only in the eye of the Colonel.

"Yes, Doctor, Sergeant Chestnutt is in my command. Mayor Shipp called me about Chestnut and all this business he became involved in. I've come all the way from Camp Maxey to talk with him about it. My time is very valuable, so I'd like for you to arrange for me to see him right away."

"I see, Colonel. You must understand, Colonel, this is a civilian hospital. We do things a little differently than the military."

"How is that, Doctor?"

"Even though we do support the war effort, we still take time to say please and thank you."

When Colonel Sanchez looked at Morris and Kinnison, they lowered their heads.

Sanchez swallowed and forced a smile. "Thank you, Doctor, may I please see your patient, Sergeant Chestnutt?"

"Why of course you can, Colonel. He's down the hall on the left, Room Two."

Loud talking and laughter erupted in the lobby, the commotion was disturbing and distracting.

"What in the world . . .?" Doc Burns stepped into the hall.

Sanchez, Morris, and Kinnison followed. They watched two girls go into the second room on the left.

"Now, those girls know they have no business going in there. Okay, Colonel, please come with me, I'll bring you to Constable Chestnutt." Doc Burns was point man as they marched in single file down the hall.

The two girls they had seen enter the hospital stood at the foot of Twig's bed.

"Where's Duke, Twig?" Odessa asked.

"They've gone to Dulfeine's."

"Daddy is mad as a wet hen," Dallas said.

"I told him the news," Odessa said.

"What news?" Twig asked.

"The baby, about the baby," Dallas said.

"I went for Preacher Adams, but he wasn't at the gin," Odessa said. "I need to tell Duke."

Stunned shock covered Twig's face. "What baby? Whose baby?"

Doc Burns led the soldiers into Twig's room.

"Constable Chestnutt, you have three visitors who need to talk with you about military secrets. Colonel, limit your visit to ten minutes. Odessa, you and Dallas need to leave these soldiers to their military business." Doc Burns held out his hand for Odessa and Dallas to precede him and they left the room. "Gentlemen, please excuse us."

"Sergeant Chestnutt, Mayor Shipp called and told me about all this mess. I brought Captain Morris with me." He made no mention of Kinnison.

"I'm fine, Sir," Twig said pointedly, "just a little shrapnel in my side and thigh. I'll be on my feet tomorrow. Hello Captain Morris. Hello, Top."

They acknowledged his greeting with nods. Their faces were solemn because they were aware of Sanchez' mission and irritability.

"Yes, of course," Sanchez said. "How are you? Where're your prisoners?"

"They left a few minutes ago. They're at Dulfeine's grocery store with my wife, Teresa. Eddy is in the Bogata hospital. He was hit in the head with an entrenching tool. But he'll be alright."

"Good God, Chestnutt, you've lost control of your prisoners. The security of the community is threatened. You've killed a civilian. This is unacceptable.

"General Pace sent me here to tell you that within the authority of the June, 1920 Articles of War, he ordered the Inspector General to conduct an investigation."

Twigs ears burned with frustration. "No, Sir, I haven't lost control. Those boys have done a lot for this community, and the community feels safe. In a matter of weeks, these German prisoners of war rushed into not one, but two burning structures to save American citizens. The people recognize their bravery.

"We've helped sheriffs' deputies find one of their own who'd been missing for over a year. During that search, one of the deputies accidentally hit Eddy Becker in the head and split his scalp. The community felt safe enough to admit him to the hospital and care for him. The deputies in Bogata are looking after him.

"I think Miss Ruby shot Eliot Thurgood because he raised his shotgun on Duke and Will. He might have killed them if Miss Ruby had not shot him. I killed the boy who killed Miss Ruby. I shot him in self-defense because he shot at me, tried to kill me."

"That will all be reviewed in the investigation. Your assignment here is finished, Chestnutt. I will order military policemen to pick up Becker and bring him to Camp Maxey. When released from the hospital you will return to Maxey with your prisoners. You will be restricted to the camp and, when called, appear before the investigators to make a statement. If the Inspector General finds cause and recommends disciplinary action, General Evans will convene a General Court-Martial, and you will face the charges brought against you, Sergeant. If convicted, you may be reduced to Private, forfeit all pay and allowances, be dishonorably discharged, and confined at Fort Leavenworth, Kansas for several years. I should have known something like this could happen with you when I learned about you permitting your prisoners to fraternize with the citizens of Palomino."

Sanchez swept his fingers at Kinnison. "Get the car ready, we're done here."

THE AFTERMATH
January 2024
Abigail Burke sworn in as 47th President of the United States of America
California, after secession, votes to divide itself into four separate countries

The lunch crowd standing in line to pay the cashier tried not to stare at the two men wearing dark sunglasses and dressed in black suits sitting at a table near the door. But movement of the secret service agents' lips drew discreet glances from customers. The agents listened to speakers in the temple pieces of their sunglasses and responded with a report on the old man and their charge sitting at a table in the middle of the cafe.

Only a few skimpy dollars lay on each cluttered tabletop for the harried waitress. A busboy moved from table to table — gathering dishes, silverware, and debris into a gray rubber tub. He arranged condiment jars, napkin holders, and wiped tabletops with a wet rag. He aligned the gratuity of coins and bills neatly and placed the money in full view. He never looked up from his work.

"This is quite an honor to meet the daughter of our President. I've seen you on TV but I think you are prettier in person, Catherine."

He looked at the agents.

She smiled. "Thank you, Willy. I know it must be hard to do, but try to ignore them. They prefer it, too.

"When you agreed to meet with me, I was thrilled. But, I have to tell you that I was heartbroken to learn about the fire. I so much wanted to see it."

"Yes, as I mentioned on the phone, it burned a year or two ago, maybe three," Willy said. "Were you surprised by what you saw in Paris? Camp Maxey?"

"Not surprised, really. More disappointed, I guess. I looked for the boarding house, but it's gone. An indoor mall and a three-floor parking garage covers that block now. I saw the front gate and a few buildings at Maxey, but the rest of the area appeared overgrown."

"It's still used by units of the National Guard."

"After we talked, I found his book," she said.

"The Colonel's book was a big success in its day. Stayed on the *New York Times* bestseller list for eighteen, twenty months," Willy said. "For many years before the place burned, we were a regular tourist detour for visitors who came to see Paris and Camp Maxey. After the fire, though, the amount of sightseers dwindled because there was nothing to see anymore. Now, it's been thirty years, maybe more, since there's been any interest in the place. Every now and then girls and boys came to do research for a college project or assistants came to take pictures and do interviews for famous authors who wanted to write their own book about it."

"I read his book twice. A copy is still on a shelf in the Houston Library. There were also some articles published in the *Houston Chronicle* a year or so after, with names of the other people. I found those stored in the paper's archives.

"After reading his book, the whole affair piqued my interest — German prisoners working in a small Texas town, bank robberies, murders, small-town secrets, and, of course, the love stories. I had to come here, I wanted to see it. I wanted to know what happened. I wanted to know the rest of the story, as Paul Harvey used to say."

"Yeah, I liked his radio program."

"As I dug deeper in my research, I learned you were the town's historian and Will's grandson. Anyway, I'm glad you agreed to meet with me. I'm excited to talk with the historian."

"As Tina's granddaughter, and our new President's daughter, you may know things about Palomino that I don't. So, it's a two way exchange."

"Bits and pieces of the story were handed down, of course. I think we do have a lot to talk about, about the aftermath."

"I favor myself to know some of the history. The newspaper here serves as the official record. But I know about the people, I have many of the journals and diaries folks kept through the years. I know most of what happened. Let's have a piece of pie and some coffee while we talk."

When the server returned with their order, she spoke to Catherine. "My name is Susan. I've seen you on TV. You're the President's daughter. I voted for your mother. I think all the women in Palomino did. Please let me know when you want something else."

"Thank you, Susan."

"I suppose you feel like a rock star with all the attention."

"Quite frankly, Willy, it's a pain. I'm followed all the time by those two or others like them."

For several minutes, they silently sipped the fresh, delicious coffee and nibbled on coconut cream pie, the house special.

Catherine stood up and pulled out her phone. "May I take pictures?"

Willy nodded and grinned. She snapped several photos of Willy and the cafe. Catherine put away her phone, sat down, and pulled a small laptop out of her leather shoulder bag.

She lifted the lid and the screen lit up instantly. She pressed keys and once the document she wanted opened, she looked up. She turned the machine so the screen faced outward between them.

"I have a high-end professional recording system on the machine. As we speak, it will record our voices and create a transcript at the same time. Is that okay with you?"

"Yes."

"Good, look at the screen. See how it wrote every word correctly?"

Willy leaned in to look. He read the text. "That's amazing. How does it handle similar words like right and write, like on paper?"

"Look and see. It's really new technology and I

don't know how it understands which word is the correct one. Even my grandmother uses it."

Willy smiled. "I can't get over that I'm talking with Tina's granddaughter. It makes my head swim."

Catherine grinned.

"I am honored, Catherine. I think I ought to be taking notes too."

They laughed. Their laughter was relaxing.

"Okay, can you start around the time the barn burned?"

"Well, you probably know about all the gunfire. Everybody had a gun. Some made jokes about it, saying it was like the gunfight at the O. K. Corral in Tombstone. The report said an extra gun was found in the ashes.

"Anyway, Eliot Thurgood survived. Ruby's bullet struck his spine, paralyzed him. Doc Burns left the bullet in him, some said out of spite. Eliot was in a wheelchair the rest of his life. He died in March of Fifty-Two, from an infection. Many blamed the infection on a piece of fabric the bullet stuck in his spine, but nobody minded. At the time, folks here said the German, Duke, should have left Eliot in the barn to burn.

"Doc Burns' report said Milton, M D, was dead before he hit the floor. Constable Chestnutt's bullet hit him right between the eyes. Folks also said the German, Will, should have left M D in the barn too. Course, his momma and daddy, Henrietta and Drayton, were distraught. They couldn't believe their boy was involved in robbing and murdering. Up until they passed away, they were mad the Constable killed their boy.

"Ruby was still alive, lying out there on the ground, when the firefighters and Doc Burns got there. They all heard her tell about the bank robberies. She confessed to all of it, a death-bed confession I guess you could say."

Willy stopped talking when Susan approached with coffee pot in hand.

"I brought fresh coffee."

"Yes, please, Susan," Catherine said.

After filling their cups, Susan served the few customers at other tables.

A man approached and spoke. "Willy, the Mayor said the Texarkana TV station wants to do a piece on our support of our troops for a pre-Fourth of July celebration. They want the Governor to come up for some photo-ops. She wants you to come to her office and talk about it."

"I like the idea of publicity for our troops. I don't like the idea of the Governor coming to steal the show. I'll go talk to Sherry about it. Catherine, this is Jerry Wilson, our Constable."

They exchanged a few seconds of pleasantries.

"Jerry's granddaddy, Henry, owned the domino hall back then.   Jerry's daddy, Harper, kept it open a number of years until television kept everybody home. Catherine is doing research for a book, Jerry."

"You're the President's daughter."

Catherine and Willy laughed.

"Everybody must say that to you, Catherine," Willy said.

"I'm sorry, Catherine," Jerry said. "It's a natural

reflex to see in person a person you've seen on the TV. Anyway, you're talking to the right person, our historian. Willy probably knows more than he should about the people of Palomino, past and present."

They all laughed.

"I'll be on my way. Don't forget to go see Sherry, Willy. Nice meeting you, Catherine."

"Did Ruby die there, on the ground?"

"No, they got her in the ambulance alright, and got her to the hospital. But Doc later said the shot to her throat caused too much internal bleeding to be able to save her. Ruby drowned in her own blood, hell of a way to go."

"What do you know about Constable Chestnutt?"

"Your great-granddad was patched up pretty good. The Mayor, Casey Shipp, called Twig's boss out there at the Camp. The boss came the next day and raised hell about the German prisoners. Seems people dying in a gunfight didn't impress him, either."

"And the Germans?"

"Well, they all went back to Maxey. There was a big investigation, but Twig came out okay. He was discharged after the war, receiving an Honorable Discharge. He came back here and the council reaffirmed his appointment as Constable.

"The Germans were released and shipped back to Germany.

"Of course, my Grandpa Will immigrated in September of Forty-Six and married my grandma, Dallas. He earned American citizenship in Fifty-One. He bought Kingston Kline's drugstore and later brought in television sets. People used to stand on the sidewalk in front of his store to watch TV.

"Even though Preacher Adams had married Odessa and Duke, the Army still shipped him back to Germany. He immigrated in October of Forty-Six and packed Odessa and their baby girl up and moved to Chicago. Duke changed his name to Don Hopper. A marketing company used him part-time to make radio advertisements. His voice was so popular and recognizable that the WLS radio station hired him the next spring. Eventually he moved into television at the station and that led to his acting career. His looks and voice were naturals for the movies. He became a celebrity, of sorts. He and Odessa had seven more children. I don't think Duke ever applied for American citizenship.

"Eddy came back in Forty-Nine for Jeannie, the nurse he met at the Bogata hospital. There were newspaper stories about him coming back for the girl he left in America. Jeannie married him and they returned to Germany. He became a popular bandleader over there. For a number of years, Eddy's band came over to appear on Lawrence Welk's television show. Eddy, with Welk's help, started a similar program in Frankfurt. His music is still popular. I have many of his old records and cassettes."

"What about Ethel and Julius?"

"You probably know that history well, because of the codicil. Ruby's lawyer in Paris drew up the paper so Ethel and Julius inherited the Porter House and your grandmother got the theater, the Palomino Palace. Well, Julius died from pneumonia in the summer of Fifty. The next year, Ethel sold the Porter House to a group of investors.   She bought a huge place somewhere near Jackson, Mississippi and started a cake baking business.   General Mills bought her company along with her recipes, and hired Ethel as a consultant. She passed away in December of Seventy-One. Her estate was valued at eighty million. I don't think the Probate Court ever found any heirs.

"The investor group promoted the house as a tourist attraction and the venture was successful for awhile, but later on wound up in a state of disrepair. Then a few years ago it burned."

"Arson?"

"Maybe. Probably. Nobody really knew or cared."

"If you'll excuse me, Willy, I need to go to the restroom. This coffee tells me to take a break."

Willy chuckled. "I feel the same way, Catherine."

When they returned to the table, Susan appeared with a pot of coffee.

Both laughed and told her no thanks.

"What can you tell me about your great-grandmother and grandmother, Teresa and Tina?"

"Well, as you know, my great-grandmother operated the *Palace* for Tina. They sold the theater when Tina graduated high school."

"To Boyd Rutledge."

"Yes, to Mr. Rutledge. Tina entered Baylor and became a dentist. It was there she met, Thorson Burke. They had two boys, Addison and Anthony. Addison married Abigail Newton in Eighty-Four and I came along in Eighty-Nine, after my two brothers. My great-grandparents, Teresa and Twig, passed away within months of each other last year in an assisted living facility in Shreveport. My grandmother lives in Arizona with Thorson and their four little dogs Terry, Chloe, Zak, and Toby."

"I think your mother will be a great President. She must have been very pleased to win by a landslide."

"That's how she won every election for the Senate, an overwhelming majority."

"Our country was ready for a change from the last two incumbents. I have great respect and admiration for your mother."

"Thank you, Willy, I will pass along your comment to my mother, it will please her. I appreciate you taking time to visit with me."

"Is there anything else? I need to go see Sherry, our Mayor, about this Governor business."

"Yes. I do have a couple of questions. I was wondering about Rayfield Pinkston and Patricia Ann Parker. Grandmother Tina often spoke affectionately about them. She always laughed when she mentioned them, saying they were the three *mustard-tears.*"

"Pinky and Patsy married their senior year in high school. They had two girls, Barbara and Zandra.

"Pinky's dad drowned in the initial wave at Omaha Beach. He never made it ashore. It bothered the boy.

"Patsy's dad was never the same after *he* came home. I think he ended up in Terrell or Rusk, one of those mental hospitals.

"After graduating, Pinky drove a truck for East Texas Motor Freight. He enlisted in the National Guard in Fifty or Fifty-One. He was a heavy equipment operator in the Guard, graders, bulldozers, that sort of thing. His unit was never activated for the Korean War, but it was for the Vietnam War. He must have been thirty-two or three when he went over there. He had been in Vietnam only thirty-forty days when a sniper killed him.

"Patsy never got over it. She packed up one night and drove away. Nobody knew where she went. Nobody heard from her, not even her girls."

Catherine nodded. They sat in silence for a couple of minutes.

"What was your other question?"

"Grandmother Tina said Twig often related a story about a sack, that a sack was the reason the two men, Eliot and Milton, came to the barn that night. They were after a sack. Did you ever find out about the sack? Or what was in it?"

"Well, no. I believe Twig and Teresa knew, they just never told anybody. I've read what folks wrote in their journals and diaries. Everybody had an opinion. Maybelle Winters and Margie Dulfeine thought Miss Parker, Patsy's mom, and Miss Pinkston, Pinky's mom, knew. The sack must've burned with the barn so we'll never know what was in it or why it was important."

374

PROMPTS
a collection of stories
Tank Gunner

Available at TankGunnerSix.blogspot.com

Available at TankGunnerSix.blogspot.com.

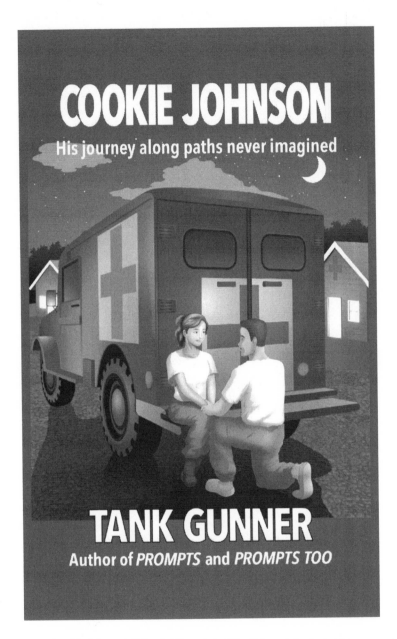

Available at TankGunnerSix.blogspot.com.